Born in the UK, **Becky Wicks**  interminable wanderlust from a lived and worked all over the w to Dubai, Sydney, Bali, NYC a She's written for the likes of *GQ*, *Hello!*, *Fabulous* and *Time Out*, a host of YA romance, plus three travel memoirs—*Burqalicious*, *Balilicious* and *Latinalicious* (HarperCollins, Australia). Now she blends travel with romance for Mills & Boon and loves every minute! Find her on Substack: @beckywicks.

Also by Becky Wicks

*The Vet's Escape to Paradise
Highland Fling with Her Best Friend
South African Escape to Heal Her
Finding Forever with the Single Dad
Melting the Surgeon's Heart
A Marriage Healed in Hawaii
Tempted by the Outback Vet*

Buenos Aires Docs miniseries

Daring to Fall for the Single Dad

Valentine Flings miniseries

Nurse's Keralan Temptation

Discover more at millsandboon.co.uk.

A DADDY FOR HER BABIES

BECKY WICKS

FROM A FLING TO A FAMILY

BECKY WICKS

MILLS & BOON

All rights reserved including the right of reproduction in whole or in part in any form. This edition is published by arrangement with Harlequin Enterprises ULC.

This is a work of fiction. Names, characters, places, locations and incidents are purely fictional and bear no relationship to any real life individuals, living or dead, or to any actual places, business establishments, locations, events or incidents. Any resemblance is entirely coincidental.

This book is sold subject to the condition that it shall not, by way of trade or otherwise, be lent, resold, hired out or otherwise circulated without the prior consent of the publisher in any form of binding or cover other than that in which it is published and without a similar condition including this condition being imposed on the subsequent purchaser.

® and TM are trademarks owned and used by the trademark owner and/or its licensee. Trademarks marked with ® are registered with the United Kingdom Patent Office and/or the Office for Harmonisation in the Internal Market and in other countries.

First published in Great Britain 2025
by Mills & Boon, an imprint of HarperCollins*Publishers* Ltd,
1 London Bridge Street, London, SE1 9GF

www.harpercollins.co.uk

HarperCollins*Publishers* Macken House, 39/40 Mayor Street Upper, Dublin 1, D01 C9W8, Ireland

A Daddy for Her Babies © 2025 Becky Wicks

From a Fling to a Family © 2025 Becky Wicks

ISBN: 978-0-263-32506-5

05/25

This book contains FSC™ certified paper
and other controlled sources to ensure responsible forest management.

For more information visit www.harpercollins.co.uk/green.

Printed and Bound in the UK using 100% Renewable Electricity
at CPI Group (UK) Ltd, Croydon, CR0 4YY

A DADDY FOR HER BABIES

BECKY WICKS

MILLS & BOON

CHAPTER ONE

Outside, the Chicago rain is hammering at the windows like it's trying to match my heartbeat. The tiny infant is swaddled in a bundle of sheets, and his chest is heaving in erratic jerks in front of me. I feel the pull on my nerves at the thought that his next breath could be this baby's last, but today, with everything I've just learned, I'm walking a fine line, not letting the shock show on my face.

"O2 sats are dropping. We need to intubate!" I call out. As the specialist NICU pediatrician, I've been called down to the ER from neonatal. No one knows what I've just discovered upstairs in my own department's bathrooms. And no one will. "Theo?"

"On it, Doctor Carter." Theo's dashed through the doors with his coat still open as if he's only just started his shift. Dr. Theo Montgomery, the ER's chief resident, takes one look at the baby's skin and agrees we need to prep for intubation. The child is a canvas of mottled blues and grays, the colors no child should be. We work side by side on the baby, swiftly, calmly, even as my head spins. He looks at me questioningly when I drop a tube to the floor, and I know that look, because I know him. He's questioning why someone who knows this department as well as her own is so clumsy today.

You'd never know from seeing Theo like this that he boxes almost at a pro level, rides his bike over fifty miles most weekends, owns a penthouse apartment with barely anything in it, adores his niece, hates all cats—even mine—and knows all the words to ABBA's "Dancing Queen." But *I* know these things. I've learned them as a result of the past four years, working with him here at Evergreen General Hospital, self-medicating on coffee alongside him in the unflatteringly floodlit cafeteria and letting him tell me about his dates as Chicago's busiest bachelor. He's my friend, my ally.

Friends don't keep secrets like mine.

"Prepping for intubation," I say while he's orchestrating his own team like he always does, with the confidence of a maestro at the front of a concert hall.

"I'm on airway," I tell him. I glance up to meet his blue eyes, and I don't miss the way Amber, my assistant neonatologist who's come to help me, fans her coat at the collar, watching him. He's the epitome of collected determination in turquoise-green scrubs. His coat is ironed to crease-free perfection. Even under the unforgiving fluorescent lights, he's a sight to behold and he knows it. Outside Evergreen, his eyes can't seem to stay on one woman past the first date, and he never talks much about his family besides his niece, unlike me. I talk about Rose all the time. How could I not? She's my twin and we live together, but somehow over the years, Theo and I have connected on a platonic, colleagues-to-friends level that I appreciate. Which is why I have to tell him my secret. But I can't. I have to talk to Rose first, and the baby's father. Oh, Lord.

My hands position the laryngoscope. I guide the tube gently past the baby's vocal cords, and the rush of adrenaline is followed by a strange flush of heat that almost knocks me off my feet. My heart hasn't settled enough yet for this.

Concentrate, Lily.

"Tube's in place," I announce, securing it before looking up for Theo's nod of approval. He gives orders for medication and Amber scurries to follow my own commands. He and I, we're the calm in the storm, always have been at work. Outside, well, things can get crazy. I guess I started at Evergreen around the beginning of my "I'm single and I don't give a crap" phase, when I was doing anything and everything to get Grayson out of my system. Theo kind of took me under his wing. Well, I'm pretty sure he had his mind on hooking up with me, but I squished that plan pretty fast. He's the biggest flirt on earth, the last person I'd trust with my heart after Grayson, but we do have fun. And the reason I'm in this mess now is because I was having fun. These are the consequences of my actions. It was supposed to be a *fun* holiday, a *fun*, one-time, one-night-only hookup with a *fun* guy on a motorcycle...

"Where are we at, Doctor Carter?"

I tell him we're not out of the woods yet.

I do my best every day to make sure no woman's world has to fall apart, so that no one has to endure the crippling loss of a child. Theo saves adult lives every day. But Dr. Theo Montgomery has no idea how much my own foundations have just been rocked. What would he do if he saw the check marks on the three little sticks in my purse in my locker? Our so-called *fun* is about to stop for good. He won't want to hang out with a pregnant lady and I can't give it up, even though it was an accident. I can't; I'm thirty-four. What if I never get this chance again?

Looking back, I was ready to start trying for a baby five or six months after meeting Grayson, back when I truly felt he was the love of my life. He certainly gave off those vibes at the start; no one knew the monster that lurked beneath the surface, especially not me! All I ever wanted was to love and care for and guide a child of my own, and that was what Grayson brought to the table, all packaged up in a wealthy, talented, handsome lover. I've often thought maybe I was blinded by my desire for a family when Grayson came along. If I'd looked harder, maybe I wouldn't have missed the sinister reality of what was really under my nose.

I draw up the precise dose of epinephrine, willing my hands not to shake as I pass the syringe to Theo. The infant's chest is tiny, so, so fragile, but he's fighting with each shallow breath. How big is the baby inside *me* at this point? No bigger than the nail on my little finger, already developing the tiny buds that'll be his or her arms and legs. He or she has a heartbeat. I'm growing another *life* inside me.

"Pushing one of epi," Theo announces, hands steady while the baby's heart dances wildly on the monitor.

"Come on, little guy," I whisper under my breath, taking his tiny hand between my fingers. The chaos begins to ebb, but the storm is far from over. I rub my eyes and blink a little too hard and catch Theo observing me. Concern etches lines in his forehead and I look away. He knows me; he already knows something's not right. His laser senses pick up on everything. At least he didn't see me almost walk into a glass door on the way in. My head was in the clouds. It still is, but now isn't the time to unravel.

"Blood gas next," I instruct, and he has it ready before I even finish my sentence. I take a swift sample from the baby's right heel. Theo nods, that familiar crease between his brows deepening.

"Oxygen saturation coming up," I report, watching the numbers climb slowly on the screen. "Heart rate's improving. Let's wean down the O2, see if he can hold his own."

Theo's gaze is fixed on the baby and I know he is willing him to fight, to stay with us. My hand goes briefly to my belly, just above my waistline, as I decrease the oxygen. The child's labored efforts soon ease into something resembling normalcy, but I'm still fighting to keep my emotions in check, seeing all this play out, knowing what's happening inside me in secret. "He's stabilizing."

There's a unanimous sigh of relief in the room. I can't stop the corner of my mouth from lifting, even as I swipe at my tired eyes. My head is starting to pound under these lights. Theo's blue eyes lock with mine for a heavy beat as he confirms we should get the baby up to NICU, the corners crinkling ever so slightly. He knows something's up. He definitely knows. So I really need to tell him.

It's at least an hour before he finds me, staring at my phone.

"Coffee, Carter?" he asks me from where he's snuck up, stealth-like, in the staff room. I ram my phone into my pocket too quickly, hiding the text I was writing to *Miami Motorhead*. I've written about nine drafts so far, but haven't sent anything yet. How do you tell a relative stranger several states away in Florida that he's impregnated you by mistake?

Theo turns those intense all-seeing eyes on me. "You okay? You're acting off today."

"Charming as usual," I say, feigning indifference to the way he's trying to read me. I search for a crease in the white lab coat over his scrubs. He's always so tidy. So meticulous. I tease him outside work. He has four pens in the breast pocket of his coat today, all lined up like soldiers ready for battle.

He steps closer and my breath hitches under his scrutiny. "I saw you zoning out." A faint trace of his cologne mingles with the antiseptic surroundings in my nostrils, and for a second I have to hold my breath. I usually like his woody sandalwood scent whenever I'm breathing it in, but it's making me feel a little ill right now.

"I'm just overtired," I tell him.

"Up late, drooling over warrior Highlanders again, were you?"

"If only I *could* time travel back to eighteenth-century Scotland. I wouldn't have to deal with you," I tell him quickly, and he smirks and cocks an eyebrow. Curse Rose for letting on in the cafeteria that we've been watching two old episodes of *Outlander* every night this week.

"Really, I'm fine, Theo." I sigh, trying to sound convincing. The July rain is still pounding the window in the periphery of my vision. He searches my face for a moment longer. Does he see through my facade? I should just tell him what I know right now...but I can't.

"Let's get you one of your frothy oat milk things," he says eventually. "You look like you could use it."

"Lead the way," I say, following him out of the room. What I really need is a moment alone to finish that text message, to wrap my head around the life growing inside me—a life that literally no one knows about except me. Rose is going to freak out, but I can't very well keep this from my twin. I can't keep anything from Rose, and not even just because we live together. I've a feeling she would know something was up with me if she lived on the moon, and I was still here on the outskirts of Chicago and we never spoke. Twin Spidey senses, and all that.

I never told her the first time Grayson started showcasing frightening narcissistic tendencies toward me, about a year into our relationship. I mean, there were red flags before that, but I pretended it wasn't happening at first, told myself I was imagining it, being paranoid. For the first eight to nine months I was completely head over heels. He was fun and complimentary, whisked me away on mini breaks, cooked me dinners, or tried to—he was never that good, even though I told him he was. He made everything too salty. That was the trigger, actually. When I told him his carbonara was too salty. It sounds so silly to say now, but the look on his face when I said that—that was the moment he changed. Or at least, that was when I decided to pay attention to the person he really was. Too bad I still loved him, anyway.

To think I spent almost four years after that, making excuses for his passive-aggressive comments and gaslighting, spiraling, growing needier by the day just to make sure he still needed *me*.

Rose called me out on it, though, eventually. My twin, as connected as she can be considering we're fraternal twins, not identical, saw the gradual decline, the way my light was dimming. She helped me get out. I have to remind myself frequently that I'm in a good place right now, a place where I don't need anyone. I'm in a happy place, a very fun place. Or at least I was. I still would be, if I wasn't accidentally expecting.

Theo gets the coffees, and I force myself not to pull my phone out while he's gone. He's talking to another nurse from another department, letting her go ahead of him in the line, giving her one of those heart-stopping all-white smiles. The nurse laughs, and damn if my own heart doesn't do a traitorous little flutter. Platonic or not, Theo shines most when he's being his real self, which is kind, considerate, attentive… Okay, fine, I like when his attention is on me. He's not a threat with it, like Grayson was.

Theo used to think he could flirt with me, but it doesn't work, and it never did. I don't date players. Just random, sexy Miami locals who pick me up over cocktails on SoBe and take me home on the back of an impressive, shiny red Indian Chief Vintage, apparently. If only we'd stopped on the villa's driveway. If only I hadn't invited him in.

"Nice work with that little one, Carter. He's going to be fine, I hope?" he says when he sits down, placing my coffee in front of me. I tell him of course he'll be fine, and realize I still don't really want to drink any coffee, but I bump my cup to his, tell him he was a hero as usual and take a sip so as not to seem off. I get another weird flutter when I picture that last baby's face. It didn't seem like just another doctor-patient case; it felt like something else entirely, knowing what I know. I thought about the mother even more the whole time; how was she feeling? How is she now? I'll go check on her, right after this, I decide.

"So, tell me about last night."

I know that's why Theo wanted to get me here. He

wants to tell me about his date. His first with some graduate student he met in Whole Foods shopping for avocados. His regular routine. I don't know how he doesn't get tired, going on so many first dates that never amount to anything.

He rakes at his hair and launches into how he booked them into some fancy steak restaurant, only to learn she was vegan, and that apparently she was annoyed at him because she swore she told him she was vegan in the vegetable aisle and he's *clearly* just another man who doesn't listen. I tell him maybe she's right, and he continues defending himself, which would usually make me laugh.

"Are you sure you're okay? You look different," he observes. My blood spikes as his tone shifts from playful to concerned again in a blink, as is his style.

"You just keep getting more charming," I tell him. I know I must look like I'm about to burst with the weight of what I know, but how can I explain this mind-blowing maelstrom of emotions about my surprise pregnancy when I haven't even begun to understand them myself?

Before Theo can press further, a familiar figure appears in my peripheral vision. Rose, my decidedly unpregnant twin sister, is the picture of professional poise in her equally well-ironed white coat.

"Excuse me, Dr Montgomery, can I borrow Lily for a moment?" she interjects smoothly.

"Please, take her away," he says, and I roll my eyes at him.

My beloved Rose's green eyes, exactly like mine, save for one tiny brown freckle on the perimeter of her right iris, look between us quickly, before she beckons me to follow her. I am fully expecting my twin to either reveal she knows via the Spidey line that something's amiss, or to relay the information that she'll be working late again tonight and can *I* make sure to feed our cat, Jasper. There's always some excuse to stay late in the fertility department. After four years of training in OB-GYN, she's all but been glued to her desk since going for the board certification in reproductive endocrinology and infertility. I'm proud of her of course; she needed something to get stuck into after the divorce. Even if a career as an endocrinologist puts her even more amongst women who are trying to get pregnant, women who unwittingly remind her that she was trying for a baby with David, before their marriage fell apart. I'm amazed by her strength sometimes. You'd never know she's deeply scarred underneath it.

She loops her arm through mine. Her touch is instantly grounding as she steers me away. I'm grateful for her impeccable timing, even as my stomach leaps in somersaults. *I have to tell her* is all I can think as she talks at me.

"So, Lils, we need to talk about Dad's party. Walk with me to the parking lot. I left something in the car..."

I knew it. I knew she was grabbing me while she could. Rose is always on the go; she barely gives herself time to breathe. Not that it matters if she's working late again. Tonight I'll curl up on the couch with Jasper and together we will go over this text message to *Miami Motorhead*. What was his real name? Something like Antonio? Anthony? Yes, Anthony, I think. It's so awful that I can't even remember but I wasn't supposed to ever have to think about him again. I was testing myself like I have done since it ended with Grayson, to see if

I could do "casual," to see if I could come off as something other than needy.

I glance back. Theo is watching us leave. His brow is all furrowed in suspicion and something else. Annoyance? Not at Rose; he adores Rose. He just senses that I'm keeping something from him. If Grayson ever suspected I was keeping something from him, there would be hell to pay— Why can't I stop comparing everyone to him, even now?

I follow Rose down the corridor and out into the rain-drenched forecourt. The trees blow wet droplets straight onto our heads as we make our way toward the parking lot. Should I tell her now? No. It would ruin her day. She's got enough going on. I'll wait, I decide, shoving down the little voice that pipes up, calling me a coward. I *have* to trust myself with this. I'll tell *Miami Motorhead* first, and then I'll tell everyone else.

CHAPTER TWO

THE SIZZLE OF bacon fills the kitchen. I try to mimic Rose's perfected method of egg poaching, but my hands are clumsy around the pan and bits of pink shell float around the whites as I break one. I'm distracted. Jasper winds around my ankles with an insistent purr, and I absentmindedly reach down to offer him a bit of bacon. Rose appears then, tutting, and tells me cats aren't supposed to eat bacon. I disagree. I think every being on earth is supposed to eat bacon, but I don't say it because she already knows what an advocate I am for the carnivore club. Theo and I try every new steak place in town the first week they open.

"Can you believe Dad's really turning sixty next weekend?" Rose says, tutting again at the broken eggshell as she leans over my shoulder. I shrug her off and she sticks out her tongue, grabbing the ketchup from the cupboard and placing it down with a plonk on the table. My heart's beating wildly as the words build up in my throat. There are so many ways I could say it now she's awake, now that it's the weekend and we've space and time. "We need to make sure everything is perfect. The catering, the guest list, especially the—"

"Rose." My voice cuts through her party-planning

monologue, sharper than I intend it to. It surprises even me, but I just can't keep this secret from her any longer.

She jolts her head up. Her eyes narrow as she studies me and tightens the belt around her plush white robe. "Do you think I picked the wrong caterer? I woke up worried about that. There's a place that does a great crawfish boil we could go with, if the Italian buffet thing is too much."

"Nothing's wrong, but…don't go for the crawfish," I say quickly. Just the thought of it turns my stomach. I've never particularly been a fan of seafood at the best of times.

"Then what is it?" She fills her coffee cup, then looks at me over it, her twin intuition on high alert. "Grayson didn't try to contact you again, did he?"

"It's not Grayson." I take a deep breath and rest my lower back against the counter, facing her. My arms feel too big in my matching robe as I fiddle with the sleeves. It's taken days for me to find the courage for this conversation, and now the words feel like boulders in my throat. "I'm pregnant."

The coffee cup she's holding clatters onto the floor. Jasper jumps in fright. She launches for a cloth and starts dragging it across the wet floor with one foot. "Jeez, Lily. You could have waited till I was sitting down!"

"What am I going to do?" I cross the kitchen and sink into the chair at the table. I feel suddenly devoid of strength. "I haven't heard back from him yet—the father. I've been waiting, giving him a chance to reply. That's why I didn't tell you sooner. I'm sorry, don't be mad."

"Mad?" Rose sinks into the chair opposite me and rakes her fingertips through her hair. She always has good hair, even when she wakes up, that silky dark mass of mahogany waves that mirrors my own. Except she keeps hers longer. I got mine trimmed to chin length before my solo vacation—the one that went so wrong. "Is it Theo's?" she asks me, and I snort.

"Theo's? Why would it be his?"

Rose looks confused, but mostly concerned now. She grasps my hand, knocking the ketchup over, and makes a big thing of looking very forcefully into my eyes. "I just assumed, I'm sorry, it's okay. Everything will be okay," she says, and I nod because I believe her; I have to. "How far along are you?"

"I was two weeks late," I murmur, tracing the wood grain of the tabletop. "I took three tests. Same results every time. So, about seven weeks."

I shake my head guiltily and she growls from the back of her throat, before seemingly remembering her lifetime role as my rock and squeezing my hand. "Lily, we'll figure this out. Together, all right?" She steps over what's left of the coffee spill and refills another mug. I see her staring out the window a second, and I know she's doing the math.

"So, seven weeks…"

"Miami," I blurt out. "The vacation you couldn't make because of work?"

"The *Miami Motorhead*? Oh, Lily, don't tell me… Wait, he still hasn't responded? When did you tell him?"

"On Tuesday."

"And today is Saturday—what a piece of…"

"Maybe he didn't get it for some reason," I interject as the implications start to swirl. I'm going to be a single mother. Either that or I abort; the thought has crossed my mind, of course, but it just doesn't sit right. I work around mothers and babies all day. I see how their arrivals, and sometimes premature departures, affect everyone involved. I know the likely state of my baby at any given moment. I can't unsee what I can't even see yet inside me.

My baby's brain has already started to develop; their facial features are starting to form. Rose reminds me we have a no-relationship pact, have done since we bought the house following her divorce and my…well, my disaster of a thing with Grayson, but I remind her that because of Grayson, this could be the only chance to be a mom I'll ever get.

"I never thought I'd be able to do this, because I'll probably never *have* another relationship, Rose."

She tuts again. "You're so dramatic!"

"I'm deadly serious. Men cannot be trusted! And now, well, look, no man! Just a baby, like I wanted. Maybe in a funny way, this happening now is fate."

She listens as I talk to her like always, but I know she's concerned for me, and I know she doesn't think it's funny. She sits back and sighs while Jasper leaps at a shadow. "You wanted adventure and fun after Grayson, Lils. But this…"

"I know," I mutter, thinking of the warm, muggy Florida night that started with cocktails and ended with sunrise out by the swimming pool. The luxury villa I was supposed to be sharing with Rose. A night of wild abandon with a man I assumed I'd never have anything to do with ever again. I was trying to live like Theo does. Maybe in a way I've always been a little jealous that Theo can live like every day and conquest could be his last. I've never been like that; I love too hard. I live too carefully. Not as carefully as Rose, mind you. Rose hasn't even been on a date since her eight-year marriage to David blew up. Sometimes I think watching the struggle I had with Grayson on top of all that put her off relationships for good, too, hence our pact.

She talks to me as she goes to the stove, retrieves the solidly poached and likely inedible eggs, instructs me on who I need to contact, what I need to eat. She tells me what my options are, as if I haven't already lived a lifetime's worth of research in a neonatal unit.

"The most important thing to know is that you won't be alone, Lily. You have me, and Dad and your friends..."

"Theo can't know," I say quickly, too quickly. "Not yet. He'd worry about me at work, and I can't—"

Rose narrows her eyes. "Is this why you just canceled on him for this afternoon?"

I pull a face. So she heard me on the phone before she came downstairs. I called him, canceling our regular biweekly Saturday plan to watch the NFL live in the Irish bar on Clark Street. Theo likes to pretend to watch the Chicago Bears while checking out hot tourists, and I actually enjoy watching the football. Just not today. I couldn't face it. Or him. How can I look into his eyes and not tell him what's going on?

Rose seems to read my thought pattern as usual. "Why don't you really want to tell him?"

"Because..." I trail off, searching for the words. In truth, I know I have to tell him. And I will. But now that the coast is clear for me to do so, I just don't want him to judge me...like Grayson did.

Rose cocks her head. "You're going to have to tell him eventually, especially if you're keeping it."

She's right. There's no way out of this. He's been looking at me funny all week in the hospital, analyzing me silently behind those blue eyes. I know him. Well, I know when he's troubled. I see it a lot after he takes phone calls sometimes, whatever that's about. It always sparks a twinge of empathy somehow, like I'm pulled to a certain darkness in him as much as I'm drawn to his light.

"I don't know how to tell him," I say aloud. Why am I getting so emotional about this?

Rose picks up Jasper and snuggles into him. "We'll figure it out, don't worry. But as for everyone else…it's probably best if we keep this to ourselves until you decide what to do. We need to find you a doctor who isn't a friend or colleague," she says, getting back to her eggs. "Someone discreet. I'll arrange it."

"Thank you," I whisper. What would I ever do without my sister?

"Code blue!" The intercom shatters whatever was left of my early Monday morning calm as I sprint down the hallway from the elevator, my scrubs rustling, my sneakers squeaking. I burst into the ER. Theo's already here, his hands moving deftly, his face a picture of determination as he intubates a tiny infant and informs me quickly of the situation while I pull on my gloves. I have to force my mind to transition from calm to emergency mode. I was just upstairs in the NICU with Zara, the young mother of the baby we helped last week. The one she's since named Tomas. We've kept them in for observation but they should both be released today.

"Bag ready, Doctor Montgomery?" I keep my voice calm as I take over, and he keeps his blue eyes laser focused. His gloves squeak against mine as he takes it and I feel a momentary jolt to my lower intestines as my secret rattles around inside me.

"Good. Keep an eye on his sats," I instruct, referring

to the baby's oxygen saturation levels. This little mite has been having trouble breathing on his own since he was born in a car several blocks away, gridlocked in traffic, only twenty-three minutes ago. I try not to let the nausea I've felt all morning affect me as I watch the monitors like a hawk and report the numbers out loud. My mind is whirring with its own countdown toward my scan tomorrow. We booked it at Dawson's Clinic, just out of town, so no one here has to do it. Rose will come with me, of course.

"Come on, little guy," I murmur to the baby, and Theo looks away just as I pull my hand from my lower belly, where it seems to keep moving to all on its own. "His sats are picking up," I announce, clearing my throat, ignoring the look he's giving me. I'll tell him I've got a stomachache if he asks. But lying won't work; he's not an idiot. Look at where he works. He's going to see right through me.

The baby's breathing stabilizes. Soon, the whirlwind of activity around me reduces to just Theo and me. He yanks off his gloves and throws them into the wastebasket across the room, as I tell Amber to bring the baby's mother in from where she's waiting right outside in a wheelchair. She needs to go to the maternity ward, and I need to finish my rounds in the NICU, where this little one belongs, too, for the meantime.

I watch the young woman's face as she strokes her little boy's cheek around the tubes. Her baby's eyelashes are fluttering, his puckered little face exploring new expressions. My eyes are starting to leak at the corners and people are going to see. I tell Amber I'll see them upstairs and try not to look back over my shoulder at

Theo. He's still watching me. I can feel it. I should take him aside on the next break and tell him, just come right out and say it. But I'm scared, no thanks to Grayson.

Far from the caring man I fell in love with in the early days, the one who was careful to remain the considerate partner so I wouldn't see through the veneer, toward the end of our relationship Grayson became someone I lived in fear of telling anything to that might alter his opinion of me further. The abuse was subtle at first, barbs and jabs inflicted with a smile or a cocked eyebrow. He would lure me to the bedroom with compliments and love bombs, then berate me for wearing the wrong color underwear, and then try to sleep with me, anyway. He'd praise my cooking, then refuse to eat it. If I asked why, he'd say he was sure it didn't taste as good as it looked, leaving me alone in silence and confusion, to box it up and bring it over to my sister.

Theo isn't Grayson, not at all, but he'll start to look at me as something broken, someone who made a terrible mistake, someone who's the opposite of everything he thought I was.

I catch myself. Theo's my friend, and this is my business. Isn't it his duty to support me? Why do I care so much what Theo thinks these days, just because those bright blue eyes might see more than I ever realized?

The last patient has been wheeled away and the weight of the longest Monday on record is a kettlebell on my shoulders as I fumble for my car keys in the parking lot. I'm almost at my car when I hear his familiar baritone behind me.

"Carter!" He jogs lightly to catch up with me. "You left before I could catch you..."

My fingers clasp around my keys in the bottom of my purse and I pull them out, turning to face him slowly. "What's up?" I say, avoiding his gaze.

"Come on... Really? *What's up?* We're really going to do this?" His tone is gentle but probing as he takes a step closer. "You bailed on our game date on Saturday. Since when do you turn down a chance to gloat over a bucket of wings?"

"That's your idea of a *date*, Theo? Hearing a woman gloat over fried chicken?"

"Depends what she's done to gloat about," he says with a smirk, and I raise my eyes to the roof.

"Oh, come on, Lily." He scowls at me till his brows touch, which somehow still makes him look impossibly handsome. "You're being weird."

"It's just a busy time, Theo... Dad's party and all that."

His blue eyes cloud momentarily. Hurt flickers across his face, and I hate how it lashes at my heart like a whip. He doesn't know Rose's words got to me more than they should have over the weekend; did she actually think this baby could be Theo's? She knows Theo and I have never been more than friends and colleagues. I guess there might have been a time when his advances were kind of tempting, once I'd moved into the house with Rose and was starting to feel more like myself again. But by then we were firmly in the friendship zone—a fling would have messed it up. And it's not like Theo ever wants more than a fling.

"Actually, speaking of dates, I canceled one myself this weekend," he says now, eyeing me down his nose.

Looking down his nose at me is not unusual, seeing as he's six foot four.

"Did you?" I ask, genuinely surprised. "Losing your touch?"

"Hardly," he shoots back with a grin that doesn't quite reach his eyes. It roots me to the spot. "I just had other things on my mind."

We stand facing each other. The space between us charges by the second with a thousand unspoken words and a truckload of tension I'm not ready to unpack.

Tell him, my brain screeches at me. *Why can't you just say it?*

Unless he knows somehow. Is he testing me? Waiting for me to say it first?

"Changing the subject," he says after a beat. "Need me to whip up a batch of my chili chocolate cupcakes for Geoff's party?"

"Your what?" I laugh despite myself. For a second there, I really thought he was going to tell me he knew about the baby somehow. "You mean the ones that sent Verity Henderson into a coughing fit last Christmas? She almost redecorated Dad's kitchen in a *very* disturbing shade of brown after eating *half* of one."

"Purely coincidental," Theo insists with mock indignation. "I'll have you know those are a surefire win at every baking contest I enter."

"Only because they're too afraid to disqualify you," I tease. "In case they ever need you in an emergency of some kind."

Theo winces, placing a hand over his heart. "You wound me, Carter."

"Get a bandage," I say before reminding him that I

know for a fact he's never entered any baking contests in his life.

"You underestimate me," he says. "If you knew even half of my talents, you'd be nothing short of intimidated."

"Intimidated? I've seen puppies more intimidating than you. You're just a prize-winning flirt, that's what you are."

His snort, which morphs into a chuckle, tells me he's enjoying our banter as much as I am, but for some reason I'm reading more into what he means by *talents* than I usually would, and now I'm thinking about what he really must be like in the bedroom. Damn Rose, getting in my head.

I unlock my car with a beep. "Just make sure those *talents* don't include food poisoning half the party guests," I tell him.

"So, that means I'm coming. With cakes."

"Affirmative," I say with a smile.

His tone softens suddenly, then turns serious, and my stomach twists. "Listen, Carter, if there's anything else—"

"I know where to find you," I finish for him, sliding into the driver's seat. I close the door on him and he crosses his arms. That serious expression on his face is gnawing at me more by the second. I'm a coward, I know I am, and if I keep this from him much longer, only for him to find out, it won't be great for our friendship. But I can't have this bond turned on its head just yet. It means too much to me.

CHAPTER THREE

I'M TALKING TO myself under my breath, deep house music blasting from my stereo. My egg whites are being whisked with a bit more vigor than is probably necessary, too. The recipe called for something like "a delicate hand," but I'll leave that to the ER. My mind isn't really focused on the fluffiness of egg whites right now. It's on Lily's latest bout of uncharacteristic silence. I didn't even bother pushing her this time; I know she hates that. And I didn't want to hear her brush me off again.

I take the bowl over to the windows and rest my eyes on the green of the trees, the two pigeons in their usual spot. My corner of Winnetka looks pretty shiny beyond the terrace this morning, shinier than I feel, considering it's Saturday and I have to be at her dad's birthday party this afternoon. I *was* looking forward to it. Lily's family is great. Usually, I invite myself over before they get a chance to; they're everything my own family is not. But something's very off with Lily. I would rather just hit the home gym again than probe and press her on it, only to be rebuffed.

Still, I made a promise. I'm already on my third batch of chili chocolate cupcakes when Taylor Swift blasts out around the room, cutting through my thoughts. My hands are still covered in cocoa powder as I fumble for my cell. My sister. "Peonie. Are you aware your daughter changed my ringtone to Taylor Swift again?"

"You shouldn't leave your phone unlocked, Theo." Peonie's voice is too energetic for the hour. She's probably been to yoga class, walked the dog and dropped Delilah off at the stables for her horse-riding lesson already. She's the mother she always wanted to be, the woman our own mother never was...and still isn't.

I brace myself for Pea to tell me what Mom's done now. It was her turn to welcome the new carer, a sweet lady called Edwina. Let's just hope this one sticks.

Whenever I think about our bipolar, alcohol-addicted mother it's a one-way ticket back to the pits of hell that constituted my childhood. Her demons succeed in every situation; even her psychologist is afraid of her. She's struggled with addiction our entire lives but as kids, Pea and I lived in complete fear of her erratic behavior, her crying fits, her bouts of rage. Oh, she'd be kind, too. She'd gush over us, tell everyone around how wonderful we were, get our hopes up. Then before we knew it, she'd be yelling and sobbing and telling us she should never have had us.

She targeted Dad a lot, until he had enough and divorced her. It's had all manner of repercussions on Pea and me over the years, but I don't talk about those any more than Pea does. She's got her family. I've got my work. All we can do is love our mother, ensure the carers who come into her home are the best we can afford, even if she detests all of them, and let her spend time with Delilah. My niece is literally the only person she tolerates.

"To what do I owe this pleasure? I'm kinda busy," I tell her. She snorts.

"Oh, really? How many women are you juggling this morning, darling brother? Cooking breakfast for one before you head out to meet another for brunch, am I right?"

I don't even bother to defend myself. I *was* a player. I mean, I *have* been, but I've canceled more dates than I've shown up to lately. It's all just getting a little tiring, especially with things how they are at work.

And with Lily, drifting away from me.

I've considered that maybe she's bored of me, but we've never been bored together ever; we have too much stupid banter going between us for that. I've been watching her. I'm pretty sure I know what I'm looking at. I just hope to God I'm wrong.

I tell Pea she's deranged and we play-bicker like we normally do for a moment before she finally gets back to what I knew was coming the second she called.

"So, Mom," Pea sighs. I can almost see her rubbing her temples as I check on my latest batch of cakes. They're browning nicely. "You know she's off the meds again."

I knew it. "Great news, just great," I say through my teeth. Same old story. It doesn't take much for my brain to serve a throwback to a million situations I had to all but drag Pea away from when she was a kid. When *I* was still a kid. I can hardly blame Dad for taking off, but no one wants to think they were abandoned, and I've tried to make it up to Pea her whole life.

Me…well, I just abandon people before they can jump ship themselves. Rip the bandage off for minimal pain all around. Isn't that how you do it?

Pea continues. "Before Edwina arrived today she locked herself in the bathroom to count the wall tiles again. Edwina is saying she's refusing the pills. She spat them out and tried to stuff them down the sofa."

I glance at my newest batch of unfinished cupcakes. We found a whole pharmacy's worth of pills down the sofa last time we checked. "All right, I'll talk to her after Geoff's party."

Pea tells me thanks and excuses herself to get back to watching Delilah practice her show-jumps. They say she's pretty advanced for an eleven-year-old. Delilah is somewhat of a child prodigy, although we might be biased. She's the best thing to happen to our family for a long time, and the one thing that gives Pea hope that Mom might change, someday. If it wasn't for how nice Mom is with Dee, and how soft Pea is, she'd probably be in rehab already.

I shower and change, box up my cakes and make my way to the party. Pea's in my head the whole time. She didn't see the half of what I did growing up. Being six years older than her, I did everything to protect her from Mom's disease. I whisked her off to our late Granny Fran whenever I could, and I thank whatever God is up there that Granny Fran took us in after Dad left and Mom stopped working and we lost the house. I know Pea is scarred like I am. But she's also an infuriating optimist. She married her high-school sweetheart, Riley, when she was twenty, popped Delilah out just eight months later, and to this day she continues trying to be everything she can be for her daughter. She does her best to give her everything *she* never had, and still never gets from Mom.

If I have to deal with more of Mom's drama just to keep Pea happy, of course I will, but if things get worse I'll have no choice but to put her in rehab.

I frown, even as I walk up the driveway. It's not just

Mom I have to worry about now. Lily's not the same lately; she's hiding something. She's definitely hiding something, and I think I know what it is. And I don't like it one little bit.

The door swings open before I can knock. Animated chatter floods my ears. The twins' place is a remodeled tenement, and its Glenview bones are at least a hundred years older than the modern furniture they filled it with when they bought it together. They got it after Rose's divorce. I think Lily's last long-term relationship fell apart sometime before that, though she doesn't say much about that—some guy called Grayson, whom she never seems to want to talk about. I don't push it. She and I met after that ended anyway, the first day she started at Evergreen, when I hit on her, of course; she's hot. She shut me down, quite rightly. So I took what I could, which was her friendship, even though we have a connection.

More than just a connection, if I'm honest with myself. She's fun, and smart and beautiful and thoughtful and kind, but I'm drawn to her for other reasons I can't explain, and I guess that's why I respect her boundaries. If I tried anything on now, it would ruin this comfy thing we've built, and it means too much to me at this point.

"Theo, hi." Rose greets me with her usual efficiency, taking the cupcakes and barely pausing for air as she whisks them away and tells me Lily is in the kitchen with Geoff.

I move through the throng of guests. My presence elicits a mix of polite nods and less subtle, appreciative glances from women I barely recognize. But as always, it's Lily's reaction I find myself seeking out. These past few days, I haven't known which reaction I'm likely to get. It's like she's become increasingly elusive with every passing day.

"Doctor Theo Montgomery!" Lily's father, Geoff is calling out from across the room, using my full title as usual. Lily is next to him, at the far end of the dinner table, nestled between cousins I've met maybe once or twice. Geoff gets up to greet me. Lily does not. She offers a faded smile as her dad and I do our usual high five that blends into a fist bump. Geoff thinks it's cool. I don't like to make him think it's not.

She touches her hair as Geoff tells me for the hundredth time what a great job he's heard I'm doing at Evergreen, and also that he knows I won my last boxing match. Did Lily tell him that? Through the window, I can see Jasper, the world's most pampered British shorthair, lounging on a pillowy shelf in his cattery. I don't like cats, never have. I think it goes back to Granny Fran's second husband always moaning about their cat's hair everywhere, then finding some in my cornflakes.

I feel Lily's green gaze on me the whole time, but I don't go over to her. I can almost feel how she doesn't want me to, which is what's eating at me. I want to at least know she's okay.

I'm swept around the room by everyone from Geoff's lawyer to Rose's hairdresser, but I can feel the tension radiating off Lily. It's concentrating in a tight ball between us and I know she feels it, too. She's wearing a thick cardigan over a wraparound dress. Even from here I can see her boobs are bigger. Swollen. She'd hate that I'm noticing things like this, the changing shape of her breasts, but I'm a doctor, and I'm human.

"Drink?" Rose asks me, reappearing like a ghost at my side.

"Water's fine, thanks." My gaze drifts back to Lily. She seems to be wilting like a flower left too long in the sun. I really hope my suspicions aren't correct, but she's also only drinking water.

"Make sure he eats something," I hear one of the aunts say about me, fussing over my plate like I am still a teenager. It's true. I've only taken a couple of small items from the Italian buffet catering that's spread about in trays on the counters. This isn't like me. Food is our thing, but Pea got to me, and Lily's getting to me, too.

"Trust me, Aunt Carol, I can fend for myself," I say, anyway, adding a wink I know she'll appreciate, and she pats my cheek fondly.

I get a sudden flashback to being eight, or nine, asking Mom if I could have a bag of chips, only for her to make me separate them on a plate into different size categories. Pea was a toddler. She grabbed a chip from my plate, as toddlers do, and Mom flew into a rage about how no one appreciates her when she tries to teach us discipline.

I couldn't fend for myself for a long time. Everything I had I gave to Pea. And nothing I ever did was appreciated, not by our mother, anyway. I guess if you were to psychoanalyze me you'd say that was why I went all out in a profession where I'd always be useful and always be rewarded for it. ER doctors don't get abandoned. We're essential workers; we're necessary. My eyes are drawn back to Lily as she stands abruptly, her chair scraping against the hardwood floor. Her hand flies to her mouth, eyes wide with panic.

"Excuse me," she mumbles. Then she makes a dash for the bathroom. The room goes quiet.

"Rose, I'll go—" I start, already stepping forward.

"Theo, it's okay. I've got her," Rose interrupts. Her

calmness would be fully convincing to most people, but it's her eyes that betray her. She's worried, and not just because Lily is her sister.

"Let me check on her," I insist. I'm an ER doctor; I am usually untouchable. So why is my heart flapping like a trapped bird right now?

"Fine," Rose concedes. She follows just a step behind as I push through the hallway and find Lily leaning against the cool tile of the bathroom wall. Her face is ashen.

"Leave us please," I tell Rose, and she cocks her eyebrow at me in suspicion as I shut the door, locking us in.

"What's going on?" I kneel beside her. "Carter, talk to me. You're greener than the Hulk."

"I'm fine," she lies, her breathing shallow. She meets my eyes, then looks away. My hand finds hers before I sweep her cheek. She's hot in my hand, clammy, and she starts peeling off her cardigan while I fill a glass with water.

"You don't look fine."

"Can we just…not do this here?" Her voice cracks as she takes the glass and downs three huge mouthfuls.

"Are you pregnant, Lily?"

The question hangs in the air like a charged particle. I watch the shock ribbon out across her green eyes, eyes that I've fallen into more times than I care to admit when we've been out talking, in bars, downing shots at the end of crazy shifts. She puts the water down too heavily on the floor. I drop to my haunches again and she covers her face.

"Theo, how could you even—"

"You think I haven't noticed? The way your clothes

are fitting differently, the way you're so tired all the time lately… It's written all over your face, every shift."

She sinks back against the bathroom wall as if my words are a physical blow, her hands fluttering to her stomach protectively. I still feel hotter than I should, knowing this is what she's been hiding from me. Why was she hiding it from me? Doesn't she trust me?

"I—I don't know what to say."

"Start with the truth," I instruct.

"Eight weeks," she murmurs. She's barely audible above the noise of my own heart in my ears. "I'm eight weeks along."

"Eight weeks," I echo numbly. I mean, I had an inkling, but now that she's confirming it I can't process any of this.

"And before you ask," she continues, "the father doesn't want anything to do with me. Or the baby. He's in Miami."

Anger flares within me, fierce and protective. A kind I haven't felt for a long time, the kind that makes me grapple for control. Lily sees it bubbling and her hand on my arm stops me cold. "I'm okay with it. I don't need him. I have Rose," she says.

I have so many questions, but I'm having to rein in my temper. This isn't about me. It's about Lily, about supporting her, no matter how much this situation makes my blood boil. If he's in Miami, this happened on that trip she took. She even told me about the guy afterward, the hookup at the villa. I think I even laughed and told her *Well done*. Right before I stood alone at the bar for ten minutes on my phone, so I wouldn't have to look at her and picture another guy all over her.

Not important. None of that is important.

"Well, now I know, Lily." I wait until her gaze meets mine again. "I'm with you, all right? Whether you decide to keep it or not."

Her eyes narrow in a flash of annoyance. "Why wouldn't I keep it? It's not like I'll ever get another chance."

I ask her what she means; she has plenty of time to meet someone and have a family if that's what she wants, but she looks sideways and mumbles something about Grayson.

"What about Grayson?"

"I just don't want another relationship, Theo. Can we leave it please?"

I shut my mouth. I know better than to offer my opinion here; it's not like I'm the father. But what the hell does her ex-boyfriend have to do with this situation, or her not wanting another relationship? What did Grayson do?

"Nobody else knows except Rose yet," she says, stopping my thoughts in their tracks. "I'll tell them today. I'll tell Dad."

"Damn it, Lily." The words blurt out with more emotion than I mean for her to hear as I sink to the floor against the wall beside her. "Why didn't you say anything to me sooner?"

"Because I was scared, Theo."

"Of what? Of me?"

"Of everything changing."

The way she says it pushes a mute button in me. I clamp my lips shut. I almost can't process what it is I'm actually feeling, but everything *did* just change. She won't need me around for much longer, not in the same way, and a prickly heat floods my veins at the thought of being shut out. A regression to a million memories of being told I'm not enough. It's my fault, not Lily's, but still, we just became two very different people.

CHAPTER FOUR

Eight weeks later

IT'S SO PEACEFUL and quiet in Neonatal this rainy late-September morning, save for the regular beeps and murmurs. I navigate the rows of incubators that each house a fragile new life and as usual, I think about the life inside me. He, or she, is making their presence known a little more each day beneath my scrubs.

I kind of like the gentle but insistent pressure against my waistband. I like the fact that my miracle skin is stretching to accommodate new life. It's almost time to get new clothes. I haven't gotten around to it yet. I know Rose is too busy to make it a priority and I guess I'm not pushing it because, like with a lot of the smaller activities that no one else thinks twice about, shopping was ruined for me once. I think about this one incident with Grayson every time I'm in a clothing store. He told me I looked beautiful in a dress I wanted to wear for a wedding. I was buzzing. Finally, a compliment! Then, when the assistant left, he told me I was dreaming if I thought he'd ever let me wear something so revealing and trashy in public.

But sixteen weeks in and I'm starting to show now. It's quite amazing. Terrifying, too.

"Morning, Ezra," I whisper to a preemie girl with a fuzz of chestnut hair. She's just waking up, her face all cutely scrunched. "How are you doing today?"

All through my rounds, my mind wanders to the little being inside me. Is it dreaming? Can it sense the love already enveloping it from this side of the world? Rose, Dad, and my aunt and Theo, too, all think I'm crazy for going into this alone, not that they're telling me. Theo's been keeping his respectful distance. I think he's weirded out by it all. I've been telling myself he'll come around, and I hope he does because I'm starting to miss him. But I don't *need* him, or anyone. I'm doing this alone by choice. I have to keep reminding myself of that.

"Looks like someone's popped," comes a soft voice. I look up into the eyes of Sheena. Her son Vivek has been fighting valiantly ever since his premature arrival three weeks ago. She's always the first in when I open the doors for visits.

"Is it that obvious?" I ask. I can feel my cheeks warming as I say it. A little pride, a little embarrassment, I suppose.

Sheena throws me a knowing smile. "Only to a practiced eye." She reaches out, her fingertips hovering but not touching my midsection. "You've got that glow, Doctor Carter. And I don't just mean the pregnant one—you always have a shine about you."

This is news to me. I saw myself as a shell for a long time, even after I left Grayson. In a way, Theo brought me out of myself. When we met, one of the reasons I was drawn to him was because he made me laugh. I already miss that.

Sheena touches Vivek's incubator. "He's been gaining weight, hasn't he?"

"Yep. He's a fighter," I affirm, watching as she strokes the back of Vivek's tiny hand with her fingertip. The baby has tubes aiding his breathing and feeding but he clenches reflexively. His miniature grip is strong. A very good sign. Sheena tells me she was so grateful when I explained the PDA ligation, even before the surgeon came to speak to her. She's referring to the procedure performed to correct her son's heart complication. "You were amazing, keeping me calm, explaining everything... I felt beyond lost."

She asks if I've picked out names yet, or if I'm waiting to find out the sex, and the question hangs in the air as I secure a blanket around another newborn. "Actually, I'm having the scan this afternoon," I admit. "At another facility."

Just as I say it, a shadow falls across the medical chart in my hands.

"This afternoon?" I look up. Theo's here. He's popped up on his break, like he does sometimes, not that he's done it a lot lately, though. A pang hits my heart like a ping from a rubber band. I've missed him. Maybe more than I thought.

Sheena makes her exit and he leans casually against the door frame. His coat is ironed to perfection as usual but he looks a little tired. I clutch the chart like a shield, then press a hand absently to my belly. "Sneaking up on me, are you?"

"Stealth is part of the job description," he says. I give him some flippant comeback, but I can't help but wonder if he's been out all night on a hot date, and a bolt of something like jealousy rocks me from my sneakers up to my throat. Why is my brain trying to trick me? Hormones, probably. Everything is out of balance. Theo's distance since Dad's party has gotten to me. He's been supportive enough around here on the brief occasions we've met, but he hasn't asked me to go to the Irish pub, or to come watch him box, or to do anything much at all out of hours, ever since. It's like he sees me as a different person, just like I feared.

"The ultrasound is this afternoon, after my shift," I tell him now.

"The big gender reveal, right?"

"Right," I echo, and there's an awkward pause as we both seem to grapple with the implications. Today it gets real. *More* real. I find out if the life I am carrying is male or female, and whether everything is developing as it should.

"Rose will be with you," he says, pulling out his phone, looking at it, then shoving it back into his pocket. He looks stressed.

"Yes. Is everything okay?" I ask.

"Mmm-hmm." He walks around the unit and doesn't elaborate, and I don't pry. I know how his mom and sister stress him out, just from seeing his face after he talks to one of them, but I don't know much beyond that. I asked once, and he shut me down. Since then I haven't probed much into his personal life beyond what he chooses to tell me. It's not like I haven't shut him down before when he's tried to talk about me and Grayson. But for some reason, probably because I have missed him, I ask him if he wants to talk about it.

He stops by an incubator and shakes his head without looking at me, and I curb the flare of annoyance from escaping my mouth. It feels like he's renouncing my right to know things about him slowly but surely, day by day.

I hate feeling so powerless, but the moment stretches until it's thin enough to snap.

"Hey," I begin, fidgeting with the hem of my white coat. "I'm kind of nervous about the ultrasound today, actually. I might take the morning off tomorrow, depending on how it goes. I'll put the locum on standby."

He looks up now, crossing the space between us. "I thought you didn't do nervous, Carter. Isn't that your superpower?" His tone is lighter, but his eyes search mine with genuine concern, and a small weight lifts from my shoulders. So he does still care, which I guess is the reason I'm telling him, to see if he does. Which is kind of pathetic. He's not Grayson, so what am I doing?

"Carrying a human inside me is my superpower," I say. "Would you do it, if you could?"

"Carry a human inside me?" He seems to contemplate it for a moment, and the look on his handsome face is already making me smile. "I don't think I would, no. Delilah is enough. She keeps changing my ringtone to Taylor Swift. It's really not ideal in emergency situations."

"I've missed you," I tell him before I can order myself not to. I can't control the tears that prick at my eyes from out of nowhere, and I swipe at them in embarrassment. Grayson hated when I cried; he said I was weak. "Sorry, gosh, my hormones are all over the place. I'm a crazy person, ignore me."

He lowers his head and looks up at me from under his eyelashes. Then he grimaces. "I've upset you by backing off, haven't I?"

"Kind of," I admit. "I mean, you said and did all the right things when you found out but then you pulled a Houdini, so yeah, I guess I'm a bit confused."

He's quiet for a moment. I can tell the wheels are turning in his head. "I wasn't really sure how much you'd *want* me to be around—" He trails off and steps closer, but I cross my arms. I won't appear weak. *Miami Motorhead*, aka Anthony, finally got in touch. He said he would support my decision, but doesn't want to be involved, just like I suspected. I left it. I don't need him. I don't need anyone. At least, I don't *want* to need anyone.

"I know you've been tired, and nauseated. I didn't think you'd appreciate me trying to make extracurricular plans. I'll make it up to you," Theo says, and the regret in his voice makes me bite back a smile. "I promise to be a better friend from now on. Do you need a foot rub? Got any weird cravings I can satisfy?"

"Like what?" I ask, and he reminds me how I once dealt with a woman who'd taken to licking dry tennis balls during her second trimester. Finally, it feels like we have our old banter back. I'm about to ask him if he wants to hang out tonight when the emergency alarm goes off in the hallway, and he's forced into a sprint from the room.

The clock reads five forty-five after another hectic day. My appointment at Dawson's is in thirty minutes. I check my watch again, pulling my jacket on, looking around for Rose. We were both supposed to be taking my car and meeting here, in the parking lot.

My phone rings, and my heart makes a dash for my throat when I see her face on the screen. "Rose?"

"Sorry, sorry, sorry, sorry, forgive me," comes her stream of despair. She's been held up after the board director dropped in unannounced. He wants to take the team for dinner to discuss potential candidates for a new role they're recruiting for soon, and can we possibly please reschedule the scan for the morning?

I can hear the regret in her voice. It breaks my heart. It's not her fault the board director is so demanding, even though it feels like she's always working these days. And what if they don't have an appointment for the morning? I'm not quite ready to take my personal affairs to Evergreen where everyone knows me; telling them I'm pregnant with a baby that the father wants nothing to do with was bad enough.

"It's more that I've been psyching myself up for this all day, and I didn't want to go alone," I tell her.

"I'm the worst sister, Lily. Forgive me."

"Where do you have to go alone? Not to your ultrasound, I hope?" Theo's deep voice makes me spin around. He's wearing that slightly worn leather jacket, the one with the sleeves a little frayed at the edges and the scuffed elbows. The white shirt he's wearing underneath is ironed perfectly, even the pocket. The look, which I'm sure he knows, screams Chicago's hottest bachelor. Even his dark jeans are crease-free. He looks like he's changed to go somewhere else, not just home. Why does this make me feel so uncomfortable?

I pull a face and tell him how Rose can't make it. Rose is still on the line. "Theo, Theo can take you, right?" she says in my ear, like she's single-handedly discovered the perfect solution. I think Theo hears her.

"Sure, I'll go with you," he offers. Then he pauses, bringing his car keys up from the depths of his pocket. "If you want me to, Carter."

I don't, actually. Until today he was distancing himself, which still annoys me more than it probably should, even though I know why. And also, attending scans is a privilege for family members and significant others. But I have neither of those today, and I really *don't* want to go alone.

We take his car. Theo's very proud of his car. He's never said it but I can tell, even though it's as sparse inside as his apartment. There isn't even a Coke can on the floor, or a book flung in the back seat. He doesn't seem to have a lot of stuff, I've noticed. I don't know why. Maybe he's as commitment phobic with stuff as he is with people.

He sends a message when we stop at the lights, but I don't see who it's for. He gets a message back, a couple, actually, but he never looks at his phone again. The Porsche's wheels hum against the pavement, a soothing lullaby that almost makes me forget the flutter of nerves in my stomach. Theo talks about the concert he's taking Delilah to. He worships his eleven-year-old niece, Delilah. I like her, too. We bonded at a museum-night sleepover a couple years back. I casually ask if everything in his family is okay again now, and he shrugs. His expression darkens for a moment but still, I don't press it. For a second he looks more nervous than I do and it hits me; I really don't know that much about Theo, and I want to.

We arrive at Dawson's at six twenty-five.

"Are you doing all right?" Theo asks me from behind the wheel. I click off my seat belt as he parks the car. He was quiet the whole drive.

"Are *you* all right?" I reply. "You seem nervous."

He sniffs. "We're finding out the sex of this baby. I'm nervous for you, Carter. What if it's an impossibly handsome boy like me who's going to cause you years of trouble?"

I huff a laugh, and he exits the car, but I know he's covering for something. I can't focus on that now, though. I'm just so grateful he's come.

The sterile halls echo with hushed voices and the occasional squeak of rubber-soled shoes as we step into the ultrasound room. I almost want to turn around again, but Theo is blocking the door, his jacket and mine draped over one arm.

"Ms. Carter?" The sonographer Dr. Priya Sharma's voice is gentle, grounding. I lie back on the examination table, the paper crinkling beneath me. Theo is still standing by the door. I bet he feels so awkward.

"You can come closer, if you like," Dr. Sharma says, and before I can tell him that he can wait outside if he wants, Theo places the jackets onto a nearby chair, steps to my side and reaches for my hand. I squeeze it, as if I can possibly transfer my racing heartbeat into his warm, steady palm.

"Are we ready to see what this little one's up to?" She starts to spread the cool gel across my abdomen. I try to steady my breathing as the monitor flickers. Dr. Sharma moves the smooth, hard tool gently around my midsection and narrows her eyes for a split second. I catch it and my stomach plummets.

Oh, no, what?

I see Theo's face next. His blue eyes widen, and he leans in closer to the screen at the exact same moment Dr. Priya does. I follow his eyes. An exhilarated smile stretches out his face, and I almost choke on my own breath.

"Twins," Theo announces, before Dr. Priya can.

She nods and lets him wheel the monitor closer so I can see better.

Twins.

The word echoes through the room, doubling itself in my mind. Twins? I turn to Theo, who's still grinning in a way that makes him look ten years younger and twenty times more handsome. Here they are, right here. Two little beings, my babies, dancing in their own private universe.

"Twins are a huge part of my family. They have been for generations, but somehow I never really thought…" My voice trails off. I'm lost in a swell of emotions now, just looking at the screen. I am completely mesmerized by what I'm seeing and soon I'm hearing it, too—two tiny hearts beating in sync.

"They're cooking along nicely, Carter," Theo says proudly.

"Would you like to know the genders?" Dr. Sharma asks. My palm is warm and clammy now from my nerves, glued to Theo's. He's still mouthing the word *twins* to himself, and there's a look of disbelief and wonderment on his face that I've never actually seen before. Am I ready? I think I am. I tell her yes. I think I'm feeding off Theo's excitement.

Dr. Sharma begins with another swirl of the cool wand over my abdomen. "You're having a boy and a girl."

"One of each, no…" Theo lets out a laugh, just as I do.

A boy and a girl. This is crazy. More tears gather in the corners of my eyes. "Just like Rose dreamed," I remember suddenly. Weirdly, Rose said she had a dream the other night, in which I announced this exact thing. I wish she were here now. She'd be wrapped around their little fingers already, too.

"Congratulations, Carter," Theo whispers. I know I'm emotional, but his words tingle my ear and send a flush of adrenaline to my nerves. I can't help missing my sister, but I'm so relieved that someone's here to witness this. That *Theo* is here to witness this.

"Congratulations, *both* of you," Dr. Priya says, making me a printout so I can show Rose. She's going to be so thrilled. Just wait till she… Wait… *What did she say?*

"Oh, no," I insert as it hits me what this lady just alluded to. "Theo's not… I mean, we're not…"

"They're going to be so loved, right, wifey?" Theo finishes for me. He's still marveling at the screen. He really does look fiercely determined now and I let the comment go.

They will definitely be loved. But my friend and colleague has just been mistaken for the father of these babies, and more concerning, for a hot fleeting second there I caught myself wishing he really *were*.

CHAPTER FIVE

"Doctor Montgomery, heart rate's dropping. Severe cord prolapse." The obstetrician's voice cuts through the cacophony of the ER. I glance at the monitor. The mother and baby just arrived five minutes ago, and her baby's heart rate is plummeting while it's being strangled by the umbilical cord. In the next room the mother's relative, or friend, is sobbing. This precious life is hanging in the balance right in front of us, tangled in its own lifeline.

"Clamp." The obstetrician's command is met with immediate action as the team rallies around us. "We need to get this baby out now."

"Prepping for episiotomy." Her hands and feet move in a blur around the gurney as she prepares for the necessary incision. "Anesthesiologist?"

"Here," Dr. Zhalo calls. I continue monitoring the fluids as he prepares to issue an epidural. The laboring woman is far too quiet. I can read the panic on her face.

Lily's just appeared. She meets my eyes as we work, on standby to get this child up to the NICU. She looks just as anxious. Would I do this if I could? Lily asked before, so I considered it. I love Delilah to death, but my own kids… I always assumed that whole "being a dad" thing was off the cards, seeing as I've never entertained a long-term commitment.

I doubt I could offer them any more stability at this point in my life than my own mother could when I was a kid, but I'm thirty-eight. A man at least has to think about these things. There was a weird moment in that ultrasound room the other week when I caught myself pretending those twins were mine, and I actually felt excited. I pictured me and Lily, too, for a moment, doing things parents do, and I didn't feel the pang of fear that would usually force thoughts like that away. Maybe that was why I took her shopping the other day, even if we only managed to hit one store. She doesn't know my past, but she always did make the future feel more bearable, whatever it might have in store.

Why can't I get Carter out of my head?

The room becomes a flurry of sterile blues. We do our best to provide all the comfort this woman needs. Lily is still on standby and I wonder what's going round in that mind of hers. I think all the time about how pregnancy must be changing her perspective on her job here, as well as her body. Her boobs are huge now. Her midsection is swollen, taut. She still looked pretty hot in that floaty dress I insisted I buy for her. She looked embarrassed, and I tried not to notice how charged the air was between us in that tiny changing room, when I did up the zipper. How my stomach clenched every time I pictured her with the guy who put those babies inside her.

"She's ready for arrival," someone calls. I take over the machines again while they work at carefully guiding the baby out. The cord is wound around the baby's neck like a vine, but soon a shrill cry tells us we're out of the woods. A regular slippery, squirming, perfect infant is going to live to take another breath, and hopefully many more after that.

"Welcome to the world," Lily murmurs. I watch her swaddle the child and tell us they'll take it to the NICU for further monitoring, just to be sure. She gives me a weary smile, and all I think is how I want to swaddle *her* and protect *her*, not that it's my duty to. I mean, it's none of my business if she wants to do this alone, but it's not going to be easy for her. She'll always have me, though. I realized that the second I saw those little beans sprouting limbs and cooking up faces on the ultrasound. It's not like me to get sentimental. I don't get sentimental about anything, not possessions, not people. The day we lost the house, when I was ten, Pea and I were marched out with nothing but a bag of clothes and a few toys each, and since then, I don't know… I still keep everything pretty minimal in my life. I don't "do" attachment. But Lily's part in my life is not minimal, and she isn't just anyone.

The rest of the morning is relatively quiet and my mind wanders. Usually, I'd be thinking about my last date. I forced myself to go to McFadden's with the cute blonde accountant last night—the one I canceled on at the last minute to go with Carter to her ultrasound the other week. But I bowed out early. My mind wasn't on it and she could tell. She kept on asking me if I had somewhere else to be. In the end I had to apologize and tell her I did. I drove to see Mom, who sat there accusing me of being nosy and disrespectful, while I gently reminded her that, despite those facts, she had to take her meds.

Then I drove to Carter's and parked up the street with a takeout hot chocolate before realizing it was 10:30 p.m. and she was probably already in bed. Maybe she did me a favor, becoming so unavailable. She'll be too busy for anything once these twins are out in the world, and now I don't have to wonder what if, anymore. What if I wasn't emotionally stunted? What if I was the kind of person who wasn't constantly walking on eggshells, waiting for the other shoe to drop? What if I admitted to myself that Lily Carter was kind of my perfect match in many ways, and she *still* didn't want me?

I tried to keep away at the start. I told her—and I told myself—that she wouldn't need me or want me around, being nauseated and swollen and tired. I assumed she saw us only as the kind of friends who do fun stuff together that pregnant women can't do. But the look on her face when I found out she was hurt... That got me thinking maybe she sees more in me than that.

Now I don't know what to think. All I know is that I was cutting myself off first, before she could do it to me. Fear has a funny way of dictating your actions, I guess. It makes you dance to a tune you can't even hear sometimes.

Hours later, I find myself in the cafeteria, mechanically filling a plate with limp salad and overcooked chicken. Across the room, Lily is sitting with Rose. They're deep in discussion about something that looks pretty serious—twin stuff, no doubt, and she doesn't see me. I'm seeing her tonight, anyway. We're doing dinner, just the two of us and Delilah. My niece loves Lily. We took her to a sleepover at the kids' museum a couple years ago and they somehow wove a whole other world together overnight. Delilah's seen her as a role model ever since.

I said I'd make us all lasagna before we take this "ghosts and gangsters" walk that we've been planning to do for ages, ever since we all watched a documentary on Al Capone. I'm already figuring out a healthy dessert. I'll have to go to Whole Foods for organic strawberries, seeing as we—or rather *she*—can't risk any nasty pesticides right now, and I'm just googling pesticides, as you do, when the spiky-haired assistant nurse who's crushing on me comes up and bats her eyelashes.

"Doctor Montgomery, you need to eat more than that. Someone like you needs to keep their strength up. Outside of the gym, I mean!"

"Someone like me, huh?" I catch Lily looking at me now from across the room. I wait for her to roll her eyes or something but I swear a catch a little pout before she looks sideways. What's that about? I tell the nurse I'm busy and hold up my phone, as if googling pesticides in a cafeteria is normal. I can't think why I'd bother to flirt back, anyway. I don't want to date her. I don't need this nurse to think *anything* about me, really.

Pea's message flashes up. It isn't good and a knot ties itself in my stomach.

Theo, Mom threw out her fan heater today. She said it was whispering secret evil messages! Then she locked Edwina out of the house.

I rub a hand over my face; the harsh lights are too bright. Poor Edwina. Mom's history with intimidating her carers looks set to repeat again, and again. Again with this insanity.

I could go mad replaying the violent storms our dad had to weather before he departed with what was left of his sanity. I swore to myself that I would never be trapped in a relationship like theirs, but Mom's refusing her meds and I'm stuck in the middle all over again.

I slide my phone away before I can type a response I'll regret later. I keep telling Pea we need to force change in some way, send her to rehab where she'll be properly taken care of by a dedicated team, but Pea won't have it.

Usually, I'd escape the hell of it all in my head by distracting myself, by arranging another date, or calling that cute nurse back over, but I can't shake the image of Carter earlier, cradling that newborn. Or how she looked embarrassed in the mirror when I zipped up that dress. I can't get that ultrasound appointment out of my head, either. It didn't feel real before that; or at least, I was able to maintain my distance. The second those tiny dots appeared on the screen it was like a switch flipped for me. I know they're not mine, but it didn't stop all the blood flooding straight into my heart, like the beat I've been drumming to my whole life skipped to the next track and started up again with a whole different rhythm.

I don't even know who I am anymore. I can't trust myself to know what's real. Sometimes, I catch myself looking at Lily and it scares me. I start to imagine a life with her—fatherhood, family, commitment. Things I never thought I'd want, especially after everything Pea and I went through as kids. I had to grow up fast, take on so much more than a kid should. And because of all that, I guess I never let my adult self so much as contemplate becoming someone's rock. It's always been about clinging on to my freedom. But now something's changing in me, and I don't know how to handle it. It's like the ground beneath me is shifting all over again.

It's six thirty. I hurry to put the tomato sauce–covered saucepan and utensils into the dishwasher, clearing the worktop before sprinkling the last of the grated cheese onto the top of my lasagna. I've just closed the oven door on it when the elevator pings in the hallway. Three seconds later, Lily and Delilah are pulling off their jackets in the hallway and Delilah, who has barely stopped to offer me a greeting of any shape or form, is talking ninety miles an hour about the special horse she's been promoted to ride next week, after winning the kids' show-jumping championship.

"Hello to you, too," I say pointedly as she holds her hand up for a high five and then promptly heads to the lounge to claim the entire leather couch and scroll her phone.

"Hope your ears don't hurt too much after all that," I say as Lily follows me into the L-shaped kitchen. "Thanks for offering to pick her up on the way over."

She's wearing the dress I bought her on our shopping trip, and my stomach performs a little acrobatic swoop at the sight of her. It falls just above her knees, a shade of mint green that compliments her eyes. I like her dark brown hair more now that it's growing back out a little, and I like how it's piled on top of her head under a blue bandanna. A few tendrils frame her face, making her look like some sort of casual bohemian goddess from a maternity wear catalog. Why am I staring at her?

"You know I don't mind picking her up, Theo. And you know I think she's great," is all she says, accepting a glass of sparkling water and leaning against the counter, pressing a hand to her bump. She seems a little distracted.

Quickly, I pull one of the stools out from the breakfast bar and she sits down gratefully, thanking me. I ask if she's okay and she says she's just tired. I say nothing, but when I check on the lasagna, she sighs behind me and starts telling me how Rose was meant to make a vet's appointment for Jasper's FIV vaccine but she forgot, and now Jasper is a week late getting it. I remind her how Jasper is an indoor cat and cannot possibly be at risk of catching a respiratory disease. I also tell her that he himself is a hazard, being a walking, purring furry hairball, and she tells me that for a doctor, I'm surprisingly unfeeling toward living creatures. There's something else going on with her. It's more than the cat.

"Rose is working a lot more lately, huh," I say eventually. I don't miss how her hand keeps moving across her belly in gentle strokes under the counter. From what I've gathered, Rose has been escaping into her work since her divorce, and while she's a devoted sister to Lily, I can see her schedule is making her forget other more important things right now. "Were you in an argument at lunch?"

Lily snaps her eyes up to mine. "Watching me, were you?"

I scoff at her, then busy my hands with the cutlery as I carry it past her to the table. "Don't flatter yourself, Carter."

She sighs. "Fine. We were talking about how she keeps canceling our shopping trip—"

"I took you shopping," I interrupt, gesturing to the dress I bought her. Her cheeks flush and she diverts her eyes, and for some reason I drop a fork to the floor, cursing as I pick it up.

"Yes, and you know I'm very grateful," she says.

"You only let me take you to one store," I remind her, and she tells me she was worried I'd get bored. I get the impression it was more than that. Maybe she felt the change in the air between us, and it freaked her out. She's carrying another man's children, and we're friends.

"Don't get me wrong, Rose means well, and I'm probably being far too needy here…"

"Needy?" I pause to look at her. "How is that being needy? She's your twin sister. You do everything together," I say.

Lily wrinkles her nose. "We used to."

I refill her glass with sparkling water, throw the garlic bread into the oven with the lasagna and she changes the subject to me and my date last night. I pretend it went better than it did, and I don't let on that her hot chocolate went cold in my car before I drove back here and benched five sets before hitting the pillow on my own.

"I'm hungry, Theo," Delilah calls from the couch. I had almost forgotten she was here.

We can see her from the kitchen, but she is too absorbed in her screen to look over her shoulder. It's only when we all sit down at the table and I'm heaping steaming hot, cheesy lasagna onto our plates that she springs back from preteen robot mode into the bubbly kid I adore.

"So have you thought about names yet?" Delilah asks, creating a cheesy tornado from her plate up to her mouth. Lily told Delilah a few weeks ago that she was pregnant, and my niece got surprisingly excited, reading up on twin babies. "What if they're conjoined? I watched a documentary on these conjoined twins in India that had to have their heads separated…"

"They're not conjoined," I say firmly, putting my fork down heavily. Lily is biting back a smile. "Do you even know how rare that is?"

"But if they were, they could be so famous on TikTok," Delilah continues. She waves her fork about enthusiastically as she talks, sending tomato sauce flying across the table. I tell her it's disturbing how much she's thought about this, and try to ignore the sauce splashes on my freshly polished surface. Usually, it would be cleared up in a flash—another echo from childhood, when Mom would fly off the handle over the smallest spill, the tiniest crease in Dad's ironing.

I won't do it while Lily's here.

Thankfully, before we've even cleared our plates, we are all discussing other stuff we've seen on TikTok, and we're laughing, and Lily looks a thousand times happier than when she walked in. As I serve up fresh strawberries with homemade chocolate mousse, she beams from ear to ear.

"Organic?" she says. "I saw the packaging. That's very thoughtful, Theo, thank you."

"I make the odd diversion from my mean-guy routine," I say, deadpan, though the fact that she's noticed makes me feel like I've reached the top of whatever mountain I was just climbing and speared a flag into the highest tree.

"I'm Marcus, and tonight we're going to take a walk on the wild side of Chicago's history—gangsters, ghosts and all!" Marcus, our tour guide, is easily the most excitable person I've met all week, besides Delilah when she talks about horses. She and Lily are listening in rapt concentration, bundled up against the October cold, eating the candy I just bought.

Marcus's tailored suit and the fedora that perches jauntily on his head are obviously supposed to invoke the spirit of Chicago's bygone era of gangsters. The tourists with us are eating it up.

We set off into the streets and I ignore my phone as it vibrates in my pocket. I already told Pea when we'd have

Delilah home, and it would be rude to answer it now. Unless she wants to tell me something else Mom has done.

"Everything okay?" Lily whispers. We've stopped by an unassuming brick wall in a quiet alley that I know already is the site of the Valentine's Day massacre. Marcus explains about the events in 1929, how Al Capone's men gunned down seven members of the North Side Gang and shook Chicago to the core. Delilah is so absorbed. She's wanted to do this tour for ages. I pull a face at Lily.

"Pea is calling me," I tell her.

She shoots me a questioning look and I tell her I'll call when we take a break. Lily doesn't know exactly what's going on with my mother, how we never know which side of her we'll be faced with. How Pea and I suffered as kids. I tend to keep my family stuff to myself after what happened with Tessa. I think I told Lily about Tessa once, the only semiserious girlfriend I've ever had, right before I started at the hospital, before Lily and I met. What I didn't tell her was that Tessa had the misfortune of being at my apartment the day a neighbor unwittingly let Mom into the building. Mom was "self-medicating" on vodka at the time. She yelled at me, yelled at Tessa and broke my kettle by throwing it barely an inch from her head. Tessa broke things off the very next day.

I've always been ashamed, really, that we've never been able to control her. She drove poor Dad to despair and he disowned us *all* because of her. I don't even know where he is, to this day. It's all too crazy and to be honest, too humiliating to try to explain to most people, so Pea and I don't even try. But I can't really ignore my phone anymore as Marcus guides us toward Lincoln Park, to the Biograph Theater.

Pea tells me she endured a half-hour rant from Mom about how the meds she was told to take made her gain weight. Now Pea is too exhausted to drive. She asks if it's all right if Delilah spends the night at my place. I tell her of course. Dee's always had her own room at my place.

When I rejoin the group, they're both absorbed in Marcus's latest story, but Lily has her hands on her lower back. Her knees are slightly bent, like she really needs to sit down. I forget about Mom instantly. I put a hand on her arm and she brushes me off, embarrassed.

"Let's go find you a seat," I say.

"I'm fine, I'll miss the tour. Was that a problem on the phone? Your family?"

I deflect her question. "You've been on your feet all day, Carter. You need to recharge your powers."

"Theo, I said I'm fine. Please don't tell me what to do."

Okay, then. I try not to look pissed while she struggles to pretend she's not getting more uncomfortable by the minute, standing in one spot with no seating in sight. I should've thought about this; she shouldn't be on her feet this long. When we finally move on, Marcus stops at Union Station, and while he's explaining how Capone had secret tunnels running beneath the city, connecting his hideouts, I take a seat by the wall and look at her pointedly. Finally, Lily sits beside me, and I smirk. She smirks back.

"You don't always have to look out for me, you know." She sniffs.

"Who else is going to, Carter?" I say before I can think. She's so stubborn.

I regret it instantly when I see the look on her face. "You think I'm stupid, doing this alone, don't you?" Her words come out a little choked and her green eyes search mine, almost daring me to lie.

"I think you're brave," I tell her carefully as Delilah sits next to me, shoving the empty candy box at me so I can dispose of it.

"Nice try."

"You're not alone, anyway. Don't expect the violins just yet," I tell her, tossing the candy box into the trash and nudging her. Instead of shoving me away, she rests her soft head on my shoulder, then buries her face in my coat. "Carter, just ask for help when you need it. Don't be stubborn."

We sit there as the cold drizzle plays in the air, and I rest my head gently on hers. I want her to ask me for help. I want to be involved. I want to buy organic strawberries and rub her feet and I don't know what any of this means. I need to get away.

The medical conference in Florida next week cannot come soon enough.

CHAPTER SIX

THE ALARM BLARES from the far incubator and sends a jolt of fear straight through me. Baby Mia Malone. I can barely see her through the plastic walls of the incubator as I pull on my gloves and maternity gown and call for Amber, all in a matter of milliseconds, but I know something is very wrong. Born at just twenty-seven weeks, she weighs barely over two pounds. My heart aches every time I look at her.

Her oxygen saturation levels are dropping—fast. I watch the numbers flash on the monitor: eighty-two, seventy-eight. Seventy-four... My breath catches in my throat as Amber appears. We can't afford to lose a second.

"We need to intubate now," I say, my voice miraculously steadier than I feel. I grab the laryngoscope, my hands moving on autopilot, and I carefully open Mia's tiny mouth. Her skin is so delicate and pale it seems like it could tear at the slightest touch. Her breaths are shallow; her chest is barely rising. I try to focus, try to block out the fears that threaten to overwhelm me now every time I encounter an emergency with someone's child. I've done this so many times before, but never with two fragile babies inside me, and I'd be lying if I didn't project every outcome onto them. It's selfish, but it's unstoppable. Rose says I need to get used to it, and she means it in the nicest possible way.

I guide the tube into her airway. Amber is quick to connect the ventilator, and I hold my breath, praying for that first *whoosh* of air.

For a terrifying moment, nothing happens. My heart pounds in my ears, and the room seems to blur around me. Mia's tiny life is in my hands. This can't be it. It cannot end like this.

And then, we hear it—the soft, steady *whoosh* of the ventilator. I glance up at the monitor and watch in relief as the numbers start to climb: seventy-eight, eighty-three, eighty-eight...

"Oh, thank goodness." I let out a breath, gently stroking Mia's tiny hand with my gloved finger. Her chest is moving more rhythmically now, but I know we're not out of the woods yet. Mia's lungs are so fragile, they could collapse at any moment, or her tiny heart could give out from the strain. I turn to Amber, my voice urgent. "Get me the surfactant. We need to stabilize her lungs."

Amber prepares the medication while I keep my eyes glued to the vitals. Babies like Mia don't have the surfactant their lungs need to stay open, and without it, the ventilator will only be a temporary fix. I can't afford to think the worst. I administer the surfactant through the tube, watching the baby's squishy face for any signs of distress. Her tiny body tenses, and I feel my own muscles clench in response. I will her to hang in there a little longer, but seconds feel like hours as I wait.

Slowly, so slowly, her oxygen levels begin to rise again. Ninety-two, ninety-five, ninety-eight... The alarms are silenced, replaced by the soothing rhythm of the ventilator. I know I'm getting far too emotional because of my condition, but I feel the tears prick at the corners of my eyes as Amber squeezes my shoulder, tells me we did it, that Mia will be all right. I know what she's thinking, though. Everyone here thinks I'm a walking liability, probably. I miss Theo. Thank goodness I'm seeing him tonight. He's finally back from his trip.

The thought makes my skin prickle in excitement, but I snuff it out fast. I've been having this thought about missing him since he left and I don't like it. I shouldn't miss Theo when he's not here, but then, it's not just at work that I've come to rely on him being around, popping up on his breaks, taking me down to the cafeteria. And I haven't really heard from him much since he left.

"Will you be all right from here?" Amber asks carefully.

"Of course," I assure her, though the question echoes in my head. Will I? The what-ifs surrounding my own pregnancy keep mounting up, selfishly. What if something like this happens to me? What if something happens to my babies when Rose isn't here? When Dad isn't here? Or next time Theo is away?

"Hey, look at you!" Rose looks up as I dump my bag on the kitchen table. "Finally wearing clothes that fit?" she teases, eyeing my new outfit.

I changed into the new pants and cozy oversize sweater before driving home. I never leave work in my scrubs if I can help it. I enjoy some separation between my work life and home life, unlike my twin sister.

"I'm sorry it took us so long to go shopping, but it's nice that Theo took you to that one store and bought you that dress to tide you over."

"I know," I say, smiling at the memory, before a shiver

of something like fear snakes along my spine and startles me. There was a moment in the changing room, when he zipped me up, when I swear my body did something strange in his presence. A feeling of longing that I totally was not expecting almost took me out. Just feeling the brush of his fingers on my skin, and his admiring eyes on me. I was so embarrassed I insisted we only go to that one store.

"I'm a hormonal mess," I say by way of an excuse, even though I didn't tell Rose how I felt. "And I still feel like I'm turning into a whale."

"Please," Rose says, rolling her eyes. I sit down at the bench and Jasper winds his way around my legs, purring. Her expression softens. "Lil, you look amazing. Makes me a little jealous, you know?"

"Jealous?" I frown at her, stirring the noncaffeinated herbal tea she puts before me. "You could still have this, too, if you wanted." I tell her she's young and beautiful and that it's not like her biological clock has hit snooze all of a sudden.

"Sure," she sighs, tracing the rim of her own cup. I know she's thinking about David and what he did. The affair stole her confidence more than her physical ability to chase her dreams. We were always the "flower girls" growing up, the "prettiest in class" according to, well… most of the guys who wanted to date one or both of us.

She sits up straighter. "A thirty-four-year-old divorcée who works around the clock. Can't you see them all lining up to date me?"

"Stop it," I say, and she knows I mean it. "You don't need a man to have a baby, anyway—look at where you work."

"It's a family I want, Lils," she sighs, and I shut my

mouth. We don't talk about Dr. David Andersson anymore; we just despise him in secret. "You need to stop working so hard, make room for… I don't know, a life."

"A life, huh? What is that exactly?" She raises an eyebrow just as her pager beeps insistently. "No time for a life, apparently. Duty calls." She stands abruptly, the chair screeching against the floor as she leans down to peck my cheek. "Evening team meet, then dinner. You'll be okay?"

"See you later," I call after her, and it's only when her coat is a blur in the doorway that I remember I won't, because I'm meeting Theo soon.

My heart does that weird fluttery thing in my throat again when I think about walking into McFadden's and seeing him in our usual spot, but I snuff it out again. I don't know what's been going on lately. No, I do… It's my hormones. My stupid hormones. Maybe my babies want a daddy, seeing as their own is not in the picture. Which is my fault as much as his. I don't need Anthony. He was a sperm donor of sorts. I'm fine with that.

I sip my tea, trying to dislodge the idea of me and Theo. I guess it makes sense that I'm overthinking it all. Hormones are one thing but also, Theo Montgomery is the only male in my life besides Dad who pays me that much attention now that I'm pregnant! I put him in the friend zone when we met for a reason, though. He's a verified playboy with more commitment issues than designer shirts, and that's saying something. And I'm not even out for a partner; I'm a terrible partner. Plus, look at Rose. David may well have been one of the country's most sought-after cardiothoracic surgeons, but his own after-hours meetings were less about performing lung surgeries and more about performing God knows what on his surgical technologist. He shattered Rose. They were trying for a baby at the time.

Rose and I might slip from time to time, wanting more, wanting men. But we know we can't count on them. That's why we bought the house. *Our* house. Our nonconventional family house, just the flower girls and Jasper, forever.

Well...until you guys come along, I think, stroking a hand over my belly in the mirror.

My silhouette is changing by the week now. Will Theo think I'm a whale, too? Why do I care so much?

Sometime later, the familiar boozy-bleach smell of McFadden's surrounds me. I untangle my scarf and remove my coat and search the crowd for that familiar tousle of dark hair.

"Over here!" Theo calls me over from a different table to the one we usually have, with its high stools. He's scored the sofa seat with the plush velvet cushions. Above us, a forgotten paper Halloween pumpkin has escaped the post-Halloween cleanup. How is it November already?

"Who did you have to fight to get this seat on game night?" I ask him, sliding my bump in beside him. He moves the table out slightly to make sure I can fit. A TV blares the NFL game on the wall and he jokes over the din about fighting a grandma and sending her back out onto the street before he stands to get me a drink. He's wearing a white Henley, tight on the chest and arms, tapering sharply down the waist to his jeans. He looks hot, but then, when doesn't he, and when doesn't he *know* he looks hot?

I lean back against his coat, which he's draped on

the back of the couch. It smells of him, and as he turns back toward me carrying my drink, my whole stomach joins in with my heart for one big flutter. No, wait. It's more than just Theo causing this. My hands fly to my bulge. "Oh, my…"

"What?" Theo's figure casts a shadow over me. I look up at his concerned face before I grin.

"I felt them. I felt them move." It feels so strange.

He looks alarmed for a second and just kind of hovers, looking at me like I'm an alien. His face makes me laugh.

"Got you a ginger ale," he says, sliding a frosty glass toward me. "Hope the gas doesn't get them even more excited in there."

"It's happening again," I tell him in awe, still laughing. This is the first time I've felt them. I'm almost twenty-one weeks now so it's normal, but still, it's unlike anything I've ever experienced. So strange and unsettling, yet kind of comforting at the same time. Like they're fluffing their little nest, making more room to grow. I keep my hands pressed to my belly over my new smart pants while Theo looks sideways, then at me, then at his drink and then up at the game.

"Wanna feel, Doctor?" I ask him. I fully expect him to shake his head and refuse. He's not my doctor, he's my friend, and for a second I feel silly for even offering—this clearly weirds him out. But I think his curiosity wins. Slowly, he reaches a tentative hand to my midsection and I press my hand over his, guiding it. Sure enough, another kick comes from within and Theo's eyes grow wide, before lighting up like they did in the clinic that day.

"They're going to be better boxers than me," he says, pressing his warm, big hand flatter to my belly. His palm against my flesh feels far more intimate than I expected, just like it did in the store changing room. His careful touch sends a flush to my cheeks before I bury it in my hair, but I'm caught like a rabbit in the deep blue hues of his eyes when he grins at me. I'm cast back to that night at his place over dinner, with Delilah. He went out of his way to prepare all that for me. And then on the tour, he was so careful to look after me… It all spins around in my head as I look at him now.

Good Lord, my hormones are putting me through it right now.

"You can teach them self-defense," I say, distracted. "I mean, if you want to be in their lives once they're born."

He looks genuinely confused and my heart soars when he asks, "Why wouldn't I?" Then he adds, "Not that they'll need my help, knowing how kick-ass you are, Carter."

The barman, Freddy D, interrupts us. We know him, of course. He tells me I'm looking great, asks if we want food and we say no, and as they talk I can't help wondering why I thought Theo wouldn't want to be involved. Grayson got to me again, like he always does when I'm enjoying being myself. I second-guessed everything I did and said around him. What would Theo think of me if he knew how long I put up with that?

Suddenly, I realize what Freddy D is telling Theo.

"That chick you abandoned here on your bad date the other week? I wanted to thank you, man. She went home with a friend of mine. They've been inseparable ever since, if you know what I mean."

Theo clears his throat. I glare at Freddy D for obvious reasons, but then his words sink in. Theo abandoned a date early? Why? Especially if the woman would have gone home with him, as Freddy so licentiously implied. Doesn't sound like him at all.

His phone buzzes on the table. It's Pea. He cuts it off. I ask him why.

"It's nothing important," he says quickly in a way that implies something important is definitely going on, something I've missed. I tell him so and my adrenaline spikes harder than it just did over hearing that Theo left a date early. Why does he keep brushing me off when I ask about his family?

"Theo, if something's going on—" I continue, but he cuts me off.

"Tell me, Carter, have you heard from what's-his-name again? The babies' father?"

Instantly, I'm on the offense. I turn away from him, nurse my drink. "I'm sending him updates. It's only polite. Sometimes he replies. Sometimes he doesn't."

"Is that disappointing for you?" He's trying to sound casual, casting an eye to the game again, which I have zero interest in right now. This mix of emotions swirling inside me is so confusing. Plus, I'm annoyed that he's clearly keeping things from me. And that I am giving Anthony updates on the twins despite the fact that he barely replies, for the simple, messed-up reason that I don't want him to think badly of me for absolutely *anything* at all.

"I don't know, Theo. He asked for updates, so as not to sound like a completely disinterested party, I suppose."

"If you *know* he doesn't care, why are you giving him updates?" He leans in, all trace of distraction gone, his blue eyes focusing intently on me. I swallow. Theo can goof around with the best of them but likewise he can be *so* intense.

"Because he's the father."

"Father of the year, Carter. Top points to him for communicating solely by text message whenever he feels like it, when you're over here a million miles away with…"

"With no one? Is that what you were thinking?"

He scowls, and the dent between his eyebrows deepens. "What about what *you* need? Won't this mess with your head down the line?"

"You think I should just cut him off?" I stare at him. Yes, I'm mad at him, but I want his opinion now, because honestly, hearing him this passionate is kind of hot. I wasn't aware he cared this much about my relationships, or nonrelationships as the case may be. I've never said anything to him about why it ended with Grayson before we met, and he's never really probed.

"I don't want to see you get hurt," he says simply, drumming his fingers on the table, the game forgotten.

"And I don't want my babies getting hurt, either. I'm just trying to do the right—"

I'm cut off by a deafening cheer as something in the game sends the bar into an uproar. Before I've even finished my sentence, or had time to move, someone, a man, is careening backward into our table and the whole thing slides toward us by several inches, right up hard against my stomach. It knocks the wind out of me for a moment. I can hardly think, let alone register what just happened, but in the space of three seconds I'm covered in sticky drinks, Theo is shoving the table away into the crowd of men who fell onto it, and somehow I'm on the floor, telling my babies and myself to breathe.

CHAPTER SEVEN

My heart throttles straight to a sprint when Lily's hands go to her stomach. Suddenly, I'm on my knees in front of her. The clamor of the bar fades to a dull roar in my ears. My hands are already on autopilot, gently probing around the area that took the hit.

"Talk to me, Lil. Do we need help here?"

"We're okay." She's sucking in deep lungfuls of air, biting her lip. Her green eyes meet mine with her customary bravado, but I see the pain shimmering from their depths and it makes my chest tighten. "It hurts a little…right here," she says. Her hands shake as she holds them just below her rib cage.

"Take slow breaths for me, all right? In and out. You're doing great," I tell her. I'm trying to keep my voice steady for her sake as I run through the checklist in my head: assess, stabilize, manage pain, but there is only one of the three I can do right here. I need to get her out.

A crowd has gathered around us, and I order them to move, then urge Lily's eyes to mine. "We're going to get you out of here. Keep breathing."

She winces and her breath hitches, but she follows my lead, her chest rising and falling more evenly after a few tries. My gaze flicks over her face, taking in every detail. Pale, she's gone pale. "Any dizziness or blurred vision?" I ask, keeping one hand on her shoulder, while someone drapes her coat over her in concern.

"No, nothing like that," she manages, gripping my arm. "Theo, we need to…"

"I'm going to help you up, okay? Can you manage?"

She takes my arm and with some effort, we get her to her feet. I move the table back even farther, and the crowd around us shuffles to make room. But just as she's stable, she wobbles, and I loop an arm around her waist to support her. On second thought, I'm not going to risk a fall at this point. Quickly, I pick her up in my arms and head for the door. Her weight is nothing compared to the heavy dread settling in my chest.

"Hold on to me," I say, more for my own reassurance than hers. "We're going to get you checked out ASAP."

"Theo…" Her voice wavers close to my ear. Her arms around my shoulders tighten. The adrenaline feels like liquid fire in my veins, and the urge to guard her with my life intensifies a thousandfold, but this is not the time to try to decipher what this weird new arrangement of emotions is every time I'm in Lily's presence lately.

"Evergreen's closest. I'm driving you." My words are a command, not a suggestion. I put her down carefully in the underground parking lot and unlock the car. She agrees, even though I know she doesn't want to mix business with her pregnancy. The other place, Dawson's, is too far away from here with the traffic. Besides, I work at Evergreen. I run the ER and this is an emergency.

Carefully, I help her into the back seat, tell her to keep on breathing, as if she doesn't know the drill already. This also means she knows that things can go wrong. Very wrong. "This is just standard procedure, you know that."

"Of course. I tell all my patients to arrive by sports car," she says through a grimace, and I tell her not to make jokes, to be quiet, to breathe.

She clasps at my hand, just as I'm about to shut the door. "I'm serious, I trust you," she says, and the look in her eyes…it's like she's lit a rocket under me. I don't break the speed limit on the way to the hospital, but I don't think I've ever reached it so quickly. The drive is a blur. My mind is already racing through protocols and potential complications. The silence between us is filled with the soft sounds of Lily's measured breaths and I can't risk saying anything else, but I know this is my fault for taking her to McFadden's. I wanted her to think we can still be normal. *I* wanted to think we could still be normal. We both know what just happened wasn't good.

"She needs attention, ASAP. Let's get her to bay two!"

I'm met on the forecourt. I've already called ahead, and two of my team members are waiting with a wheelchair. I help Lily into it and rush to park the car so I can get inside. It takes me all of four minutes.

I find her in bay two and I pull on my scrubs in record time.

"Doctor Montgomery, you're not on shift," a nurse tells me, trying to wave me away.

Lily's voice stops her. "It's all right. I want him here."

Several team members look between us in confusion.

"Sorry if I'm a drama queen," Lily says next, and I frown in her direction. "I'm not used to being on this side of things."

"Stop apologizing. Why do you always do that? Focus on yourself," I tell her, and she presses her hands to her belly, wincing. For someone so set in her ways about certain things, she can be surprisingly self-sabotaging sometimes. "Did they move again?" I ask her.

"I think so."

"That's a good sign," I remind her, and she presses her lips together. We both know the alternative is just not a viable option.

"Doctor Montgomery," one of the techs acknowledges me. "What do we need?"

"We need an urgent ultrasound. Please page radiology right away. Also, page the on-call OB-GYN specialist to come down to the ER immediately."

Lily's on the gurney in seconds, her face all pinched in discomfort. I watch with my heart in my throat as the sonographer appears and preps the equipment, and Lily helps smear the cold gel around her own stomach. I fetch a bunch of paper towels and rub it from her hands for her; she shouldn't have done that, but I know she's probably not thinking clearly. I hear her take a sharp intake of breath as the cold tool is placed upon her, and without thinking I take her sticky hand.

The hum of the machine fills the space as images flicker to life on the screen. Two tiny hearts beating. Relief washes over me but it's premature, I know—I have to wait for the final word.

"Vitals are stable, Doctor Montgomery," a nurse reports.

"Keep monitoring her," I instruct, never taking my eyes off the screen. I want this to be over for her. People are looking. Let them look.

I've flirted and hit on her before, but I've always been happy with Carter as my friend, really. Nothing else would work, anyway, not least because of Mom. Tessa proved that. I'll never forget her face when she was forced to duck that flying kettle. Every time we hear of something else she's done to send a carer packing, I'm thrown right back to the boxing ring we called a living room—me in the corner, Pea's face pressed into my chest while I inch us closer and closer to the door so we could finally make a run from whatever Mom was using as missiles to launch at Dad that day besides words. But every time I back off from Lily lately, something draws me back even stronger. I spent the whole time at that conference in Florida wondering where the baby daddy was, thinking how I should go out, meet some women, get this weird new set of emotions out of my system, and then doing nothing about it.

"Looks like they're determined. They're not hurt at all," the sonographer finally announces. I blink as her words settle into reality. Lily lets out half of a strangled sob before covering her mouth.

"Thank God," she breathes out, and my heart thuds as she exhales deeply with her eyes closed. The connection is something beyond friendship now; for me, anyway. I can't make complete sense of it. It's visceral, a tether that feels like it tightens with every moment we share, including this one. Before I know it, everyone's left the room except me.

"You're gonna be okay, Carter," I say, resisting the urge to sweep a few matted strands of damp hair from her face. I know I should excuse myself now, leave as more doctor than friend, but her eyes root me to the bedside and I can't help imagining, under different circumstances, if things *were* different, I'd probably kiss her forehead or something right now. Why the hell do I want to kiss Lily's forehead? As if that wouldn't just make me want to kiss her mouth.

"Theo," she says, and her eyes are full of the kind of questions I don't know how to answer. What if something else like this happens? What if next time it does, there's no doctor present? Doing this alone is not a good idea, not as good as Lily thinks it is, but it's not my place to always be there, just in case. I'm her friend. Nothing more.

Her phone buzzes, and I catch the name on the screen. Anthony. Him, the father.

I bite my lip. I mean, I guess it's her prerogative if she wants to involve him. And her kids will one day want to know who he is, probably, but it's causing her additional stress. Stress that I shouldn't add to by questioning her about it.

"What you said before, about involving him. I'm sorry things got so…heated," I say.

She looks away. "Maybe you're right. Maybe I shouldn't be involving him."

"Look, don't listen to me," I tell her. "I don't know anything about what you're going through."

"The same as I don't know anything about what *you're* going through, Theo," she says pointedly.

"Me?" My shoulders tense. She sighs in frustration.

"All the calls? All the messages. Is your family in the secret service or something? I don't want to impose but it's hard to be around you sometimes, knowing you're keeping things from me. At least I'm telling you about Anthony, even if it makes me an idiot."

"You're not an idiot. Stop all this self-deprecating talk. What is that about, anyway? It's not just your hormones, Lily."

She tuts at me loudly. "Stop changing the subject."

I search for the right words to say. I hate that my secrecy is upsetting to her; I hate that more than anything. I've learned to protect myself by keeping people at arm's length, avoiding emotional vulnerability to prevent the pain of abandonment I felt as a kid. It's textbook psychology, a blatant manifestation of my fractured emotional intelligence, which Lily has noticed and interpreted as righteous entitlement. I'm allowed to know her, but she can't know me. She's right; it's not fair.

I open my mouth to speak but I don't actually know what to say. At least, I can't put it into words; it's complicated. Telling her anything means telling her everything. I study the poster for the upcoming annual fundraiser on the back of the door. We both went last year. We drank champagne and dared each other to do terrible moves on the dance floor. I think I won. Those were good times. Way less complicated.

"Theo?"

I hold my hands up. "I guess there's some stuff I never talk about when it comes to my family."

"What kind of stuff?"

"It's my mother—" I start, racking my brain as to how to explain. I'm interrupted, however, by the door. It bangs open with such force it reverberates against the walls and Rose barges in, her eyes storms of fury. "Theo, what the hell?"

"Rose," I start, moving to intercept her, but she's a cyclone of indignation, stepping around me, straight to Lily's side. "Are you okay?"

"I'm fine," she assures her, adjusting her pillows again before I take over.

"We were at McFadden's," I explain. "You know how it gets on game night…some guys got a little too excited—"

"It happened *so* fast," Lily repeats, almost on top of me, but Rose is only looking at me now.

"McFadden's? Theo! You took my pregnant sister to a bar full of drunks?" Her voice scales up and I rub my jaw, feeling Lily tense beside me. Her fingers brush mine briefly. Rose's eyes catch the movement and she purses her lips together, seemingly composing herself. "You scared me," she says to Lily. "Both of you." She glares at me again.

"It wasn't Theo's fault," Lily tells her. "He knew I wanted to do all the things we used to do…"

"But you can't, Lily."

Lily closes her eyes, and I know she's holding herself back from snapping. "I'm just grateful he was there. He drove me straight here."

Rose just glowers and Lily lowers her voice. She's doing her best not to make a scene. "What was I meant to do, Rose, stay home alone again? I'm pregnant. I'm not disabled."

I step back as they glare at each other, forces of nature, alike in so many ways you'd almost think they were identical. Eventually, Rose huffs some kind of apology. She reaches down to stroke a hand along her sister's cheek. "I'm just so relieved you're all right."

"Thanks to Theo."

I watch as Rose's features soften, the rigid lines of her mouth relaxing. She takes a deep breath, then turns toward me as I straighten some equipment needlessly at the other end of the room. Her eyes are still glinting with the remnants of worry and something a little like gratitude, maybe. It's hard to tell. It could be loathing. "Thank you for being there," she says, finally, slowly. "I should've been more available."

"Rose…" Lily reaches out, grabbing her sister's hand. "You're here now. That's what counts."

Rose tells her she will put her and the babies first from now on, and I excuse myself, giving them space. The weight of the day and everything we've now left unsaid feels like a bowling ball pressing heavy on my chest. Seeing Lily loved and cared for eases some of the tension knotting my insides, but the knots are also a reminder of why I've kept these kinds of feelings at bay since that whole thing with Tessa. Mom is a liability; I'm not in a stable place; I'm not what anyone needs, not as far as anything resembling partnership is concerned. I have to let Rose step up and remember my proper place as Lily's colleague and friend.

CHAPTER EIGHT

WHAT A MORNING. Not only have I been experiencing severe back ache since 7:00 a.m., but I've also just attended an emergency C-section down in ER and the sight of blood, for the first time in years, made me feel quite queasy. Heading for the elevator, I'm picturing the bubble bath I'll be pouring myself when I get home when Theo's voice calls me back.

"Carter, glad I caught you. Do you have a moment?"

The air between us crackles with a new energy the second I meet his eyes. I get that familiar flash of warmth, the one that just bubbles up now whenever he is near. Something changed that day at McFadden's, maybe even before our heated words about Anthony. Neither of us has brought it up, and I can tell he still doesn't want to talk about whatever he has going on, either. I wonder if that's why he's been extra "busy" lately. Or maybe he's been busy with his secret life, whatever it is that's going on with his mom that he never finished telling me about. I've been wanting to ask, but he's made sure that we've hardly seen each other.

Anyway, now is not the time to analyze his actions, or my own wild heartbeat around him.

"We thought it was appendicitis," he tells me, ushering me back into the chaotic ER, toward a closed curtain.

"But the ultrasound showed us otherwise." He keeps his voice low as he continues, handing me the chart. "She's seventeen, Carter. She doesn't know she's pregnant."

A scream takes all the words from my mouth as he sweeps the curtain aside. A teenage girl with matted brown hair and a clammy forehead is clutching her abdomen, crying out in pain on the bed. I'm just stepping around to speak to her when Theo takes my arm. The shock in his eyes throws me. "She's crowning."

My heart thumps erratically, adrenaline flushing through me as I process the words. The teenage girl on the stretcher before us has been completely oblivious to the life growing inside her until this very moment.

"Wh-what's going on?" she stammers, her eyes wide with shock as people flurry around her and I take her hand.

"Sweetheart, you're going to have a baby," I say gently, locking eyes with her. "Right now."

"Baby? But I—I didn't know... I can't be..." Panic weaves through her voice, crescendoing into an almost hysterical pitch as the pain takes hold again.

"Easy, we've got you," Theo reassures her.

"Where is the OB-GYN? We need them here, stat!" I call out.

"Called for, but we don't have time," Theo replies tersely, glancing at me. "We have to do this, Doctor Carter."

"Of course," I acknowledge, my hands already moving to gather what we need. "Okay, you're going to feel a lot of pressure, but you need to push when I tell you to," I instruct the girl. "Can you do that for us?" I squeeze her hand for emphasis and she nods, tears spilling down her cheeks. I can't help but admire her bravery. This poor girl is so scared and unprepared, yet here she is, about to become a mother in the most unexpected way possible. Imagine!

"Ready?" Theo glances at me again. I support her legs, encouraging her through each contraction, while Theo remains focused, guiding the baby.

"Almost there," I cheer her on, while sweat beads along my brow in sympathy. My back still hurts like hell, but this is not about me. "You're doing amazing."

"Next push, come on," Theo urges, and with one more monumental effort, the cries of a newborn pierce the air and it feels like I can finally breathe, too.

Theo passes the newborn to me, his eyes locking on to mine again. "Doctor Carter, NICU, now."

"Is—is the baby okay?" the girl asks as I take the baby from his hands.

"We're going to make sure he's just fine," I hear him say as I head for the elevator.

My head is whirling. That poor young woman must be in a state of complete shock. What will she do now?

Hours later, after the chaos has settled and the baby is safe under my colleagues' supervision, I find myself walking alongside Theo through the empty parking lot. He's talking about the young mother, asking if she's getting help, and I tell him everything I know. I can't help how the whole thing made me feel even more grateful that I have so much support around me, even though I'm going through this without a man. I also can't help the way my mind goes to Theo now, whenever I do picture a man at my side, despite the fact he's been distant again lately. It's crossed my mind that maybe he feels a little guilty that the last time we hung out I got hurt.

He's changed out of his scrubs and ironed coat into jeans that hug his thighs just right, and a simple black T-shirt under his thick winter coat. The words *effortlessly handsome* spring to mind. He's perfected the kind of casual that makes my heart do a traitorous little flutter. I should not be letting my raging hormones get the better of me. I have enough to deal with right now without reading into Theo's push and pull approach to our friendship at every given turn. Besides, Rose wants to take me to a pregnancy yoga class tonight, and ever since she's decided to put our sisterhood first—as much as her schedule will allow, of course—I've been enjoying our twin time.

He asks me what I'm doing tonight, and the question breaks the silence as he digs for the keys to his car.

"Yoga for whales," I tell him, trying to focus on anything but the way his shirt stretches across his chest as he moves. It's a futile attempt; my mind betrays me, flashing back to the warrior Highlander–like protection of his arms around me as he carried me out of McFadden's the other week. I remember his familiar scent, clean like his apartment, how I breathed it in for comfort. He was comfort. I needed him and he was there. He was more than there; he was my hero.

"Is that right," he says, stopping by his car, giving me that look. "Both the flower girls, together?"

"Yep, it was Rose's idea."

He waits for me to talk, because he knows as well as I do that Rose was less than impressed at me going out to bars, and anywhere, in fact, where trouble might befall me. It wasn't him she was mad at specifically. I know that, and I'd hope that he does, too. She was mad at herself for not making more time for me, to look after me, like we promised each other we always would.

I don't tell him how it's starting to feel like it did before I met Grayson, because he doesn't know about what I put myself through with that man—he'd think me an idiot if he did. Instead, I tell him how it feels like it did before *she* met David, before David started stealing her away from me at every chance. It's tough when the closest person to you in the whole entire world meets someone else who's simultaneously trying to be the closest person to them in the whole entire world. Her ex didn't understand the twin thing, but then, not many people do. We are cosmically bound to each other. Each little fracture, like a minor falling out, or a boyfriend who demands all your time, needs healing for the world to be right again.

When I stop talking, I realize Theo's head is slightly cocked and he's looking at me with such interest, it feels like I've just been beamed down for inspection from a spaceship. "Well, I'm happy you two are getting your vibe back."

"What are *you* doing tonight?" I ask. When he smiles like this, with his lips still tight and a twinkle in his eyes, I get that same warm flush throughout my whole body, and this time it doesn't stop at my skin. It goes between my legs and makes me shuffle awkwardly on the spot. Curse these raging hormones.

"Going home. Eventually," he answers. I can see a glint of something unreadable in his blue gaze now.

"I get it, Theo," I say stiffly. He's clearly going on a date right now, and it bothers me more than it should. "Well, have fun on your date. I guess I'll see you tomorrow."

I start to head toward my own car.

"How do you know I'm going on a date, Carter?" he

calls, and I pause with my back to him a moment before turning around.

"Because you don't look as shabby as you usually do," I say. "Did Delilah dress you again?"

"Not this time."

The light from the lamppost casts a halo around him, and he stands there smirking at me infuriatingly in his designer navy wool coat, still unzipped, despite his breath casting little clouds every time he speaks. Why does he have to look at me like this? Maybe he always has, but now the emotions are tangling up with each other inside me—intrigue, excitement and something else, something I don't think I'll ever dare go for again, not after Grayson. It feels a lot like desire.

He takes a few more steps toward me, away from his own car. "From your admirable attempt at wit, Carter, am I right to think you're jealous?"

"Please," I scoff, rolling my eyes, even though something in my chest tightens at the thought.

He leans casually against my car as I search for my keys. I am quite jealous. This is wild. And I do have to talk about what's going on, because if I don't I'll go crazy, and I'm sick of holding things back.

"Listen. Ever since that night at McFadden's—" I start, then I hesitate. Do I really want to go there with him looking like every woman's dream and me feeling like a tired, hormonal mess? But something compels me to continue. "You've been distant again, Theo. Don't tell me I'm imagining it."

"I thought it was best for me to give you and Rose space to work things out. And look, it's working," he explains calmly. He locks his eyes on to mine with an intensity that makes my heart stutter. I wonder if he's really just been going on another endless stream of dates without his pregnant friend killing his mojo, which, to be fair, he has every right to do. He can do what he wants.

"It's been working," I confirm. Whatever's going on, I'm glad he understands that there was something to work out with me and Rose in the first place. The twin thing is a mystery to a lot of people; it always was to Grayson. "You told me something was going on with your mom," I say now, crossing my arms. "Is that still the case?"

He scratches at his chin and finally zips up his coat. He does it a little too hard. "It never ends, Carter," he says.

"What never ends? What is it?"

"She's pretty sick," he replies, and I swallow, pressing a hand to my bump.

"I'm so sorry. Why didn't you say anything?"

He tenses. "Because, what we have, Carter, is an escape from all that, and I don't particularly enjoy talking about it."

I'm jarred for a second by the fact that he's never seen what we have as anything more than an escape, but then…he's been an escape for me, too. I was always too ashamed to tell him much about Grayson. We've both been keeping things from each other.

"Theo, how sick is she?"

He pulls a face, tells me it's nothing anyone can control, and I fire a couple more questions at him, which he deflects expertly until I'm annoyed again. Rose would have a field day with this, I think. She's been poking and prodding about Theo ever since I told her he carried me out of the bar and personally drove me to the hospital. I wasn't exactly thrilled to find myself at Evergreen that night. I guess I feared the whispers and pitying glances and the fact that I was taking up space. But they've been nothing but supportive ever since, whereas Theo's done that disappearing act thing again, physically and emotionally. My getting hurt is one possible reason for the distance, but maybe he's picked up on my new feelings toward him—the last thing the eternally single bachelor probably wants to deal with. Pressing him like this puts me on edge as much as it apparently does him. Our proximity feels charged now, like the air before a storm. His posture has changed; he's guarded.

"Okay, well, don't let me keep you," I say.

I finally unlock the car and lower my weary body into the seat, careful to fit my bulge behind the steering wheel. Theo watches through the window. Then he taps on the glass and I roll it down.

"The fundraiser thing over the weekend. Black tie, silent auction, the whole deal. You've seen the posters."

"Same as last year, different venue," I remark, turning the key in the ignition.

"We're going again, right?" he says.

I frown at him. "You want me to go with you? Why? Did your date cancel?"

"I didn't ask anyone else," he admits, rubbing the back of his neck.

"So, you want *me* to be your date?"

"I want you to be my better philanthropic half. My wingwoman," Theo clarifies quickly.

"Your wingwoman? Really, looking like this?" I'm kind of laughing now but the word tastes strangely bitter on my tongue. I've been his wingwoman many, many times before and it's never bothered me till now, now that he's retreating, forcing out my clingy side, damn him. On top of my hormones, this is doubly bad.

"Think about it?" he asks. "It'll be fun. I said I'd help with the banner. Some of Delilah's horsey friends are helping to paint it. I'm also putting the gift baskets together."

"Look at you, getting all involved," I tease, although how sweet is it of him to volunteer?

"I'm more about getting the gossip like we did last year. And the free dinner." He winks at me and I smile. It does sound fun, actually. I haven't been out to anything like this in ages.

"I'll think about it," I reply. Why is my pulse racing?

"Great," Theo says. "I know you love helping out for a good cause."

"I'll wear my maternity superhero cape," I add, and suddenly I'm presented with a flashback to a friend's art exhibition that Grayson took me to, several months before I ended things for good. I wasn't allowed to speak to anyone there except him, and he took me aside at regular intervals to either praise me for how well I was doing, or berate me for making too much eye contact with people. It was after that, when I came home visibly shaken, that Rose confronted me, and we hatched the plan for me to move my stuff out of his place and into the rental she had at the time.

Theo glances at his watch. "I should probably get going."

"Hot date can't wait, right?"

He nods, lifting his weight from my car. "Inexcusable acts of tardiness don't go down well with my sister, Carter. She's not the forgiving kind. Neither is Delilah."

I open my mouth to respond, then close it as my cheeks

start to flush. Okay. So he's meeting Peonie and his niece tonight. And now I feel like a total idiot. I almost put my serious face on and demand he tell me what's really going on with his family, but he's just reminded me I'm the "fun friend" to go out and get the gossip with, the one to eat free dinners with, the one who teases him about who he might be dating, and suddenly I'm biting my tongue, pressing a hand to my bulge. That's how he sees me. The fun friend, who's expecting another man's babies. I won't embarrass myself by slipping into some unwelcome counselor or partner role; he clearly doesn't want that from me. And I can't seem to stay mad at him.

"Have fun, tell them I say hi," I say as I slip into gear. I am utterly exhausted. At least I have a "bit of fun" lined up with him, even if it's the platonic kind, as usual.

CHAPTER NINE

THE CLANK OF metal on metal reverberates through the penthouse as I heave the dumbbells above my head. It's one way of shedding the weight of the morning shift just now at the hospital. We managed to bring a kid back from the brink in ER, a hit-and-run. We spoke to the police and the kid, too, when we brought him round. Dark stuff.

I like the feel of my own sweat sliding down my torso, soaking into my shorts at the waistband. This morning I really enjoyed waking up with nothing on my body at all, and turning around to see her there in the doorway, in a see-through white dress…three seconds before I woke up all alone in the bed with a hard-on.

I can't be sure but I'm pretty sure she was jealous the other day in the parking lot, when she thought I was going out to meet a woman. Crazy. I still don't know what I think about that, which is why I let her think I *was* going on a date for a minute. Then I caved, told her I was meeting Pea. I should have just come out and told her I was meeting her because Edwina left. After getting locked out, she quite rightly said she couldn't help someone who didn't even want her there, so we have to find a new carer now. I don't know why I didn't say that to Lily, or anything, really. It feels like we're past the point of pretending with each other now...not that I know much about her ex. Something tells me there's more to that than she's letting on. I guess I don't want to seem all vulnerable and have her looking at me differently because of my past. It would only bring us closer, make me want her more, when we could never be anything more.

She's pregnant, so a fling wouldn't be fair to propose. And I don't want anything serious!

I have to admit, though, I've been thinking a little differently lately, picturing myself in the partner role instead of stuck in the friend zone.

Chicago is snowier than a Christmas movie out my windows. If it wasn't zero degrees outside I'd go running now, straight into the skyline, run Carter out of my system. I drop the weights. I've had enough. I'm tired. But if I didn't work out every day I'd go insane, especially now. How does she unravel me without even trying lately? It's not like anything could happen even if I wanted it to. She deserves forever with someone who can give it to her and the twins. I'm not a forever kind of guy and she knows that. This attraction is undoing me, the way she's been looking at me. Maybe it's all in my head?

I wipe a water splash off the counter the instant it spills, and pour hot water over a lemon from the kettle—which has never been tossed at a date by the hands of Elizabeth Montgomery.

I've asked myself if it's some strange new attraction to pregnant women, now that I'm heading for forty. Is it some deep-rooted longing to see someone raise kids the way Pea and I should've been raised, with love and respect and attention? She's twenty-four weeks pregnant, but that's almost irrelevant at this point. It's not about what she looks like, either. It's the emotions and truths coming out of her along with all of this, the way she's forcing new emotions out of me. I almost told her about Mom… I mean, I probably would have already, if I even knew where to start with it. I don't know what to do with this, wanting to keep Lily close and have her out of my way at the same time. I have to figure it out or I'll lose her.

My phone's ring slices through the silence. I snatch it from the bench, swiping to answer without checking the caller ID—a rookie mistake. My music cuts out.

"Hi, honey!"

It's Mom. She seems to be in a good mood, but I'm instantly on edge. She talks to me, tells me she's excited to spend time with Delilah later this week, and I finally relax a little.

But in a flash her tone turns ice-cold. "Theo, while I have you, do you know how much you hurt my feelings, reminding me to take my meds? You sound like Edwina, before she abandoned me like all the others."

Here we go. My knuckles clench.

"Can we not do this right now, Mom? I've been up since dawn saving lives, and I need to unwind before tonight."

I know my tone will piss her off, especially the bit about saving lives. She never thought I'd become a doctor. It's childish, I know, but my patience with all this is at new levels of low. I'm pissed at myself for not putting my foot down sooner and insisting that something changes. Pea still doesn't want her going to some soulless facility, but at least she'd be getting round-the-clock care and not directing all this vitriol at me.

I end the call while she's still raging, right after she reminds me that she wishes I'd left when Dad did, and toss the phone aside, the screen lighting up with a missed call. I catch that it's from Lily, just as the screen goes blank again.

"Get it together." All it took was seeing her name. What is my problem?

The intercom jolts me back to reality. My heart is still hammering from the workout, never mind what Mom just said. She always knows how to hit where it hurts. It shouldn't get to me, it's her illness, I know that, but it's crippling having to hear what a terrible excuse of a son I still am to her. I shouldn't answer the door. I don't want to see anyone right now, not even the delivery guy who's bringing up my protein shakes.

When I answer, it's not the delivery guy.

"Your neighbor buzzed me in. Theo, I—" Lily cuts off. Her gaze lands on my sweat-slicked torso as she shakes snow from her coat. Her eyes widen when she sees my eyes. "What's wrong? What happened? I just tried to call you to say I was on the way…you were already on the phone."

I look at her blankly. She's my friend; why can't I tell her what just happened? She wouldn't look at me like I'm weak; surely, we're past that, I think. But she doesn't need my problems piling up on top of her own right now. "I lost track of time," I say as my inner voice chides me for being a coward, still choosing to let her see the version of Theo everyone else sees—a problem-free version that doesn't even exist right now. Then I catch her eyes on my skin, trailing downward slowly, then up again to my face. I watch her neck as she swallows, the way her cheeks change color like flowers in the sun, and damn… I'm sweaty, and I'm hardly wearing anything.

"They ran out of paint at the store," she says, clutching a giant snowy zip-up bag to her chest over her bump. I assume it holds her dress for the event tonight. "I was going to start on the nursery, which technically *was* supposed to be our yoga studio but, you know we never really use…"

She fiddles with her hair and fumbles over some words about how she needed something to do, so she figured she could help me with the other jobs if she came over early.

"Right, for the fundraiser." I clear my throat. "Come on in."

"You seem…on edge," she observes as she steps past me and takes off her coat and boots. I'd forgotten what just happened with Mom for a moment. I was thinking about dream Lily in the white dress, her hair all messed up, her lips all swollen. Her shampoo and perfume smell floats around us now as I tell her I'm fine. She looks at me like she doesn't believe me, so I make for the shower before I tell her anything at all about what my mom just said, or how she's said the same thing, about wishing I'd left with Dad, since I was ten years old.

"Theo?" Lily calls out. I'm still standing under the hot shower like I've moved to a waterfall in Hawaii. How long have I been in here?

"Yeah?" I shout back, hitting the taps off and stepping naked into the steam. Part of me wants to throw the door open and let her see me, let her want me. I could do it, force this mad attraction out into the open where we both have to address it, but I don't.

"I'm starting on those gift baskets," she says, and I can hear her lips almost up against the door. Is she teasing me now?

"Did you need a medal, some kind of reward?" I say, toweling myself off too hard. The words *gift baskets* have never sounded like such a turn-on before, which is not a great start to the day we're about to spend together.

"Very funny. I'm just telling you what I'm doing."

Telling me what she's doing? Okay, she really is teasing me. The way she looked me up and down earlier told me everything I needed to know. I've seen how women look when they want me. But she's Lily. She's being controlled by her hormones more than anything else, surely.

"If that's what you want to do, Lily, then you should do it," I say, toweling my hair and hot neck. Damn this. She doesn't need to know what I want right now. I want to do things that would ruin both of us.

There's silence for a moment. I can hear her shuffling on the other side of the door.

"Is there something else you want to be doing, Lily?" I ask. Then I regret it. What am I initiating here? I have to cool it. Mom's wound me up. All I want to do when she gets to me is bury myself in something else to forget it. I know I've done the same to a string of women before, but I won't do that to Lily. My family's issues won't become hers, or anyone else's. Sometimes I wish I *had* left when Dad did and taken Peonie with me.

My best intentions are somewhere out the window now with the snow. Somehow, I'm inching closer to the door, my mouth by the paneling, waiting to hear her voice up close. Then it comes, in my ear.

"I want to be drinking champagne and squeezing into a hot dress, Theo. But that's not going to happen. And you really have been in there a *very* long time."

"Ri-i-i-ght." I pull a black towel around my waist and open the door. Lily jumps back and clutches her bump.

The look on her face almost makes me laugh. I walk toward her in nothing but the loosely clamped towel, and she keeps on stepping backward till she's up against the bed.

"We've got loads of donations from local businesses to sort through for the baskets," I tell her. My voice comes out huskier than I was expecting, and her eyes rake over my body, up and down, then up again to my eyes. We're an inch apart. Her thigh is between my legs and she doesn't move. She just runs her gaze along the towel again, upward to my navel, till I catch her chin between my fingers. "They're near the couch, by the blinds," I tell her.

"I'll find them," she says, but her words are more a choked-up whisper. She leans softly into my fingers, then starts sinking backward to the bed, like she's on a spring, till I'm waiting for her to catapult up and fly out the door. The towel is barely masking my turn-on at this point, and she looks at my hand on it while her bottom lip quivers. I can read her face. She's not telling me to stop, but she's not laughing. This is no joke. She wants me. She came into my room and up to that door for a reason. I lower myself over her slowly, till she's pressing both hands to my flesh over my heart. She's not pushing, but somehow she's urging me closer with every breath. Everything in me screams to stop this, it's everything I said I wouldn't do with my friend, but she's driving me mad.

"I'll start organizing them," she says, right on theme, right as my knee lands between her legs. She's flat on the bed now, lasering my eyes with hers, reaching for me.

"Make sure you categorize them by value and theme," I instruct as her fingers start to weave and tangle in my hair. She's breathing so hard I can feel it on my face. My lips are on a course to hers and I need my hands. So I release the towel.

"Theo—"

Her hands slide lower down my chest, softly across my nipples. She lets her fingers whisper inquisitively toward to my navel and I feel my own breath catch as she traces all around my thighs, across my bare backside, like she's exploring me, inch by inch, taking it all in, taking her time. I watch her face the whole time, the way she masks a gasp when she finally gets a full handful of me. I'm so hard, it's all I can do to just let her look and touch me. I lower myself farther over her, careful not to squash her, and the way she strokes and rubs me so softly, almost curiously, definitely appreciatively, almost makes me come into her palm. I roll to my back; it's the only way I can stop myself.

"What are we doing, Theo?" She's up like a flash, off the bed.

I groan, half at her, mostly at my own stupid self. "I know, I'm sorry, it's my fault, you were…"

"It's *my* fault," she counters. "I was… I don't know."

She stumbles on a shoe, almost trips over the towel I just tossed. She grasps the door handle, but not before I've caught her and spun her back to me. Her hands land against my chest as I set her right, and she tries to laugh at her misstep, even though nothing is funny right now.

"Are you okay, Carter?" I say.

She doesn't look okay. She looks like a deer in headlights now. "Yes," she assures me without moving her hands. "I just… I haven't been in a situation like this since my ex." Her words come out all fast and flustered.

"You never really told me anything about him," I say.

"I've been trying to forget," she says. "It's not you, Theo…it's me."

That old line?

I'm still naked, holding her arms, but she keeps looking over my shoulder, like she needs to escape. She reaches for the towel and hands it back to me, swipes at her eyes as I cover myself and sink back down to the bed. My heart is pounding as she leaves the room.

CHAPTER TEN

THE MOMENT THE LAST wicker basket is squeezed into the trunk, Theo slams it shut and opens the passenger door for me. I climb in past him, careful of my babies, and he leans over me to adjust the seat. I need more space than I did last time I was in his car.

I try not to breathe him in or touch him while he clicks in my seat belt. Instead, I tell him I'm perfectly capable of doing it myself, and then I wish I didn't have to find ways to mask the absolute panic I am feeling. What the hell just happened in there?

I got complete confirmation that Theo is considerably well-endowed, that's what happened. There was something about his face, though, when he let me into the apartment, like he'd just walked through hell to get to the front door. I was worried about him; it led me to him; it led to *that*. We sat there afterward, making the gift baskets for the fundraiser in the living room. I didn't kiss him. We left it all in the bedroom, didn't even bring it up. If we had kissed, I think it would have been even more intimate and way harder to come back from.

I huddle into my coat. It's a half-hour drive to the fundraising venue at the Grand Avalone Hotel. Every nerve ending feels like it's buzzing. We're going to have to talk about it; we both know it. But I don't know what I even want to say. No one told me pregnancy could make a woman so horny, even for her platonic male friends. Well, all right, the soaring levels of estrogen and progesterone, an increase in blood flow to the genitals—it's no secret all that can lead to heightened sexual desire, but this is Theo. And it's *my* blood flow that's supposed to be the issue here; *my* genitals, not his!

There's a reason he initiated it. He's a sex-mad single bachelor.

We merge onto the freeway, and that's when we hit it—a colossal traffic jam, the kind that transforms highways into parking lots and regular humans into furious honking ogres. The cars are bumper-to-bumper, horns blare through the snow. It's actually snowing again now. Theo's knuckles whiten on the steering wheel and his jaw clenches. I know he wants to wind the window down and curse at full volume out the window.

"Where's the siren when you need it?" he mutters at the windscreen, before we merge back into silence. The stillness gives me way too much room for my mind to wander. Sex with Theo *would* be amazing. And different. Grayson would never look into my eyes, or invite me to explore him slowly and erotically like Theo just did. It was like he gave up all desire to actually connect with me, until I started fearing connection. I was scared of it, scared of doing something wrong, scared of being belittled or rejected or both. It was so warped and twisted, the mind games!

That back there with Theo, though. That was…

"This is bad, isn't it, Carter?" Theo says.

My insides rearrange themselves at the sound of his voice. "It's a little awkward, yes—"

"I didn't think the traffic would be this bad."

Oh, he means the traffic. "It's not your fault." I force a smile. "At least the chocolates won't melt. If this was a summer ball situation, it would be a different story."

"I have a story to make this traffic jam more interesting," he says, before launching into a tale about Delilah as a toddler and a story he would read to her about a mouse princess and a grasshopper prince and a dragon. I guess we're still not going to address what happened in his bedroom.

"Good thing this princess brought her ball gown to change into," I say, more to distract myself from his mouth than anything. I wanted to kiss him all afternoon. I'm glad I didn't. Sort of.

"And your prince here still has his stallion waiting patiently," he replies, deadpan except for the smirk, tapping his fingers against the wheel.

The sound exits my mouth before I can form words, something between a snort and a squeal. "Did you just refer to your penis as a stallion?"

"We were working to a theme. Princes ride horses!"

"I get it," I tell him, and thank goodness we're laughing. It feels good.

"Listen," he says, and my stomach flips as his tone turns serious. "I'm really sorry if I made things weird."

Silence. I can barely gather my thoughts enough to answer. "I...um..." I turn to him, willing myself to be honest.

Tell him you wanted it, my devil voice screams.

"I don't think we have to analyze it, really, do we?" I say instead and he nods at the road ahead, tapping his fingers to the wheel.

I'm a coward. I don't know why I told him that. I *want* to analyze it now. I just don't want it to seem like I expect anything, or need anything. This is uncomfortable. And there's another pressing issue now, too—one that simply cannot wait out a traffic jam. "Theo…" I begin, shifting in my seat. "I really need to use the bathroom."

His eyes flicker to mine and he frowns. "Here? Now?"

"Blame the babies," I say. "They're pressing all sorts of buttons."

"I know better buttons."

"Stop it, Theo!"

"Okay, okay. Let me think." His gaze scans the vicinity along with mine. We're probably looking at an impossible situation. There's so much snow and concrete and cars.

"I don't think the babies care about traffic laws anymore, Grasshopper Prince," I tell him. "Summon your dragon. Find us a way."

He salutes me dramatically. "I will not fail you, Mouse Princess."

I'm laughing, but I wish I weren't because it makes me need to pee even more. I clutch the handle as he edges us toward the shoulder, inching past the honks and a thousand glares until we are safely—sort of—out of the direct line of traffic.

"Privacy is going to be a little bit of an issue here, Carter." He turns to rummage through the back seat and I warn my fingers not to touch him again. "But I think I found my dragon."

He pulls out the oversize fundraising banner that Delilah's friends made and I feel my eyes grow to the size of satellites. "I can't pee behind this…it's got pictures of kids on it."

"They're pictures, Lily."

"It says *Together for a Healthier Tomorrow* on it,

Theo. There's nothing healthy about me peeing behind it on the highway."

"Do you need to go or not?" Quickly, he drapes the banner from the door and beckons me forward. It's the side farthest from the oncoming traffic, so I guess no one will see, but honestly, do I even have a choice? I'm bursting.

I hold my bump as the freezing wind and snow blows around my legs, and Theo creates a makeshift stall, instructing me to squat.

"This is so undignified," I tell him.

His eyes shine with something wicked before he turns his back, and if I didn't have to pee and safeguard two tiny humans inside me I might pull him down on top of me. This is weirdly exhilarating actually, but, oh, Lord, I am already a terrible mother.

"Make it quick, Carter, and try not to pee on your boots."

I manage the quickest roadside relief in history while Theo stands guard, humming the theme song to some eighties action movie. It is quite ridiculous. And exactly why I'm feeling all this about him. I never really saw our connection for what it is before. We have something rare, I think. It's friendship but it's also trust and respect and fun, and being there when you really, really have to pee. He still hasn't told me what's really going on with his mom, though. He still doesn't trust me *enough* to tell me anything, even when I ask. What is it that he's so afraid to talk about, I wonder? What don't I know, besides the fact that he doesn't seem to be as big of a playboy as I thought, lately. He could have brought anyone here today, but he chose to bring me. He also chose to open that door, drop that towel…

"Mission accomplished?" he asks as I emerge from behind the banner with what remains of my dignity.

"Your gallantry knows no bounds," I retort, while the fact that I'm wondering things I've never wondered about this mad, intriguing, infuriating, talented, unpredictable man takes on new shapes and forms and colors in my head until I miss his next words completely. "What did you say?"

He rolls the banner back up and puts it in the back seat. "I said I'm going to auction off this banner when it comes to raising funds for your maternity leave party. You've put a dent in its value, but we should still be able to secure some supermarket flowers."

"I hope you tell them a princess used it."

We drive on and talk about work and I'm so glad some of the weirdness has gone. I shouldn't try to sweep what happened under the carpet, though. Even if he doesn't romanticize or analyze sexual encounters like I do, it doesn't mean what's going on isn't real for him, too.

His phone blasts more Taylor Swift. He mutters "Delilah..." as he hits the decline button.

"You hung up on Delilah?"

"No, she put Taylor as my ringtone and I keep meaning to... Never mind."

The phone is relentless. It rings again almost immediately. "Come on, Theo, answer it. We're stuck here, anyway." I push the call through to the speaker without waiting for his consent.

"Theo!" The female voice that explodes around us makes me physically jump. Theo's arm comes up across my chest like he's expecting this woman to appear in the windscreen.

"Mom," he says, a forced calmness in his voice.

"Do not cut me off again! How dare you…?"

My hands go to my bump as she carries on ranting. She goes on and on, yelling, crying, so much emotion, so much vitriol, and it's hurtful, horrible. I think she's intoxicated, too. The things she says to him make my heart pound with so much secondhand embarrassment for him and pity for *her*, that I can't look at him anymore. He sees my face.

"Mom, I'm driving." Finally, he cuts her off.

"Theo, the things she said… She sounds like she…"

"Like she hates me."

I stare at him, shaking my head. "Like she needs some serious help. Why didn't you tell me it was this bad?"

"Well. Now you know." He presses his lips into a line and swallows back whatever he's trying to say but I know what he needs. He's stressed and embarrassed over whatever his mom's suffering from, and he needs space for his thoughts, and he also needs me not to press him.

Finally, we pull up to the venue. "All right, let's get this over with, Princess Mouse," he says.

I put a hand to his arm and he lets out a sigh from somewhere deeper than his bones. "I'm here, if you want to talk," I say.

"I thought we weren't analyzing it."

"Not about us, Theo."

"So there's an us, Lily?"

"No, there is no us. Stop it."

His eyes don't leave my lips and I see the way he stops himself from leaning in to kiss me. It happens in a fraction of a second, and in that fraction of a second his eyes sweep up over mine and I swear I feel like I could melt right into the seat, despite all the snow outside. I swear he wants to melt into me, too, if only so we can both take some of his pain away. I see how his jaw shifts as his tongue moves behind his lips; how he lowers his eyes then pulls away until the connection is broken.

The moment passes like it never happened. He pops the trunk and slides out of the car.

For a moment I'm truly shocked that he didn't just kiss me. Or that I didn't kiss him. Then I have to laugh at myself and my open mouth and my racing heartbeat. This is how he does it. He's such a goddamn tease, such a good flirt. Really, truly, the best I've ever had to face. He wipes my brain of everything else, and I love it. When I'm not freaking out about it, I love how playing with him makes me feel. Grayson never...not even before he changed and sucked my soul dry. It was nothing like this. But Theo is hurting, too. I see him clearer now than I ever have. How long has his mom been acting like this?

A guy arrives to help unload the baskets, and Theo greets him with his trademark high-five shoulder bump. He only ever does that when he really likes someone, which now that I think about it is only maybe this guy and my dad. He truly must be going through hell in secret if he gets treated like that by his own mother. He could have been on the phone to her when I arrived at his place earlier. Maybe *that* was why he looked like his psyche had just taken a bullet. What I witnessed in the car was a continuation of her tirade, which was probably one of many, if his reactions to my questions are anything to go by. I'm not going to let this go. The woman clearly has some kind of mental disorder, maybe alcoholism or bipolar disorder. Why is she not getting treatment?

"This place is something else," I say, attempting to take a basket from him as the valet drives off with the

Porsche and we crunch across the snowy gravel. He refuses to let me carry anything, even though he's balancing the banner over his shoulder along with the bag containing my dress. "Let me help," I say as we step over the threshold. He grunts a no, then ignores me.

The entrance hall is like a film set with its splendor. The chandeliers sparkle over us as I walk beside him across the checkered floor. People are milling about already, placing welcome glasses on special tall stands. I tell him I want a grand staircase like the one here, someday. It sweeps up to the second floor in a marble dance toward the domed ceiling. From somewhere the strains of a string quartet meet my ears. A tingle creeps along my arms and I catch Theo looking at me.

"You look cute in an opulent setting. Did I ever tell you that?" he says, heading for the staircase. "I should've switched McFadden's for more fancy establishments sooner. Looking at your face is almost worth the parking fee."

"Oh, you're good," I say, but I'm already thinking about my dress, how I wish on this one night I didn't have a bump to squeeze into it. I catch myself and curse. I didn't mean that. Gosh, I'm awful. I didn't mean that.

He's lugging the banner up the stairs beside me suddenly, and I try to take the other end of it.

"You didn't wash your hands, remember," he says, moving it out of my reach.

I laugh. We both know I didn't get pee on it, but he's making it a thing. "You're the one touching it, Theo!"

"I need to wash it, and you need to wash your hands. And your mouth."

"Why would I wash my mouth? You didn't kiss me."

We're at the top of the spiral steps now, the mounting crowds bustling beneath us. Theo props the banner against the railings and turns to face me. Stepping to my toes, he leans in so close I can feel his lips brush my neck when he speaks, and my heart shoots up to the very spot where his breath warms my skin, till it's thudding in my ears.

"Did you want me to kiss you? Did you want to carry on with what we started in the apartment?"

Someone sweeps past us. My heart is hammering now.

"I think you did," he says. "So did I. We both know I want you, I'm not denying that, but we also both know I won't be good for you, Lily. You were the one who stopped it and I think you were right to."

"I did stop it," I manage. "And I have all kinds of reasons. But I'm more concerned about you, if I'm honest. You're being abused. That's what it sounds like."

A darkness crosses his face. "She's my mother."

"I know what abuse sounds like, Theo. It doesn't matter where it comes from."

A storm is raging in his head. I can see it in his eyes. I draw a breath, and I'm surprised at the emotion that escapes when I speak, the way my voice cracks. "I promised myself that tonight would be perfect. We were meant to escape together, Theo, have some fun, and you know what? Even stopping for that emergency pee was more fun than I've had in ages, but…"

I falter suddenly, closing my mouth. I can't stop thinking how Grayson took so much away from me for so long, drained the fun-loving side of me clean away. I let him do that. And now Theo's mother's condition is putting his own mental health in jeopardy.

"Don't let this illness of hers take over your life, too.

She needs help," I finish. Theo just scowls at the floor, then at me.

"You don't know the half of what's going on," he says eventually.

"Because you've chosen not to tell me," I counter, forcing my anger below the surface. I'm mad because I didn't press him enough sooner, and because he's shut me out. "You've chosen not to tell me! Look, Theo, I was a victim of abuse for a long time, and it completely sucked the life out of me, so yes, I kind of want to know that she's getting help, and I really want to know that *you* are okay, too."

Theo stares at me. His eyes are a million questions, all layering up in the blue, multiplying as he processes what I've just said. "What are you telling me?"

"Grayson," I say. Just vocalizing his name makes me rub my arms against a sudden chill.

"What did he do to you?"

I can hear the hurt in his voice, the confusion. My mind keeps spinning over and over. He asks me again through his teeth what he did to me, and I can feel the heat between us burning something down. "It wasn't physical," I tell him. It wasn't; it was worse. I can feel my shutters coming up now, and Theo's, too. This is not how I wanted this night to go.

"How long were you with him?"

"Four years," I tell him. "We need some space."

His eyebrows shoot up incredulously. "Us? Here? How will that even be poss—?"

"Figure it out, Grasshopper."

I leave him at the top of the stairs and try not to fall over. I shouldn't hurt Theo. He's being hurt enough by this situation with his family, but yes, it's what Grayson did to me, and when Theo shuts me out it brings it all back; the way I felt alone, surrounded by people. I was so alone, always, and *I'm* still hurting, too.

CHAPTER ELEVEN

OF COURSE WE'RE seated next to each other. For hours she's avoided me, talking to this person and that person and ignoring me, even when I purposefully pulled a face at her while I was stringing the banner up across the banisters.

She's impervious to my charms as I pull her seat out at the table, and she doesn't look at me, even as she slides in next to me. "Thank you, Doctor Montgomery," she says coolly, for the sake of the eight other important people around the table.

"It's good to see you after all this time, Doctor Carter," I try, but she doesn't crack.

All right, so I should have told her sooner about what exactly is wrong with Mom, before she was forced to hear it for herself. But she knows now, some of it at least, and I'm more torn up about what she told *me*. She was with a guy for four years who had zero respect or appreciation for what he had right in front of him, who *abused* her in some way? I don't know the details and she probably doesn't want to tell me, but how have I never known this? How has she never told me she was in an abusive relationship? I feel helpless, angry for her, even though I know it's in the past.

She does look hot in that dress, though. The color of

the trees in spring, all sparkly with lace crisscross stitches and matching green earrings that people might say bring out her eyes. Her eyes don't need enhancing in my opinion. I kind of like it when they burn me.

I arrange my napkin on my knee. She mirrors me, so I tap my foot to hers. She tuts and moves it, so I tap it again until finally, she cracks a smile. Just a flicker but it's there behind her Ice Queen agenda. She picks up her fork and I can't *not* see it again... Her hands all over me before we left the house, her eyes burning into mine, wanting me. I never once touched her. I didn't need to... She was doing it all on her own and she loved it. Right until she didn't—she ended up with her ex in her head. Grayson. I swear I'll run an ambulance over him *and* leave the scene without him.

Dr. Robert Simmons, widely regarded as one of the best cardiothoracic surgeons in the country, has dedicated his career to the intricate field of heart and lung surgery, and he is absolutely loving that everyone knows it. He fills her glass with sparkling water as he talks and I ignore my phone vibrating in my suit pocket. I watch her mouth as she listens politely to the doctor's story, pecking at a bread roll. We didn't kiss yet; her mouth never touched me. I don't know how we managed that at my place, or earlier in the car, but I don't want to treat her like some dispensable item I can use and cast aside. I won't.

I can't resist a real beer. Lily eats her salad like a bird when it appears, nodding in all the right places as Simmons reminds us all how he attended Johns Hopkins University "back in the good old days." She still barely looks at me. I carve into my steak, only half tasting it. From somewhere across the room I hear my name mentioned. Two female execs are whispering, looking right at me.

Lily whispers to me…actually it's more like a cat from a cartoon: sultry, seductive, with the perfect amount of spite. "Don't you want to go over there, Theo? Remind them how being with you is a terrible idea? Or don't you say that to one-night stands?"

"Oh, so you've decided to grace me with your words now, have you, Princess?" I smirk. She's pissed about what I said, when I told her I'd be no good for her. She knows I'm right, but her pride took a hit, and who knows what else that Grayson guy put into her head? A lot more things are starting to make sense about Carter now.

I catch her looking at the execs again over my shoulder. I should make a point of going over there just to wind her up, but what would that achieve? She's the one I want now, even if there's stuff we *both* don't particularly want to discuss. I press a hand to hers under the table, holding it against her bare knee, and twist my chair to hers. "Let's go somewhere and talk, Lily."

She puts her fork down calmly. "I'm eating my salad."

I run my hand along her inner thigh, softly, slowly, till she hides the smallest moan behind her hand and swipes me away like a pesky fly. "We'll get pizza on the way home," I say.

"What makes you think I'm getting back in a car with you?"

I lean in closer, whispering into her ear. "Because I'm the only one who will untie that banner up there. And bring it back downstairs through *all* these people. And put it in the car and make a shelter for you with it when you need to stop. I am the *only* person who will do that, Carter. Come with me."

She pushes my hand away. "Don't tell me what to do."

"Okay, this is stupid. Seriously." I take her hand back and hold it tighter to her knee. "Don't compare me to him," I tell her before she can pull away from me. "I don't know what he did to you, Lily, but you know I'd never hurt you."

Her eyes gloss over as she looks away. Then Dr. Simmons's scratchy beard appears over her shoulder and she almost leaps off her seat into my lap.

"Forgive me if I'm stepping out of line here, but did you say your partner wasn't here tonight?"

I scratch my chair loudly as I reposition my seat. Oh, this will be good.

Lily sniffs and then scratches her chair just as loudly to face him. "My partner?"

"The father of your child?" Dr. Simmons presses, and I don't miss his eyes moving to me. This is amusing me more than it should.

"What makes you think that my *partner* is also the father of my babies?" Lily says next, and a woman at the table presses her hands together, addressing us all.

"Why *do* men think they can probe us like this?" she asks, like we've just sat down for her TED Talk. I see now that she's pregnant, too, and she's also here alone. Oh, this is going better than I expected. I hope someone's filming.

It's finally Dr. Simmons's turn to speak, but unfortunately he's cut short, because a huge commotion is breaking out across the room.

A man. Middle-aged. He's staggering from his chair, clutching his chest over his suit. His face is contorted in pain. I can see the sweat beading on his forehead from here.

"Stay here," I tell Lily as I stand, but of course she gets right up after me, gathering up her dress.

"He's having a heart attack. Call emergency," I bark at the nearest onlooker, a woman who fumbles with her phone in a panic.

There are other doctors here amongst the sponsors but Lily and I synchronize, largely without words, as the room fades into the background. All that matters is the man gasping for air on the floor. I check his pulse and order others to clear the space.

"Sir, can you hear me?" Lily asks him.

"His breathing is shallow. We need to start CPR," I say as someone mentions a defib stored downstairs. We work together, counting compressions and giving rescue breaths. It's strange how everything else disappears when the world is narrowed down to the task of keeping someone alive.

The AED is here now, hustled over to us by Dr. Simmons, and in seconds I'm cutting off his shirt and lining up the pads. "Clear!"

I brace myself, letting another jolt out. This is not how this gentleman must have thought this evening would go. His losing this battle would destroy his wife, who's staring at all this and shaking like she's never been more afraid in her whole life. Then…

"Carter, we've got a pulse."

I can already hear the sirens outside.

The paramedics filter in and I step back with Lily. I reach for her hand as he's carried away on a stretcher. If I'm exhausted after that, Lily must be ready to drop. She won't let me take her hand.

"I can take you home if you want?" I tell her, just as the MC hops onto the stage and announces that we've done all we can for the moment, and the show must go on. Of course, what else would they say? We have a hospital to fund. The band starts up, and people start filtering to the dance floor.

"You should dance," Lily tells me, lowering herself to a seat. "Go find those execs."

"I'm not going to do that, Carter."

"Do it."

"Don't tell me what to do," I tell her, and she rolls her eyes.

"Touché."

It's not long before I'm lured to the dance floor, anyway, and I don't even know why I stay on it, following her orders. What is wrong with me? But I do like watching her turn away every single man who approaches her; even the attractive ones who might possibly be single. I wait maybe ten minutes before returning, and she cocks an eyebrow.

"Dance with me?" I say, holding out my hand. "I assume you have now washed your hands."

"That's the least romantic thing anyone has ever said to me. Thank you, I won't be doing that."

She stands, anyway, when I put my hand down to her, but I can see the weight of her thoughts in her eyes. I cup her chin again. "You can stand on my feet if you're tired," I say, but her expression almost breaks me. This is not the time to make light of anything. I curse my bad habit of deflecting discomfort with humor.

"I'm sorry," I tell her. "I'm sorry about what happened at my place, how you found out about Mom, it's a lot. And your ex. But you know I'd never hurt you."

"Not on purpose, maybe, but I'm pregnant, Theo," she announces as if it's not blatantly obvious. She lowers her head and sighs at the floor. "You were right before. This wouldn't be a good thing to explore…"

"I wasn't hitting on you!"

"But you want to. You admitted it. I have to think about my babies."

I close my mouth. She sighs heavily again, and I force myself not to say a thing. Kissing in her mind leads to commitment, and the fact that I can't offer it, and I should let it go. Except my mind is going to the exact same place—if I kiss her, I'll want more, and this isn't me. At least it didn't used to be. She's messing with my head.

"When I walked into your place earlier," she says, "you looked like you had the weight of the world on your shoulders. Was it your mom then, too?"

I nod solemnly. So she guessed that?

My phone vibrates in my pocket. It's the hospital with the update we've been waiting for. "Doctor Montgomery, good news. The patient you sent over is stable and recovering well."

"Thank you," I breathe out. "Thanks for the update."

Someone hears and wants me up on the stage. I tell Lily to wait where she is. This conversation isn't over. "I'll drive you home. To your place."

"I'm serious, Theo, I want to go on my own. I really think we need some space."

I'm ushered onto the stage, where the MC hands me the mic. I tell the crowd our man is stable and he is going to be just fine, and the room erupts and decides it's the perfect time for the gift basket auction. Lily's eyes find mine across the applause. She's standing in the doorway now, holding her coat. By the time I've made my way through the throng of people and out into the snowy open air, she's gone.

CHAPTER TWELVE

WE WORK THROUGH the days now, avoiding each other for the most part. Theo does his thing and I do mine, and when we have to work together at the hospital, we're polite and efficient but it doesn't go beyond that. For almost two months, as my belly's grown bigger and my body more tired, I've refused to let it. But I have thought about the fundraiser every single day since.

What happened in his bedroom plays over and over and over in my dreams. The memories only make my already crazy hormones fire into overdrive. It wasn't right how we left things. He shut me down, then I shut *him* down, and now we're at an impasse. I had to shut him down, though. Things were getting too complicated. I'm about to give birth, and my days are about to be nothing but babies…more babies than usual and that is a lot.

At thirty-one weeks, I'm even bigger now than I thought my body could possibly get. Beach ball doesn't cover it. I feel like there's a baby elephant curled up inside me.

I walk around my little patients, all sleeping so peacefully in their incubators. I reach through to one of them, gently stroking the fingers of Baby Jay, another preemie barely weighing two pounds. He is one of the most fragile in our unit. He had a heart operation just a few days ago.

"Doctor Montgomery is the biggest charmer in Chicago. Do you think he would've taken me seriously?" I tell the tiny infant. "And if we really had...done some wicked things that only adults do...he only would have made light of it afterward. Then where would we be?"

The baby's innocent face scrunches up adorably, like he understands. But even I don't understand. I'm saying all these things about Theo every day, mostly in my head, but I don't always believe them. I miss him making me laugh, the way we forged a real, undeniable connection through all the recent chaos, and maybe that's what scares me the most. He told me he would never hurt me. I fell into his eyes when he said that, in a room full of all those people. I truly, honestly believed him. Then that poor man had a heart attack and everything went crazy, and my mind made a huge deal of *everything* that happened, and the only way out was to set fire to it all and run. I did the right thing, though, didn't I?

Baby Jay blinks and crinkles up his tiny eyes and mouth. I adjust his tube and press my palm to the incubator. "I told him I needed space and he's only being respectful by giving me it. Truthfully, I think I'm afraid of liking someone too much after my last relationship was such a mess. I can't afford to lose myself to another guy, or to anything. I have my babies to think about."

The infant gurgles at me softly, fixing me with his big brown eyes. He gets it, I can tell. I can't help but huff a laugh as I give his hand one last gentle stroke. I tell him I hope my own babies are such good listeners. And then I realize someone is standing in the doorway.

"Theo. You snuck up on me again. Why do you do that?"

"I'm on a break. Sorry, can't help my tiny, silent footsteps," he says, before stomping heavily toward me with a completely straight face. Somehow, his shoes still barely make a sound on the floor.

"Did I order a clown in here?" I ask him, but I can't fight the start of a laugh as it bubbles up, damn him. Then he steps dramatically carefully and quietly forward to check on Baby Jay, and my heart does a somersault at the forced proximity. I never know if it's going to be another weird, awkward silence lately, or if we're actually going to have a conversation. Is it bad that even though I asked for space, I can still picture every inch of him naked?

I adjust the tiny knit cap on another infant, searching for something to ask him. But it's Theo's voice that breaks the silence, and of course my traitorous heart leaps when he casts his blue eyes to me.

"I actually did seek you out for a reason." He follows me as I walk to the end of the incubators. I get a lungful of his cologne, just how his bedroom smelled. Exactly how he smelled when he carried me out of McFadden's in the worst possible scenario that may or may not have intensified a mounting crush on my friend. The cologne no longer makes me nauseated, that's long gone, but it makes me think bad thoughts that I promised myself I would never think again.

"Should I be scared of this reason?" I ask him.

"It's about tomorrow."

I stiffen slightly. I just *know* what he's about to say before he says it. "What about tomorrow?"

"Your maternity leave celebration. I can't make it." His gaze holds something like an apology, but it doesn't mask the flicker of something else—regret, maybe? Guilt. I won't show how disappointed I am; it's not like we've even been speaking lately.

"So much for raising money by selling the banner," I say instead. The pangs from his rejection make me shuffle in place.

"I decided to keep that for myself, for the memories, you know." He lowers his voice, brushes my shoulder with his as he leans in. "I put it up on the ceiling, over my bed."

"Hilarious," I tell him.

I hate that I like the way he does this, switches so casually between joking with me as a friend and reminding me that he's clearly still thinking about that moment when we blurred the lines. He must know I'm still thinking about it, too. Before he can elaborate on why exactly he can't make it to my gathering, if he was even going to, his phone distracts him and I catch a glimpse of the caller ID—his mom. Again. He's programmed her name to come up as "Just be kind!"

I shouldn't feel sidelined by the persistent intrusion of his family drama; that wouldn't be fair. I can see how he's sick of it, too. It's all over his face. He doesn't want to look at his phone all the time, especially not here, but he can't help it; he feels like he has to. Like I always gave myself a minimum of three rings before I picked up to Grayson. If I took any longer than that to pick up he would simmer on it and bring it up later, accusing me of being too busy for him, which of course I was most of the time. I work at a hospital.

Just how bad is his mother's condition, whatever it is? After that call I overheard in the car, I haven't been able to stop thinking about it, and how much it all just reminds me of being stuck under Grayson's thumb.

Theo writes a text, and I watch his face as he shoves the phone back into his coat.

"So, we *are* trying to get help for my mother," he finally says, but his eyes dart away and he dashes his hands through his hair. "We have an appointment at a place tomorrow. It's taken two months for a spot to come up."

"A place?" It's the vaguest response from him on a serious matter that I think I've ever had. "Do you want to tell me more?" I encourage, but the Taylor Swift ringtone cuts me off this time. It's very quiet, and he doesn't startle the babies, but it's a melody that is still far too upbeat for this moment.

"You really need to change that," I tell him, and he replies that I need to show him how, exactly, before he excuses himself to talk to Peonie. There is always something with him. Every time he takes a break and turns his phone on, it's a flood. How can he handle all that on top of his job? I turn my attention back to the little fighter in the incubator. Just looking at these infants makes it even more real that two little lives will soon turn my entire world upside down. And with everything being so crazy, I still haven't gotten around to painting the yoga room. Rose agreed that it should become the nursery, and we finally got the paint delivered from the store, but that's about as far as we've got.

Theo steps back into the room. "So, the place?" I ask him.

He nods, folds his arms across his perfectly ironed coat like he's putting up a safety barrier all of a sudden. "It's called Serenity Pines. They specialize in DBT."

"Dialectical Behavior Therapy," I add. I know about this a little at least. It's commonly used in more individualized cases of depression. It tackles the extreme emotional thoughts that exist in severe cases. He tells me he's been trying to get her help for years beyond a revolving door of caretakers who come to her house and wind up leaving soon after, but that she doesn't think she needs it, and I can tell this is having a huge emotional impact on him. I feel so guilty now that I haven't been around for him, that we've been stuck avoiding each other like this. I'm the one who's been selfish.

"It must be a relief, knowing she might finally get some help," I say. He still has his arms folded over his coat like a barrier. Is it wrong that I want to hug him now and tell him things will be all right? "I don't know the half of it, like you said at the fundraiser, but it seems like something you've been wanting to fix for a while," I add.

"Yes, but it's not just down to me. It's complicated," he says, and he turns to one of the incubators now, moves some tubes, and the silence stretches between us. I'm not going to push him for more information now. This is more than he's ever said about the whole situation, so that's something. He's been trying to get help for two months, which means our blowup at the fundraiser made some impact. I'm actually proud that I might have helped in some way. It's already more than I managed to do for myself when I needed it.

"So, what's been going on with you?" he asks eventually, changing the subject. He draws the last word out as he sidles closer to me. "How is everything in baby world?"

"A lot, and they're not even here yet," I say. Then, because we're here and he's asking, I tell him how I still need to get car seats and paint the nursery but I don't even have a ladder or any paintbrushes yet.

"I assume we're *not* going for pink and blue?" he

says. "Someone like you…you picked a glitter paint, didn't you?"

I smile and tell him most certainly not on both accounts, and then he digs his hand in his other pocket and pulls out an envelope. He holds it out with purpose and I stare at it. "This is for me?"

"Just a little something, because I'm missing your thing," he says.

"A peace offering, you mean?"

"Just open it." He's trying to be casual, like he gives me little gifts every day or something, but I can tell by the way he watches me open the envelope that he's nervous about giving this to me. It's why he came in here to find me in the first place.

I pull out a voucher for a massage and a facial treatment at a place in my neighborhood I've never been to called Elysian Wellness Spa. It's for two people. He tells me how it has a salt pool float that's specially designed to ease the weight of pregnancy, and three different mud baths, and if I'm good I might even get some jasmine tea.

"I thought you and Rose could go," he says.

I hold it to my chest. "Theo, this is… I don't know what to say."

"There's nothing *to* say. Just go and relax."

He looks at me a moment too long, just a little too close, and I can feel everything we started the day of the fundraiser taking up the space between us all over again. "Lily," he starts, and I can tell he's going to say something serious. "I know you said you needed space, and I respect that, it's smart. So you don't get all magnetized to me again…"

"You flatter yourself."

"I've been thinking a lot about what you said, about Grayson," he continues.

My shoulders tense and I sniff at him.

"Four years, isn't that what you said? I can't get my head around it, Carter. How did I not know?"

"I don't tell you everything, Theo, the same as you don't tell me everything. Anyway, it's in the past," I say quickly, and before I even have the chance to tell him why just the mention of Grayson sends my blood levels through the roof, the sudden blare of a monitor alarm cuts in. Theo's head snaps up. His eyes dart to the incubator at the other end of the room.

"Baby Jay," he says, and I follow him quickly. Baby Jay was just fine! I tell him so, but something's wrong now, very wrong. His chest is rising and falling erratically beneath the translucent incubator. His skin has turned a frightening mottled purple in parts, and his little fingers keep clutching for an invisible lifeline as Theo checks his levels.

"It's okay, Carter, you've got this."

"Oxygen's dropping," I say. I can't seem to stop my fingers from trembling as I adjust the flow of oxygen. "Help me, please."

Somehow, my foggy brain knows where to take my feet and hands. Theo places the oxygen mask over the baby's face, while I prep an intubation kit. Baby Jay is still struggling for breath. This is breaking my heart.

"Pipe," I tell him, and I hand him a tiny endotracheal tube, which he slides deftly into place and secures swiftly with the surgical tape I hand him next. I'm actually shaking. This should not be happening…we were watching him!

"I was watching him," I tell Theo now, and he presses a calming hand to mine.

"Breathe," he says. The warning flickering in his eyes sends me back to silence. He's right, I'm getting too emotional. I'm taking this too personally, and he's reminding me of that, whilst also being my rock. God, I've missed him. But this is not supposed to be happening.

Finally, after what feels like hours, but is likely only a few minutes, Baby Jay's heart rate stabilizes and his breathing grows less frantic. I'm so emotional now, though. It feels like everything is piling up on top of me and I'm pretty sure Theo's bringing up Grayson is contributing to it. Grayson's left a mark on everything and if I don't watch my step, the way he haunts me will haunt my babies, too.

Theo catches me in the corridor. "What happened in there, Carter?" He frowns.

"It got on top of me, I'm sorry."

He sighs at me, takes me by the elbow and walks me down the corridor. "Don't apologize," he says. "You're pregnant. You're allowed to be emotional."

I nod and smooth down my coat, and I tell him thank God I'm about to go on maternity leave because I'd hate for anyone here to see me crack the way he just did. He asks if he can do anything, and if I want to talk about everything. The hope in his eyes ties my stomach into a knot for a thousand reasons and I tell him no.

"I can't, I'm really busy."

He bobs his head, looks away and I can feel the walls coming straight back up again. I want to hear more about Serenity Pines. I know it's selfish not to ask, but it's always been like drawing blood from a stone. Who knows if he'd even tell me what he's been through to get to this point? "You've been drip-feeding information for months, Theo, and now you want to talk?"

"Better late than never," he says. He wants to ask me more about Grayson, too, I can feel it, and I feel sick just thinking about how he'll look at me when he discovers all the crap I put up with before leaving.

"I can't do this right now, I'm sorry," I say, and I hate how disappointed he looks, but I need to start sticking to my boundaries. I need to focus on my babies. I tell him thanks again for the spa day. I tell him I hope it goes well at Serenity Pines, and then I excuse myself. I don't see him again for over a week.

CHAPTER THIRTEEN

"Uncle Theo, do we have any orange juice left?" Delilah has just emerged from her room, rubbing her eyes. Taylor Swift smiles at me from the back of her pajama top, which reminds me—I still need to change that damn ringtone.

"Bottom shelf, behind the milk," I reply, going back to flipping my omelets. She stayed over after I took her to a show last night, but Pea's picking her up to go shopping soon. My head is all over the place as Delilah talks to me, and I feel bad that I can't really focus on what she's saying. I keep reflecting on that disaster of a first appointment at Serenity Pines.

We eat mostly in silence until Delilah puts down her fork. I watch the frown line her forehead when she tells me she misses Lily. "Where is she?"

"Maternity leave," I tell her, pushing my food around on my plate. I should be starving after my workout but there's too much on my mind. They only take new patients at Serenity every few months, so we had to wait, and when that new intake appointment came up on the same day as Lily's leaving thing, what was I supposed to do? As it was, Mom reluctantly agreed to check the place out, but freaked out at the last minute. She made a huge scene outside the car before we'd even left the city, got a cop sprinting over to see how we were "hurting her," which obviously, we were not. Pea and I had to go alone to the facility and talk to them.

"Did you do something to upset Lily?" Delilah's question catches me off guard. She waggles her finger at me. "You did, didn't you? What did you do?"

"What makes you think I did anything?" I say, though admittedly, she's probably right. I've kept my distance from Carter. It hasn't been easy, I hope the spa voucher wasn't pushing it, but I think I'm getting a clearer idea of why our hookup…our almost-hookup…was some kind of defining boundary line for her. She's been through it. This Grayson guy put her through it. The fact that she's about to become a mother has her on high alert. I don't blame her for thinking I'd run a mile from her if she gave me an inch, and I know my reputation doesn't help with her trust issues. Especially when I'm still keeping things from her.

"She was around a lot, and then she wasn't. I miss her," Delilah says again.

"I miss her, too," I tell her, taking a dishcloth to a piece of egg right as it falls off her plate. I *do* miss her. It's been strange at the hospital, not seeing her around. I've seen Rose, obviously, in the cafeteria, on the rare occasion she breaks away from the tight-knit bubble that constitutes the Fertility Department upstairs. She told me they still haven't painted that damn nursery.

Lily being on mat leave only makes me think about her more. She was the one who finally got me to push Pea into doing something about Mom. I didn't think Pea would agree, she never has before, but I think she saw the emotional impact it's had on me, on top of all the stuff with Lily.

"Are you going to see her today?" Delilah presses. "It's Saturday."

"Why are you so invested?" I ask her, and she looks at me like I'm crazy, tells me Lily is—and I quote—"the only one who gives me hope that maybe my uncle won't be alone forever."

Sassy, but for a girl turning twelve next month she's more clued into things than I ever was. Her words rattle around in my head long after Pea's collected her, till I find myself in the garage, hauling a ladder and all the painting supplies I own to my car.

"Theo?" Lily answers the door in surprise, one hand resting on the curve of her belly. Her eyes trail along the ladder over my shoulder and the buckets at my feet. "The auditions for shirtless decorator were last week," she says through a tight smile.

"What makes you think I'll be taking my shirt off?" I reply as Jasper appears and starts curling around my ankles. "I charge sixty bucks an hour and my clothes stay on. Do we have a deal?"

Her lip puckers under her teeth as she fights another smile and steps aside. The cat weaves around us like he's daring me to drop my tools as Lily leads me to what will soon be the twins' nursery. I set down the ladder and force my hands not to swipe at the cat hair I know will be all over my jeans. She pads around barefoot and cracks open a window. It's cold as hell outside but we're going to need the air. I need air already.

She's always been hot, but pregnancy seems to have transformed her into some ethereal creature these past couple months. Her hair is loose and shiny around her face. The maternity dress is a pink I've never seen on her, a feminine print with tiny white flowers.

We make small talk about the attendees at her leaving party while we both try to ignore how we're enclosed in a small space, and how Rose isn't home. Should I have come over here? She didn't tell me to leave, I guess, and she really does need help with this.

"I didn't expect you, Theo." She glances behind me now, presumably at my car parked out front, then meets my eyes.

"And I didn't expect to be here," I admit. "But Delilah..."

"Delilah?"

"Never mind," I say, making for the three cans of paint in the corner. The room is bare except for two cribs and a changing table, and they've gone as far as putting a plastic sheet across the floor at least. "So, what's the color?"

"Sunset blush," Lily answers, stepping close as I crouch to my haunches and inspect the paint. "Warm and neutral, not overly girly. No glitter."

"Shame," I tell her. "But we can always add that later. If they're anything like you, they're going to love to party."

"Party? What's a party?" she asks with a tired sigh as I pop open the can with a screwdriver and stir the paint with a stick. Lily disappears and comes back dressed in an old T-shirt and shorts. My eyes fix on her slender legs as she walks toward me. I get a flashback to them wrapping around me on my bed and I stand up straight, only to find myself an inch from her face. She holds my eyes for just long enough for the live wires to start sparkling up my forearms and over my chest, but I keep my expression in neutral till she looks away, shaking her head.

"What did I do?" I ask her, pouring paint into a tray.

"You know exactly what you *do*," she replies, stepping away from me to unwrap a brand-new roller. I honestly have no clue what she means, but before I can ask, her phone beeps and she grabs it up from the windowsill. I watch her eyebrows rise, then knit together, and I pick up another roller, ask her who's messaging her. Usually, I'm the one fielding calls that turn my face like this.

"It's Anthony," she tells me. "He's been texting me a bit. More than he used to. I think he wants to visit."

"The baby daddy?"

"If that's what you want to call him, yes." She says it as a question, like she's not sure of *who* he is to her, exactly. A flood of mixed emotions swoosh over my senses as she pushes a lock of hair behind her ear. I ask her when he started messaging her regularly and she tells me about a month ago. We stand side by side on the plastic sheeting, rolling color onto the walls. "Should I let him visit when they're born?" she asks me. "I know you weren't so keen before but…"

"It's not up to me," I tell her. This is not what I came here to talk about. I came here to finally discuss us… and this guy's intrusion irritates me more than it should. "I don't know, Carter, what does he want from you?"

"Why does he have to want anything?" she asks, and I sniff at the wall, rolling my brush over it too hard, sending paint splatters onto my shirt. Damn it.

"Well, does he want to support you going forward, or does he want one look at his creations before he disappears again forever into the sunset, on his bike?"

"He has every right to see them, I suppose," she says with a shrug. I put my brush down.

"He only has the rights you give him. You don't owe

him anything, Lily. But I guess you have to ask yourself what *you* want."

She looks confused and sad for a second, and I know she feels conflicted. I lean the ladder against the wall and climb up. We paint in silence for a while before she stops and lowers herself to her knees on the floor.

"Grayson used to say I was too needy," she says quietly. I stop painting. A leaden ball has just formed in my stomach. She doesn't look up at me while she speaks. "He said a lot of things that stuck in my head and now I guess I overcompensate in some ways. I don't want to *need* anything or anyone, but I don't like cutting people off. It's not fair."

"I know you don't want to *need* anyone," I tell her softly. She's running her hands over her stomach and I step back down the ladder. This is the first time she's really said anything about what this guy did to her.

"I shouldn't have compared your situation with your mom to me and him," she says.

"It's okay."

"It's not okay. I don't know what you're dealing with exactly, Theo. I shouldn't have done that, it wasn't fair. Grayson was in a league of his own. He would reel me in, then shut me out. He'd tell me he loved me, then tell me I was a waste of space. I did everything I could to reach him, to make him realize he needed me. But I just came off like I was desperate and I ended up hating myself."

She pauses, and this time the tears really do come loose in her eyes. I lower myself to the floor beside her. We sit between the ladder and the paint cans, and Jasper looks on from the doorway, licking his paws. "How could I explain all this to *you*, without you thinking how stupid I was not to walk away sooner, Theo?"

"It's not easy to walk away. Trust me, I know," I tell her. "They get into our heads. There are good moments, when…" I swallow, I'm suddenly too hot. I've never said any of this out loud to anyone and it's making me more emotional than I want to be. "There are good moments when they love us, and it makes us think everything's gonna finally be all right."

"I used to cling to those moments so hard," she follows. "It only made the rejection worse. He wasn't always like that. I loved him for a long time. It's why I stayed…"

"I can imagine." I take her hand in mine and hold it tight. My heart beats a violent drum against my rib cage. She's been keeping all this inside her, and it's probably been eating away at her, too, the same as all this with Mom has been eating at me. "I know all about that," I say, turning my whole body to face her now. She turns my hand around in hers and looks at me sideways. The live wires spark again up my arms beneath the paint splatters.

"Listen, Lily, I owe you an apology," I begin. "I said I wouldn't hurt you, and I know my silence about all this has done that. I guess I also find it hard to talk about."

"Theo, you don't—"

"No, let me finish," I insist.

Jasper can probably tell my heart is hammering under my shirt, because he pads over and starts nuzzling me, before moving to Theo. Somewhat reluctantly, Theo pets his head while he talks about what's going on with his mother. I can't believe what I'm hearing.

He tells me how she refuses to take her meds, and how she refused to attend that appointment at Serenity Pines the day of my mat leave party, forcing him and Peonie to go on their own. He tells me how his whole childhood was a living hell, just waiting for her next flare-up, how he spent the whole time plotting the next escape in case he had to run, to protect his sister. He tells me that his mother got so mad at him once that she threw a kettle at his date, which broke so close to the woman's head that she blocked him at every angle soon after and refused to speak to him ever again.

He tells me how his father left without ever looking back. I can't even imagine the pain and damage that would have caused. The sense of abandonment. Theo is acting as mediator to this day. He's still looking after Pea, still concerned for his baby sister's welfare, and Pea's own family's, too. A new respect for him blooms around my heart, till I can hardly stand not touching him.

He rubs a hand across his chin and mouth, and I realize I've been staring at his lips since he started talking. "It's a mess, Carter."

"Your mess is part of you, and you've been nothing but supportive of my own mess," I remind him, running my hands over my bump softly. If I don't touch myself, I'll touch him.

His blue eyes lock with mine. There's a warmth there, a gratitude that makes my heart swell and forces a flock of giant butterflies to buzz around inside me. For a second I feel myself leaning in ever so slightly. I'm drawn to him like always, even more so now. I understand him, why he is the way he is, why he was reluctant to tell me any of this before. He was ashamed, like I was, for letting Grayson control me.

I catch myself, and I can't help a little laugh escaping

from my throat. He cocks his head and asks me what could possibly be funny.

"The fact that you told me all that, and now I understand—"

"You understand why I'm an emotionally unavailable bachelor with a deep-rooted fear of abandonment by the people who claim to love me. Is that right?" Without warning, he picks up the roller and flicks it at me lightly, sending an arc of paint flying right at my face.

I shout out as speckles of sunset blush land on my cheeks and neck and on my shirt. He looks at me with a mischievous glint in his eye. It turns me on more than it should, and I retaliate with a swift flick of my own roller.

"Not fair!" He scrambles to his feet just as I do and I raise the brush again.

"Okay, okay, truce!" he laughs, holding up his hands in surrender. Then he takes a step closer. My breath catches as he removes the roller from my hands. He drops it to the tray and faces me, and I watch his pulse throb at the base of his neck. Just his eyes on me now are undoing me. I am right back in his bedroom, hands against his hot skin, his muscles tightening under my fingers. We didn't kiss. We haven't kissed, ever, but I think I might die if I don't.

"Do you still think of me like that, Carter?" he asks. "Emotionally unavailable."

I falter a moment. My instinct is to tease him, tell him leopards don't change their spots. But he's here; he came to help me. He came to talk to me, and he's opened up more than I thought he ever would. "I care about you. A lot. I think you know that," he says.

My breath catches in my throat. It feels like my blood has turned into pancake syrup now. His eyes track mine and I can see the intensity of our conversation blowing like a storm in his gaze. He didn't have to tell me everything, the same as I had no intention of opening up about Grayson, but here we are. Something else just changed between us, an indelible line was drawn up between who we were and who we are. My pulse throbs at full throttle under my hot skin as I finally reach a hand to his face, trace a finger across his lips.

"I care about you, too," I admit, but there's an edge to my voice. I know he can see that protective shield around my heart. "It's complicated."

"Very," he agrees, leaning into my hand before catching it and holding it to his cheek. He closes his eyes, then brings my hand to his lips himself this time. My internal alarms are blaring, reminding me of all the reasons why this could be a disaster. He kisses my fingers and the action sends lightning bolts across my skin.

"Theo, we shouldn't," I whisper, though every fiber of my being screams otherwise. It's maddening, this pull toward him.

"We shouldn't," he agrees, his voice low, his breath mingling with mine. My body is short-circuiting; his eyes are electrifying my nerves. How does he do this? How do I let him? We're closer than ever, and I'm struggling to keep my resolve.

"This is *really* complicated."

"We've established that." The intensity in his gaze is almost too much, but I can't look away.

"I'm about to have twins, Theo."

He looks deep into my eyes. "I know that, Carter." He presses his forehead to mine, and I cast my gaze down to my bump between us. His voice is a caress, soft and sincere, and I want to give in. I want to taste him. But this is only going to end badly; how can he not see that? He thinks he's changed, but has he? Will he feel this way when my babies arrive? I'll only start needing him, and then I'll be left for dust.

"Theo, I—"

Before I can protest, before I can even think of how to build up another wall, his lips find mine. Logic completely vanishes out the window. My arms wind around his neck as if they have a will of their own. The kiss isn't just a meeting of our mouths; it feels like the crashing together of everything we are—friends, confidants, colleagues, two people who have more in common than we ever knew before. It's so passionate, so all-consuming, that absolutely everything shrinks right down to the way his tongue dances over mine, and how his hands are sweeping along my back, up and down through my paint-splattered shirt, then tousling hungrily in my hair. I feel myself urging him closer, digging my nails into his skin, but there's only so close we can get with my bump between us. Still, we're totally lost in each other, breathless as our mouths grow more urgent, our teeth sinking into each other's lips softly, then releasing. Then…

"Ahem."

The sound jolts us apart. Reeling, I turn to see Rose standing in the doorway.

"I…um… I see I'm interrupting something," she says as I smooth down my shorts. Theo runs his hands through his hair and picks up the roller.

"Rose," I manage, heat flooding my cheeks. "We were just—"

"Painting," Theo finishes lamely, and he grimaces as he looks at me, which for some reason only makes me laugh. My heart is still thrashing wildly in my chest, and my legs still feel unstable. I lean against the wall as Rose studies us. Her lips twitch, and her knowing look informs me she's amused rather than disapproving, but I can't shake off the embarrassment.

"I thought you were out for the afternoon," I say, lamely.

"I forgot my book," she replies, holding up the textbook.

"Right, well, I should probably get back to it, too," I say quickly, gesturing toward the half-painted wall. Theo is painting again already, three rungs up the ladder.

"Of course, don't let me stop you." Rose backs out of the room, still smirking to herself, and I pretend not to see the pointed look she throws me as she leaves. I am going to hear about this later.

I turn to Theo, my heart still racing. "You should *not* have done that," I manage to whisper.

"Are you sure?" he shoots back at me. He waits for the front door to shut behind Rose and climbs back down the ladder.

"Yes," I tell him. I don't move an inch. My lips are still pulsing from our kiss. I want to tear his shirt off, roll in paint and command he makes love to me in the middle of the room, but…this is all so crazy. "I'm sure," I add, but the wobble in my voice betrays me.

I wait until he's inches from me, brushing loose strands of hair from my face. I have paint all over me, and so does he, and I know he knows I'm lying. The second I open my mouth to speak, a groan escapes instead and I pull him close again by the front of his shirt. In a heartbeat we're back in each other's arms, and in minutes our clothes are strewn around the room and all the inhibitions I thought I'd have, being the size of a bus and hornier than I've ever been in my life, seem to evaporate as we take it in turns to pleasure each other in ways I don't think I've even dared to envision with a man this ridiculously hot and into me. The only reason we don't have full sex is because it's so physically awkward, and I tell him I'd rather wait.

"Some things are worth waiting for," is his reply.

For the next month, we do this more than we probably should, falling into each other's arms as soon as we're alone, and sometimes even out in public. We go on actual dates to exhibitions, to parks and museums. He cooks me for after his shifts, rubs my feet. We talk a lot, about everything and nothing, and sometimes I can't imagine how we were only friends all this time, because I've never felt like I can be myself with anyone like this before, really, besides Rose. It's comfortable, but it's electric at the same time.

People stop to ask how "our" babies are doing, and every time I can't be bothered to explain, Theo puts on a straight face and tells them, "They're going to be TikTok influencers. It's all we've ever wanted for our children."

I don't think I've ever wanted to sleep with anyone as much as I want to sleep with Theo, but he doesn't push for it, and I tell myself as long as we don't do that, I won't fall in love. I'm getting pretty good at lying to myself, but I can't afford not to. I think I'm starting to need him, and I still can't stop the niggling feeling that with everything he has going round that head of his—with his mother, his sister, his work—that myself and my fast-approaching new role as a mother of twins will all prove too much for him eventually.

CHAPTER FOURTEEN

The sun is a warm caress on my hatless head as Lily takes my arm and we watch another dog run for a ball along the Riverwalk. Finally, we're heading into spring. The skyscrapers glint in the sun, the river is sparkling and the tourists can't get enough selfie-stick photos of Chicago the way it was designed to be seen. An undeniably magnificent mile.

This is our fourth Sunday morning coffee walk in as many weeks. Seeing as Lily is almost thirty-six weeks into her pregnancy it's more like a waddle, then a sit-down, then another waddle, then another sit-down. It's at one of these sitting down points that Pea calls me. I'm seeing red by the time I hang up, but Lily is engrossed in something on her own phone now, so I hold in the fact that Delilah has reported her grandmother *sounded drunk this morning*. It was 10:00 a.m. when they spoke.

I fume in silence, watching the boats glide past on the water. It's too nice of a day to bring Lily down. It's been a month or so of trying to reschedule things at Serenity Pines, and Mom still refuses to even entertain the notion of visiting, let alone staying there. We *can* force her. We can have them come collect her. But Pea is having second thoughts again, maybe because she's seen how happy I am these days.

I fix my eyes on another tourist boat that's drifting a little faster than the others toward the dock, but I'm pulled to Lily when she sighs at her phone. My jaw tightens instantly. She's messaging the motorcycling baby daddy, who suddenly seems to see himself as a candidate for Father of the Year. She looks at me sheepishly before sliding her phone back into her purse, and I stop myself from asking her what he wants. I know she hates it when she thinks I'm telling her what to do, and I know more about *why* she hates that now. Anyway, I'm more concerned about Mom being drunk at 10:00 a.m.

"You look displeased, Grasshopper," she observes, turning to face me properly.

"Sorry, there's trouble in the kingdom again, Princess," I reply, and she gives me that sympathetic frown that tells me I don't have to say any more. I kiss her, wrap my hand around hers on her lap. Right away, some of the tension floats from my back and shoulders and she smiles under my mouth.

"I thought you were still annoyed that I canceled on you for maternity yoga last night."

"Oh, I am," I tell her, scooping a hand behind her head and urging her closer. "But I used the time to dream up some other fun positions we can try."

"I'm looking forward to it," she tells me, but then she winces and presses a hand to her midsection and tells me the babies are kicking. When we resume our path along the waterfront I'm wary of every person coming toward her. If I could conjure a protective bubble around us, I would. I've never felt this way about anyone before in my life. Who'd have thought *not* having sex would make me more invested, more raw, more available? I guess she thinks I won't like making love to her like this, but I'm only concerned she'd be uncomfortable. I'm taking this thing one day at a time. Our emotional connection is so strong, it's like we make love with our minds sometimes. I can only imagine what the sex will be like in the future.

We've just rounded the corner when an almighty crash sends us staggering backward. My arm goes around her. Screams echo out ahead of us, followed by more anguished sounds and a lot of splashing. "What the—?"

I look at Lily, then we both start hurrying toward the dock. A small tour boat must have lost control, its engine sputtering before crashing into the Riverwalk with a sickening crunch. There's fiberglass everywhere, luggage floating in the water, and people floundering.

"We need to get them out!"

Lily looks stricken as she races for the edge with me, still clutching her bump. The impact has thrown the boat's passengers into the water like ragdolls and they're flailing about, grappling for fallen cases and swimming toward the sides.

"Help! Somebody help, I can't swim!" A scream pierces the air and I zero in on a young woman in the water, clutching the edge of the dock. I call for an ambulance quickly, tell Lily to assess the situation with the injured, and instruct a bystander to get some medical supplies from a nearby restaurant. I drop to my stomach at ground level and reach for the woman's hand. Her face is shock white and her eyes wide with terror as she grapples for my hand, just out of reach. Elsewhere, strangers are pulling others out of the ice-cold river, but just as I finally clasp this woman's fingers, she gasps and drops back in, and immediately she's floating out of my reach. I strip off my leather jacket and shoes, and

I only just make out Lily calling my name before I dive into the water.

I reach the woman within seconds, turn her to her back and propel us back to the side with one arm. She's shivering, and so am I. This water is still freezing cold. "You're okay, ma'am. I've got you."

Two guys help haul her out and she drops to the deck, where someone drapes a towel over her shoulders and helps me back out with one hand. There's more chaos unfolding here than in the ER on the Fourth of July. A crowd is already taking photos, while others kneel to help the people on the ground.

"Theo, over here!" Lily's voice. I turn dripping wet to see her kneeling beside a man with a deep gash on his forehead, blood streaming down his face. She's already applying pressure with a scarf.

"Keep talking to him," I instruct, moving to assess the situation better. "Sir, can you hear me?"

"Y-yes," he stammers, wincing as Lily presses harder. I can see he's not okay.

"Good. You're all good," I tell him, anyway. Lily's brow is furrowed in concentration as she tears a gauze we've just been given. Even at nearly full term, she's a force to be reckoned with.

"His pulse is weak," she tells me, her voice strained. I can see she's struggling almost as much as this man; she's in no shape to be doing this but I know she would never forgive herself if she didn't. The cops are here now, ordering people this way, sending reporters and a TV crew in another. An ambulance is inching through. I can hear the sirens in the distance, too.

"Hang in there, Carter," I say, then I turn to a distraught young woman who's just been pulled from the water. "Ma'am, what's your name?"

"Angela," she gasps, shivering uncontrollably. "I can't find my cat!"

"Angela, do you have any injuries? Can you move everything?"

"Just cold…and my arm hurts," she whimpers, cradling her right arm protectively. "I need to find my cat… he's in a crate!"

"Okay, let me see." I snatch up the jacket I took off before and wrap it around her shoulders for warmth. "Lily, how's your guy doing?" I ask her as my eyes scan the dock and the water for a crate that might be holding a cat. I'm not even going to ask why there was a cat on a tourist boat…cat people are strange.

"Theo, he's losing consciousness!" Lily's voice sharpens, pulling me back to the man in her arms. He must have taken a big hit from the boat.

"Stay with us, buddy. Help is almost here," I coax as his eyes flutter. "What's your name?"

"A-Abdul," he rasps.

"Abdul, Doctor Carter here is good at this. Hang in there."

Lily has located more gauze and tape from the supplies going around the scene. Despite her cumbersome form, she works fast alongside me, wiping sweat from her brow. She's hot, and I'm freezing. I'm only just feeling how numbingly cold that water really was, when Angela's voice comes at me again over the wail of the sirens.

"Over there! My cat!" She and her friend are pointing over the side, beside themselves. They look like they're going to jump back in.

"Dammit," I mutter, glancing at Lily. "Can you handle things here?"

"Go," she urges, her eyes fierce. "I'll take care of them. Theo, be careful."

"You be careful," I warn, squeezing her hand before diving back into the chaos.

The icy water shocks my system all over again, but the adrenaline keeps me moving. The cat is alarmed and unsurprisingly feisty as I grab for the crate and drag it back with me. Angela takes it in floods of tears, sobbing, "Thank you, thank you, thank you!"

"Over here!" a man shouts now. How did we miss him before? He's trying to keep a child afloat, his son maybe. I thrash back through the water, grabbing the boy first.

"You're safe now. I've got you." I'm trying to reassure them but the cold water is seeping through my senses, slowing me down by the second. It's all I can do to haul his son to the side and lift him high into the waiting arms of a paramedic, but I have to go back for this guy. He's even colder, even weaker. Every muscle screams in protest, but I push through. I have to help everyone I can. On the dock, past the police car, the ambulance and the frenzied crowds, I see Lily, still on her knees, attending to someone else now. A middle-aged woman.

"We need more blankets," she yells as I haul my soaking body out of the water. "She's going into shock!"

I sprint back to Lily, dripping all over the boardwalk. I can't afford to think about how cold I am right now. I just wrap warm blankets around the shivering woman and help two paramedics load her onto a stretcher.

"Theo, you need to get warm," Lily tells me. I tell her I'm fine, that other people need them more than me.

"How are *you* holding up?" I ask her as I cast my

eyes around the scene. I'm doing my best to regulate the pounding in my chest but I can hear it in my own voice.

"Pregnant, not helpless," she shoots back, before draping a blanket around me and holding me close. Her warmth seeps into me immediately. She pulls me harder into her, and for a brief moment as the cold air leaves my lungs and I press into her heat, I am completely, utterly, irrevocably hers. It has been a long time since a woman I cared about cared about *me* this much.

"Move aside, please!" More paramedics swarm the scene, taking over the care of the people we've stabilized. One of them I know, and he looks between Lily and me in concern, asks if we're okay.

"We're okay," Lily breathes, finding my arm and guiding me to the side away from the crowds. Her hand lingers on her stomach for just a second too long. Any warmth she's just transitioned to my body chills over when her face crumples up.

I step closer. "Carter?"

"Yeah, just—" She winces again, clutching her belly. "Theo, something's wrong."

"What's happening?" I demand, cupping her elbow.

"Feels like...contractions," she gasps. Her face is paling now. I drop the blanket from my shoulders.

"Contractions? Are you sure?"

Now, of all the times that this could happen. It's too early.

She shoots me a look that's almost apologetic, right as she doubles over under another wave of pain.

"Not here, please, my loves," she wheezes under her breath. "It's too early. There are too many people. This is not your moment."

"Maybe they weren't getting enough attention," I say,

and I wrap an arm around her, start guiding her through the throng of onlookers. Journalists are already hovering, cameras flashing, microphones thrust forward.

"Miss, can you tell us what happened?" one reporter calls, her eyes zeroing in on Lily.

"Not now!" I snap, shielding Lily with my body. "She's in labor!" I flag down a paramedic, who rushes over with a stretcher. His eyes widen as he takes in Lily's condition.

"She's having contractions…she's thirty-six weeks," I explain urgently. "We need to get her to the hospital. Now."

He signals his team. They lift Lily onto the stretcher, securing her quickly.

"Theo?" Her eyes dart around the chaos for mine, and she reaches out for my hand. "Don't leave me."

"I'm here," I tell her, clasping her hand tightly. "I'm not going anywhere."

CHAPTER FIFTEEN

I DO MY best to breathe through the pain and panic, to focus on the squeak of the rubber-soled shoes against the sterile floor, the voices all around me in Evergreen's corridors. I can hear people talking about what's happened on the Riverwalk. Already there are photos online, apparently, of me and Theo. Theo saved a cat.

Focus on that, I tell myself, holding my belly as I draw deep breaths on my back and the familiar hospital walls rush past me.

"Contractions are five minutes apart, preterm labor," Theo barks at the nurse who's jogging alongside me. He's not holding my hand now. He's in full ER doctor mode, despite being soaking wet and no doubt freezing cold, and while I'm grateful there were paramedics already on the scene out there, this is even more complicated than I ever thought it would be. I should have been taken to Dawson's but there was no time, and with the city streets all clogged because of the accident at the dock, here I am. Theo. I need him with me, whatever happens next. I don't want to do this alone.

As if reading my mind, Theo stops at the doors to room three. "You're in good hands, Lily. You know they'll look after you."

"No... Theo." Another contraction makes me flinch,

then yell out as I'm rushed into the room, but Theo follows. He is tired, wet and visibly cold but he knows I need him.

"I'm not going anywhere," he tells me, and I nod and try to concentrate on my breathing. My babies are coming early. I can tell they're desperate to get out. Why did they choose today? Another contraction almost cripples me. I don't even know how long I lie here. I'm losing track of time now. It feels like hours pass. Sweat plasters my hair to my forehead. My throat feels raw from screaming, and the room is a blur of scrubs and surgical masks, and the sterile smell of antiseptic blending with my own fear. I'm told to push. I'm so weak. No one can prepare you for this.

"Doctor, heart rates are dropping," a nurse says.

I don't like her tone one bit but I trust her. I trust everyone here. Why did I want to go to Dawson's in the first place? I don't recognize the locum obstetrician but she knows who I am, like everyone here. Theo is at my side, and somehow I manage to move my hand from my bulging belly and into his. I need his strength.

"Let's move quickly. We need those babies out now," the obstetrician warns. Her voice is steady but strained. "Lily, you need to focus. Push!"

"Come on, Lily," another nurse encourages, patting my leg gently.

"You're all good, Carter," Theo follows. I focus on his eyes. "You're almost there. You're doing so well, come on, make me proud."

Proud? He's proud of me? Tears stream down my face as my body struggles to comply with the things he and all these people are telling me to do. How exactly do I do this? I bear down with every ounce of strength I have left, feeling my body stretch and strain until I hear the words I've been dying to hear.

"Here comes Baby A."

A high-pitched cry fills the room. Relief washes over me.

"Baby A is just fine! Let's get ready, Baby B," Theo says, before anyone else has a chance.

His eyes are wet with tears and he's not even trying to hide them. Despite the pain ripping through me I am utterly lovestruck seeing the pride on his face. He looks like he might actually be their father; no one on the outside right now would have any reason to think otherwise. I can do this.

"You're almost there, Lily," he says, still squeezing my hand. "Keep going."

I can do this.

The glare of the overhead lights bears down on me as I pace the corridor. People who know me try to make conversation, try to congratulate me for being a hero on the dock, saving a cat as well as a kid; I can hardly believe it. And now this. My mind reels and spins with the magnitude of the day's events. I'm still cold and damp, and my hands are still trembling with the remnants of adrenaline. I shove them deep into my pockets. The muffled sounds of urgency seep through the closed doors of the delivery room and I want to go in there but I can't just yet. Rose is in there now, doting on her new niece and nephew.

I'm not leaving. Pea tries to call again, but this time I don't answer. I'm a wreck.

"Doctor Montgomery?" Eventually, a nurse's voice cuts through my thoughts. I'm told that I can see her again, and my heart lodges in my throat as I enter the room. There she is. Lily is pale, exhausted, but beaming, too. Rose is at her side. In Lily's arms, swaddled in the trademark hospital cotton, are her two tiny, perfect-looking babies. For once in my life, I can't seem to find any words. It almost feels like they're mine somehow, after knowing Lily the way I'm starting to know her. I'm connected by way of my connection to Lily.

I edge closer, and the air around us charges with something indefinable. My finger brushes against a tuft of dark hair that's so much like Lily's, and their smallness staggers me. A surge of protectiveness washes over me. It's so fierce it leaves me reeling. These babies, part of our story—they matter more than I can articulate. Rose shares the news with their dad, Geoff, on the phone, and I watch her watching me as she talks to him from across the room.

"Hey again," I say to the tiny boy and girl in Lily's arms. "Let's make it official. I'm Theo. You just couldn't wait to get here, huh?"

"Aren't they perfect?" Lily breathes out, her green eyes meeting mine.

"You did good, Carter. They *are* perfect," I tell her truthfully. We've already been told they're a little jaundiced, that due to the speedy birth and the distress they were in, it's best if they stay in the NICU for a while. It's nothing to worry about; Lily knows that. Rose knows that. She's still watching us together. I straighten up and my hand goes to swipe self-consciously at my jaw. I didn't realize how emotional I was till now. I had no idea how I'd feel in this moment. How is it possible that I feel so attached already?

"I'll leave you to rest," I tell Lily as the twins are removed from her arms, ready to be moved to the NICU. I refrain from kissing her in front of everyone we know, even when she leans into me out of exhaustion, probably.

I've barely made it outside into the sunlight when Pea's name flashes up again on my phone. "Pea? Lily's fine, the babies are fine."

Pea was concerned about the boat incident and seeing me on the news. She has no idea that Lily has just given birth—why would she—and I'm forced to tell her what happened. I tell her the twins are fine but will have to spend a little while in the NICU, and Pea tells me it's not my fault. The second she does, is the second I wonder if it *is* my fault. I put Lily in danger again, letting her help, even though she wanted to. I put the twins into distress mode.

I can't shake the thought now. It strangles me as I walk toward the bus stop; we didn't take my car to the city and I rode in the ambulance here. I must look like a damp, disheveled disaster who's just dropped from the sky in a rainstorm, and I can't face the thought of talking to a cab driver.

On the bus, Delilah calls me. Pea said earlier that she went to a friend's house this morning. Maybe she also saw me on the news? Or TikTok, most likely. I call her back, and what she tells me almost makes me stop the bus. She's not at a friend's house; she's with my mother. Or rather, she's only just managed to escape.

"Escape what?"

"I'm telling you, Uncle Theo, because I don't want to upset Mom!"

I can barely believe what Delilah is telling me. She went over to her house, to give her one of her riding certificates, hoping her grandma would be proud of her and frame it. It escalated after Dee found a bottle of vodka in the laundry cupboard and tried to hide it. Mom caught her and it all blew up. After the argument to end all arguments, Mom locked her in the utility room for two hours. Dee's only just managed to escape through the window, relocate her phone and call me. This is bigger than any of us now.

When I'm home, I call Pea again. As predicted, she's upset. Very. I tell her we need to do something once and for all, no messing around, and absolutely no more taking no for an answer. Mom needs help if she's going to get better, if things in our *family* are really going to get better. I want to be there for Lily and the babies with all of me, with all of my attention. I owe them that. I need to at least *try* to get my life back.

They're so beautiful. I know I'm biased but they are. I trace the delicate outlines of my twins' faces, their tiny fists curling and uncurling in their amazing little dance of newborn reflexes. I've become obsessed with observing it already. My heart swells with a love so fierce it almost hurts every time I look into their soulful eyes. In the NICU's soft light I can pretend for a moment that everything is perfect.

"My loves," I murmur. "You're both so loved, you know that?"

My gaze flicks back to my phone, resting on the edge of an incubator. Still no messages from Theo. I've heard nothing for almost two entire days. When I call, it goes to his voice mail. The silence from him is deafening, especially after what happened on the dock. I don't even know if he's all right. Each passing second is a confirmation of my worst fears. I expected too much from him, practically forcing him to stay with me during the birth... I went too far, like I always do, and now, not only have I scared him off with my neediness and impending list of maternal responsibilities, our friendship is most probably in the toilet, too.

Rose appears in our private white room with fresh flowers. I force a smile to my face as she arranges them in the vase Dad brought in last night, and peers over the babies. I still can't quite believe that my own children are here in the neonatal unit. Despite Theo's noticeable absence, I'm beyond grateful that I accidentally switched to Evergreen for their care.

"Have you decided on their names?" Rose asks quietly as her hand lands gently on my shoulder. My twin has been a steady anchor these past couple of days. She's reassured me I can do this on my own...well, with her help of course, but I still don't want to admit how much I need Theo. My gaze flits between the two sleeping forms.

"I thought I'd decided on Ollie and Winnie. But now they're here, I'm not so sure."

"Names are identities...destinies, almost," Rose says, and I arch my eyebrows at her. It's not like her to say stuff like this.

"Getting sentimental, are you?"

"It's my niece and nephew. Of course we have to give them the perfect names! Take your time, Lils. It'll come to you."

I nod and sigh, trying to channel peace as my mind goes to Theo again. For a few silly seconds you could have convinced me that he and I were... Ugh. The only thing we ever were was predictable, spontaneous, a disaster waiting to happen. He couldn't have run away any faster after the twins were born. I hate that I'm surprised, when I should be anything but.

I wish I could stop thinking about him. I reach out for my phone again, but the screen is dark and silent. I resist calling him, but I do quickly reply to the message from Anthony, aka *Miami Motorhead*. He wants to take a ride here from Miami on the bike, and he seems pretty serious about it. I figure what's the harm? I know I want nothing from him, or nothing to do with him, really, but I still don't think it's fair to deny him the right to see the twins if he wants to. I don't want them growing up and finding out I refused their birth father when he offered to come visit.

We're just discussing more potential baby names, like Amelia and Harley, maybe, when my phone rings and sends my heart catapulting up to my throat. But it's just an unknown number. The same number that has now called a few times. I decline it as usual.

"I take it that's not Theo?" Rose asks, scowling at the floor a second.

"Probably just someone selling new windows, or car insurance like last time," I tell her. No, thanks. I'm too tired for that. I have enough to deal with right now without pushy salesmen on my back. Theo is probably busy being a hero after the boating incident, soaking up the spotlight from female reporters and fans. He's probably finally figured out the magnitude of what this all involves for me, and for him, too, should he stay involved. Players will always play, and I've been well and truly played. If I wasn't so exhausted, I'd be furious at both him and myself.

Rose chews on her lip, fiddles with her glasses, then crosses her arms. I know this look.

"Maybe there's an explanation," she says. "But then again, maybe it's time to accept that Theo *isn't* going to be the rock you hoped for," she adds softly. "It's you and me, Lily. The twins have us, and we have each other—we are all we need, remember?"

"We are all we need," I echo, even as the sting of tears threatens to spill. I thought I knew him, or was starting to, at least. I thought I was different. I thought he promised to never hurt me.

"Hey." Rose nudges me. "First one to make the other laugh changes the diapers for a week when we're home."

"Deal," I reply. I love how she's here for me. She knows I'm devastated, but she's not about to let me dwell on it. She didn't want to ruin my fun with him while it lasted, but she knew, and I did, too, I guess, that Theo isn't built for anything long-term, no matter what he says or likes to think.

Rose doesn't say another word, but when my chin wobbles her arm comes up around me. It's all I can do not to cry into her arms, and it's pathetic. I am pathetic for thinking we could actually be something, but I bolted all doors shut against the possibility of another betrayal years ago, until Theo Montgomery, of all people, forced them back open.

"Men," Rose scoffs eventually into my hair. Her voice is laced with a bitterness I know stems from her deep-seated pain over what happened with David.

"Men," I mutter, brushing away a stray tear. The ache in my chest seems to deepen, till a cocktail of hormones and hurt makes it hard to breathe. The doctor on shift arrives to ask when we're leaving, and whether we need anything arranged, and I try to curb the hope in my voice as I ask her whether Theo has checked into his shifts in ER.

"Doctor Montgomery called in sick yesterday," she tells me, looking over my babies. "Haven't seen him since. He was quite the hero, diving into the river for those people, and the cat! Maybe he caught a cold."

"Maybe," I echo hollowly as Rose presses her lips together and looks away. I know she wants to comment but she knows she shouldn't; not here. We both know if Theo was really sick, he would at least be checking his phone. Has he actually taken time off work sick in order to avoid me? Anger courses through my bloodstream till I have to remind myself it doesn't matter. All that matters now is my babies, keeping them safe and protected. I am all they have.

Later, when Rose is helping me pack my bags, I send Theo a message, which he will no doubt see once he decides to acknowledge me. No point getting emotional, or questioning him or begging, not like I did with Grayson. I need to get out of this one with my dignity intact. I won't let him break me. I have two little people relying on me now and they need me to be strong.

Theo. Now that the twins are here I think it's best for me to take some time to get to know them by myself. I'll forever be grateful for our time together. See you when I'm back at work. Lily.

I'll let him off lightly if that is what he wants. Me, however? I will take my two tiny precious gifts from

God home, where I will resume my new purpose, to make their lives as wonderful as possible, without Theo Montgomery or *any* man getting in our way.

CHAPTER SIXTEEN

THE YOUNG COURIER hands over the package that contains my new lifeline. "Sign here, please, Doctor Montgomery," he says, extending a small electronic pad toward me.

"Thanks," I mutter, scribbling my name with more force than necessary.

The moment he leaves, I tear into the paper and soon the phone buzzes to life. I insert the new SIM card connected to my old number, leave it all to update while I pour myself a glass of water and stare at Chicago through the windows. My old phone is somewhere on a rooftop belonging to one of my neighbors, along with Pea's. If I knew Mom was going to toss them out there, I'd have locked them away before she got here, but at least *she* is safe now, and so is Delilah and so are we. She won't be leaving Serenity Pines for a while, and hopefully by the time she does, she won't still be out to throttle me.

The past few days have been hell. The confrontation with my mother was more like a detonation of years of pent-up frustration on my part, and denial on hers.

"Theo Montgomery!" Mom spat my name out like it was poison. For a moment I truly thought she was about to throw the kettle at me. "I am *not* going to rot in some institution!"

"Mom, it's specialized hospitalization, in a nice place. It's more like a retreat—" I tried to reason with her. She was the Elizabeth Montgomery I remember from my childhood, the one I would have done anything to protect Pea from, and she was not about to be reasoned with.

"I am your mother! Don't you care about me at all? How can you lock me away like an animal?"

I told her she won't be locked away, that she'll be cared for by the best team north of Chicago. She didn't know then that there were people due to arrive at my place any second, or that Pea had lured her here for collection, where she wouldn't be able to make a scene in public.

"You think because you play doctor all day, you can diagnose me?"

"Enough, Mother, I've had enough!"

Pea's voice shocked us all, even her. It was nothing like I've ever heard from my sister.

"Theo has only ever tried to help you, and me. He is a good brother and son. Either you accept our help, or I'm done, and you'll never see your granddaughter again."

I have to admit I was impressed. It was a standoff after that, like the Wild West minus the pistols. I moved the kettle. Mom snatched up my phone instead. She had the audacity to look me in the eyes as she tossed it right out the window. She managed to get Pea's next and awarded it the same fate.

"Try and get them to collect me now!"

She had no idea that the long-suffering Pablo had already agreed to help us, and was waiting outside to bring the people from Serenity Pines upstairs. We tried our best not to react in anger about the phones; it would have only made it worse. And then, the dam broke. Mom's shoulders slumped and I watched the fight drain out of her like air from a punctured tire. We argued for a while, until finally, she relented. She was no doubt fueled by the thought of never seeing Delilah again.

The aftermath is a blur—slammed doors, hushed conversations in a locked van, more tears, a whirlwind trip to Serenity Pines the next day to see her in her new pine-scented Lake Forest home away from home. Pea felt wretched. Her big heart is totally broken by what she's had to do. I've spent the past two nights with her and her husband, and Delilah; no phones, just each other. I've barely come up for air until now, and I'm sure Lily and I have a lot to catch up on. I tried to call her from the Serenity Pines landline a few times, but she didn't pick up. I could've left a message but I was all up in my head with a thousand things to say and in the end, it was better not to bother her with my issues. She's got her hands full, I'm sure. I'll talk to her when the twins are home.

Finally, my new phone has updated. My heart is a riot. The world narrows down to the glow of the screen as I read the last one from Carter.

Now that the twins are here I think it's best for me to take some time to get to know them by myself...

Wait. What?
I read it again, then again. She cannot be serious. I stare at my phone like it might ping more answers at me but it doesn't. She sent this yesterday. I call her instantly. The phone rings out, so I try again and finally she answers.

"Theo—" She sounds surprised. Behind her I can hear gurgling and laughing, and the sound of a guy talking to

Rose, I think. She lowers her voice, hisses at me. "Theo, where have you been?"

"It's a long story, Carter, but I just saw your message. Are you serious? You want more space from me *now*?"

She's silent for a long while. I hear her walking to another room, closing a door behind her. "Who's there with you? Are you at home?" I ask. I don't know why but my instincts are primed for some kind of reply I'm not ready to hear. None of this adds up.

"You weren't here," she says slowly. She almost sounds confused before she sighs heavily. "You never even *called* me."

"I tried to," I protest but she cuts me off.

"Theo, I meant what I said, okay? I just need some time with the twins, to get to know them. And you clearly have a lot going on. You don't need me, or this."

I refuse to hear this. I have to swallow hard to keep my tone in check. "Lily, something's happened. What's going on?"

"Theo, we both know this was never going to be anything more than two friends messing around. I have to get serious. I'm a mother now."

"Stop it, Carter," I tell her. Abandonment and rejection don't just sting; they burn. My fists clench as I walk back to the kitchen. I tell her I can explain everything, but she cuts me off, distracted.

"I have to go, Theo. Take care, okay?"

The call ends and I stand rooted to the floor. *Take care?*

I scroll through the log of missed calls and messages. She called me a couple times before sending that message. Maybe she did want to talk it through in person...or maybe she *was* just waiting to yank the bandage off and end it over the phone. Either way, I spent my whole life backing off, letting other people who claim to care about me dictate my fate. I'm not letting Carter off this easy.

The traffic on Maple Avenue is a slow-moving serpent. I drum my fingers on the steering wheel. There's a gnawing restlessness in my chest that I've never felt before over a woman. I hate it, but I love her. It crept up on me but it's true. The sight of the slow-down sign flashes a memory at me—Lily, laughing, crouching behind my car in the snow, her pregnant self behind the banner while I kept watch. That feels like ages ago already. I loved her then, too. Maybe I always have. How did this go wrong? Maybe she does still secretly blame me for the twins being born into all that drama and stress, for putting them at risk?

I park on the street outside her house. There's a shiny red Indian Chief Vintage parked outside and all right... it's a *nice* bike. I can tell it's seen some miles. I grab up the fresh flowers and the stuffed giraffe and antelope I bought her weeks ago in secret at the zoo, and step onto the street.

I'm actually admiring the bike up close when a shadow in her front window makes me pause. There's a stranger in the house, a man cradling one of the twins. He looks so effortlessly dad-like with the baby that my heart stutters somewhere around my throat, then sinks. He lifts the baby high, mouthing a coo of affection and... I know who it is. The bike belongs to him. How did I not put two and two together before now? He must have ridden all the way here on it from Florida. This was who I heard laughing with Rose just now over the phone.

Something inside me shatters. Maybe everything. I can't go in there now.

I drop the gifts back to the empty seat. My hands clench the steering wheel until my knuckles turn whiter than white. Lily has been unreachable and now…well, it's pretty obvious why. She's been wanting to ask this guy here for months, I've seen her on the phone to him! How could I have been so sure of "us," as to think she wouldn't want to at least give things a go with the actual father of her babies, especially after what I did, or didn't do at the dock? After I kept everything about Mom from her for so long.

I should drive away, but I can't seem to look away from the window. He's tall with a mop of curly, thick hair that screams bohemian artist—someone who can simply hop on his bike and be anywhere, whenever he chooses. But somehow, he still couldn't be *here* till now. And she's choosing *him*! It feels like a punch to the gut. I'm swallowing back more betrayal and hurt than I can even try and fathom, watching him cavort around the living room like he belongs here. I want to storm in and demand answers.

Think, Montgomery. Flying off the handle won't help anyone.

What right do I have, anyway? Lily is a free agent. She can invite anyone she damn well pleases into her home, into her life. It's just that the panic clawing at my chest is way too much like the feeling I knew as a kid, knowing my dad was gone, knowing Mom wanted *me* gone, too. There's no way I'm letting that agony consume me again.

With a last searing look at the window, I put the car in Reverse and drive away. To think I was going to ask Lily

Carter to be my girl, officially. I was actually going to admit to her face that I've fallen so deeply in love with her that I've started wishing with all my stupid heart that I could raise those kids with her, together.

CHAPTER SEVENTEEN

"Amelia, no, no, no…"

My voice cracks as I stare at my baby girl in the crib. Her tiny chest is heaving and her forehead is burning up. I quickly check Harley. He seems fine, sleeping like a log, but Amelia…

Fear scratches like nails at my throat as I swallow it back and tell myself to breathe. Just moments ago I was humming a lullaby to Jasper in the kitchen, and now, now something is really wrong. I tear open my medical bag. Two months into caring for the twins at home, I'd just been getting used to not needing it.

The thermometer beeps, and the numbers scream danger: one hundred and four degrees. Febrile seizure territory. Rose isn't home; she's off at some conference, and this is the first time I've been left alone since they were born, since I booted Theo out of our lives and Anthony rode off on his bike. I force myself to calm down. This is what I do; this is what I have to handle…

Theo. He's probably at the hospital. All I can think is *I need Theo.*

"All right, Amelia, Mommy's got you." I wrap her in a cool towel, pushing past the terror. As her little body shudders, Theo's steady hands flash into my mind again.

This is not the time to be dwelling on the way he used to hold me, but I need him. I need him *now*.

I bundle up the sleeping pair and somehow fix the car seats in place. Jasper looks at me startled, and I tell him to guard the house while we're out. The drive is a blur of stoplights and honking horns, but my focus stays laser-sharp on the rearview mirror, where Amelia's car seat is strapped in tight. At every red light, I twist around to check if she's still breathing. "You're going to be fine, baby girl."

The familiar sterile smell hits me as I burst through the doors. "Help, emergency! I need help here, please!"

Despite this being the place that molded my professional status, I don't even know who I am right now. All I can think of is my baby. Again, I tell myself to maintain even a small glimmer of calm but I must look like a crazy person, holding one child and swinging around with another strapped to my chest. Heads turn, and then he's here—Theo, his blue scrubs clinging to him like superhero garb under his white coat, his blue eyes locking on to mine. Thank God. I almost fling myself onto him, but somehow I manage not to.

"Theo, it's Amelia. She's—"

"Exam room four, now," he cuts in, taking charge as he runs for a gurney.

He barely looks at me, but still, somehow he's all I need to feel safer, calmer. I follow him as they take over. Awkwardness hangs between us, thick and tangible after so long apart, I can feel it, even if he can't, but this is about Amelia.

"Talk to me, Carter," he says as we hurry alongside the gurney. Nurse Amber offers to take Harley off my hands. Gratefully, I accept and untie him from my chest but it does nothing to regulate my breathing.

"High fever, sudden onset. I'm worried it's meningitis... or..." My words trail off and I struggle to maintain my calm.

"Okay, let's get her stabilized," he says, and when his hand brushes against mine, a jolt of familiarity pierces through the chaos. We haven't touched in months, but his presence is still as grounding as it came to be before... well, before I told him and myself I didn't need him. I pushed him away, I know I did, and I've been agonizing over it ever since, along with dirty diapers and screaming in the middle of the night and accepting that I only have time to shower every two days. But it was the right thing to do; I didn't want to need him, only for him to pull away from me *and* my babies yet again.

We're in room four now. "Doctor Montgomery, she's seizing!"

Someone holds me back and ushers me to the corner of the room. I feel like I'm stuck in a bad dream.

"Get me two mgs of lorazepam, stat!" Theo barks.

The monitor beeps erratically, and I've no doubt my heartbeat is the same. I can help, I know I can. Theo knows I can, and this is my baby! But he doesn't let me close and neither does anyone else, of course. It's all I can do not to be thrown from the room as he starts an IV line.

"Come on, baby girl, stay with us," I hear him say. "I need a CBC, blood culture and lumbar puncture on deck. Temperature's spiked."

Everything becomes a blur around me as my gaze flicks between my baby and Theo's face. This is not exactly how I pictured a reunion. I don't deserve one at all, probably.

"Seizure's subsiding," he declares suddenly. His shoulders lose some of their stiffness as the meds take effect in front of us. Amelia's little chest is rising and falling more evenly now and finally, I can breathe a little more normally myself, even as the tests are done and I walk with them to the neonatal. He doesn't speak to me, and I don't speak to him. Why would he speak to me at this point? He's doing his job, but he must think I'm awful. I was angry and insecure when I sent that initial message, and then, when he called me I had Anthony in the house, I was distracted and in shock. I've been so selfish. I did to him the one thing he must hate most in order to save face. I was the one who served him his worst fear on a plate. I cut him out, made him feel like he didn't matter. But then, he didn't try to reach me. He didn't try at all. I haven't heard from him.

With a few colleagues surrounding us now, I don't miss how their eyes flit between us, like they're sure something is about to happen. My chin is doing a strange dance as I will it not to wobble. I'm just so exhausted. It feels like forever passes by as I wait for the tests that prove she's in the clear, drumming my already bitten nails to the chair in the private room Amber ushers me into, along with a vat of tea that I can barely touch. She's fine, it was just a febrile convulsion. I should feel a bit silly really but all I feel is even more exhausted and close to tears. I'm about to leave the room when Theo appears, and sees I'm alone.

He steps in and shuts the door behind him, pulling off his gloves.

"You saved her life, Theo," I choke. Finally, I can let

all these crazy emotions free and it's more like an avalanche as he steps toward me, jaw clenched. His breath ruffles my hair and my nerve endings tingle as he leans into me.

"I would rather die than let anything happen to them, or you. Don't you know that?"

All the breath leaves my body. The second he looks away, his eyes glaze over with something like despair and it almost breaks me completely.

"Theo, I'm so sorry," I manage. I'm standing here in front of him, a few rooms down from the bathroom where I first found out I was pregnant, and I'm falling into more pieces than I did then. His arms come up around me, awkwardly at first, then tighter, till the four pens in his pocket are digging into my breast. I don't even care.

"It's okay, Carter," he whispers. He sighs against my hair, and his hand comes up to cradle the back of my head. "She'll be okay, I promise, don't worry."

The gesture, the familiar warmth of him, and the promise in his voice make me want to kiss him right here, pressed up against the cold porcelain sink, but I don't. I just fall back into his eyes. "I thought I was going to lose her… I couldn't handle it," I admit. "Not on top of losing you."

"I've been here the whole time, Carter," he says. "You just…you made your choice."

"My choice?" I try to stay afloat in his eyes, where everything used to make sense. But the world feels like it's spinning out of my control again. Outside I can hear Harley's guttural howl. Amber is still with him while I gather myself back together, but he needs feeding. I need to get back to my duties. I don't want to need this man in front of me, but I do. I don't want to risk more rejection but I also can't continue doing all of this without him, even if we just go back to being friends.

"Can we talk later?" I say, one hand on the door now. I feel so helpless. Harley is still screaming. I'm a terrible mother, but I love this man, and I can't just let this go.

He lowers his eyes, and my heart breaks as he shakes his head. Then, he sighs long and hard, so hard I feel the fabric of my shirt move around my collarbone. "Let me know when it's a good time to come over," he says.

I knew I still wanted her as more than a friend the second I saw her in the hospital with Amelia. I know it even more now that her door's swinging open and she's standing barefoot in front of me. I don't know what I'm doing exactly. Lily is with someone else, which maybe went into my decision not to buy her flowers this time, but I agreed to talk and she agreed to have me over, so here we are. I guess if we can salvage a friendship I'll have to be all right with it but seeing her now just makes me realize how much I've missed being more than her friend.

"Theo...you're early."

"Believe it or not, the traffic was fine, and no one had to hold me up by stopping to pee."

"Well, that's a good thing, seeing as you hung the banner up over your bed," she says dryly, but the smirk on her pretty mouth makes my heart speed up.

"I come bearing gifts," I tell her, lifting the stuffed toys for her to see, and she motions me past her into the house.

She's wearing a plain white shirt, tucked into denim shorts. Maybe I got used to seeing her bump, but her slender frame is kind of strange now. She almost looks the same as she did before the pregnancy; slim, petite, with legs like a damn gazelle. Her hair's all loose and longer now, and I like how it falls around her shoulders as she leads us to the living room.

"Motherhood suits you, Carter," I say before I can stop myself. She looks at me and a soft blush creeps up her neck and onto her cheeks. "I'm serious, you look good."

"Thank you," she replies, looking away quickly. I'm nervous as hell right now and I don't even know why. I know I messed things up, not following up after I saw her with that guy. I couldn't even bring myself to send a message; she made her choice. She didn't message me, either.

There's a double crib in the living room, I assume, so she won't have to keep the twins in the nursery all the time. My breath hitches as I catch sight of them snoozing peacefully.

"Harley and Amelia," I murmur, stepping closer. They're so perfect. I send a silent prayer to whoever's listening that Amelia is good as new after that scare. The tiny girl stirs. Her little fist punches the air before her arms reach up as if she recognizes me. Does she? Lily lets out a huff of surprise, like she's wondering the same thing. I know it's impossible, but awe turns into annoyance at myself as I watch the baby's face scrunch and un-scrunch. I've missed two months already.

Lily picks up Amelia and asks if I want to hold her. I'm not sure if I do. I'll only get attached. But Lily places her into my arms and her little mouth puckers, and her big eyes stare up at me, and I'm attached again, just like that. Great.

"Harley usually sleeps like a log. But Amelia... Rose says she's got a sense of people," Lily says as she crosses to the open kitchen to make some tea. Her voice is tinged with pride and tenderness, and a thousand layers of maternal love I never got to witness as a kid myself, and I know why I'm here. I want to be a part of this, whatever that means. Even if Carter's with…him.

"So, did you name Harley after the bike?" I ask, placing Amelia back in the cot. Her hair is the cutest tuft of dark brown. Her skin, soft as silk and warm, gives off a scent you could only describe as baby. I hope this motorcycle man is good to them both. I hope he appreciates what he's got because her last guy didn't and neither did I, for a long time.

"Why would I do that?" Lily's hands are steady as she passes me the cup, but I can see the flutter in her eyelids, the way her gaze darts away just before our fingers brush. I open my mouth to explain, but stop myself. An ocean of unsaid words seems to stretch out as she sits at the other end of the couch.

She picks up the blue giraffe I brought, along with the cute red antelope. "I don't know why I expected a grasshopper," she says. I can hear the nerves in her voice as she turns it over in her hands. I sit back in the couch.

"Well, I did bring flowers for you, too, last time…but they're dead now. Obviously."

"Flowers?" Confusion laces her voice. Her brows knit together. "Last time?"

"Yeah, I drove here, after we spoke on the phone," I confess. "I wanted to talk and explain what happened with Mom, why you didn't hear from me for two days after they were born. But I never made it to the door."

I watch the realization dawn on her face. "Theo, I had no idea."

"How would you?"

She lowers her head; she's embarrassed I saw them, I bet. "I'm sorry," she says eventually. "The message I sent you… I didn't mean… I know it must have hurt after everything you've been going through with your mom."

"It's all right." I cut her off before she can spiral into an apology that neither of us needs right now. It's easier to play the part of the rational one than to admit how much seeing that guy here stung that day. "I should've known you'd need someone with more to offer. Like the babies' father."

The words still feel like lead on my tongue. "How's it going, anyway? The long-distance thing between here and Miami?"

I casually mention seeing the motorcycle outside last time, and seeing him through the window with the twins. I brace myself for her response. I have to be ready to hear about the life she's building without me in it. But she's looking at me like I've grown a second head.

"Theo, he's not involved at all! He came by once after they were born, offered to set aside money for their college fund each month, in case they need it later, but that's it. We agreed I wouldn't get any other help from him—it was my choice to keep them after all. My decision to do this alone. Besides, he's seeing someone."

I'm listening to all this from some place outside myself, processing what she's telling me. All these little pieces of a puzzle that have been floating around in my skull since that day, they're coming together. I shift closer to her on the couch.

"He only came by the one time?" I ask her. I need this clarified. I need to understand if what I'm hearing is true.

"I know you don't like that I let him, but he had every right to see them. I make my own rules, Theo."

"Of course you do," I tell her.

"He must have come by at the same time you did." She taps her fingers to the cushion between us like they're looking for somewhere to go. I take her hand and draw it to my lap and she shifts even closer.

"This is my fault," she says, meeting my eyes. "I was trying to give you a chance to get out of what we started before you could do the same to me. I compared you to…him…and what he would have done, and that wasn't fair."

"Well, maybe I should have fought harder for us, whatever it was I thought I saw with you and Anthony. I was just overwhelmed, I guess. There was a lot going on."

"I hurt you," Lily says, and she presses a hand to my face. "I shut you out, Theo, and I'm so sorry."

I want to tell her it doesn't matter, but we both know it does, that we're both sorry for getting the present all tangled up in the past. I tell her exactly what happened with Mom and Serenity Pines, and how Pea has really come into her own since Mom was forced to finally get treatment. She's excelling at work, and I don't have to dread seeing her name flash up on my phone anymore. We both know things can't ever get that bad again, but Mom is slowly returning to a slightly more manageable and tolerable version of herself under supervision, and hasn't attempted to use any kitchenware as weapons, which is a very good sign.

Lily tells me all about the struggles of single parenthood, but also how it's the most rewarding thing she's ever done all by herself. When we lay all these issues bare between us like open wounds, I just want her more. Somehow, throughout our conversation, we've closed any remaining space left between us and she's pressed up against me now, her leg to mine, my hands in hers.

Our words run dry until we're just sitting here, and she's looking into my eyes like she wants me to kiss her.

"I think I love you. Tell me I've finally lost my mind," she says eventually.

My heart lurches upward so hard it almost leaves my mouth, but I manage a laugh as I lean in to her. "If you've lost your mind then so have I, because I'm pretty sure I'm in love with you, too, Carter."

She moans softly into my shoulder a moment. "Theo…"

"And I still want to be here for you and the twins." My gaze flickers to the sleeping twins, then back to her. "If you'll let me."

"I think you mean if *Rose* still lets you," she says with a smile, but she's pressing her forehead to mine and inching a kiss down my nose. When our lips meet, the world tunnels into the softness of her mouth, the surrender of her body against mine. I can tell she's not going to let anyone come between us, but I will prove to anyone who needs it that I'm worthy of this woman and these kids. I want all of it, the mess, the chaos, the midnight diaper changes. Maybe a kid of our own; it's crossed my mind. I want to continue rebuilding my family with a solid foundation of love, and yes, that includes my mother. I also want to keep on adding to it, so no one has to *ever* think they're alone.

Lily pulls away slightly, studies my eyes. "There's one thing I need from you, if we're really going to make this work."

I frown at her. "No, I will not remove that banner from my ceiling. I want you to look at it every time I make love to you and remember how we started."

She grabs fistfuls of my hair, and I pull her astride me as she laughs. We both know there's no banner on my ceiling but I'm never going to let her forget that day. "That's not how we started, Theo," she says.

I remind her that that was the day I started falling in love with her, because looking back I think it's probably true. I tell her when I saw her at the fundraiser, challenging that doctor, then helping a man through and out the other side of a heart attack...what could possibly be hotter than that? For some reason, it only makes her kiss me harder. It's only when the cat pads in and attempts to curl round my legs that she remembers.

"Jasper was here first," she tells me. "And he and his fur are not going anywhere." She holds my hands above my head now and clenches her thighs around me. "I need to hear you say it. Jasper is King."

"Jasper is King, my princess," I tell her without missing a beat.

I don't mean it at all, but when she kisses me like this, I'll say anything. Besides, I'll probably even wind up *liking* the cat eventually, because I plan on being here a whole lot more from now on.

Almost a year later

Theo walks into the room. I stop with my stitching. It's proving beyond my current skill set to attach the newest patch onto the quilt that's taking up the entire dining table. He checks the cake he's baking in the oven, which already smells amazing, then he leans against the wall, playing with the string of a balloon that's floated up to the ceiling.

"You'll still be trying to stitch that when you're a hundred years old at this rate," he says, and when he sees I'm looking, he bends down to pet Jasper and makes a thing of *not* pulling a face and *not* rubbing his furry hands on his shirt after. "I could have learned to build an airplane faster."

"Why don't you learn to build airplanes, then?" I tell him. "You really don't have any recognizable skills, you know, except for the boxing and the doctor stuff—"

"Doctor *stuff*?"

I laugh as he puts his arms around me from behind and kisses the side of my neck about six times in a row. Then he whispers in my ear: "I think I've proven my many skills to you at this point, but please, let me know if you need me to trial any more with you."

I push my chair back and put my arms around him fully, and he lifts me onto the kitchen counter, standing between my legs. We kiss while we're laughing but soon, as it often does, our laughter morphs into something not entirely suitable for a kitchen that's expecting guests any second.

I push him off as Rose's footsteps sound out in the hall. Theo smacks my backside on the way back to the nursery where the twins are napping, and I pick up my stitching as the blush paints my cheeks. How is today their first birthday already? How has it been a whole year since their arrival, and almost a year since Theo and I decided to give things a shot, as more than friends?

Rose looks exasperated as she finds me. She's wearing a blue tailored blazer and smart suit pants and she throws her purse on the couch and flops down beside it. She's only just gotten home from her breakfast coffee date with a guy she met on a dating app, at Theo's encouragement of course. He loves to tell her that anyone who looks like *me* can totally score the second best-looking, second most successful man in Chicago.

"I give up. That was a complete waste of a morning," she declares, covering her eyes with her palms and groaning.

"Another bad date?" Theo ventures, coming back into the room with a spare balloon that floated outside to the hall.

"It was disastrous. He thought it would be *fun* to bring his pet snake to the diner. A snake, guys! He said he had an appointment at the vet after meeting me…two birds one stone kinda thing."

"Okay, no, that's not normal." Theo frowns. "Was it wrapped around his neck like a scarf?"

I set aside my sewing as they discuss the pitfalls of dating people with pets, and again Theo makes a thing of reminding me how much he loves Jasper now. Then Rose pulls a small green envelope from her purse.

"I forgot. I prepared something else for the time capsule when snake guy left."

Theo perks up, intrigued. The time capsule was his idea. We've been adding stuff to it for months with the idea being that we'll bury it today and open it when the twins turn eighteen. Part of me was reluctant at first, because…well…does Theo really anticipate being here with me to open it eighteen years from now? I know that's my old issues struggling for attention, though. Sometimes they try to surface when I least expect it, but he hasn't gone anywhere, and instead we've kind of built a comfortable routine around him visiting me here, and me visiting him at his place. Sometimes I take the twins. Sometimes I leave them with the nanny, or my dad. I hate to admit it but those are my favorite times, not because I don't enjoy the twins being around, but adults need alone time. And Theo's bedroom is my absolute favorite place for us to be alone. He was lying about the banner on the ceiling, obviously, but when I'm with him I wouldn't notice anything, anyway, even if a million spiders were up there spinning webs and watching us.

"It's a letter," Rose explains, putting it down between us. "I wrote to them about everything that's happened to their favorite aunt this year. Figured it would be nice to have something personal from Madame Spinster Rose to read when they're older."

"Oh, stop it," I tell her. Rose wants kids of her own, which of course has to start with her getting back on the scene. I don't want her to give up. I want her to find a love like Theo and I have found, as impossible as it once seemed for either of us. But she doesn't believe it could ever happen. She says we are one in a million. I say she's crazy...we are four in a million, because we wouldn't be so in love if Amelia and Harley hadn't come into the world.

"Eighteen years will go so fast," I say. I can already picture them as teenagers. It really doesn't seem that long ago that I was eighteen myself. If I'd known what I'd have to endure to get to this point, would I have done anything differently? Sometimes I wonder. If I hadn't gone through all that, I wouldn't be with Theo now. We wouldn't have smashed all our stupid walls down to uncover the absolute best in each other.

"Do we want chocolate icing, or vanilla?" Theo's heading to the kitchen counter. He's obsessed with making cakes now.

"Both," I tell him.

"And raspberries," Rose adds.

"Your wish is my command, ladies."

Rose disappears to change for the twins' party. I smile as I keep on sewing, and Theo whips up icing in comfortable silence while I sneak looks at his backside and remind myself not to pinch it when our family is here. Delilah loves us together, but she has her limits.

There was a time when all of this would have scared me, when accepting Theo's love also meant living in fear that he might leave me. I guess he felt the same way for a long time, and somehow, through constant open communication and honesty…and amazing sex…honestly, it's the best…we've found what we really need in each other. Everyone at work has been so supportive of our relationship, too, since I started back at the NICU.

The doorbell chimes. I guess the party has started. I stand up, but Theo catches me, pressing a chocolatey kiss to my mouth that makes me swoon. "Is it wrong that I want them to leave already?" he whispers against my lips, right before grabbing my backside and urging my hip bones hard into him. I tell him no, not at all. He flashes that mischievous look that sends shivers down my spine. And then…

Peonie and Delilah step in from the hallway, arms laden with brightly wrapped gifts.

"Where are they?" Peonie exclaims, her voice ringing with excitement as she hands me a soft, squishy gift-wrapped parcel. "Where are my beauties?"

"Napping, they'll join us later. Peonie, these are…" I trail off as I unwrap the parcel and pull out two tiny onesies, and Theo gets up to take the cake out of the oven.

Delilah smiles softly. "Grandma made them," she announces.

They all look so proud all of a sudden, and peaceful. I sigh, holding them up. "They're gorgeous…we'll dress them in these when we visit next."

Theo goes a little quiet, pouring on the icing while we chat around the table, but it's only when he puts the cake down in front of us that I realize something is going on. He looks…not like himself.

"Okay," he starts. "Before we devour my latest creation, and while we're in a celebratory mood…"

Everyone at the table quietens down. I feel my own heart miss a beat or three, as every pair of eyes lands on me. "Theo, what are you—?"

My breath hitches as he drops down onto one knee. A small velvet box has somehow materialized in his hand. The room seems to shrink until it's just us.

"Lily Carter," he begins, and even though I know him to be the master of emergencies, his voice wavers and he's vulnerable and raw, the man I fell in love with a hundred times over. "I've been your wingman through double shifts, diaper disasters, roadside emergencies and pretty much everything in between for almost a year and that is long enough for me…"

He trails off as my hand lands softly over my mouth.

"It's long enough for me to know that I am yours, and you are mine and we belong together, Carter. Will you take me off the market forever? Will you do me the greatest honor imaginable and marry me?" He leans in, so only I can hear. "I promise, it will be your one and only wedding, and it *will* be spectacular."

I can barely breathe. Rose is squealing suddenly. So is Peonie, but luckily, from the way she's slapping him on the back, she's still ecstatic. Tears blur my vision, but his blue eyes are imploring through the haze, waiting for my response. My hands tremble, reaching for his.

"Yes, Grasshopper. Yes, I will do you that honor."

Delilah pulls a face. "Grasshopper? What?"

Theo ignores her. "Good, because I don't think I could return the ring at this point," he says. Then he winks at me. "It was *very* expensive."

He takes my hand and slips the diamond onto my finger. I gasp, tell him it's gorgeous, which it is, no joke. How on earth did he keep this a secret? How long has he been planning this?

Then, as if on cue, an indignant wail pierces our celebratory bubble, followed by another. The twins are perfectly synchronized as usual.

"I can hear they're critiquing my proposal," Theo announces, standing swiftly, taking me with him. "Let's go appease our pint-size critics, will we, future wife?"

The cries dissipate as soon as we enter the nursery. Theo cradles Amelia and I hold Harley, admiring my ring the whole time we change them. He just proposed. Theo Montgomery will be my husband! What will everyone at Evergreen say on Monday?

"Ready to go back in there?" Theo's question pulls me back to the present, and to our family, waiting in the kitchen.

"In a minute," I whisper, leaning into him. I think I need another minute.

His lips find mine and he kisses me in a way that promises forever without him saying a word. It's a perfect slice of serenity… I wish I could bottle it and keep it forever. I can't remember *ever* being this happy.

* * * * *

*Look out for the next story in the
Twin Baby Bumps duet*
From a Fling to a Family

*And if you enjoyed this story,
check out these other great reads
from Becky Wicks*

Nurse's Keralan Temptation
Tempted by the Outback Vet
Daring to Fall for the Single Dad

All available now!

FROM A FLING TO A FAMILY

BECKY WICKS

MILLS & BOON

CHAPTER ONE

I’s 8:39 A.M. I lean my elbows on the counter, peering into the back, looking for Margot. She's the owner at Brewed Awakening and she usually has my smoothie waiting by now, but she's nowhere in sight. My first appointment in the fertility department is in twenty minutes. I'm already exhausted thanks to one of the twins—I think it was Amelia—screeching myself and my sister, Lily, to consciousness at 5:00 a.m. The terrible twos are real, double real in our case.

"Sorry, sorry, Rose!" Margot hurries out from the back in her trademark maroon apron, juggling three coffee cups and a bagel in two hands. She sees me and throws an apologetic smile my way before offloading the breakfast items to the people waiting. "How are you?"

"Busy morning," I say needlessly as she reaches for my premade smoothie.

She says I can pay tomorrow, and I thank her, finally making my way back to the door. Chicago's busiest and best café just happens to be on my route to Evergreen General, by way of a small two-street detour and a free short-stay parking space in an old client's driveway right next door. It pays to be one of the city's best known, and thankfully well-liked, endocrinologists.

I swing open the door, just as a tall, strapping black man steps inside. He's looking down at his phone. I'm secretly admiring his height and impeccable bone structure when his elbow unwittingly catches mine, sending both our phones to the floor. I bend down to catch mine, just as he does the same, knocking my drink sideways with his hand. Before I can right myself, the smoothie tips straight from my hand and sends the vivid green liquid splattering all the way down my white shirt. Oh, my...no!

I don't even have any words as I stand, watching the green droplets slowly drip from my clothing onto the gray checked floor.

"Oh, man, I'm so sorry!" The guy quickly picks up his phone and stands back to give me some space. The embarrassment is acute as I try ineffectively to wipe the green smoothie from my front with a handful of napkins someone hands me. The coffee shop has gone oddly silent. My face flushes hot. My pulse drums in my ears. The man looks genuinely horrified. His deep brown eyes have gone wide with shock. "I didn't see you coming," he says awkwardly, running a hand through his cropped black hair.

"Don't worry about it." My voice is tight and clipped as I swipe at the mess, and he winces visibly at my tone, but doesn't back off.

"Let me buy you another one," he insists, holding out his hand for my empty cup.

Bristling at his pitying gaze, I snatch it away from his outstretched hand. "That's not necessary," I tell him sharply. I don't need a man pitying me, whatever the situation. But despite the awkwardness I find myself unable to look away from him as he continues to mop more green juice from the floor with napkins. Underneath the mortification and annoyance simmering in my belly, I'm quite thrown to experience the unexpected flutter of something else. He is undeniably attractive, strapping and handsome, broad and striking, and I haven't seen him around here before. I thought Lily and Theo had set me up with every sexy bachelor in town by now, which must mean only one thing. He is either married, or new in town.

He's brushing away an errant piece of avocado pulp from his own sleeve now. "I insist. Let me buy you another one."

His offer triggers another unexpected flutter in my stomach as I take a moment to really look at him: cropped black hair, smooth ebony skin, a short beard with just the smallest sprinkling of salt-and-pepper gray. No wedding band. His kind brown eyes are full of compassion and a touch of mischief, too, shining behind sleek, black, oval-shaped glasses, which suit him perfectly.

"I'd prefer a dry-cleaning voucher," I say quickly. Laughter bubbles up from the crowd behind us and even *he* smiles, a warm laugh lifting the corners of his dark eyes.

"Right," he says, grinning, seemingly unfazed by my sarcasm. "I would need an address, to know where to send that."

I stare at him, open-mouthed this time. Is he seriously hitting on me after that? Asking me where I live? I should be offended, but instead I'm just confused. I take a step back, glancing down at my stained shirt one more time. This is not how I envisioned starting my day. I mumble that I have to go and quickly deposit the smoothie cup with a disgruntled Margot. I'll pay for it tomorrow anyway, but right now I'm late, and I've nothing else to change into. It's going to be a long day at work, looking like I just had a bust up with a bucket of green paint.

In the consultation room that doubles as my office, I rest my elbows on the desk, stacked neatly with pamphlets and medical journals. Across from me, thirty-nine-year-old

Mrs. Emily Hanson is here for her post-surgery ultrasound. She's wringing her hands. "Nathaniel can't be here today," she says.

"You're not alone," I assure her, squeezing her hand. Emily has experienced two miscarriages, both requiring dilation and curettage to remove the pregnancy tissue. Unfortunately, further testing revealed Asherman's syndrome, in which scar tissue forms inside the uterus. It wasn't an encouraging outcome and she needs our ongoing support.

"How are you feeling now, a month since the hysteroscopy?"

"I don't honestly know," she says, reaching for the box of tissues on my desk. Emily had a hysteroscopy to surgically remove some of the scar tissue. We hoped it would restore the uterine environment.

"Well, let's take a look, shall we?"

I make a little small talk while I perform the ultrasound, ask her about her work, her weekend plans. I smile when she tells me she had sex for the first time since the op on Thursday. My patients often get personal with me, considering my profession. If only they knew my own sorry single status. I'm the biggest walking irony in Chicago—a single thirty-six-year-old fertility doctor in her second round of secret IVF, via a sperm donor at a different facility all the way across town.

As Emily talks about Nathaniel and how amazing he's been through all of this, I can't forget what happened the last time I put my trust in a man. My eight-year marriage went up in flames thanks to his stupid affair. I was so sure David and I wanted the same things. Turned out he wanted his twentysomething surgical technologist—Harriet from Shropshire, England. Maybe it was the accent. Maybe she was just more available and not married to her work. Whatever it was that made his eyes wander, it was pretty clear he didn't want a kid as much as I did, and I'm no spring chicken. Sometimes you just have to be proactive. I always longed for a family, maybe more than Lily did. I want one as much as Emily does, even if I do it alone.

"Well, the good news is that the uterine lining is regrowing properly, and I don't see any new scar tissue forming."

Emily breathes a sigh of relief. "That's good."

"Like I said, it's very good." I smile. Already she looks less nervous. I recommend a second diagnostic hysteroscopy after another menstrual cycle, just to be sure, and tell her we'll then see about our next steps. She puts a hand to my arm by the door, gathering up her purse.

"Thank you, Doctor Carter. You always make me feel better."

"Please, call me Rose," I tell her. "And I know what you're going through. I'm always here."

Empathy is my secret weapon; it disarms fear, builds trust. Lily says I never lost it, even after what David did, and I guess I didn't. My work has never been affected by my ex-husband's betrayal. My work is my life. Although I admit it's been a struggle since the divorce, gathering up all the pieces of me and patching them back together, creating this new version of myself. A single version, who was trying to get pregnant with a loving husband once, just like Mrs. Hanson is now. I still feel gutted when I think how we were trying for a baby by night, while he was having his way with Harriet by day, behind my back.

Only my twin sister, Lily, and her husband, Theo, know I'm trying for a baby alone. I can't sit around waiting for my dreams to come true, or for my prince to ride up on a white horse. Most princes are frogs in disguise, and who needs a man, anyway? Well, okay, I need a man. For sperm. But for everything else, I'll handle it, thanks.

If only the IVF was actually working.

Emily Hanson heads out the door and I follow, slipping into the bustle of the hallway. The sterile antiseptic smell mingles with the low murmurs from several nurses at the station, and I tighten my white coat around me to hide the smudge of green from this morning's little incident. I'm still annoyed I never actually got any of that healthy juice into my system, and I will have to wash it off my shirt tonight instead. But I can still picture that guy. Now, *he* was my idea of a prince: tall, dark, handsome—

"Doctor Carter?" A voice catches my attention on the way to the ladies' room. It's Janet from HR, her clipboard hugged to her chest like a shield. "There's someone you need to meet."

"Sure." Curiosity piques as I adjust my lab coat again. Then I remember the new OB-GYN who's starting with us today. He's moved here from New York, where he was leading some impressive research studies at NYU Langone Fertility Center, on top of his exemplary primary care and surgical responsibilities. They conduct some truly pioneering research in reproductive endocrinology over there. He'll be continuing some of those studies here as he works alongside me.

Oh. My. Goodness. All the breath leaves my lungs for a moment when I realize who's in front of me. It's *him*. Of course it would be him.

My eyebrows shoot up when I spot her, recognizing her immediately. She looks just as surprised, though she covers it quickly. I can't help a bit of a smirk—half amusement, half...

well, I'm not quite sure what. I extend my hand, giving hers a firm shake, confident but not over-the-top.

"Pleasure to meet you," I say smoothly, pretending we hadn't already crossed paths this morning.

She plays along. "Likewise." Her gaze lingers a beat longer than usual, taking in my cropped black hair, my face, my eyes. I'm used to that look; people tend to watch me, like I take up a bit too much space. And here, at Evergreen, I feel that sense of command more than I did earlier at Brewed Awakening.

Janet clears her throat, adding, "As you know, Doctor Bennett is our new OB-GYN." There's a bit of pride in her voice, like she's welcoming some kind of heavyweight into the department.

Dr. Rose Carter—I remember her name now, saw it on a few papers while I was doing my own research—flashes a polite smile. "We've all been looking forward to your arrival, Doctor Bennett," she says.

So she knows a bit about me. Well, I did some reading on her, too. A respected career, a few impressive publications in reproductive endocrinology and infertility. She's worked her way up the hard way—that much is clear. No shortcuts. I respect that.

"I've heard a lot about your work here, Doctor Carter," I say, my tone sincere.

Rose nods, but there's a guarded look in her eye. I've seen it before—people who've put in years of work, who guard their space fiercely. I get that. My own journey from New York to Chicago, and now here, wasn't exactly without its costs.

And then there's the way she looks at me, a little too closely, like she's wondering what she'll have to put up with. Like maybe she's had to deal with one too many inflated egos. But that's not me. I'm here to contribute, not compete. And to forget about Mabinty—her tear-stained face when she called around unprompted and saw I really *was* packing my bags to move states. I think that was when she realized it was really over. Maybe that was when we *both* realized we'd reached the end of the road, despite my breaking things off months before. Mom and Dad weren't impressed, having known us as a couple for pretty much our whole lives, but who meets their soul mate when they're a child?

You did, Lucas! said my mom, in tears. *You were perfect together!*

I beg to differ. People grow apart. I said that to Dad, looking for backup. He just held up his hands, went to his office and shut the door, as usual. I can't even count the times I've wanted to saw that goddamn door off its hinges and make him talk to me, his only son. Has he even noticed I've left New York yet?

"I'm looking forward to collaborating with you," I say, keeping it professional, though I notice a flicker of something cross her face. Her cheeks go a bit pink, and for a moment she looks almost vulnerable. I'm not sure if she's embarrassed by our earlier encounter or just wary of me, but she squares her shoulders, regaining her composure quickly and mentioning a few of my research papers and how much she enjoyed them. Respect.

She gestures down the hall. "Shall we, Doctor Bennett?"

"Please, call me Lucas."

"Lucas," she repeats, my name rolling off her tongue with surprising warmth. There's something about the way she says it that I can't quite place, but I like it. I like how intrigued she seems to be by all my research, too. Mabs was never all that interested in my work, in all the years we were together—she had her own ambitions, I suppose, in the tech world. Mabs could never wrap her head around how I could work in a fertility department and still not want kids, either. To her, it seemed hypocritical, impossible to reconcile—even though she knew about my dad. How his indifference toward me taught me that kids only end up standing in the way of your ambitions.

I don't want to think about Mabinty, not here.

I follow Rose down the hall, and I find myself thinking a little too hard about her instead. The green of her eyes, and the green of that smoothie on her shirt that I know she's hiding.

CHAPTER TWO

The door to the consultation room swings open, and the assistant presents us forty-one-year-old honey-blond Mrs. Denise Caldwell, dressed in slim-fitting jeans and a designer jacket. "Nice to see you again. Please, take a seat," I say.

"Thank—" Mrs. Caldwell's gratitude is cut short when she clocks the presence of Lucas Bennett, filling the space with his authoritative presence, even from across the room. He was leafing through some of my journals, and admittedly I was half watching him, half texting Lily about this morning's mishap and his surprise reappearance when the door opened.

"Lucas Bennett, meet Mrs. Caldwell," I introduce them briskly, gesture for him to sit in the chair next to me. "He'll be joining us today, and I've brought him up-to-date on your file. I believe he has some insights for you."

"Of course." Mrs. Caldwell nods, her eyes flicking between us with subtle interest. Lucas is so tall his knee knocks mine softly as he settles into the chair.

"Apologies, Doctor Carter," Lucas murmurs with another polite nod, shifting further away in his chair and continuing to explain his credentials. The echo of the contact lingers on my skin, a kinetic spark pulsing through my veins.

It's a sensation I definitely did not expect. I stutter on my words when I take over.

"We've, um…we've got your latest hormone panels back," I begin, sliding the paper across the desk. My finger traces the numbers. "Your insulin resistance is still a key player here."

I pause for a moment, letting the information sink in. "These levels—" I point to the fasting insulin and glucose numbers "—are still quite elevated, and that's impacting your ovulation and overall hormonal balance. It's one of the main reasons your cycles have been so irregular."

Lucas leans forward, no doubt seeing the confusion on her face. "When insulin is out of balance, it creates a cascade effect with other hormones, especially androgens—that's what we're seeing here. High insulin can drive up androgen levels, which then disrupt ovulation."

I glance at our patient, making sure she's following. She seems to be. Lucas looks at me to continue and I nod in agreement, picking up from where he left off. "This isn't unusual for patients with polycystic ovary syndrome, which we've discussed before. We'll need to address the insulin resistance head-on to increase the chance of conception."

"But the positive side is that we can absolutely work on this," Lucas chimes in. "We can see about adjusting your current treatment plan."

He looks to me, and I do my best not to sound as surprised as I am as he brings up a new medication used to treat insulin resistance, one that is fresh out of trials and proven to help lower insulin levels, which in turn might improve our patient's ovulation.

Denise looks interested. She's practically bumping heads with Lucas over the table now, looking at her charts. "And look, your testosterone levels have started to decrease a bit from the last check, which shows some progress. We just need to keep moving in this direction."

"We need to be patient, though," I add, looking Denise in the eye, while I can feel Lucas looking at me. He's keen and I like it, but we also have to be realistic. Too many people get their hopes up when it comes to getting pregnant, like me. I can still picture my kindly doctor's face when she tried not to break my heart last week.

I'm really sorry to have to tell you this, Rose, but the latest results show that the IVF cycle wasn't successful this time.

I push the thought from my mind, before I can dwell on it. It might be successful next time. It can take a while sometimes.

"Hormonal balance doesn't happen overnight. It could take a few months for your insulin and androgens to stabilize and for us to see improvement in your ovulation patterns." I lean back slightly, gauging Denise's reaction. "The goal is to get you ovulating regularly without us needing to rely heavily on medications or injections."

"I know this can feel like a lot," Lucas says, his voice softer now. "But remember, these numbers don't define your chances of becoming a parent."

I realize I'm as hooked on Lucas's words as our patient is. His manner is kind; his input is insightful. I have nothing to complain about here, which unnerves me further. Why? I wasn't ready for this new recruit to be so…what is the word? All I can think is *sexy*.

Mrs. Caldwell seems relieved and pleased as she gathers her belongings, and a tentative smile blooms on her lips as she looks between us. "Thank you, both. It means so much to have such dedicated doctors."

"We're right here with you," I assure her, feeling Lucas's approving gaze on me.

Once the door clicks shut behind her, I turn to face him. Our eyes lock again.

"That went well," he comments, breaking the silence with a smile. He has a nice smile. I noticed that this morning.

"Indeed," I return. Why am I suddenly so flustered in my own space? "Shall we review the next file in the cafeteria? I think you should try the apple pie before it sells out."

"Is that a thing?"

"It's a thing, if you promise not to throw any on me."

He stifles a smile. "Lead the way, Doctor Carter."

"Rose," I correct him, extending the same informality he offered earlier. We're almost at the door when he clears his throat and looks at me sideways from over his glasses.

"About this morning—"

"Don't worry about it. It was an accident," I tell him quickly as the blush hits my cheeks again. "No one has to know."

"It'll be our secret," he replies. Then he leans in slightly, in a way that shifts something around in my system. "But I still owe you a drink."

Somehow, I keep my expression neutral. "What if I'd still prefer a dry-cleaning voucher?"

He grins, and I enjoy his pearly white teeth and sense of humor even more than before. My phone's vibration sends me back to the desk. It's Lily.

"Sorry, I'll keep it quick, just checking if you still have those pearl earrings for the dress fitting this weekend? I can't find them."

I tell her they're in the safe like a bunch of other stuff we don't want the twins to pick up and chew, and Lucas goes back to looking at the books and certifications on the wall.

"Something important?" Lucas asks when I hang up, pulling me back into the present.

"Just sister stuff," I say, smoothing my lab coat. "My twin, actually. She works here, too, up in the NICU."

His eyebrow quirks. "So, there's *two* of you?" The way he says it is nothing short of awed, and his tone sends a lightning bolt up my spine.

"We're fraternal, and she has twins of her own," I explain. I tell him all about Lily and Theo, who also works here in the ER, as we head for the cafeteria. I tell him we also live with a very demanding cat called Jasper, who the twins equally adore and annoy. I probably tell him too much but he looks so interested that I can't seem to stop. Oh, help me. This is the last thing I expected when I woke up to my screaming niece at 5:00 a.m. But I won't say it's the worst surprise I've ever had.

"Stand still for just a second," I say, tugging at the hem of the ivory silk cascading down Lily's slender frame.

"Okay, okay, I'm trying." Lily laughs, her eyes meeting mine in the mirror. "But it's harder than it looks to be a mannequin."

"Trust me, you're a natural." After adjusting the veil, I step back to observe. "This one's beautiful on you," I say. Then I frown. "But it doesn't scream 'Lily' to me."

The dress is a stunning, intricate blend of lace and light, but it's not the one—not yet, I don't think. You know when you just know. My twin nods. "You read my mind," she admits, turning around to admire herself anyway, just as Amelia and Harley shriek in laughter from the pen behind us. The assistant is dangling a lace glove between them, tickling their noses with it, and they love it.

The people at Love Lace, the wedding dress store, have been so nice to let us set it up so we can watch them here, on the nanny's day off. "Do you love the gloves, Amelia?" Lily asks, sticking out her tongue playfully. "Maybe we'll make a doctor of you yet."

"Theo would love that. Next!" I announce, thumbing through the garments on the rack. I can't help the twinge of jealousy at my sister, who has it all. The adoring fiancé, and the adorable twin babies and the wedding of her dreams soon approaching. They've had a long engagement; they wanted to wait till the twins were old enough to know what was going on, and no doubt to ensure they both enjoyed it without tending to newborns all day. Lily and I are alike in every way, except for…well, all of that.

As the next candidate—a softer number with delicate beading—slips over her head, we lapse into comfortable silence. We've been each other's constant, two halves of a whole from the start, and now her wedding feels like another chapter in our collective story. I should be happy for her. I am happy for her.

"Can you believe it?" she murmurs as I zip her up. "This is actually happening. Theo actually chose me."

"He's punching above his weight and he knows it," I tease her. They are perfect together. "Gosh, Lils. Remember how we planned out our dream weddings with those ridiculous scrapbooks?"

"Ugh, yes." She chuckles. "I was going to marry a prince, and you were set on that astronaut."

I laugh, tweaking a loose curl beside her ear, picturing the *prince* who surprised me by showing up in my department last week and threw me off balance for a second time. How has he been there a week already?

"Well, I'm thrilled you found your man, but I don't need one," I say. Weirdly, I'm still thinking of Lucas when I say it and it doesn't quite come out as convincingly as I intended.

"Rose…" She manages to frown at me, despite her reflection glowing with love. I cut her off before she can start.

"Nope. I'm skipping the man part, having a baby on my own. We've discussed this. The next round of IVF will work."

Lily presses her mouth closed. She knows I'm more disappointed than I can afford to admit by it all, by what David did, by feeling forced to do this pregnancy thing solo. But I've tried the dating apps, more than once. I don't really think it's me; you can't feel someone's energy, or your chemistry, if you meet via a screen, and if it's not there in person when you finally meet, it's just awkward.

Anyway. At least choosing motherhood on my own terms gives me full autonomy over my reproduction and family-building plans. I've built a nice life without a man. Yes, it could be a little more exciting, but still, it's a nice life.

"What about the New Yorker? What's his name? Lucas?"

His name from Lily's mouth sends a jolt to my heart. "What about him?" I say, too quickly. There's a glint of mirth in her eyes when she shakes her head. She reminds me that I spent longer than I normally would earlier last week describing him.

"I don't date colleagues," I tell her simply, and she pulls a face.

"If I didn't date colleagues, I'd never be getting married now," she reminds me. "Don't overlook what's right under your nose!"

I tut at her. "That will hardly be possible. He's going to be under it a lot."

"Then get him under *all* of you." She laughs and I pretend to thwack her with a very expensive shoe, right before Harley calls out to her.

I watch as she heads for the toddlers, her dress trailing across the floor, and annoyingly I picture Lucas and the way he smiles. I do love his smile. But I really couldn't date a colleague. It would be far too complicated. Besides, I've already decided that I'm going to be a mother. That is going to be my life. I will be a very happy single mother with the support of my friends and family. I can't just be an aunt forever. I want what my sister has, and I want it now.

I'm on the recommended fertility medication at the moment, in the hope that it will stimulate egg production and increase my chances of successful fertilization on the next round. All I can do is be patient, keep up my clean eating, exercise, meditate. Pray for a miracle?

"Hey," Lily says softly, catching my hand. She can always tell when I'm getting too deep into my thoughts. "Whatever happens, you'll always have me."

What would I do without my sister?

CHAPTER THREE

"Needles, hope and hormones," I mutter, scrolling through Emily Hanson's chart. She's due in any second. "Isn't that the unspoken love language of fertility?"

"You make it sound more romantic than it is, Doctor Carter," Lucas says as he leans over my shoulder. His proximity creates a sudden warmth at my back that spreads throughout my chest like it's been doing for the past few weeks. Every time I walk into a room to find him there, my eyes seem to gravitate toward him right before my feet do.

"Let's not scare Emily off. It's her second diagnostic hysteroscopy today," I warn him.

"I'll do my best, Doctor Carter." He catches himself. "Sorry, Rose."

I suppress a shiver when he says my name, not from the cool air-conditioning in the clinic, but from the closeness of this man—this infuriatingly charming new recruit who everyone has kind of fallen for around here.

"So, I've managed to secure a spot for Evergreen at the Dallas conference," he tells me. "I'll be presenting my research on novel treatments for gynecologic cancers. Started it last year at NYU Langone, and..."

"You're continuing it here, I know," I interrupt. "No pressure for me, trying to keep up with all your achievements, right?"

I am only half joking but Lucas grins. "From what I've heard, you can hold your own."

I arch a brow. "I've read everything you've published. Really impressive work."

Lucas feigns shock. "Thanks, but...all of it? Even the dry stuff? And here I thought no one read my papers except my mom."

I fold my arms. "Well, I don't have a lot of free time, so consider that a compliment."

Lucas leans in, smirking. "Consider it received. And if you've read that much, then you know I work better as a team."

"Or a power couple." I catch myself, flushing. "Professionally speaking, of course."

He nods and his smirk lingers, but there's a flicker of something serious in his eyes as I watch him, like he's remembering something. I feel a strange need to fill the silence.

"So, um... New York to Chicago. That's a pretty big move. Why here?"

Lucas shrugs, looking thoughtful. "Could ask you the same thing. Why do you stay in Chicago when you could go anywhere?"

"Touché. But for me, it's family. My sister, my dad, the twins—they all keep me pretty busy and grounded." I'm kind of telling the truth. My life could be more exciting, I suppose.

Lucas nods. "I get that. Family keeps you...real." He pauses and rubs his jaw. "Sometimes painfully real," he adds, pulling out his phone for a second, then putting it back into his pocket. I'm about to ask what he means, but he's still talking. "Anyway, I like the idea of stirring things up a bit here. Evergreen's got some serious potential, and I want to be part of that."

"Well, you're definitely making waves. In a good way," I say, wondering if my secretly mounting crush is making me too complimentary.

"Glad to hear it. But I wouldn't want to be *that guy* who barges in with all the answers."

I smile. "If you turn into *that guy*, you'll be the first to know." I nudge him playfully, then immediately feel a bit self-conscious and pull back.

Lucas notices and leans just a bit closer, making my heart pound. "I'll hold you to that."

There's a charged pause, and I can't quite shake the feeling that he sees right through my attempt to pretend I'm not enjoying this flirty exchange. But we need to keep things professional here. Thankfully, I'm saved. A knock on the door has me stepping away from him.

"Doctor Carter," Emily greets us with her husband, Nathaniel, this time. Lucas leaves, and soon Emily's legs are in the stirrups—never a comfortable position.

"Emily, I know this isn't easy. I'll walk you through everything, like last time. We're just checking how well your uterus has healed after surgery."

The screen flickers on, displaying a grainy black-and-white image. I'm very pleased, actually. "The scar tissue has reduced significantly, and your uterine cavity is much clearer. The lining looks healthier."

Emily exhales, visibly relieved. I point to a smooth area on the screen. "Your endometrial lining is still a bit thin—five point five millimeters. For successful implantation, we need it closer to seven or eight."

After the scan, she's dressed, and Lucas returns. He discusses the plan for high-dose estrogen and the whole time he speaks, I can literally feel my body reacting to his presence. I can't help comparing him to David, back when we met. The way my pulse would race like this whenever he came near me.

He was deep into his fellowship at Northwestern Memorial Hospital, destined to become one of the country's most sought-after cardiothoracic surgeons. I was on my OB-GYN residency, living a permanent cycle of clinical rotations. It was during one of the surgeries that we met and then our paths kept crossing. I thought it was a sign from the divine whenever I'd catch him in the hallway or the cafeteria. I can still picture the way he'd look at me, peeling off his gloves like he was thinking of much better ways to use his fingers.

We bonded over late-night shifts, shared frustrations with coursework and all the camaraderie that comes with the intensity of medical training, I guess—he had a wicked sense of humor. It was infatuation, lust, my first true love. Everyone noticed the chemistry between us. It was the kind I thought would see us through forever. Everyone saw how it broke me when the truth came out.

Despite what Lily thinks, I'm not about to get too personal with another colleague. I've worked too hard here to risk something like that messing anything up again. Lily and Theo are the exception when it comes to being colleagues and lovers but to be fair, they don't even work in the same department. They make being together, raising the twins and working in the same building seem like a breeze, but they don't have to see each other all day every day; not like me and Lucas.

All that said, it doesn't mean I can't look at and admire, and maybe have a little flirt with, a handsome new colleague, does it?

Lucas is still walking through his treatment plan. I watch as Nathaniel takes one of his wife's hands in his lap and rubs his thumb gently across the back of it, and I recognize the twinge as envy. Ridiculous. My fingers find the silver chain around my neck as I try to will my eyes to stop darting to Lucas's sexy profile. Those lips...so full and delicious-looking.

Ugh, what?

I don't need to be thinking these things about any man. Maybe the next round of IVF will be successful this afternoon. I have to have hope, don't I?

I barely notice the drive to the clinic. My mind is busy on the things I have to do, including a bunch of stuff for Lily's wedding, but my brain goes blank the second my embryologist, Dr. Beaumont, welcomes me into the room.

The walls inside are lined with serene images of nature, a squirrel holding a nut, three galloping horses in a meadow. I'm sure to some people these things are calming. I see straight through them; we have nothing like this at Evergreen. Still, I appreciate what they're trying to do.

"How are you feeling today, Rose?" Dr. Beaumont asks me.

"Just...a little nervous," I admit, forcing a smile. "I really want this to work."

She nods at me empathetically. "That's completely understandable. We want the best outcome, too. Let's take it one step at a time, okay?"

After a brief consultation about the meds I've been on, I'm prepped for the procedure. As I lie back on the examination table, my heart tries to pound out of my chest. I hate this part. The room is equipped with the most unromantic array of advanced technology, and I can hear the soft hum of machines as well as my own heartbeat as she stands over me.

I suddenly wish I'd accepted Lily's invitation to come with me today instead of being so stubborn, but I didn't want us both leaving Evergreen at the same time and people asking questions.

"So, as you know, today we'll be transferring an embryo created from your eggs and the donor's sperm," Dr. Beaumont explains, reviewing her chart. "We'll be using one of the embryos that survived the thaw from your last cycle. Are you ready?"

I nod, swallowing hard. Of course I know what the procedure entails, but she doesn't have to know that. I was careful not to reveal too much about myself. I guess out of embarrassment more than anything. The thought of anything surviving a *thaw* is even more unromantic than the soundtrack of machinery all around me. Why didn't I just give dating apps another chance?

I have to pull myself together. Remain a sacred vessel. "Yes, I'm ready."

I find myself holding my breath as she proceeds with the transfer. Again, it's entirely unromantic. I could be having sex instead with a hot stranger...but ugh, that would have been even more complicated, and who's to say it would even work? I guess it worked for Lily, getting pregnant from a one-night stand, some guy she met in Miami, but that was Lily. I'm different. I like things to be done, well, my way.

I wince at the slight discomfort.

"Take a deep breath," Dr. Beaumont encourages. "You're doing great."

As the procedure continues, I close my eyes, visualizing this working, picturing myself months from now, carrying a healthy pregnancy. Manifest. That's what Lily would say. Think it, believe it, it will happen.

I'm told to rest for a few minutes once the transfer is complete and I lie still on the bed, feeling a strange blend of vulnerability and empowerment swirl through me. "This could be it," I whisper to myself and the ceiling. I close my eyes again, and Lucas's face flashes into my brain. God help me.

After a while, the doctor returns. "Everything went smoothly, Rose, well done. Now it's time to start the waiting game again. You'll take a pregnancy test in two weeks."

Right. I nod, trying to steady my breath. I appreciate her kindness and empathy, and the fact that she's probably resisting the urge to ask why I'm doing this alone when I could go out and meet a guy. It takes time to meet a guy, though, and more time to trust him enough to try for a baby, and more time to observe him after he's agreed to it, to see if he's changed his mind… No. I don't have that much time. This *will* work.

I'm cornered the moment I step out of the elevator, before I can even slip on my white coat.

"Doctor Carter, glad I caught you. There's been an issue with the Dallas conference next week."

I blink at our receptionist and admin assistant, Maddy, and I know I must look like I'm on another planet, but my mind is still spinning after my appointment across town.

"Sorry, what kind of issue? I'm not involved in the Dallas conference. That's Doctor Bennett and Doctor Lin."

Maddy pulls an apologetic face and follows me into my office. "Doctor Lin has a conflicting arrangement we seem to have overlooked when we were finalizing the schedule. Rose, Doctor Carter, you're the best person to fill in."

She drops the file on my desk with an air of finality and I blink at it. "But my patients, they're expecting me—"

"I've already cleared your calendar. You're all set."

"All set?" The words echo in my head like a ticking bomb before my eyes are drawn back to the door. Lucas is leaning against the door frame now, his dark eyes locking on to mine with an unreadable expression.

"Problem?" he asks, managing to sound both casual and concerned at the same time. I still don't know how he does that.

Maddy tells him what's happened, and he nods like he already knows and tells us Dr. Lin approached him earlier. His elderly father's having heart surgery on the same day. I can hardly blame him for pulling out of the trip.

"Timing's tight," I admit, flipping through the itinerary. "My twin's wedding is coming up and…" I trail off. I realize it must sound like I don't want to go, which isn't ideal, but then, I really don't. I don't particularly enjoy conferences or airport lounges, or soulless hotel rooms and small talk. I'm a creature of comfort. A homebody. I'm also trying to get pregnant.

I'm acutely aware of Lucas's eyes on me as I struggle for an excuse. The thought of the two of us going somewhere, anywhere outside this hospital feels too personal somehow, even if it's for work, but if I say anything I'll look entirely unprofessional. I just have to suck it up; it's only for two nights and three days.

"Let's grab lunch when your schedule allows," he suggests, and I meet his eyes again as my heart does a tiny hop. "To go over the presentation," he continues. "I'll give you some time to look it over obviously, but I'm sure you'll have plenty to add."

"Right, yes. Perhaps. You're the expert."

"Well, you're also an expert," he counters, and he has that look on his face again now, the one that makes me think he sees through me. I try not to let my gaze linger on his broad chest, the pen in his pocket. I'm annoyed at myself. Obviously, he meant a business lunch. What did I think he meant?

He keeps his dark gaze on me as he closes the door softly behind him and steps toward my desk. My heart starts stammering the second we're alone.

"Forgive me if I'm out of line, Rose, but you seem a little uncomfortable with taking this trip. If you really don't want to go I can…"

"It's personal," I tell him. Then I wince. That was worse than lying. "Sorry," I add. "Like I said, wedding planning is a constant nightmare, not that I'm not happy for my sister, of course, and for Theo. It's just a lot."

Oh, Lord, I am making this worse by the second. "I'll make it work around the trip. I'm looking forward to it."

The corners of his mouth twitch, threatening to form a smile. He folds his arms across his chest and levels me with a piercing gaze, like I'm suddenly a specimen under scrutiny.

"All right, then," he says in a calm, measured tone.

"All right, then," I repeat. This is so awkward, but his smile is contagious. Without saying more than *all right*, we seem to have reached some kind of understanding.

For some reason my heart keeps pounding madly as I exit the room. The thought of heading to Dallas with this man is already putting me on edge.

CHAPTER FOUR

I LEAD ROSE through the crowd to the notice board listing today's events, talks and workshops. "Our presentation's one of the last," I say, glancing at her.

"So many people again." Rose sips from her cup, her gaze skimming the crowd filling up the conference center, and I can't help wondering what's going through her head. She's quiet, keeps to herself, so I barely know anything about her, other than they call her and her twin sister the "flower girls," and Lily has twins herself. Twins everywhere. She went back to her hotel room early yesterday, no doubt to call them, while I discovered a great restaurant with some of the guys. She missed out. And I found myself missing her.

"So, big plans after this?" I ask, testing the waters, hoping to draw her out a little. "Maybe join us for a drink tonight?"

She gives me a half smile. "I'll think about it. Let's see how the presentation goes."

"We're going to kill it," I tell her.

"Okay, Mr. Confidence," she teases, and for a second the storm in her eyes disappears. What is she carrying? Even though I know better than to get too close to a colleague, I'm drawn to her. She's so different from Mabinty, too. It's messing with me a little.

The place feels like a beehive of buzzing medical professionals all trying to make their mark along with new introductions as we head for one of the lecture rooms. We're just squeezing through the third row in search of empty seats when a voice booms out from behind me.

"Doctor Bennett, I had a feeling I'd see you here. Congratulations on the new position!" It's Thomas Marx-Sampson, another ex-colleague from way back in my fellowship days. He extends a hand over the seats and we shake, while I rack my brains as to what he is doing now, and where. I've been to so many of these things, sometimes I lose track.

"This is Doctor Rose Carter," I introduce her, my hand finding its way to the small of her back against her blue blazer—a guiding touch more than anything else, though I don't miss the way she leans into it, only slightly. "We could all learn a lot from this woman."

"An honor, Doctor Carter." There's respect in his eyes and smile and I can tell Rose feels it from me, too. I notice the slight blush across her cheeks before she does that thing she does, where she threads the chain of her silver necklace between her fingers. She's nervous about something.

"Are you nervous?" I ask her as we move through the throng and take our seats with our coffees.

"Maybe," she answers honestly.

"Why? About our presentation later?"

She shrugs, then sighs. "Not that. I'm with a professional, remember, Mr. Confidence?"

"Then what?"

She shakes her head like she doesn't want to bother me with it, but I want to know now. Several people call out to me, or wave my way as they did outside, but I'm continuously aware of her presence right beside me—poised in the blazer and dark blue dress pants, scanning the room with those perceptive green eyes. "We are going to make some real waves with our research later," I remind her, adjusting my tie and nudging her.

She exhales, half laughing. "Let's hope we don't put them to sleep instead."

"No one would want to sleep with you up on a stage."

The words come out well intentioned, but I'm quickly aware of the double entendre and she doesn't miss it, either. "No one would want to sleep with me, huh?"

"That's not what I meant. Oh, wow, I'm making this worse, aren't I?"

"It's okay." Thankfully, Rose is laughing. She asks to see one of my research papers quickly, so I hand her the mobile version on my phone, and our fingers brush. A spark flies up my arm and I do my best to focus on the task at hand, which is to appear like the professional she thinks I am. Or thought I was, until I told her no one would want to sleep with her. Which is not true. Not at all.

"So you seem to be quite the celebrity around here," she says, once I've finished yet another conversation with a guy in the row behind. I note the smile playing at the corners of her lips and try to ignore how the curve of her mouth in my direction sends a thrill to my heartstrings.

"Real star quality, me. That's what my mom says," I reply, flashing my trademark grin, or so Mabs used to call it. Rose rolls her eyes playfully.

"Doesn't it get exhausting? All this…schmoozing?"

"Sometimes," I admit. "But it's part of the job, right?"

"Of course," she says, nodding, understanding flickering in her green gaze. She really does have the most remarkable colored eyes.

"Though, I must confess—" I lean in slightly, dropping my voice to a conspiratorial whisper "—I'm more interested in discussing where we're going to eat after the conference. I know you've never been here before, so I know you've never met real Texan food. You missed out last night."

"Doctor Bennett," she says, her eyes meeting mine, the faux-serious intensity matching my own. "Are you asking me out to dinner when you haven't even bought me my dry-cleaning voucher yet?"

The chatter around us fades and for a moment, it's just the two of us. We're half joking, but we are clearly going to have dinner together tonight.

"Why would I go out alone?" I play on. "Aren't you concerned I might be kidnapped by cowboys?"

She pretends to think long and hard about this and I take her empty coffee cup and place it on the floor under my seat to take away later. Before I can list the steakhouse I have in mind, we're forced into silence. Dr. Lars Henriksen is on the stage. He speaks fluently about how womb-lining receptiveness can be better assessed with the new protocols he's about to trial in Denmark. Rose seems utterly engrossed and scribbles notes right through to the end. I want to know more about this flower girl than I should. Tonight I will be on my best behavior, but I won't let her slip away.

Hours later, I snap the lid shut on the last container of promotional materials. The satisfying click echoes through the now silent auditorium, which will soon be filled with people attending our own lecture. Rose is across the room, double-checking the projector alignment. I can't help but watch her for a second, the way she moves.

"Everything good on your end?" I call out to her.

"Perfect," she responds without looking up. "Presentation is loaded and ready. Oh, hi, Doctor Henriksen."

The Danish doctor has recognized me, but it's Rose who

corners him after I've given him an info packet. I wonder why she's particularly interested in him, and it hits me: maybe she thinks he's attractive. He's smart, but he's also not completely awful to look at. I'm comfortable enough in my own skin to appreciate a fellow good-looking man when I see one. I know nothing about Rose's type, but as I watch them talk I spot the tendrils of jealousy creeping over me. Crazy! I'm jealous. I haven't felt jealousy in a long time and it doesn't sit well.

People have started filing in now. Rose slips out to apply some lipstick and I make casual conversation with some of the attendees in the front row. When she reappears, I have to do a double take. From her laid-back look of a blue blazer and dress pants, she's totally transformed herself into a commanding figure in a sleek, formfitting navy blue dress. Every detail exudes confidence and elegance, power and sophistication. Wow.

Her feet are higher than they were earlier, too, but there's no sign of discomfort on her face as she walks in the heels. Instead, there's this newfound confidence in her stride that makes it clear—Rose Carter is here to own the room. As she passes by on the way to the podium, she pats my arm reassuringly. "Showtime," she smiles.

"You look—" I trail off, shrugging farther into my suit jacket, which I pulled on over a crisp clean white shirt earlier. I couldn't help but notice *her* watching *me* for just a few seconds too long.

"How do I look?" she replies, before reaching across and straightening my tie. Her fingers brush against my neck as she adjusts it under my collar, and a red-hot shiver shoots right down my spine. Well, this is just great. This crush is growing faster than I can rein it in.

"Um… You look very nice."

Really, Lucas, is that the best you can do?

Jeez, this woman is getting to me! But she is all business. Her wavy brown hair, that earlier flowed over her shoulders, is now pulled up into a polished updo that draws my eyes to the graceful arch of her neck. A neck I, by now, have spent far too long looking at. Her full lips are highlighted by that bold red lipstick and they're so close now, while she fiddles with my tie. It's all a little too distracting. My brain is about to short-circuit.

Rose's eyes are focused and determined, even as she performs this one small act of attention to detail about my neck, and I catch a whiff of her perfume. It's a subtle mix of floral and spice that reminds me of walking through a souk in Dubai with Mabs… Why am I thinking of Mabs again?

I step back from her, smoothing down the sleeves of my jacket. In the background, the hum of conversation grows louder as more attendees fill out the room.

"You also look the part," she says, appraising me from head to my brown leather-clad toes. "Very suave."

"Thanks to you." I smooth down my tie unnecessarily before following her lead toward the presentation area. The dimming lights signal us to begin, and Rose takes one final look at me before turning to address the room. I can only look on in awe. So this is Rose Carter, the most commanding and charismatic presenter I've ever shared a stage with.

I'm not just impressed—I'm inspired.

Finally, we find ourselves standing alone, side by side. "Well, that went surprisingly well," she says on a sigh.

"You were amazing up there," I reply sincerely.

She shakes her head slightly. "I can't take all the credit. You were pretty impressive yourself."

"But your ideas on how we might continue targeting

those *specific* molecular profiles... You have to admit you enjoyed coaching me," I respond with a wink.

She laughs, waves it off. "Oh, please, you didn't need my ideas. And if anything, you coached me. I shouldn't even be here."

I feel a sense of pride swell inside me at her words. "Let's just agree not to tell Doctor Lin how well we both did," I reply.

We bounced off each other on stage, sharing the spotlight and questions effortlessly. It was like we'd been practicing and collaborating for weeks instead of just a few days, and I can't help thinking Rose and I did a better job at hooking the crowd than Dr. Lin and I would have done, purely because Rose is so magnetic up on stage. There are so many sides and layers to Rose, I can hardly keep up.

"Is it weird that you kind of remind me of my dad?" I say, before I can hold it in. She is going to think I'm crazy.

She raises an eyebrow, smirking. "Remind you of your dad? Is that another one of your compliments, Lucas?"

"No, no, well, yes, it's...it's a good thing," I say. "He had all these sides to him, you know? People loved him. He could impress anyone, even me." My gaze drifts for a second, tangled in a memory.

Rose's voice softens. "He passed away?"

I nod. "Six years ago."

She frowns at me, sympathy all over her face. "Sorry to hear that. Sounds like he must've been a pretty great guy."

"Yeah, he was," I tell her, wondering how on earth we've reached this point, out of nowhere. "It's just a shame he barely came out of his office when I was around. He could put on a show for everyone else, but he was more of an occasional teacher than a father to me, I suppose."

Her eyes don't leave mine. "Maybe he didn't know how to do both."

I hold her gaze, letting the words sink in. "Maybe."

I stop before I add that for a long time, I thought I could make him see me differently if I just became someone worth noticing. Even graduating med school didn't seem to make him proud, though; he was so self-absorbed.

"You're worth noticing," she murmurs now, her voice gentle. It shifts something monumental inside me and the tension makes me awkward.

"Careful or I'll start thinking you actually like me," I say.

She smiles, holding my gaze again. "Who says I don't?"

"Hey, Lucas!" The familiar baritone cuts into our conversation. I turn to find Ayden Hartlett approaching, his hand risen for what I know will be an exuberant slap on the back.

"Doctor Hartlett," I say, bracing for impact, "good to see you, man."

"Likewise! Been a long time since the Cornell days, huh? Kings of the Upper East Side." Ayden always had this infectious energy about him, like he could make even the dreariest lecture seem like a Broadway show.

"Too long," I agree, rubbing where his friendly gesture landed.

Ayden's gaze drifts past me to Rose, and I introduce them quickly. "Pleasure to meet you," he says, offering Rose a firm handshake.

"Same here," she replies coolly, and I suppress a laugh at the look on her face when he goes in with his standard iron grip.

"I saw your lecture. Impressive stuff. New York's loss is Chicago's gain, right, Doctor Rose?" Ayden remarks. Then he turns back to me. "Speaking of New York, how's Mabinty? Last I heard she was crushing it in the tech world—something about a cutting-edge cybersecurity start-up?"

"Thriving, as usual," I say quickly, though a tightness knots in my chest at the mention of Mabs.

"You guys are still good with the long distance and everything?" he asks.

Rose's eyes flicker to mine momentarily. I can tell she's curious suddenly and I feel completely put on the spot.

"Actually, man, we're not a thing anymore. It's been a while now—"

"Okay, good stuff." Ayden nods before checking his watch. He looks completely distracted. I'm pretty sure only Rose registered what I just said. "Looks like the next lecture's about to start but will I see you for dinner out at Hank's?"

"I don't know yet." I shrug. I got the invite, of course. Even packed my "uniform" for the event, but I was hoping to hang out with Rose tonight.

Rose tilts her head as he tells me he'll see us later and hurries off, her eyes scanning my face for a moment too long. "Hank?"

"Doctor Henry Jackson Merrick," I explain, pointing at him over the crowd; he's pretty hard to miss. "Most people just call him Hank or Tex. He's another friend of ours from way back, an ex–trauma surgeon. He quit his medical practice to build a quiet life out here, on his family ranch."

"Sounds a lot less traumatic."

"The dinner is kind of a regular event. He just aligned it with the end of the conference this time. So, you wanna go?"

"I'll pass, thanks. Got some reading to catch up on."

Disappointment unsettles me but I do my best to keep it

off my face. "Are you sure? Could be fun. It's always fun. You don't want to miss this food, either."

"Then why am I only just hearing about this? I've nothing to wear." She shakes her head, a strand of wavy hair falling from her updo into her view while I scratch my neck. Busted. I didn't tell her earlier because from the way she retreated from the crowds last night, I had a feeling she wouldn't want to go, and I wanted to hang with her *somewhere*. But I'm not going to say that.

"We can go back to the dinner plan, just the two of us?" I try.

"I'm pretty tired," she says. "It's been a long day…my feet are killing me."

"That'll be your choice of shoe," I remind her, and she winces.

"No pain, no gain, Lucas."

We walk to the elevators. We've seen all the lectures we were planning for today and I admit I'm tired, too. Nothing a nap won't fix for me, but Rose seems to have made her choice. I respect that, even if I don't like it. Maybe it's even for the best. If anyone else plans on bringing up Mabs, I'd rather she didn't hear it. I can do without that following me to work, and there's something fresh and new about Rose that I don't want tainted by my past, even if she's subtly telling me that she doesn't mix business with pleasure whatsoever, anyway. If only my heart would accept defeat as fast as my brain.

CHAPTER FIVE

THE TAXI PULLS to a stop on the crunch gravel. I take in the lights from the porch that's wrapped around the homely-looking, tree-hugged farmhouse. I can't believe I'm here, on an actual ranch in Texas. I can't believe Lily persuaded me. I also can't believe Lucas is actually wearing cowboy boots.

"I'm kind of glad I didn't get this memo," I say as he opens the door for me. I gesture to the light brown leather boots he's tucked faded jeans into. His plaid shirt stretches like a tight tease over his sculpted, broad frame, and he flashes me that grin that almost knocks me off my feet whenever I see it, shutting the door behind me and placing a tawny-brown cowboy hat on his head.

"Oh, you'll get it soon. Trust me, ma'am," he says with a nod of his hat that makes me laugh despite myself. Then his hand finds the small of my back again, like it did earlier in the lecture room. The contact sends the same bolt of red-hot adrenaline up my spine as he guides me past the paddocks toward the path. What am I doing here?

I had every intention of lying low in my hotel room again and catching up on my reading, and praying that a miracle pregnancy might occur inside me if I just keep still and quiet. Besides, Lucas unnerves me for reasons I can't afford to contemplate any further. But when Lily called, her reaction was not what I'd expected.

Are you crazy? You would rather sit in your hotel room alone than have a fun night out with your sexy colleague under the stars? You never have fun, Rose. Go have some, I beg of you.

She's such a romantic. I had to remind her that *my sexy colleague* is exactly that, a colleague, and therefore not someone I should be contemplating sitting under any stars with.

I told her, *No, Lils, remember what happened with David? Getting personal with any more sexy colleagues is not on my agenda.*

Then I had to finally admit that, yes, okay, I am madly attracted to him. I just wish I weren't, *especially* considering I am—hopefully—about to become a single mom!

"Lucas, my man, so good of you to come!" Hank finds us as we step onto the porch. His booming voice echoes out over the guests who are already here, mingling in the muggy evening air. His arm shoots out to wrap Lucas in a bone-crushing embrace. Hilariously, he's also clad in the quintessential rancher's attire and now that I'm looking around, I notice that every guy here has dressed the part. In fact, if someone typed in "show me a group of ranchers," I'm pretty sure Hank and Lucas, and everyone else on this porch, would appear in the search results.

"You must be Rose!" he booms as his eyes land on me. Then he envelops me in an unexpected hug. It's like being embraced by an affectionate grizzly. "We've got some good old Texas barbecue waiting for y'all later, but in the meantime, can I offer you some refreshments?"

He leads us across what suddenly feels like a cowboy costume party, toward a rustic wooden table laden with bottles of wine and platters of home-cooked food. Through the window I can see into the cozy kitchen, where more people are standing around mingling and laughing. I wish Lily were here. She's the social one, not me. Before her ex, Grayson, killed all the joy left in her soul, which was long before she met the amazing Theo—who has since instilled it all back in again, thank goodness—she had no qualms about heading out places on her own and just seeing who crossed her path.

Lily lives by the mantra that a stranger is a friend you haven't met yet, whereas for me, even standing in an elevator with more than one person fills me with dread. Somehow, I can switch it on when I'm at work. I show them the side they need to see. It's called playing the game…like Lucas with his schmoozing. Although secretly, I think he enjoys it. There's more to him than I first thought. When he told me about his dad passing away earlier I felt his pain. It's obvious there is something unresolved there, too.

"Hank, you always were the host with the most," Lucas is saying now, accepting a cold beer from an ice bucket. No drinking for me. I have to stay a healthy vessel. I opt for a soda water and steal another glance at Lucas, who seems completely at ease here beneath the wide Texas sky. As for me, I feel a little underdressed now in simple jeans, a loose white shirt over a tank, and feminine sandals. After today in heels my feet aren't yet back to normal.

Lucas catches me looking around. His deep brown eyes hold mine and he shrugs lightly, a half smile pulling at one corner of his lips. "First time at anything cowboy themed?" he asks.

"How did you guess? I didn't even bring a hat."

"Well, we can fix that." He puts his beer down, removes his hat and deftly places it on my head. My breath catches as he steps up close and adjusts it, and I feel another flutter somewhere around my heart that zips me right back to when I fixed his tie earlier. I don't know what possessed me to do that, other than a need to be close to him, to fill my lungs with his cologne and have him look every inch like my partner. My professional partner, of course.

I step away, lowering my gaze. I should have stayed in the hotel room. But I can't lie; I'm intrigued to know more about him now, especially after learning he has a recent ex. Lucas looked more than a little disgruntled to hear that name brought up. What was it? Something exotic. Mabinty?

I knew there was another reason he left New York, besides the job opportunity at Evergreen. Maybe it was a really bad breakup. So bad that he felt like he couldn't stay. Maybe everything in the city reminded him of her. Okay, I'm getting carried away, letting my imagination create the story, but from the look on his face I could tell whatever happened with Mabinty hit him hard. Maybe as hard as the breakup with David hit me. I wonder what happened.

As if I've conjured him with my mind, Ayden nudges his way through the throng and slaps Lucas's shoulder dressed, as predicted, in a flannel shirt, jeans and boots complete with buckles. I'm accosted by one of the women, but as I sip my soda water and make polite responses, I can't help but overhear some of their conversation.

I'm pretty sure I hear the name Mabinty again, but I can't make out the context this time. I can only keep sneaking glances at Lucas's face. Uncomfortable doesn't cover the look on it. Why am I itching to nudge back in there and listen for real? It's absolutely none of my business. I have no reason to want to know anything about Lucas's personal life, and I need to remember that. I'm choosing motherhood over men. *Especially* men who are colleagues.

* * *

By the time we're told to gather around the huge dining table on the porch behind the house, I'm feeling better about being here. It's actually nice to talk to people I've never met. How did I forget what new perspectives that can bring?

"I knew there'd be hay bales," Lucas says with a smirk when we spot them scattered around the dance floor. A stage just off the porch seems to be featuring a rotation of wannabe musicians from guitarists to saxophonists and someone with a harmonica who only seems to know one song. Next to it, a bucking bronco sits in the corner on a padded platform, daring anyone to try their luck. The air is thick with the smell of barbecue, and I sneak in a message to Lily.

Is it weird that I kind of want a Texan ranch of my own now?

She replies:

I told you you'd have fun. You should trust me more often, sis. How is Lucas looking tonight?

You wouldn't believe me if I told you.

After I reply I shove my phone away as Lucas leans in. "So, Rose," he says up close to my ear, giving me another whiff of his cologne and sending a tingle through me. "I'm guessing you're not a fan of country music?" He lifts his hat off my head and puts it back on his, then gestures toward the stage where a guy is setting up a guitar and a mic.

"I wouldn't say I'm a die-hard fan, but I wouldn't turn it off, either." I smile, refusing the bottle as he goes to add a splash to the waiting wineglass by my checkered place mat. Despite my best efforts to maintain composure, I can't help but steal glances at his biceps straining in his rolled-up shirtsleeves as he tops up someone else's glass. I notice he himself has switched to iced tea. He catches me looking and I pull my eyes away quickly.

The sun dips lower as we tuck in to the feast. It's nothing short of mouthwatering: smoked brisket, fall-off-the-bone ribs and spicy sausage links sitting alongside the bowls of creamy coleslaw, baked beans and buttery cornbread. Juicy steaks sizzling on the grill, sides of creamy mashed potatoes and a medley of freshly picked vegetables smell so good. I promised to eat healthily, give my potential baby what it needs, but one night off won't hurt, will it? I'll just add a few more vegetables than meat chunks.

As we dig in, conversation flows easily among the group, though I'm acutely aware of Lucas's presence next to me. His laughter is rich and genuine, and it's hard not to be drawn in. I wonder what Mabinty looked like. I wonder how long they were together.

"Rose, try the cobbler," someone suggests, snapping me out of my thoughts.

"Thanks, I will," I reply, accepting the bowl as it's thrust at me. The sweet, tangy taste of peaches melts with the crumbly, buttery topping and I wish I'd bought some plastic containers for leftovers.

"My sister would love this. She's such a foodie," I tell Lucas, spearing a slice of peach. "She goes to every new steakhouse the moment it opens with Theo, and they always share every dessert wherever they go. They're obsessed."

He smiles, carving into his steak with precision. "And what about you?"

"What about me?" I say.

"What are you obsessed with?"

The way he says it makes me swallow too hard, and for a second it's a struggle not to choke on my peaches. "I guess I'm obsessed with details," I tell him. Why can I command an entire auditorium of people to hang on my every professional word, yet I can't hold a conversation with an attractive man without turning into a hot mess?

"Details?"

"I like to know things are in order," I tell him. God, I sound so boring. He must think I'm so dull. "I guess it's some form of undiagnosed OCD, or maybe I'm just a control freak," I continue, while simultaneously willing myself to shut up and stop talking. I'm not painting an attractive picture of myself here. But he's still smiling.

"What do you do when you're not working? Do you have any bizarre hobbies? Do you crochet while using a Hula-Hoop? Do you have a secret passion for taxidermy, or maybe you're a silent pro in the competitive dog grooming world on weekends?" His brown eyes sparkle with amusement as he swirls the ice cubes around in his glass.

I laugh. "Well, I wouldn't call my hobbies bizarre per se. I do like to garden. Our house has a small lawn out back that I've turned into a sort of urban oasis."

Again, yawn.

"An oasis in Chicago? That's impressive," he remarks. He sounds genuine.

"I wouldn't go that far. I have a couple of rosebushes and some herbs. It's not much, but it's enough to keep me busy and clear my head from all this baby stuff."

I pause. I didn't mean to say that.

"You mean with Lily's twins?" he asks, frowning. "Aren't they toddlers?"

"Yes…yes…toddlers. I just can't help still thinking of them as babies, you know?"

He nods again over his drink. Yikes. I hope I covered that up convincingly. It's a little too soon to tell him I'm trying for a baby on my own, so far with zero luck. It really is the worst situation for a control freak.

"Gardening can be a kind of therapy," Lucas responds thoughtfully after a pause, stabbing at a peach slice absently with his fork. He's watching a man climb onto the bucking bronco, and a few others follow him, crowding around. "My ex used to grow these tiny little tomatoes on our balcony. They never got sweet enough for us to eat. The birds didn't mind them, though."

"Mabinty?" I say. The name slips out before I can stop myself. Lucas shifts in his seat. A muscle twitches along his jawline as he takes another long sip of iced tea, the cubes clinking against the glass in the quiet that descends. Even the laughter around us sounds distant now.

"Yes," he says, setting down his fork with finality. A tension simmers under the surface, and I regret prying.

"It's just…your friend Ayden," I explain. "Sorry, I didn't mean to—" I start, but Lucas interrupts with a dismissive wave.

"It's okay. Ayden knows her, too, obviously."

The silence stretches out a moment longer and verges on uncomfortable. I have a feeling I should keep my mouth shut, but now I just want to know. "So, is she the real reason you moved to Chicago? I know bad breakups can make us switch gears pretty fast. I went through one myself, not long ago. Well, actually, I guess it was quite long ago now but you never really get over the big ones, do you?"

His eyes flicker with something unspoken, and for a second, something tender as he studies my eyes then looks away. "Let's not talk about this right now," he says coolly. "I was having a nice time."

Oh, no.

I maintain my composure as usual, but the heat creeps out from my shirt and up my cheeks as I sit back in my chair. I crossed a line. As for my babbling on about myself, too, why did I say all that?

Cries of laughter echo out from around the bucking bronco. A few people move to the dance floor and start kicking up their boots, and the moonlight shimmers across the pond behind it. I wish I could swim in it. It's the kind of pond that looks like it would be perfect for a moonlit swim; maybe I could sneak off there and hide in it for the rest of the night.

More food is brought to the table on giant heaped plates. This never-ending spread is a feast for the senses, but suddenly, I'm not even remotely hungry. This could be the perfect time to use the bathroom.

"I should probably—"

"I tried my hand at guitar once," Lucas says, halting me in action just as I'm about to excuse myself from the awkward silence. The guitarist on stage has started to play a country tune now. "My fingers didn't agree with it, though, so I switched to piano instead."

"Piano?" I raise an eyebrow in surprise. "That's something I wouldn't have guessed."

"I'm full of surprises," he murmurs. "I'm sure I also don't look like the kind of person who'd creep through a window of an abandoned building just to check the mail."

I can't suppress a smile. I'm so glad that the awkward moment has passed. "What are you even talking about?"

"There's something beautiful about places forgotten by time, don't you think? Forgotten treasures, rusty and torn-up clues about the people who used to live in them. You never know what you're going to find."

I look at Lucas for a moment, picturing him in full explorer's attire, rummaging around dusty old attics and breaking into locked basements, before shaking my head. "Well, well," I say, running a hand through my loose hair. "Doctor Bennett, you *are* full of surprises."

He nods. "The thing is it's pretty hard to find anything unexplored or abandoned in a big city. You usually have to get away into the suburbs or outskirts. The Midwest is the best, so I've heard. Maybe I'll find some fun places outside Chicago. You'd be amazed how many factories, schools, even whole neighborhoods got abandoned when places like Detroit and Toledo went under. There's this group I'm in—we travel around the country checking them out. It's called urbex. Urban exploration. Total adrenaline rush."

"I'm hooked already," I say, leaning closer. "So tell me… What's been your favorite exploration so far?"

Somehow, my earlier slipup is forgotten. My legs have swiveled on their own to face his, and his have done the same to mine.

"Well, closer to my old hood in New York, there was this abandoned mayonnaise factory on the outskirts of Brooklyn," he starts, his brown eyes lighting up with excitement. "It was massive. Completely dilapidated. Mesh metal walkways, dripping pipes… We had to climb through broken windows and crawl under rusted machines to get inside."

I listen intently as he describes the eerie atmosphere of the place and how they found a bunch of old machinery and equipment still inside. "But the best part was this old office, completely untouched," he continues, his face breaking into a grin under his cowboy hat. "There were papers scattered everywhere, like whoever worked there just got up and left one day and never went back. We found some jars of mayo, too, but we didn't dare open those."

"That's crazy," I say in amazement.

"We found some old documents and letters dating back to the nineteen-fifties. A warrant for evacuation. Reminders of unpaid rent."

"Wow," I say. "You have the best way of bringing these places to life, like I can actually see them."

His eyebrows lift. "You *can* actually see them, if you like?"

"Maybe," I say, swirling my drink. "Not that I'm into urbex or anything, but... I don't know. Sometimes I feel a bit like I've let other things in my life stay on the sidelines, you know?"

He leans in a bit, genuinely listening. "Yeah? So what's holding you back?"

I laugh lightly. "It's probably just me. I've shut myself off more than I thought, especially since the divorce. Most people don't see it—David knocked my confidence, you know? But you seem to have this...freedom."

He watches me for a moment, processing the fact that I'm divorced. I think he's going to ask me about it, like I asked about Mabinty, but instead he gets a mischievous spark in his eyes. "Maybe you just need someone to show you the ropes, as an urbex newbie."

I raise an eyebrow. "You volunteering?"

He grins. "Ever heard of any good abandoned spots around Chicago?"

I think for a second, then shake my head. "No, sorry."

His smile widens. "I'll find somewhere. Then maybe we'll go on an adventure together. See if there's a new urban explorer at this table, hmm?"

I laugh, feeling a flicker of excitement. "All right, if you promise not to get us arrested."

"Deal," he says, eyes twinkling. "Just don't blame me if you get hooked."

My heart jumps at the idea of being somewhere exciting with him. "I won't get hooked, don't worry. I'm too sensible."

"Ah, yes, there she is. The control freak." He winks, and I shove his shoulder playfully, making him laugh.

"I'm teasing you! I'm a control freak, too, goes back to my childhood. Anyone will tell you."

"Oh, yes? Why?"

His grin fades for a moment, and he shrugs. "Aren't all kids control freaks in a way?"

I look at him maybe longer than I should, eyebrows quirked, but he doesn't elaborate. I ask if he has any siblings, because I realize I don't even know.

He tells me no. "It was just me, Mom and Dad. They were both only children, too. So I had no siblings, no aunts, no uncles, no cousins."

"Then you did get to control everything," I say with a smile.

"Nah, my father did," he replies quickly, before looking away and swigging his drink.

"Oh?" He's got that darkness on his face again, the same one he had before when he talked about his dad, and it sparks a need to know more, even though I also know it's probably not the time to go into our personal histories; not that deeply, anyway.

I need to loosen up a little myself. Everything has been so intense lately, what with all the fertility stuff, and Lily's wedding planning, not to mention work. But it doesn't have to be my entire life. Maybe I *could* be the kind of person who climbs through windows with a flashlight and rummages through cobwebby corners for trinkets. At least I'd contemplate it with someone like Lucas.

What is going on with my brain? That would be a terrible idea! For a million reasons!

Before we know it, it's almost midnight. We have barely spoken to anyone else at the table and Lucas says we should go watch the guys take turns on the bucking bronco. His light, steadying touch on my lower back again makes my breath catch. It's been ages since someone has escorted me anywhere with such casual intimacy. The sensation is foreign yet comforting, and it ignites another flutter in my stomach, the kind I thought I'd never feel again after a string of terrible dates over the past couple years.

"Watch your step," he says as we approach the rodeo arena. His grip firms to guide me over the uneven ground and I can't help thinking he likes touching me as much as I like him doing it. The butterflies are mounting, causing a riot.

The cheers crescendo as another guy, who's all swagger and denim, mounts the fake bull. I think someone's put it on the highest setting because it bucks wildly in a manic dance of man versus mechanical beast, and for a moment I'm swept up in the collective thrill witnessing this bizarre spectacle. What on earth would possess someone to want to do this? Maybe Lucas is planning on it, I think in both horror and excitement. He'd look hot up there.

Then, a snap of reins and the cowboy is airborne before he's crashing down hard beyond the protective surface of the padded surroundings. The crowd's elation morphs into gasps of horror.

"Lucas!"

I don't think. I just react.

CHAPTER SIX

THE COWBOY IS lying crumpled with his leg at an unnatural angle. The pain is etched across his face as he tries to clutch his knee to his chest and fails. "I can't feel my leg too good," he grits out, panic sharpening his Texan drawl.

"Everyone, give us space!" Lucas barks to the onlookers. They obey, parting like the Red Sea. Most of them are medical professionals here and one has gone to fetch a bag already. A couple of the others are on their phones. Lucas drops to one knee beside the man right next to me.

"Keep still," he commands, stabilizing his neck, while my hands palpate for fractures.

"Sir, can you tell me your name?" I ask, needing him lucid, needing to gauge his awareness.

"Ty," he chokes out. The sweat is beading his brow. His hat is lying facedown in the dirt several feet away and his right leg is twisted unnaturally. He's clearly in agony. Hank appears through the crowd, unzipping his trauma kit, but like many of the guys surrounding us he's slightly unsteady on his feet thanks to downing a few too many cold beers, so Lucas takes over and begins preparing the necessary equipment.

"Open fracture. Lower leg—looks like the tib-fib," I tell him.

"Yeah, that's a nasty one," Lucas agrees, already pulling

out gloves and gauze pads. "Bleeding's not too bad, Ty, but we've got to splint you up pretty fast, okay?"

Ty is a medic himself from what I'm hearing in not so quiet conversation snippets all around me, and he's doing his best to cooperate through the searing pain. His eyes close suddenly and he drags a deep breath through his nose, and then another through his teeth before trying to move again.

"Hey there, can you hear me?" I keep my voice calm but firm. "I need you to stay as still as possible, all right?"

The man grimaces, beads of sweat dotting his forehead. "I'm trying, Doc…"

"Doctor Carter. Rose."

"Rose. My leg… It hurts so bad."

"I know, I know. We're going to fix you up," I reassure him while taking his pulse, checking his level of consciousness. He seems a little dopey on top of his injury but then, everyone's had a few drinks tonight. Hank leans toward the radio he has somehow produced.

"We've got a male, early forties, open fracture of the right tib-fib. Prepping him for transport. Is someone coming? What's the ETA?"

"I'm going to immobilize your leg first," Lucas says. He is already wrapping a tourniquet above the break to control any potential blood loss, and a woman is pushing through the crowd to reach them. Ty's partner? "Ready for the splint?" Lucas says, while the woman shrieks at the sight of his leg. His wife is apparently not a doctor. She's just come back from the bathroom to find her husband on the ground.

I hold Ty's leg carefully to keep it steady while Lucas's hands move deftly to place the inflatable splint around it. We all know his leg needs to stay absolutely still before they can transport him. Ty knows, too, but when you're in this much pain it's hard to think straight. Hank leans over him, his broad frame blocking the light momentarily.

"Ty. You're doing great. Okay, man? Just breathe."

Lucas meets my eyes and I bite back a smile. Hank is the trauma doctor here, but he's too drunk. Not that this was anyone's fault; accidents happen. Ty grits his teeth, but nods. "I can't feel my toes now."

I sense my expression tighten for a moment as I check his toes for any signs of circulation. "Pulses are still weak, but present," I confirm to Lucas.

"Got it. Let's get him on the backboard before the pain gets worse," he replies, grabbing the board from the three or four men who are hovering with it on the periphery, awaiting our instructions. I let them help Lucas with this one. "On three?"

Ty still doesn't quite appear to know what's going on, exactly. All he knows now is pain. "Ty, we're going to lift you now. Try to keep still. It'll hurt, but it's important."

"I know," he breathes, bracing himself.

The guys move together smoothly, lifting Ty onto the backboard, careful to keep his broken leg in the proper position.

"Ambulance is en route," Hank informs us.

I adjust the oxygen mask over Ty's face. "You're doing great. Ambulance is a few minutes out, and they'll get you some strong pain relief once you're in the truck."

Within moments, the wail of sirens cuts through the air, and the ambulance pulls up. The team moves swiftly, transferring Ty into the back of the vehicle. His wife hops in with him, and Hank shuts the doors behind them.

As the ambulance speeds off, I'm filled with both relief

and adrenaline, and beside me Lucas is wiping the sweat from his brow and putting his hat back on.

"Just another day at the rodeo," he mutters, and I can't help a snort of laughter escaping my mouth. I'm just so tired now; that was mentally exhausting.

"Everyone all right?" Hank's voice cuts through the quiet. He's still swaying slightly on his feet but his concern is more than genuine despite the alcohol that meant Lucas and I had to jump in just now.

"How are you feeling?" he asks me.

"I'm fine," I assure him, brushing back a loose strand of hair with a shaky hand. I said too much to Lucas before all that. I almost let it slip how much I want a baby, not that that's a bad thing to want I guess…but if he knew I was already in the process of doing it alone…

Why do I suddenly care so much about what he thinks?

Around us, the remaining guests are murmuring their relief. Their faces are all lit by the soft glow of the lanterns strung above the now vacant rodeo ring. "We should probably get a cab back to the hotel," I suggest.

"Sorry, guys," Hank begins, steadying himself against a nearby post. "No taxis will come out here till morning now. Stay the night, whoever needs to! Rose, Lucas, you're the heroes of the hour. I have rooms all made up in the guesthouse."

Oh. "No taxis?" I look to Lucas, searching for any sign of his own discomfort. His deep brown eyes give nothing away.

"Appreciate it, Hank," he says. Then he turns to me. "He's right. That little situation took us past the cutoff point for cabs. We could stay and get a ride back first thing in the morning? At first light, if you want?"

Hank tells us there are toothbrushes, towels, lotions and

even swimwear and robes in the drawers if we need them, and though I wasn't planning on this at all, I am kind of intrigued as to what the guesthouse might look like. Plus, the long ride back to the hotel sounds less appealing by the second. I'm exhausted.

"We'll take the rooms. Thank you," I say, just as a guy I recognize from the dinner table walks up to us and explains he has had one too many beers to drive, and so has his colleague.

Hank ushers us all toward a building in the direction of the pond. The guesthouse is a rustic little place with cedar walls that seem to blend into the surrounding greenery, and in the moonlight it looks like something out of a storybook. A carved wooden sign dangles from the eaves, engraved with the words *Eagle Lodge*.

The interior is simple but comfortable, filled with homey touches like a wood-burning fireplace and handmade quilts on the plush sofas. I look up at the ceilings with their authentic, old-fashioned wooden rafters. Then I see the giant taxidermy eagle, wings spread from its mount like it's about to take off.

"I feel like I just stepped into a movie set," I say to Lucas, and he snickers.

The guy from dinner and his colleague disappear down a hallway, leaving Lucas and me standing in the living room with Hank. "Well," Hank says, removing his hat and running a hand through his hair. "There's just one problem."

I stiffen, my heart pounding in my chest. Somehow, I know what he's going to say.

"I've only got the one room available now," Hank continues, oblivious to my horror. "You'll both have to share."

"I see," Lucas says without missing a beat. There's an

unreadable look in his eyes as they flicker toward me in the dim light. "So, we're roommates, then?"

To his credit, Hank doesn't wink at Lucas or anything. He's still trying to remain upright by the looks of it. My mind reels as I look at Lucas, hoping for a way out of this predicament, but his expression is inscrutable. For reasons I can't quite articulate, the thought of sharing a bed with Lucas fills me with a growing sense of equal dread and excitement.

"No problem, Hank," he says, "I can take the couch."

Oh. Of course he'd take the couch. Why on earth did I think he would choose to share a bed with me, as if I would have agreed, anyway? Where is my mind at?

"I can sleep anywhere, trust me," he says, shrugging at me, and I sigh and tell him thanks.

"Night, folks. Rose, your room is through there." With another somewhat weary tip of his hat, Hank lumbers off toward his own quarters, leaving us alone.

Lucas drops to the couch and removes his hat again. I drop to another padded armchair, my fingers tracing the patterned upholstery. "Well, that was…intense."

"Yeah." Lucas rubs his temples and I watch his big hands move across his head. "But you were incredible out there. On the stage, at the rodeo in a crowd of drunken cowboys… What can't Rose Carter do, huh?"

There's a dreamy quality to his voice that's both tired and awestruck and I look away as my face heats up. "Team effort," I remind him. I can't exactly accept individual praise when it was our joint capabilities that made the difference to Ty.

"Still," he insists, "you've got this…poise under pressure."

"I guess I have to, living with toddlers," I quip, trying

to deflect the compliment and his obvious admiration with humor. He's making me feel things I shouldn't be feeling, things I cannot afford to contemplate right now.

He nods, and his gaze is thoughtful, distant for a moment. For a second I am quite certain he's going to bring up something from our earlier conversation, when I as good as told him I've stayed single and pathetic, living with my sister and her children since my relationship failed. However, he merely grabs a few cushions and starts plumping them around his head with his fist before shaking off his chunky boots and lying horizontally on the couch. "Good night, Rose."

I stand as his yawn transfers to me. "Good night, Lucas."

The room is cozy enough, with warm hues of brown and orange splashed across the wallpaper, embroidered horse pillows and vintage cowboy hats hanging on brass hooks, but for some reason, I can't sleep at all. I rustle the cowboy-themed linens as I toss and turn on the bed, trying to ignore the ringing silence and the fresh rush of anxiety I can't quite place. It's been such an eventful day. And Lucas is on the other side of the wall. It's the closest I've been to a sleeping man in a long, long time, and I can't get our conversations out of my head, or the feeling that he might feel a slice of this attraction, too. He even invited me to go on some kind of urban adventure with him, as if I ever would!

Why wouldn't I?

I don't actually know. I don't know what these feelings are all of a sudden.

My eyes catch the wooden dresser in the corner of the room. Curious, I rise from the bed and open the first drawer to find an assortment of neatly folded clothes—plaid shirts, jeans, even a fringed suede jacket. It looks like an entire cowboy wardrobe. I smile to myself—Hank really has thought of everything. The second drawer presents another surprise—the swimwear he mentioned. I roll my eyes at several bikinis in various colors and patterns that wouldn't look out of place on a beach in California, along with matching sarongs and beach towels. A soft, fluffy robe lies on top in a deep shade of blue.

I hesitate for a moment before pulling out one bikini—a simple yet elegant black two-piece—alongside the blue robe, which feels invitingly soft. Well, why not? Slipping into the swimwear makes me realize how long it's been since I last enjoyed an unplanned moonlit activity like this, but the pond outside is calling me now.

Wrapping myself tightly in the robe, I step out through the back door onto the porch. The ranch is quiet. Only the chirping crickets and a distant hoot of an owl reach my ears. The moonlight bathes everything in its silvery glow as I step toward the pond, only to find there's someone else in the water.

CHAPTER SEVEN

I PUSH MY body through the water, focusing on each stroke that slices the pond's surface while my heart thuds against my rib cage. I thought I was exhausted but the adrenaline is still surging through me, from both the incident with Ty and…her. I needed to swim off my thoughts about Rose. It was killing me, knowing she was sleeping just beyond those wooden walls.

I insisted she take the bedroom, playing the gentleman of course, while I took the couch. It was the right thing to do, but damn if being that close wasn't testing my self-control. Her green eyes seem to linger in my thoughts like an unshakable melody lately—they have done since the moment we met, but she's getting to me even more after today.

I shared too much about my life, too much about my hobbies, my love of sneaking into abandoned buildings with my internet friends. Mabinty hated me doing it. Rose probably thinks I'm crazy, too, or stupid, or both. At least the fact that I never once left the table to mingle tonight meant I avoided talking about Mabs with anyone else who knew us as a couple. I still feel so damn guilty whenever someone mentions her name.

How was Ayden supposed to know I broke things off months ago? I told him tonight, but no one knows it ended in my heart long before I grew the balls to end it in person.

How do you tell your childhood best friend, teenage lover and adult partner all rolled into one that you just don't see a future together? That the thought of bringing babies into the world together makes you want to run a mile?

Above, a dome of stars shines over me, brighter than anything I ever saw in NY or Chicago. My mind runs over Rose on that stage earlier; she looked amazing. She's hot, she knows how to command a room, but whereas many women like her would have an ego the size of one of Hank's hay bales, she's got this calming energy about her that's nice to be around. And she's divorced. I wonder what that David guy did. Whatever it was, he's an idiot.

A rustle from the sidelines makes me stop in my tracks. My feet find the pond's squishy, slippery bottom and my muscles tense, ready for anything—anything except her.

"Sorry, didn't mean to startle you." Rose is looking at me almost sheepishly from the cool grass, standing there wrapped in a dark blue robe. "Looks like we had the same idea."

"Great minds," I quip, keeping my tone light, my position strategic. The dark waters are my ally now. They are hiding my current naked status. With her in the bedroom, I didn't have easy access to swimwear or a robe, and I didn't exactly expect anyone else to be out here.

"I hope you don't mind?" she says, but there's no real question for me to answer. She's already unfastening the soft belt from around her middle. I watch it slide from her slender shoulders to the ground.

"Not at all," I manage. My voice comes a shade rougher than intended. "The water's perfect."

I swallow a groan, sinking lower into the pond. Here she is, moonlight dancing on her skin, clad in a bikini that leaves little to the imagination. I force my gaze upward, toward the endless starry sky and the full white moon as she slips into the water, but it's no use. Every cell in my body is acutely aware of her presence and how little she is wearing, and the fact that I am wearing absolutely nothing.

Get a grip, Lucas. I swim to the opposite side of the pond, putting some distance between us. I can feel her watching me, her curious gaze like a physical touch on my skin.

"Sorry again," she says finally, breaking the silence. "I couldn't sleep, and I really didn't know you were out here."

"It's okay," I reply automatically. "I couldn't sleep, either."

We are both quiet for a moment, just floating in the water.

"You know," she says suddenly. "I can't believe I've never been on an actual ranch before."

I chuckle softly, grateful for her light tone. It makes a little of the awkwardness melt away, at least. "What do you think so far?"

"It's beautiful," she answers sincerely, spinning slowly in the water to take in the night sky above us. "And peaceful."

"That's one of the things I love most about it," I admit. "That and the peach cobbler."

She smiles. "That was divine. But really, I can see why he swapped the city for a place like this."

"Uh-huh." I can't seem to find any more words. Should I tell her I'm completely bare under these deceiving ripples? No. I let the secret sit heavy between us. Something else is growing by the second now, too, seeing her in this bikini. I need to say something.

"So...you said you were married once?"

Great, Lucas. That's not going to make things awkward at all.

She pauses, the water around her stilling as if awaiting her response.

"Sorry, I didn't mean to pry," I say, my words quick. "That must have come out of left field, but it's been on my mind since you said it. I know I kinda cut you off myself back there at the table, when we touched on relationship stuff."

"You said you didn't want to talk about it," she replies, floating onto her back, causing her breasts to stick out of the water and taunt me.

"I did say that." I smirk. "So I don't expect you to talk about it, either. Forget I asked."

"It's okay." Her sigh is laced with a weary kind of acceptance. "I was married once, yes—to a surgeon. Met him during my residency. We lasted eight years, before he cheated."

Her openness surprises me and her honesty pulls at something in my chest. I can almost sense the things she's not saying about her surgeon, and empathy makes me move a little closer before I remember my naked state. I move away again.

"I'm sorry to hear that," I tell her. "And I can't believe any man in his right mind would divorce you."

The words are out before I can help it and she smiles to herself, but I can see she's embarrassed.

"So, were you ever married to Mabinty?" she asks, turning the spotlight on me.

Her name from Rose's mouth is jarring, but I shake my head.

"No." I swim around her carefully as she looks at the sky. "We were together a long time, but it never got to that point."

We continue to float. The silence now is loaded despite

a roar from the cicadas. She's making a conscious effort not to float too close, not to touch me at all. I feel like she's waiting for me to talk more, and I wouldn't usually; I had no intention of even bringing it up... But something about the way she let me talk so easily earlier at the dinner table, and how great it felt to have her listen, makes the words fall out of me.

"Mabinty and I, we go way back," I start. "Since we were kids."

She turns to me. "Really? How did you guys meet?"

"She was playing soccer with some of her friends and I was just walking by when she kicked the ball a little too hard. It ended up hitting me right in the face. I cried."

"You *cried*?"

"I was eight, it hurt."

She laughs, covering her mouth before settling back into the water. "What an introduction."

"Yeah," I agree with a smile. "But that's what started our parents talking. They're from Sierra Leone." I pause a minute as the flashbacks hit me, how I'd be so excited when my father finally dropped his work to spend an hour or two just being a dad, and a husband and friend, only to watch him play the part and then go right back to his study and close the door on me.

"My parents went there once on one of Dad's business trips, a West Africa trip. I don't know...they just clicked over the connection, I guess," I continue. Rose doesn't need to know the details of how I was left with the nanny, how I begged and begged to be allowed to go, just to spend more time with my father outside the house.

"It grew into dinners and meetups for them, play dates for me and Mabs. We grew up together and then when we turned fifteen or sixteen..."

"It grew into more. That's so cute. Sounds like you two had a great relationship," she says, almost wistfully.

"We did," I reply, trying not to let my emotions get the best of me. The arguments toward the end were anything but cute. Mabinty couldn't understand my reasons for not wanting kids, because I had trouble articulating why that was, exactly. I work as hard as my father did now—a way of maintaining control of my life, I guess, and maybe if I'm honest, avoiding the chaos and emotional vulnerability that comes with parenthood. I've spent my whole life trying to justify why my dad was the way he was…why he had a kid, only to ignore him for the most part, but who knows how I'd handle having kids myself? Maybe they'd annoy the crap out of me, too. Maybe I'd also prefer to focus on my work forever. "Sometimes things just don't work out," I say.

"I know all about that," she says softly. "So, what happened?"

"She wanted to start a family," I hear myself say. The admission hangs heavy between us. "And I realized I didn't."

I glance at Rose. She's frowning slightly at the sky, like the moon just did something to upset her, and my mind flashes back again; this time to the doomed Dubai trip, the last trip I took with Mabs. The tears in that hotel room when I finally blurted out that we needed to break up for good. I didn't tell her that not only did I not want kids, I had also fallen out of love with her. How could I have told her what I knew would hurt her more?

"We were kids when we met, you know?" I say. "The two of us just…started wanting different things."

Rose turns to me, her gaze steady. "What do *you* want?"

Her question hangs in the air, bold and direct, almost like a challenge. I take a breath. "Honestly? I'm not sure."

She watches me, waiting, and I feel this pull to keep

going, even though the truth is messier than I'd like to admit. "There was always this understanding with Mabs. Like, we'd become parents someday. But it felt so far away, something for the future. And then suddenly, that future was right now, and I just—" I pause, struggling for the words. "I couldn't do it. I didn't want it."

Rose is still staring thoughtfully at the moon. "So, what happened? You ended it because of that?"

"It wasn't just that," I say, my voice dropping. "It was like, if I couldn't be the man who wanted the same things she did, then I didn't even know who I was anymore. I'd spent so long picturing this future with her, and when that fell apart, I kind of…fell apart, too. I also felt heartless, which I hate."

She looks at me, her frown deepening. "It doesn't make you heartless to admit something isn't right for you."

I glance away. Am I saying too much? She's so easy to talk to. "Sometimes it feels like it, though. Like I let her down."

Rose shakes her head. "I think it makes you honest. And brave, actually. You only get one life. You walked away from something that wasn't working."

I let her words settle over me, along with the weight of them. "I don't know about *brave*. I'm still figuring out who I am, what I want…after spending so long thinking fatherhood was just this obligation waiting to happen."

She tilts her head. "Maybe it's not about knowing exactly what you want yet. Maybe it's just about being open enough to figure it out."

I smile back as a strange sense of calm washes over me. "You are so wise. How did you get this wise?"

"I watched a lot of Oprah," she says with a smile.

I go on to explain that while Mabs and I were the picture

of a perfect couple who knew each other inside out, cracks had started to appear years before it all blew up. Behind closed doors we were barely together. All the nights she spent in the lounge drinking basil-infused cocktails with her egomaniac tech friends, while I pored over new medical studies in a different corner of the house, using earplugs so as not to hear their insufferable music. My fascination with the intricate world of genetics was more than an academic pursuit. It was my calling, my form of meditation. Like Rose's gardening. The millions of nucleotides holding the secrets of life was a world that mystified and enthralled me as much as my urban escape adventures, and Mabs didn't understand any of it. Nor did she really care.

I tell her how Mabinty went full speed into tech development while I was consumed by my medical studies. She helped launch several start-ups, even built an app that ended up trending. By our late twenties our lives had started to diverge completely, but we kept pretending everything was okay. We went out for ice cream as we always did, spent weekends playing board games or hiking in the mountains, yet the connection was fading. Our core differences grated on me for so long before I spoke up and broke her heart.

"Did you ever want kids, before your divorce?" I ask Rose. We've been talking so long now my fingers are shriveled but I don't care.

Her breath catches, and she looks away, her hands tracing patterns on the water's surface to her sides. "David and I were trying for a baby," she confesses. "That's when I found out about his affair."

"While you were trying for a baby?" My heart clenches. Instinctively, I move to comfort her, but then I halt.

Boundaries, Lucas, I remind myself.

"How long ago did this happen?"

"Six years ago."

We're quiet for a moment, processing. This guy really is an idiot.

"I ended things with Mabs six months ago," I tell her. "And you were right before. It *is* the biggest reason I left New York. I thought it would make things easier for both of us. And when the role at Evergreen came up… I just went for it."

"Are you still in touch?"

"Not really. We made a clean break," I say. "It was for the best."

Rose nods slowly. "Sorry," she mutters as if she's coming out of a daze. "I didn't mean for us to get that…personal."

"Well, neither did I, but here we are," I reply, and I meet her gaze, just as I realize I have drifted close enough to touch her, and she hasn't moved away. "Just two people in a fishpond, baring their souls."

She huffs a laugh, then puts her feet to the bottom.

"There aren't any fish in here, are there?" she says next, looking around her warily.

Now it's my turn to laugh. I'm less than a foot from her now. My fingers itch to reach out and confirm she's as real as she is raw and beautiful. This attraction is crazy; the way we can talk is so…different. I feel strangely, emotionally connected to this woman in a way I can't go back from now, and I'm pretty sure she feels it, too.

Our knees touch just for a second before I pull away and dunk under the water, needing to reset myself. I said I wouldn't do this, and she'd think even worse of me if I hit on her now, right after telling her everything about Mabinty. I'm not that guy. At least I don't want to be.

When I emerge from the water, Rose has swum to the shore. She climbs out and pulls the robe back around her, leaving me naked and alone once again. "I should at least go try to get some sleep before the sun comes up," she says, tying the belt around her waist with a definitive knot.

"Good night again," I say.

"Good night again," she says with a smile. She turns to go and right as I'm about to follow her in all my nakedness, she spins back around and I'm forced to duck back under the water. "Thanks for tonight," she says. "You have no idea how much I needed it."

CHAPTER EIGHT

The moment thirty-five-year-old brunette Sarah walks into my consultation room, I can sense her anxiety. She fidgets with her wedding ring and her glasses, and her eyes dart around nervously. I offer a reassuring smile as I gesture for her to take a seat.

"I'm fine, Doctor Carter," she says, when I ask her how she is. Then she lets out an aggravated gurgling sound before pressing her palms to the desk between us. "Okay, I'm lying. I'm nervous as hell. I… We've been trying for so long. So many times a week…sometimes several times a night, and nothing. What is wrong with me?"

I bite back a smile. This is not uncommon. Women always open up to me about this stuff. My heart aches for her, though, the second her eyes cloud over, and I feel instantly guilty that when she alluded to all the sex she's having, I started thinking yet again about Lucas. I haven't stopped thinking about him since that night in the pond two weeks ago, though I need to, badly. He is no match for me, despite every atom in my body reminding me our chemistry is off the charts. Now he's not just a colleague, he's another man who doesn't want a family. Not a good match, Rose!

As Sarah tells me about her journey into attempted motherhood, I jot down notes. Eighteen months of trying. Multiple negative pregnancy tests. The same crushing disappointment each month when her steady cycle refuses to be disrupted, despite keeping close tabs on it and having a very enthusiastic partner.

It's a familiar story, one that resonates deeply in my bones. I haven't been having any sex, obviously, much to Lily's chagrin—she wants nothing more than to see me coupled up again, or at least out having "fun"—but it's not like I haven't been doing my best to prepare my body for the art of growing and carrying a child.

I have been eating all the right things and not drinking all the wrong things, with the exception of that one night off in Texas two weeks ago. I've been doing yoga with Lily, taking folic acid, vitamin D, omega-3 fatty acids, spiritual advice from podcast hosts. Yet, according to my doctor across town, with whom I sat just yesterday, I am still not pregnant. The test was negative. I'm no closer to becoming the ideal sanctuary necessary to host a living being than I was this time last year. But I'm doing my best not to dwell. I'm keeping busy.

"We'll start with some basic tests," I explain to Sarah, leaning forward. "Hormone levels, ultrasounds, the tubes test. For your husband, we'll do a sperm analysis. Is he here?"

She scowls. "He says the problem isn't him."

That's what they all say. I almost tell her this, but of course I don't. Sarah's shoulders relax slightly. "We can arrange that," I say instead.

I walk her through each option that we might explore down the line, from medication to stimulate ovulation, to IUI or IVF, watching as hope slowly replaces the fear in her eyes. It's moments like these that remind me why I chose this field. Why I come here every day and help all these women, even though I still can't help myself. Why was my test negative, *again*? They're running more tests. I'm on more meds. Same story as before. I feel like I'm stuck in a loop, going nowhere.

As I schedule Sarah's first round of tests, my mind drifts again to Lucas. The sound of his voice, his laugh, everything he said about Mabinty, everything I said about David. I haven't opened up like that to anyone in a long time; nobody except Lily. It felt so freeing somehow. And I can't stop thinking about him now.

Dammit. I need to stop this!

The second Sarah's gone with armfuls of information and restored hope, and a planned stern talk with her husband about his sperm, Lucas's head pops around the door. He looks excited and my heart rate spikes. "Good news about Emily Hanson," he says, stepping into the room. "She's pregnant. She just called to say she did a test. She's on the way in."

I feel my mouth fall open for a second, before I remember to paste on a smile. "That's fantastic," I say, hoping my voice sounds genuinely excited. Of course, this is fantastic news. She's only been on the estrogen for a couple of weeks! She's been sticking to Lucas's revised treatment plan, too, and apparently, it's worked.

Lucas's eyebrows furrow slightly. "You okay?"

"Everything is great," I lie, shuffling papers on my desk. I'm having to force down the bitter taste of envy suddenly, and the fact that the second he's close to me, my own hormone levels do their best to prove they're not faulty in any way whatsoever. They are far from perfect. My body stubbornly resists every treatment I've tried. But I can't tell Lucas that. I'd feel so embarrassed. Already this is complicated.

He's still looking at me in suspicion as he pretends to leaf through a file.

"Such good news for Emily. She must be thrilled," I add quickly. "No doubt your amended plan had something to do with it."

Lucas's dark eyes search my face, his expression softening with concern. "Are you sure nothing's wrong? You seem…off."

His gaze reminds me of that night in Texas, the way he looked at me under the stars, and I feel a flutter in my stomach. I squash it immediately and wave away his words. He opens his mouth as if to press me further, but his eyes suddenly shift to something behind me.

"Wow. Those are something else. I'm surprised you don't have a swarm of bees and butterflies in here with *that* dominating the space."

I turn to follow his gaze toward the massive bouquet on the windowsill. I know what he means. It's a completely over-the-top, beautiful-smelling and brightly colored riot of sunflowers, daisies and bluebonnets. It is, in fact, a distinctly Texan arrangement.

"They're something else indeed," I say. "Ty sent them as a thank-you for helping him out after that unfortunate bucking bronco incident."

Lucas's eyebrows rise slightly. "Ty?"

Is it my imagination, or does he sound a little jealous?

"Yes," I reply, keeping my tone casual. "He wanted to show his appreciation. It was a nice gesture."

Lucas nods, his expression unreadable. "Very nice." His voice is carefully neutral. Then he grins, his white teeth flashing against his dark skin as he steps farther into the room, closing the door behind him. The soft click of the latch sends my heart racing harder, and I silently chide myself for this involuntary reaction. I shouldn't feel this way in his presence. This is how I started feeling around David in our early days, before we started sneaking into store cupboards to make out...before he decided our entire relationship and marriage was a disposable object he could have his fill of, then toss into the trash like a chewed-up apple core, leaving me floating round the halls like a ghost of myself, terrified of bumping into him.

"Speaking of Ty," Lucas says, pulling out his phone, "look at what he sent *me*."

"He sent you something, too?"

"*Something* is the word." He holds up the screen, revealing a photo of an enormous gleaming belt buckle, even bigger than the one Hank was wearing that night. It's pure Texas kitsch—a silver longhorn skull surrounded by intricate rope work and studded with what looks like genuine turquoise stones. I mean, it's hideous.

I can't help but laugh. "Oh, my God, that's..."

"Ridiculous? Amazing? Both?" Lucas chuckles, his eyes crinkling at the corners. I like how his eyes smile.

"Definitely both," I agree, studying the gaudy accessory instead of him, despite the fact that it's getting harder every time I see him now. "I'm starting to think you dress like a rancher every day and we just don't know about it in here."

"Damn, my secret is out," he teases. "Well, now you know, why don't you come over to my place sometime and we can break it in properly? I'll make us some authentic Tex-Mex."

My stomach does a little flip, especially when he looks away to the floor, then scratches at his neck, like he's embarrassed that an invitation like that just slipped out of his mouth so spontaneously.

Unless he's been thinking about me since Texas, like I have been thinking about him.

I can't fight the small smile that finds my mouth as I catch his gaze again quickly, before we both look away and heat flames up my neck. I can't stop imagining him in that moonlit scenario, his cowboy shirt gone, bare skin glistening in the water. Droplets cascading down his chiseled face, merging with the pond, every muscle defined against his smooth, dark skin. His eyes are usually cheerful, if analytical, but they held a new layer of intensity under the moon that night we talked, and talked, and talked. I wanted him. That's why I had to force myself out of the water the second he dunked under. I can't have him.

Before I can formulate a response to his invite, a notification pops up on his screen, obscuring part of the belt buckle photo. It's Mabinty.

Hey, I'll be in Chicago in two weeks' time for a conference. Want to meet up?

A sudden chill snakes around me, as if someone's opened a window in the sealed room. Lucas's ex. The woman he was with for years, the one he wouldn't have children with. Why is she asking to meet him now?

My eyes flick up to his face, searching for a reaction. Whatever's going on, her timing is impeccable. He more or less just asked me out. At least, he asked me over to his house, to cook for me, which Lily will say is still classified as going out, because it's outside this hospital. I am way more flustered than I want to be.

"Are you going to see her?" I ask, trying to keep my voice neutral.

Lucas blinks, running a hand over his short, cropped

hair. The mood has darkened now. He's probably forgotten that little moment we just shared. "I don't know. She still has some of my things at her place in New York. It might be a good opportunity to get them back, at least."

"What kind of things? She's not exactly going to drive here in a removal van and deliver your antique couch, is she?"

He grunts a laugh and I curse myself for the way that just sounded. I sounded like a jealous idiot. Jealous and cold, great. I don't trust myself to speak now. I'm too grouchy and emotional after the news about myself and selfishly, the news about Emily. It's not my business if he sees her on not. And yet, I can't help the overwhelming rush of envy I feel coming at me from every direction.

My pager tells me Emily and her husband, Nathaniel, have arrived, and I really have to psyche myself up. I can feel Lucas's presence beside me as we walk, even when he says nothing. That message from his ex is on his mind now, I can tell. Was it just one of many she's sent him since the breakup?

I remember how David hounded me before we finalized the divorce. He was more concerned about me damaging his reputation in the industry than he was about destroying our marriage. The fact that we'd been trying to get pregnant while he'd been screwing someone else seemed to elude him. I often wonder if he ever wanted it as much as I did, if my longing for motherhood was what caused his eye to wander in the first place. Lily hypothesized that he probably saw fatherhood as the end to all his fun, the nail in the coffin of what was left of his free time, and he just didn't know how to say it. Instead, he made a statement by pursuing someone else, forcing *me* to leave *him*. Coward.

Is Lucas like that, too? He doesn't seem anything like David.

Emily sits nervously in the chair opposite me, her fingers twisting in her lap, hope and anxiety battling for dominance on her face as her husband takes her hand. I explain how we'll do the ultrasound, and then, when she's on the table and the grainy black-and-white screen confirms she is indeed, somewhat miraculously in my opinion, pregnant, I watch Emily's face. The joy, the hope, the excitement—it's all there, shining in her eyes. It's everything I've dreamed of feeling myself, everything I've longed for. I watch Nathaniel, too. He seems elated. I used to long to see that look on David's face.

"Do you have any more questions, Emily?" I ask her, once I've explained what happens now, the scan appointments, the follow-up tests. She shakes her head, still beaming. "No, I... I'm just so happy. Thank you both so much. We are over the moon."

I answer all her questions as best I can. She's concerned the pregnancy won't reach full-term, of course, but I assure her we'll be here every step of the way, while a new heaviness settles in my chest. Everyone seems to be getting their chance at happiness. Lily with her wedding fast approaching. Emily with her pregnancy, Lucas potentially reconciling with Mabinty...

The thought of that upsets me far more than it should.

"That guy Nathaniel is gonna be a great dad," Lucas says when they've gone, interrupting my spiraling thoughts. "You know when you can just tell?"

"How?" I hear myself ask him, distracted.

"They're both already so invested. That's a good start, trust me."

There's something in his tone, a hint at a darkness I don't think I've ever heard from him except for our conversation in the pond, and when he talks about his relationship with his dad. That's affected him more than even he lets on. I watch him making notes in their file. I'm distracted again, this time by his handwriting. Neat and clear, precise and deliberate. There's a sense of order and clarity that I wish I felt inside. Instead, I just feel like I'm unraveling. Am I not a family person? Do *I* need a family, as in, a husband to do this? Can I even keep going through all this on my own, all this heartbreak? What if I just can't have children?

I force a smile when I see him look up. "Sorry, what did you say? I'm a little—"

Oh, no. Maybe I should start accepting the fact that I'm probably not built to have babies in any way, shape or form. Maybe I just can't have kids, full stop.

I think I'm having a panic attack. Oh, no, *no, no*, this is no good.

"Excuse me," I manage, just as my chin wobbles. He looks at me in alarm as I cover my face and hurry from the room, and he calls something out but I don't stop. I rush to the nearest empty room, barely making it inside before the tears begin to fall. I heave deep breaths into my lungs, trying to calm myself down. This isn't professional at all, but it also isn't fair. Why do I have to struggle as a single divorcée while everyone around me seems to be either getting pregnant at the drop of a hat, or getting the good news I so desperately want to hear? It's not fair.

I wipe my face, press my hands to the basin in the corner, then sink to the bed to try to compose myself, but the floodgates have opened and I can't seem to stop crying now. I feel like such a failure—as a woman, as an ex-wife, as a doctor. How am I supposed to go on helping others when I can't even help myself?

I am still trying to collect myself when there's a soft knock on the door. "Doctor Carter? Are you all right?" It's Lucas's voice, so full of concern now it makes my eyes pool with a fresh wave of self-pity.

"I'm fine," I call out to him, swiping at my face, trying to sound convincing. I know I keep telling him this when I probably sound anything but. He's not an idiot. I scramble for my phone to buzz Lily but it's not in my pocket. I left it on the desk. Sucking in a breath I unlock the door. It opens and Lucas steps in. He looks at me with worry etched all over his handsome face and it only makes more tears well up in my eyes.

"You don't look fine," he comments, shutting the door again behind him.

I shake my head and let out another sob. "I'm just... I'm so sorry."

Lucas steps closer. For a long moment, or so it feels, he looks like he doesn't know quite what to do with me. Then to my total shock he wraps his arms around me and against every ounce of my professional demeanor, I lean into it. "It's okay," he says softly. "I'm here, Rose."

His chest is hard under my cheek, a wall of warm human strength. I allow myself to be cradled in his strong, safe arms, nestled against his heart, which is beating now, fast, hard, like mine. In this moment with Lucas holding me tight, and without me saying a word, all my emotions come pouring out—the frustration, the sadness, the anger...all of it. It feels like I'm emptying my soul in the silence, and he's just soaking it all up. I needed this.

"I'm not usually so emotional," I mumble, my voice muffled against him. "I don't know what's wrong with me. Well, actually, I do. I can't—"

"What is it?" His hand lingers on my back and I let out a shaky laugh, tearing up again, swallowing hard. The thought is too painful to voice out loud.

"Can't what?" Lucas asks gently, stepping back to look at me more closely.

"I can't have kids," I finally blurt out. The words hang heavy in the small white room. "I don't think so, anyway."

"Oh," Lucas says softly, understanding washing over his face. He looks at me for a moment longer before his gaze drops to the floor and he nods slowly, understanding dawning in his eyes.

"I'm so sorry," he murmurs at last. "I didn't know." There's an apology in his voice and I'm taken aback by the sincerity there.

"How would you?"

"Well, we talked…in the pond."

"I wasn't just going to come out and say it, was I?"

"Okay." He nods, but I can see him processing. "You know this for sure?"

I shrug. "Not one hundred percent, no. It's just looking likely right now. Ironic, huh?"

Lucas looks like he wants to say something more but instead he takes a step forward and reaches out to gently brush my hair back from my face. His touch is soft, almost tentative, as if he's worried I might shatter into pieces any second. As if sensing my surprise, he quickly pulls his hand back, reaches for the dispenser and pulls more paper towels out. He hands them over, and puts his hands to my shoulders gently as I dab at my eyes.

"Do you want to talk about it now?"

I shake my head resolutely. The last thing I want is

pity from anyone, especially Lucas. "No, thank you. I just need…"

"Go home," he tells me. "I'll cover for you. Go home, make a big hot cup of tea and don't think about coming back until you've taken all the time you need."

I sigh. I can still feel the trace of his fingers on my skin. "Okay."

He peers down at me over his glasses. "Doctor's orders."

"Fine, thank you."

I don't understand why I just told him that; it just felt like I could, or should. I don't know a thing about what's going on in that head of his but somehow he has the power to get into mine, and I don't know what to do with it at all.

CHAPTER NINE

I SET THE grocery bags on the kitchen island, the rustle of paper echoing through the loft. Floor-to-ceiling windows frame the glittering Chicago skyline beyond my grand piano, but my mind is far from the view. Rose's words replay in my head as I swing open the refrigerator.

I can't have kids.

It's a complete surprise knowing all this now, considering how long we spent talking in Texas, but she must have her reasons for not telling me.

The organic kale crunches as I stuff it into the crisper drawer. Should I call her? Check how she's doing? It's only 6:30 p.m. She'll be home. I told her to rest. My fingers hover over my phone, hesitating.

A notification pings. It's not Rose. It's Mabinty.

Lucas, I know you said no, but please reconsider meeting me when I'm in town. I miss talking to you.

I sigh, sliding a carton of almond milk onto a glass shelf. Mabinty's coming for that tech conference. I think she's showcasing her fertility-tracking app. Ironic, given our history, or maybe not. She asked me years ago what kind of app I thought she should develop to help the most people, and this was the first thing I thought of.

The app's good, I'll give her that. Uses AI to predict optimal conception windows, integrates with smart devices. But seeing her? That's a minefield I'm not particularly ready to navigate again, even if she does want to bring me my collection of records and my vintage record player. I miss that thing; it's the only thing Dad ever gave me from his heart, instead of out of duty. I left them behind in my haste to leave New York. They're sitting in her Upper East Side apartment, collecting dust. I choose records over TV any day, but music doesn't sound the same from a stereo as it does from that old record player.

I reach for an apple, pressing my palm around its cool skin. Rose's face flashes into my mind again, the way her green eyes clouded over. Heartbreaking. I pulled her into me on autopilot, couldn't help it. My chest tightens. I didn't ask her anything more, like who is she trying for a baby with? Is she doing it alone, at a clinic somewhere else? How long has she been on this journey? I have a thousand questions now, but really, I just hope she's all right.

I want to text her and ask how she's doing. But is that overstepping? We're colleagues, nothing more. Even if I can't stop thinking about her.

The phone feels heavy in my hand. Mabinty's message glows accusingly. Rose's number tempts me. This is not an ideal situation. I take a bite of the apple, its tartness barely registering. What the hell am I supposed to do?

I settle on the couch, balancing a bowl of quinoa salad on my lap. I can't keep leaving Mabinty hanging, and the guilt gnaws at me even as I type out a response to her. I want my records back. But I have to do what's best.

I appreciate you reaching out, but I don't think meeting up is a good idea. Take care at the conference.

Send. Done. But the unease lingers. She doesn't just want to give me my records back; she wants to talk about what went wrong. She wants to ask me again why I suddenly decided I didn't want kids. She wants to remind me I'm not my father—of course she knows how my father barely looked at me when we were living in the same house—and then we'll fight and wind up in exactly the same place we are in now, because I never could find the courage to tell her how I fell out of love with her, and that *that's* the overarching reason why I wouldn't have *her* kids. I guess I've never thought about having a family with anyone else; I've never really let that sit. It was always gonna be me and Mabs, or no one.

Until I held Rose in my arms. She sends my brain to strange territories.

My thumb hovers over Rose's contact. Before I can overthink another situation, I start typing:

Hey, Rose, how are you doing?

The dots appear almost immediately. My heart rate picks up.

I'm OK. Sorry about earlier. I shouldn't have unloaded on you like that. I'm embarrassed.

No need to apologize.

Thanks, I appreciate that.

I put my bowl down on the coffee table, bring my phone closer.

Hope you're doing something fun to take your mind off things?

Oh, yes, absolutely. Having a blast.

I frown, sensing the sarcasm. What could she be up to? I know I should leave it here, but I'm enjoying waiting for her messages, knowing she's home but still talking to me. Knowing in some way I'm making her feel better.

Intriguing. Care to share?

She types again for a while, stopping and starting, and I realize I am fixated on the screen, waiting like an addict till her message appears.

I'm knee-deep in my sister's kids' finger-paint masterpiece. It's everywhere. Including my hair.

I can't help but grin to myself, picturing Dr. Rose Carter—always so put together at work—covered in rainbow splatters. Besides never feeling like I'd do fatherhood justice, I haven't spent much time around kids. I kind of kept my distance when our friends all started popping them out. I guess I never really know how to *be* around kids, how to act. Like my father? His awkwardness extended to me and there's no base to it, really; it's just how it is, how it's always been.

My only involvement with children and babies so far has been helping other people conceive them, which a psychologist would have a field day with, I'm sure. Lucas Bennett, bringing kids into the world so parents can love them, in all the ways *he* wasn't.

I type back.

Sounds like a real Picasso situation.

It really is. Thanks for checking in, Lucas. It means a lot.

I stare at her last message, warmth spreading through my chest. *It means a lot.* I like that. The quinoa salad sits forgotten on the table as I contemplate what to say next. Should I leave it there? Or...

My fingers hover over the keyboard. Indecision gnaws at me. The urban exploring event this weekend flashes through my mind—the abandoned Riverview Amusement Park just outside the city. It's been on my bucket list for ages. Exploring its decaying roller coasters and overgrown snack stands with the group, and Rose, would be fun. I'll bet she's never done anything like it.

But should I ask her? The rational part of my brain screams no. I'm her colleague, her ally. There are lines we shouldn't cross. She's trying for a baby! But I care about her now. She's snuck into a special place in my heart, and she needs something to lift her spirits, doesn't she?

Before I can talk myself out of it, I type.

Actually, I might have an idea to cheer you up. My urban exploring group is checking out the old Riverview Park on Sunday. Want to join? Promise it'll be more fun than finger painting.

I hit Send, my heart pounding. What am I doing? This is a terrible idea. I should follow up, tell her to forget it—

The three dots appear. My breath catches. They disappear. Reappear. Vanish again.

I stare at the screen as the silence stretches on. I cross to the piano, sit behind the keys. Each second feels like an eternity. What is she thinking? Is she trying to find a polite way to say no? Or worse, is she uncomfortable that I asked at all?

The dots pop up once more. I lean forward, gripping the phone so tightly my knuckles turn white.

My fingers hover over the phone's keyboard. I glance up at Lily, who's perched on the arm of the couch, peering over my shoulder while running her hands along their cat Jasper's silky back. He's purring so loudly I swear he has something to say about this situation.

"Well?" Lily prods. "Are you going to say yes or what? Don't keep him waiting!"

I chew my lower lip. "I don't know. It's complicated."

Theo, Lily's husband, looks up from where he's sprawled on the floor, building a tower of blocks with Harley and Amelia. He likes to tire them out mentally before bedtime. "Come on, Rose. When's the last time you did something spontaneous?"

I remind them how I borrowed a sexy bikini and took a moonlit dip in a pond a few weeks ago, which only wound up with me getting closer to Lucas than I should have, and then, as if on cue, one of the twins toddles over and plops a plastic dinosaur in my lap. "Rawr!" Amelia growls, grinning up at me.

I sigh through a smile, running my fingers through her cute curls. "You think I should go, too, huh?"

"Absolutely she does. Your niece is never wrong," Lily chimes in. "It's just an outing with a friend, anyway. No pressure, no expectations."

I let my fingers hover over the phone again. He knows

now what a mess I am. He knows I'm trying for a baby and he must have a million questions about that, which I don't expect to get away with not answering for long. At least this adventure would give us a chance to talk properly again outside of work, and it's not like we'll be alone. He goes to these things in a group, he told me. Besides, he's probably getting back with his ex; he's only trying to be nice to a colleague in a new place he's never lived in before.

I let a small spark of excitement ignite in my chest. Exploring the old fairground sounds just the right amount of dangerous and risky to be fun. "You know what? You're right. I need to get out of my own head."

Then with a newfound determination, I type.

Count me in!

I hit Send before I can second-guess myself, even as anticipation flutters like a flock of sparrows in my stomach.

"There," I say, setting down my phone triumphantly. "I did it."

Lily lets out a whoop of joy, startling the twins, who giggle in response. "That's my flower girl!" she exclaims, pulling me into a tight hug. I fend her off; she's always so dramatic. "Invite him for dinner after? We're doing Theo's famous lasagna on Sunday."

"I'll get the good cheese," Theo promises.

"I'll think about it," I tell them, although there's absolutely no chance I'll be asking Lucas to dinner with this lot of crazy people. I shouldn't even be going to the abandoned park with him, all things considered, but…well, screw it. It's just one day out. What could go wrong?

CHAPTER TEN

I watch Rose's green eyes widen as she takes in the skeletal structure looming against the crisp blue sky. The rusted metal of the abandoned roller coaster is creaking slightly in the breeze, and she pulls out her phone to take a photo, smiling. I adore her smile.

"Incredible, isn't it?" I say, unable to keep the excitement from my voice now that we're here. The thrill of urban exploration never gets old, but sharing it with Rose today is adding a new dimension of exhilaration. I love when someone else seems to enjoy this stuff.

She nods, snapping another photo. "It's...beautiful, in a way."

I beam at her enthusiasm. "I'm glad you came, Rose. Not everyone appreciates places like this." I can't help thinking of Mabinty as I say it. She came with me precisely once, to an old abandoned prison, and wound up calling an Uber after ten minutes, deeming it cold and creepy, which it was, but that was the point.

We're standing at the edge of Riverside Park. This sprawling space was once a bustling fairground on Chicago's outskirts, but these days it's a ghost of its former self. Overgrown weeds are pushing through cracked concrete, and faded paint peels in all directions from derelict concession stands.

"I can picture it how it used to be," Rose says, narrowing her eyes as she looks around. "In fact, I think Dad brought me and Lily here when we were kids."

The rest of our group is clustered around the base of the roller coaster, snapping photos and debating its structural integrity. I gesture toward a quieter area of the park. "Do you want to explore over there?"

Rose nods, following me down a weed-choked path. The crunch of dead leaves under our feet fills the silence between us.

"So," I begin, keeping my tone casual despite the nerves fluttering in my stomach, "how are you feeling? After the other day, I mean."

Her shoulders tense slightly. "I'm fine. Work's been busy since I got back."

I nod, sensing her reluctance. "I know. And we haven't had a chance to talk about…you know, the baby thing."

Rose's pace slows, her gaze fixed on the ground. "Lucas, I—" she starts, then stops abruptly.

My heart rate quickens. I want to know more, to understand what she's going through, but I don't want to push it. "You don't have to talk about it if you're not comfortable," I offer and she sighs, running a hand through her wavy brown hair.

"It's not that. It's just…complicated."

I sense she's nervous. We pause beside a rusted merry-go-round, looking together at the dull and chipped horses that were probably so vibrant and colorful back in their heyday. Rose traces a finger along one of the poles, lost in thought.

"These things are never straightforward," I say. "We should know."

She looks up at me. Her green eyes are filled with a mix

of emotions I can't quite decipher now, and it makes me study her harder while I get a little lost in her gaze. "No, they're not," she agrees softly after a moment, pulling her eyes away.

I hesitate, then ask the question that's been nagging at me. "Forgive me for asking this, but why are you doing this alone?"

She laughs, but it's a hollow sound. Her fingers trace along the back of a horse and its saddle as she contemplates her answer. "I guess, after my divorce, I didn't think I'd find anyone in time. And honestly? I learned not to trust men." She grimaces as she says it, flicking her gaze to me. "No offense."

"Ouch," I say anyway, feigning offense.

Rose is usually so composed, but I can see how deeply her ex-husband's betrayal has affected her. I want to tell her not all men are like that, but platitudes probably won't help, nor will they be appreciated. And I crushed Mabinty's dreams of being a mother, too, didn't I? Not by cheating, but still. The guilt still haunts me. I could have broken it off sooner, given her more time.

I listen as Rose describes her latest IVF attempt. She had more test results back this week. The embryo didn't implant, the same story as the first time it failed, a case of the uterine lining being too thin. "After all the hormones, the procedures…the fact that it failed again because of something so basic is just so frustrating. Maybe I'm just not cut out to carry a child."

"Don't say that," I tell her, leaning against the merry-go-round, being careful not to put too much weight on the aging structure. The weight of unspoken words hangs between us instead, and I find myself wishing I could do more, say more. An idea crosses my mind.

An ex-colleague of mine is starting a new trial that might help with Rose's exact issue. It's a novel approach, using platelet-rich plasma to improve endometrial receptivity. Early results have been promising, especially for women who've had previous implantation failures. He was supposed to present at the conference in Texas but something came up, otherwise she would've heard about it. I consider bringing it up, but wouldn't that be going a step too far with my colleague?

The idea plays in my head as we walk on, and I gesture toward a dilapidated fun house in the distance. "Want to check that out?"

Rose nods. "As long as there are no clowns in there. I hate clowns."

As we walk, I can't help it all spinning around in my head, like the carousel once did. The doctor in me wants to offer solutions, to bring up the trial, which I'm pretty sure could be done from Chicago, too, while the man in me, who is irrevocably attracted to this woman who's set on having a baby alone... Well, that's a complication I don't know what to do with.

"So, how did you..." I pause, not really sure how to frame it. We stop by the fun house. Its warped mirrors reflect our distorted images and Rose takes a deep breath, intercepting my question.

"I went with a sperm donor," she says.

I turn to her, surprised by the sudden admission. "Oh?" I keep my tone neutral. I don't want to spook her.

She nods, her eyes fixed on the cracked pavement beneath our feet now. "Lily went with me to choose. It was an interesting process."

"I'm sure it was," I say carefully, bending down to pick up a flier as it blows past. It's an old one, dated from the late nineties, and I show her it, before putting it in my pocket. I am genuinely curious to hear more about her donor process, even if a twinge of something like jealousy sparks in my chest as she continues.

"It's not exactly like shopping for groceries. You're looking at medical histories, hobbies, interests, physical traits. It's surreal, trying to pick the genetic makeup of your potential child from a catalog, like designing a new kitchen or something."

This is so wild, to be jealous of a guy I've never met. Who *Rose* has never met!

I listen and tell her I think she's brave as we venture inside the old fun house.

"You think I'm brave? Or are you just being nice because I said the same thing to you about breaking it off with your ex?"

I feel another twinge of guilt over telling Mabs I couldn't see her, but I forget it once she starts describing picking out the right "father" with Lily. I do think she's brave, but there's a part of me that's kind of angry on her behalf. She deserves someone amazing, someone who wants to build a family with her. Someone like me…except, that's not what I want. I'm single for the first time ever. I want to enjoy it! As soon as I find some time.

The scent of mildew greets us. Our warped reflections stretch and twist in more polished distortion mirrors lining the corridor.

"So, you definitely don't want kids of your own someday?" she says quietly, as if she's reading my mind. "Not even if Mabinty wanted to get back together?"

I frown at her. Why on earth would she think Mabs and I would get back together?

"Honestly? Growing up as an only child, I never really

got the appeal of a big family," I tell her. "It was just me and my parents, and that always felt like enough."

Rose gives me a curious look. "Really? No part of you ever wanted siblings?"

I shrug. "Not really. I mean, I overheard them more than once saying how expensive I was. Like they could barely keep up with one kid, let alone more."

Her brow furrows. "Ouch. Did they really say that?"

"Yeah," I say, trying to keep it light. "They didn't mean for me to hear it, but as soon as I did, I couldn't help feeling like a bit of a burden. Like having kids was something they might've regretted."

She nods, scowling to herself. "That's heavy."

"Exactly," I agree, a little relieved that she gets it. "It's hard not to carry that around, you know? Thinking maybe you'll end up making someone else feel like that without even meaning to."

Rose looks at me, her gaze steady. "But that's not who you are. Just because they felt that way doesn't mean you would."

I glance down, letting her words sink in. She has this strange way of making me contemplate things logically without me ever feeling judged. It's daunting, but refreshing, I guess.

I concentrate on carefully picking my way through the debris. The space looks strangely beautiful in its decay. Mirror shards catch stray sunbeams as they fracture light into fragmented rainbows across the dusty floor and she takes another photo, this time with me in it. Then, as if she's conjured it through her fear alone, a giant clown looms out at us in a button-up suit, and Rose shrieks, then trips on something in the darkness.

Laughing, I instinctively grasp her hand, offering a firm

hold as we turn around the corner. Her fingers are cold but they warm up quickly in my grip. Looking down, she's laughing, but she mutters a bashful apology and attempts to let go. I hold on. Not only is the path unclear here, but our interlaced fingers feel more right than I ever imagined, like holding her felt the other day when she cried.

What is happening to me?

Then, a piercing scream cuts through the air, stopping us both in our tracks. My body reacts before my mind catches up. I'm already turning, running back the way we came toward the sound, Rose right beside me. Her face is set in determination. All traces of our previous conversation have evaporated in the chilly air.

We round a corner of the dilapidated fairground. Rusted metal creaks under our feet as we enter an area with a no-entry sign on its gate. The source of the scream is getting clearer now: a young woman from our group, another newbie to the explorers who is maybe in her early twenties. She's sprawled at the base of a half-collapsed ticket booth.

The woman looks up as we approach and tell her we're doctors. Her face is pale and streaked with tears. "I... I was trying to get a better photo. The floor just gave way."

Rose is already kneeling beside her, her voice calm and reassuring. "I'm going to check you over, okay? Can you tell me your name?"

"Mia," the woman whimpers.

I scan the area, noting the jagged edges of the collapsed flooring. "Rose, watch out for any exposed nails or metal," I warn. The last thing I want is for her to get hurt, too.

She nods, her hands moving expertly over Mia's limbs. "Any pain when I touch here?" she asks, applying gentle pressure.

I crouch down on Mia's other side. "Mia, I need you to

follow my finger with your eyes, all right?" I check for signs of concussion, my mind running through potential injuries. This is not the first time something like this has happened on one of these adventures, unfortunately, but these are the risks we take. I hope I haven't put Rose off for good; we had just stared to have fun, despite the serious talk, and the clown.

"Her right ankle's swollen," Rose reports. "Possible fracture or severe sprain. No obvious head trauma, but we should be cautious."

I agree, impressed by how quickly we've fallen into sync, like we did at the ranch that night. "Mia, we're going to help you up, but we need to move slowly. Any dizziness or nausea?"

Mia shakes her head, wincing as we carefully help her to a sitting position.

"Lucas," Rose says, her voice low. "We need to get her to a hospital for X-rays and a proper exam."

I nod, already pulling out my phone. "I'll call for an ambulance. Can you stay with her?"

Rose's hand on my arm stops me, her fingers digging into my biceps. "Wait. The hospital is at least thirty minutes away. We could drive her ourselves—it might be faster."

I hesitate, weighing the options. "You're right. Let's do it."

CHAPTER ELEVEN

The hospital doors sweep open as Lucas and I rush Mia into the ER.

"Over here!" I guide Lucas, who's supporting Mia's weight. Her face is pale and her eyes are worryingly unfocused.

Theo, Lily's fiancé, emerges from behind a curtain, his expression shifting from surprise to concern in a heartbeat. "Rose? What happened?"

"Possible concussion, possible fracture or severe sprain to her right ankle," I explain quickly. "She fell during our... outing."

Theo's eyebrows rise slightly, but he's all business as he directs his staff. "Get her to bay three. I want a full workup—CT scan, the works."

As they whisk Mia away, the adrenaline roaring through my body starts to ebb but my hands are shaking. I hadn't realized how worked up I was until right now. I've been operating on autopilot. Lucas has been, too, I think. He sinks to a plastic chair and I sit beside him until Theo returns with his clipboard in hand. "She's in good hands. Thanks for bringing her in, guys."

"Thanks, Theo."

Theo glances at his watch. "Listen, I'm off in a couple of hours. Still on for dinner at the house tonight?"

I blink, momentarily thrown by the shift in topic. "Oh, right. Yes, of course."

Theo's gaze flicks to Lucas, then back to me. There's an expectant pause and I can literally feel the pressure building. Before I can overthink it, I blurt out, "Lucas, would you like to join us?"

Lucas looks surprised, then conflicted. "I wouldn't want to impose," he says slowly.

"You wouldn't be," I assure him, though part of me wonders if I'm making a mistake, pushing the topic when he really just doesn't want to come. I feel like I've fed him enough information today to warrant him running a mile. "It's lasagna," I hear myself say, anyway. "Award-winning, so Lily says. She's never elaborated on which award."

"Because it's a secret award she likes to give me in private," Theo says, deadpan with zero shame, and I screw up my face, tell him I didn't need to know that, and he laughs. He must have broken the ice because Lucas is smiling now. Finally, he nods.

"All right, then. Thank you. I'd love to join."

Theo looks pleased, of course. He knows exactly what he is doing here. "Excellent! I'll see you both later, then. Now, if you'll excuse me, I better get back to it."

I settle into the passenger seat of Lucas's car, my heart racing in a way that has nothing to do with the adrenaline from the ER or what just happened with poor Mia. The leather seat is cool against my back, and I draw a deep breath. I couldn't have *not* asked him to dinner, with Theo standing over us expectantly.

"That was wild, huh? Now, what's your address?"

He types the house address into his phone on the dash, and as we pull out of the hospital parking lot, my mind wanders back to our conversation earlier. I told him everything, and never once did it feel like he was judging me. In turn, he told me some stuff that hints at why he doesn't want kids...stuff that definitely stems from the way his parents were. And now I'm just conflicted. I think I am starting to want more. More than Lucas could ever give me, even if we didn't work together.

"I hope I didn't overshare earlier," I say, breaking the silence as we hit the freeway again. "About the donor and everything."

Lucas glances at me, his expression softening. "Not at all. You make me think that maybe..." He trails off, chewing his lip.

"What did I make you think about?" I ask him.

He shakes his head. "Never mind. Look, I can't show up to your place empty-handed. Mind if we make a quick stop?"

"Oh, of course not," I reply.

He pulls the car into a small shopping complex and parks. "I'll just grab a bottle of wine. Won't be a minute."

As he exits the car, I let out a breath I didn't realize I was holding. Being in an enclosed space with this man is starting to do strange things to my body and brain.

His phone buzzes on the dash, and I can't help seeing the message notification. It's from Mabinty. My stomach tightens as I read it.

I'll bring your record player. Just let me know where you want to meet.

Annoyance flares up from deep in my bones. So they *are* planning to meet.

Lucas slides back into the driver's seat, a brown paper bag in hand. "Got a nice Cabernet. I hope that's okay?"

I force a smile, pushing my thoughts about Mabinty aside. Why torture myself? "Perfect. Lily loves red wine."

He pulls a face. "You're not drinking. Right."

"It's all good," I tell him. "It's not like I'm pregnant." I can't help the way it comes out with a tone of defeat, and I roll my eyes when he turns to me. "Sorry, this must be so weird for you. I won't talk about it anymore."

He throws me a long look that tells me that it's all right, and also that there's something else he really wants to say, but doesn't know how. I question him with my eyes again, but again, he shakes his head and starts the car. My heart thuds all the way home.

The living room is a whirlwind of color and chaos as usual. Lily's started cooking and Lucas and I have settled in the lounge, where the twins are playing. Stuffed animals and building blocks litter the floor, and Lucas is sitting cross-legged amidst the mayhem with a purple feather boa draped around his neck. He's helping Harley stack a teetering tower of blocks. I can't say for sure, but it certainly seems like he's having a nice time, and it's a joy to watch them playing.

"Higher!" Amelia squeals at him, her chubby hands reaching for the sky.

Lucas grins, his earlier reservations nowhere to be seen. "Okay, but if it falls, we're blaming your aunt Rose."

I tut but I can't help the smile tugging at my lips. It's unexpected, seeing him so at ease with children. From what he was saying earlier, he hasn't really spent much time with them, and watching him now, a pang of longing hits me, sharp and bittersweet. How can I not imagine him as a father figure? But it's not what he wants. He broke up with his ex because of it, and now if anyone's going to change his mind, it's Mabinty, not me. Ugh, I need to curb this crush.

Lily emerges from the kitchen with a plate of apple slices. "Having fun, Lucas? I think the twins have found a new favorite playmate."

Before he can respond, the doorbell chimes. Theo's arrived. He has a key but out of respect he always rings the doorbell in case we're doing what he calls "lady things," whatever those are. As Lily goes to let him in and the twins reach for the apple slices, I catch Lucas's eye. He winks from within the feathers around his neck, and I feel the flush creep up my face. I busy myself with picking up some stray toys, trying to quell the butterflies in my stomach.

As usual, Theo runs upstairs to shower and when he emerges ten minutes later, his presence fills the room. The twins lunge at him, encircling his legs and waist with their little arms. "Good news," he says to me and Lucas, hauling Amelia into his arms. "Mia's been discharged. She's resting at home now, just a sprain, no lasting damage."

Lucas stands, carefully extricating himself from the sea of toys. "Well, that's good to hear. Though I'm afraid it means Rose will never want to go urban exploring with me again."

I feel my cheeks burn as he sits next to me on the couch, acutely aware of his presence beside me, in my home. "I think I've had enough excitement for one lifetime, thanks."

Lily, ever the instigator, pipes up, extracting three apple slices from Harley's fingers and replacing them with just one. "Oh, I don't know. Maybe you should keep asking her, Lucas. Who knows? She might surprise you."

I shoot my sister a look that clearly says *traitor*, but she just grins innocently and flicks her hair, curse her.

"I'll keep that in mind," Lucas says as Harley offers him

the apple slice. His tone is light and even, but his brown eyes are a low level of intensity as they meet mine, and I have to look away. I busy myself with cleaning sticky fingers and making sure no apple slices get stuck between the sofa cushions.

Over dinner, once the twins are upstairs in bed, the conversation shifts to safer topics, thankfully. Lucas grins as he digs into the lasagna. "This is seriously good. Best I've had in ages."

Lily leans in. "So, Lucas, where did you grow up? How did you get into urban exploring? Have you ever—?"

I kick her under the table. "Lily!"

Lily just grins, turning back to Theo as they start their usual back-and-forth banter, half ignoring the rest of the table.

Lucas leans into me now, voice low. "So…if I haven't completely put you off, a few of us are planning to check out the Old Prairiewood Asylum in about a month. It's this abandoned place from the nineteen-thirties, meant for the criminally insane, way out by the Cook County Forest Preserves."

I feel my eyes widening. "You serious?"

Lucas smirks. "Dead serious. There might be a séance, too. Some of the girls in the group are into that."

"All right, you've got my attention. I'll think about it."

In truth, I would probably go if he asked me, but I don't want to appear too keen. Lily turns to us. Her eyes light up as she starts to discuss their upcoming wedding.

"So, we've been thinking about how to involve the twins," she says. "We want them to be part of the ceremony, but…"

Theo chuckles. "But we're not sure how to wrangle two energetic toddlers down the aisle."

I lean forward just as Lucas does, intrigued. "We need a plan."

Lucas's face breaks into a mischievous grin. "How about if you attach crates or baskets to a couple of cute ride-on toys. They can zoom down the aisle on them and scatter petals as they go."

The image makes me laugh. "That's brilliant."

He gives me a sideways smile and I catch Theo and Lily looking at each other tellingly. "Speaking of the ceremony," I add quickly, "I'm auditioning three pianists early next month for the music."

As I speak, I notice Lucas looking at me even more intently. Our eyes meet, but Lily jumps in. "Lucas, don't you play?"

"How do you know I play piano?" he asks my sister.

My cheeks flame as Lily looks pointedly at me, then back to him. I'm going to murder her. She might as well come out and say that I've told her every single thing I know about him so far. Lily is shameless, though. "We wouldn't want you playing all night but maybe you could perform one piece at the wedding…"

"No pressure," Theo interrupts. "Obviously, we're inviting loads of staff from Evergreen, seeing as we wouldn't have met without them. It'd be so great to have a special piece from one of the staff who actually plays!"

Well, this is just fantastic. They're not so subtly trying to push us together at every given opportunity now. Lucas is never going to want to socialize with me anywhere again, let alone at their wedding.

"Guys, don't put poor Lucas on the spot," I say, attempting to change the subject. Thankfully, there's a scream from upstairs, and Theo excuses himself, quickly followed by Lily.

By the time they come back down we're making tea and talking about whether a séance is really likely to summon up any long-dead patients in an asylum on the outskirts of the city. Theo and Lily remain on their best behavior until finally, Lucas announces it's late and he has to go. I didn't even realize the time.

I walk him to his car, my heart racing in the cool night air. The silence between us feels charged now, like it always does when we find ourselves alone. He stops at the end of the driveway, turning to face me with his jacket in his arms. "I had a really nice time," he says. "The twins are great."

"They loved you," I say truthfully, and he nods, fixing his eyes on mine, which makes my heart start fluttering wildly. Then he lowers them down to my mouth, which makes it worse. This crush is irrevocable now. For a moment, I think he might actually kiss me, the way he's studying my lips. My breath catches and I feel my lust like a living thing, hot and hopeful in my throat. Maybe he wasn't scared off. But he also has that look on his face again, the one that tells me he wants to say something important and serious. He is going to address this attraction, I know it. He's not one to just kiss a woman, especially a colleague. He wants to talk about it first, and he knows by now that I'm not exactly the spontaneous type.

Or maybe he's going to announce that he and Mabinty are reassessing their relationship. I brace myself.

"Rose, there's something I wanted to mention," he starts, and I feel the prickles of anxiety start up my arms. I shouldn't do this... Look what happened with David; look how independent I've become ever since, how I've scraped myself back up from rock bottom to the point where I'm ready to be a mother, all by myself. I shouldn't. But oh, I want to...

"I wasn't sure whether to bring it up," he starts as I find myself inching closer. "But I actually know someone conducting a trial that might interest you. It might help your cause. Doctor Mei-Ling Tan."

Oh.

I root my feet to the street as Lucas continues telling me about this doctor's new approach, using platelet-rich plasma to improve endometrial receptivity that might help me, and I'm not sure what to think as my medical curiosity piques, momentarily overriding my bitter disappointment over the non-kiss.

Lucas's eyes are so dark and intense in the streetlights. "Early results seem promising, especially for women who've had previous implantation failures. I thought... well, you might want to know more about it."

I'm touched by his thoughtfulness, even though part of me kind of still hopes he'll stop talking and kiss me. I'm so torn right now, I have to keep my head on straight. I don't need a man to kiss me. I need to get pregnant before it's too late. And if he wants to help me, then, great... I guess.

"That's... Thank you, Lucas. I'd definitely be interested in learning more about this."

He smiles, and I can't help a twinge of despair as I see how happy this is making him. He doesn't want to kiss me at all.

"Great. I'll send you Mei-Ling Tan's details," he says, and he lingers a moment, holding his jacket in his arms like a barrier until he nods again and gets into the car.

As he drives away, I'm left with a swirling mix of emotions that I don't really know what to do with. I'm disappointed that he didn't just kiss me, and excited about the potential of a medical breakthrough. And more than a little concerned that my newfound independence is being threatened at every turn by my growing feelings for Lucas Bennett.

CHAPTER TWELVE

I HOLD THE ultrasound wand steady as Rose examines the screen. Denise Caldwell is biting her lip, her eyes flicking between us and the monitor. The room seems to be humming with anxious energy, but it's not all because of our patient, who's returned to see if her new treatment plan is helping.

"There," Rose says, pointing. "You can see the follicle. It's a good size."

Denise's face lights up. "So, I'm ovulating?"

Rose smiles, a warm, reassuring curve of her lips. "It looks very likely."

I wipe the gel from Denise's abdomen and help her sit up. "This means you have a real shot at conceiving naturally, Denise. Keep tracking your cycle and continue with the yoga and Pilates. And the early-morning smoothies?"

She laughs. "Green ones, every day, Doctor."

"Great," I say. "We're very optimistic."

Tears spring to Denise's eyes suddenly. "I am so beyond grateful. Thank you, both of you. This is just…the best news."

Rose hands Denise a tissue and they chat as my phone pings in my pocket. I know instinctively who it is and I feel my shoulders tense. Mabinty has sent three more messages, each one a little more insistent than the last.

I open the thread and type.

I'm sorry. I can't do this.

I hesitate for a moment, then delete it. Instead, I write:

Let's talk later.

I owe her that, I think. I send it and put the phone in my pocket.

As Denise leaves the room, Rose's shoulders slump ever so slightly. I've noticed she's been more tense than usual, ever since I brought up the trial at her place and she agreed to find out more. Her appointment with Dr. Mei-Ling Tan is today.

"How are you feeling about your call this afternoon?" I ask her.

She pauses, fiddling with a chart, then with her necklace, which tells me she's nervous. "I really appreciate you setting up the call, Lucas."

I nod, but something knots in my stomach. "You'll be in good hands. Just remember, it's still experimental."

"Every treatment was experimental once." She closes the chart with a snap. "I need to believe in something." Then she sighs and perches heavily against the desk. "Do you really think I have a chance with this?"

I rub the back of my neck, buying time. "It's not that I don't believe in the science, Rose. You know that. It's just… I don't want you to go through any more heartache. You have enough on your plate as it is."

The words fall out of me before I can stop them and I curse my stupid mouth. I just made it very obvious I've been thinking about it. And her. I cross to the window, stare too long and hard at the trees outside. There's vulnerability in her voice when she speaks and it twists my insides.

"Why do you care about this so much, Lucas?"

The question hangs in the air like a live wire. I force my back to stay turned so she can't see my face. This is an invitation. She wants an answer, an acknowledgment that there's something here, maybe? It's pretty hard to ignore how the air buzzes whenever we're alone now. It's another gamble on her part to even be asking me this, but I have to stay strong. This woman is having a baby and it's not going to be with me. Never mind that I've started to imagine a future where she's more than my colleague. Or that I'm terrified that if she fails at this, it will break her, and I can't stand the thought of her broken.

"Rose," I say, choosing my words carefully. "I care because I like to think you're my friend. And because I know what it's like to want something so badly that it consumes you."

Does she know I'm talking about her now? I think of the dinner at her house, how natural she looked holding Lily's babies, how her laughter made me feel more at home than that amazing lasagna. I'm already too involved in this woman's affairs. I should take this whole trial thing as my cue to walk away, to squash this crush once and for all. She'd never cross the line with a colleague after what happened with her husband, and we don't even want the same things.

Rose is still studying me. "Are you okay?"

"Me?" I say, taken aback.

"How are things going with Mabinty? You're meeting up when she's in town, right?"

I frown at her, scratching at my chin. The silence stretches. I'm shocked that Rose even remembers Mabs has that conference in Chicago this week.

"I didn't say I'd see her," I admit.

"Don't you want to get your record player?" she continues, and I feel myself bristle. How does she know about the record player?

"I saw a message pop up on your phone when I was in your car, on the way to my place. She was pretty sure you were meeting up, but you never said anything to me so… Oh, gosh, it's none of my business, is it, if you did or if you didn't?"

She looks at her hands now, embarrassed. So she saw that message and said nothing? I don't know how to take this. I swipe my hand across my head and jaw, also embarrassed.

"Sorry," Rose says now, flustered. "I should go take this Zoom call. Wish me luck."

I am still reeling from her words, but I catch her forearm as she walks past and squeeze it in support. She freezes under my grip. I want to say so many things. I want to show her how Mabinty is my past and not a concern for her at all, but I can't cross any lines here. She's made her decision to get pregnant on her own, and I have offered her this chance with the trial, and now I have to ignore how much I want to spend more time with her *outside* this hospital.

"Good luck," I manage.

I watch her leave the room as the knot in my stomach tightens.

It felt so unexpectedly nice being at her place the other night, playing with the twins, getting all caught up in their games and chaos. I didn't think I could ever feel so at ease in that type of situation, but with her, and Lily and Theo it just felt…natural. I want to believe that everything will work out for Rose on her own, that the science will hold, that her hope will be enough. But I also know it's a long shot, and there's me, too, now, stuck in the middle of it all.

I don't know how to feel about any of this, not about her, not about us and not about the family I've spent so long convincing myself I didn't want.

The rest of the afternoon blurs together: consultations, a quick surgery, more consultations. I catch glimpses of Rose in the hallways, in the staff lounge, always moving, always focused, but I like to think I know her a bit better now. She's a workaholic. So am I. It's one of the reasons we've worked well together since I joined the department. But like me, she works to escape whatever else she's got going on, the things she can't control as easily. Like getting pregnant. I want to ask her how the call went, but she has to come to me. It's not my business.

At five thirty I retreat to my office and close the door. I'm tired, but I still have files to look at. I lean back in my chair and stare at the ceiling, letting my mind wander. It soon wanders back to Rose.

The thing is I've always admired Rose. Even before I met her, I read about her work. She's published, respected. But over the past few weeks, that admiration has shifted gears and all I want to do sometimes is kiss her. Those eyes undo me. I see the woman behind the accolades now, too, the one who tends to a garden to keep her demons at bay, who buys feather boas for her niece, who still flinches at the mention of her ex-husband. I see her, and I care. More than I should.

My phone buzzes on the desk, pulling me from my thoughts. It's a text from Rose.

Can we talk?

My heart does a stupid little lurch.

I type back.

Sure. Where?

Her reply is immediate.

Your office.

I don't have time to wonder what she needs before there's a soft knock at the door. I open it to find her standing there, arms crossed, an unreadable expression on her face that's jarring.

"Come in," I say, stepping aside.

She walks to the center of the room but doesn't sit. I close the door and wait.

"I thought I should let you know how it went," she starts, then stops. "But, Lucas, I don't want to put you in an awkward position."

I fold my arms across my chest so as not to do something silly, like reach for her and tell her it's probably too late for that. "What do you mean?"

She takes a deep breath. "Is it something you even want to know about?"

Is she testing me? I swear she is testing me.

"Rose—" I pause. No. She's a professional. We are at work. She is probably only involving me because I'm the one who initiated her participation in the trial. And if I revoke my interest now it would only seem selfish and cold. "Tell me," I finish.

She studies my face, searching for something. Maybe she finds it, because she nods slowly and some of the tension in her features eases. She tells me how the preliminary data is promising. How so far they've seen significant improvements in endometrial receptivity in a majority of participants.

"I asked about the risks, of course," she continues. "There are risks of infection and complications, but they're minimal. Doctor Tan's biggest concern is the emotional toll. They have to make sure all participants are fully prepared for the possibility that it may not work. I have a psychological examination later this week, and then I guess we will take it from there."

I watch the flicker of doubt and fear cross her face. She feels like this is a last resort, which it shouldn't be, but that's not for me to say.

"Even so, my background makes me an ideal candidate, apparently. He said he'd be thrilled to have me on board."

"That's great, right?" I do my best to sound as happy for her as I should be.

Silence. I can almost hear Rose's thoughts whirring, calculating, weighing. "It is…great," she says after a moment, but I see the conflict blazing in her green eyes. Something beyond my control forces me to reach out a hand again. I press it to hers and she looks at it before letting out a long sigh. For the smallest moment she leans in toward me, as if she wants to rest her head against me. Then she seems to think better of it and steps away quickly, shaking her shoulders like she's shedding a weight.

"This is weird," she says, casting her gaze back to mine.

"It is, a little," I agree, but I don't know if we mean the same thing anymore. This whole situation feels like it's getting out of hand.

I think of Mabinty and the fights we had about children, and about the life we wanted to build before we started taking different paths that only led us further away from each other. Before we grew up and grew apart; not that she'd admit that's what happened. She accused me of being selfish in that hotel room in Dubai, of putting my career above everything else. Maybe she was right. Or maybe I was just scared, like Rose is now.

I've been scared my whole life that my father's emotional neglect when I was a kid might somehow transfer, that I also work too hard to give a kid the attention it would deserve, that I'd regret it, if I brought new life into the world. Rose is scared of a lot worse, but she's doing this, anyway. She is carving out a future for herself that can't involve me. All the more reason to take a big step back.

CHAPTER THIRTEEN

THE PAST SIX weeks have been a blur, thanks to work, the wedding plans and a chaotic whirl of blood tests and treatments involving multiple trips across town to yet another clinic. I can't believe how quickly time has passed since I joined the medical trial. I'm not pregnant yet, but I have more hope than ever before, and I can't stop thinking how I've got Lucas to thank for it. Not that I've had much to do with him lately.

"Everything looks great, Emily," I say, studying the ultrasound as the wand hovers over her swollen abdomen. She's ten weeks in now, and the screen shows a tiny flickering heartbeat. "Your baby's growing right on track. Look at this cute little bean. Your blood pressure is a little high, but we're monitoring that."

Emily's eyes light up and I'm happy that for the first time in a long time, I actually don't feel quite as envious of another woman's success. "I can't believe it. After so many tries, it just feels unreal, Doctor Carter."

I squeeze her hand. "Believe it. This is the home stretch for the first trimester."

"I can believe it. I keep craving red meat. Nathaniel's getting a reputation at the butcher's," she laughs, and I tell her to eat what her body asks her for. We're just discussing the potential merits of indulging in more chocolate bars when the door opens and Lucas walks in. My stomach tightens.

"How are you doing, Mrs. Hanson?" he asks our pregnant patient, flashing a warm smile.

I step back, letting Lucas take a closer look at the screen. "Emily's doing wonderfully. Strong heartbeat, perfect measurements," I announce, while watching his brown eyes crease at the corners. Why does he have to be so handsome?

I watch Lucas as he explains how the hormone support is still crucial, how and why we'll continue the progesterone, how high blood pressure is more common in pregnancies from fertility treatments, noting how my heart does its usual traitorous leap every time he looks my way, or asks me a question.

He's been distant since he told me he cared because he was my friend. I dwelled a lot on that word, the way he said *friend*. I thought there was something more in his eyes and in his tone when he said it, but maybe I was just seeing what I wanted to see. I made myself believe he wanted to kiss me. Then I made myself believe he didn't. Then I forced myself to focus on the trial and my amazing independent self because who needs a man?

If only my heart wouldn't keep calling out for something else.

As Emily leaves, I steal another glance at him. He's already looking ahead, his mind somewhere else. Back with Mabinty, possibly? I guess if he was, it would explain why he's pulled back. I keep telling myself it doesn't matter, that I'm used to being alone, that I should have learned my lesson with David, but his emotional absence stings more than I'd like to admit. I had to give him a chance to tell me if he felt the same, a chance to hear if he also thought there was something between us. But he never wanted anything more than friendship.

"How's the trial going?" he asks suddenly, charging into my thoughts.

I pause, frowning. I can't help a little bitterness seeping into my words. "You haven't asked about it until now."

He rubs the back of his neck. "I didn't want to overstep."

"It's going well," I say, feeling a bit awkward. Then I turn to him, crossing my arms. "I'm feeling pretty good, even if I've missed our conversations lately."

He nods, then shifts his weight on his feet. He waits a while, apparently considering his next words. "How's the wedding planning?"

I shrug. "I found a great pianist."

"Excellent," he says, but he looks almost uncomfortable. Was he expecting me to ask him to play after Lily and Theo almost forced him into it at our house that time? I bite my lip.

"Did you get the invite?" I ask, filling the silence. "All the staff received one."

"I got it. I'll be there," he says. "I can't miss the twins riding down the aisle, throwing those petals."

I can't fight my smile just picturing it. Theo is super excited to put Lucas's suggestion about that into action. A small part of me wishes Lucas and I could go to the wedding together, as each other's date, but that would not look in the least bit professional to the other Evergreen attendees, and of course, neither would he want to. At least I'll see him there. I try to sound casual when I ask, "Will you be bringing a date? Mabinty?"

"No," he says, and there's a finality in his tone that makes me believe him. "We've been over for a long time. I thought you knew that."

I shrug, not wanting to admit that I've been keeping tabs on him. On them. I also can't afford to notice the way he looks at me even more intently, almost questioningly, as he says it. I searched for her on social media. I know all about her fertility app, her awards for various tech accomplishments, but she's surprisingly quiet on the topic of romance. "But you met up with her, right?"

"No," he says, like he's drawing a line under it, and I bite my tongue.

"Sorry, it's none of my business."

"Is that why you keep asking?" he retorts, and I feel the blush creep right up my chest to my face before he studies me so hard I can almost feel his eyes pressing into my cheek.

"No," I say, willing my entire face to stop flaming like a forest fire. "But I'd like it if we could be honest with each other. I was starting to value our…friendship."

Friendship. Oh, why did I have to say that awful word? I need him in the friend zone, though. He's safer there. I'm safer there.

"How's the urban exploring going?" I ask. Anything to lighten the air in here, though I don't miss the smirk on his face, or the way he's picked up a pen and started tapping it absently to his thigh, as if to distract his fingers? I know mine are itching to touch him, to feel like I did when his hand was in mine that one time…that one time I've clung to. I am a crazy person. I need to stop reading into everything he says and does—this is so not me.

He drops the pen with a click of its tip. "A few friends are coming into town for it this weekend. If you're not put off by the last time, you could join us. We're finally going to the Old Prairiewood Asylum."

I hesitate. The last time I went with him on one of these

things, it didn't exactly end well with that poor woman ending up in the ER. It was reckless and stupid and…whatever, it was fun. And I've missed his company. "Sure. Why not? I love a good séance."

He looks taken aback for a minute, like he fully expected me not to accept his invitation. He stands up. "Well, I can't promise the séance but…"

"I was joking. I can't think of anything worse. Please, no séance."

He laughs and, oh my, his eyes when he laughs. I'm gone. What am I doing?

"Great. I'll text you the details," he says. Then he looks at me differently, almost apologetically. My heart falls out of step when he says, "For the record, I've missed our friendship, too, Rose."

I bite down hard on my cheeks. The word *friendship* makes me cringe, every single time, no matter which one of us says it. But it's for the best. And if he does only want to be friends, then surely I can at least try to start feeling the same way? I'm going to be a mother soon. I can feel it. So I might as well start having some fun as a single woman…in an asylum?

The door swings open, making me start. We're summoned outside to where our next patient is sitting, patiently waiting. But it's clear we have to see to someone else first. A nurse is on her knees in front of her, taking her details, but I know her.

"Ms. Tallison, what's going on?"

The black-haired woman in her midforties looks up at me. Her face is pale and her hand is gripping her stomach, the other fumbling for something to hold on to.

Lucas is on her in a second, his voice calm but clipped. "We need to examine you, Ms. Tallison. Now."

We both guide her into the exam room and shut the door behind us. She sinks into the soft chair right by the door, as if she can't move any farther. I can see it in her eyes. Panic. Real, raw panic. She's pregnant. She was trying for a year before going with IVF. She was ecstatic to get pregnant and everything seemed to be going to plan. But now something is very wrong.

"The pain," she gasps, her breathing shallow. "It wasn't this bad when I left the house. I mean it was bad, but not this…" She falters as her face scrunches up and my stomach tightens.

"Where's the pain?"

She presses her palm hard into her lower abdomen, wincing. "It's bad, I can't…"

Lucas kneels beside her, hands already moving across her abdomen, assessing. I grab the doppler from the cart and come closer, locking eyes with him for just a second. I know what he's thinking.

"Can you manage?" Lucas says, encouraging her up. His voice is steady but the set of his jaw says everything right now. "We need you to lie down."

The woman nods but hesitates, gripping the chair as if letting go will make the pain worse. I pull over the ultrasound machine. "Take it slow," I tell her, guiding her up along with Lucas, and helping her down to the exam table.

"Breathe with me," I say, setting up the machine. "Deep in through your nose. Hold it. Out through your mouth."

She tries, but the pain hits her again, hard. Her back arches, her hand flying to her stomach, her nails biting into her palms, then into Lucas's arms. Lucas moves quickly, positioning the probe on her abdomen as I adjust the screen. The image comes up, grainy at first, and then—there. The baby. It's early, but it's there. Heartbeat strong. Relief flickers through me, but it's too soon to relax. Her ovaries. That's what we need to see.

I scan lower, biting the inside of my cheek. There. The left ovary. It's swollen, twisted. Ovarian torsion. Damn.

"Lucas." I point at the screen, my voice low. He sees it, too, and his eyes narrow.

"We need to operate," he says, no hesitation. His hands are already pulling off his gloves. "Doctor Carter, can you prep her?"

Ms. Tallison's eyes widen, her breathing speeding up again. "Operate? But—but the baby—"

I step closer, keeping my voice calm but firm. "Your baby's fine. We need to untwist your ovary. It's necessary to protect the pregnancy at this point, and your future fertility. It's a quick procedure, but we need to act now."

Her lip trembles, tears welling up, but she nods, trusting us. She doesn't have a choice.

I call down to the OR, my fingers moving even faster than my thoughts. Lucas is already in motion. He glances at me, giving a quick nod, and for a second I catch a glimpse of something beneath that calm. Worry. We have to move fast.

Lucas makes the first incision. The rest of the room fades out. The ovary is twisted like a rope on itself and her blood flow is severely compromised. Time is running out.

"Clamp here," I say, handing him the instrument. He does, and for a moment I forget about the fact we've barely spoken outside work lately. We're a team; this is why we are here. Nothing else matters. I get into my head way too much when I don't keep busy, always have done. It's why I keep myself on busy mode, always.

He untwists the ovary carefully, too carefully for the

amount of time we have, but I don't rush him. We're too close. One wrong move, and she could lose it.

"Blood flow is returning," I say as the color comes back. It's like watching the life crawl back into a body. We're not out of the woods yet, not at all, but it's a start.

Lucas exhales slowly, his shoulders dropping just a fraction. He looks up at me, and his deep brown eyes are sharp. "Good?"

I nod. "Good."

Lucas closes her up, clean, efficient. By the time he's finished, it's like the whole room exhales with us. The tension breaks. Ms. Tallison is stable now, thank goodness. The baby is safe. We got to her just in time.

Outside the OR, we strip off our gowns. I lean against the wall for a second, trying to let the adrenaline drain out of me, but my heart's still pounding in my ears. Lucas glances at me.

"You all right?"

I nod and turn away, excusing myself from his presence and making for the restroom. I don't quite trust my voice just yet. There's nothing to say, not really. We did our job. That's all that matters.

I scrub at my hands. They're shaking. This will stick with me for a long time, maybe forever; the way she looked at us, the fear in her eyes. Ms. Tallison is divorced. IVF was her last shot. She's older than even me. This is literally her last resort, her only shot at motherhood.

It's not enough just to get pregnant. There are a thousand things around a pregnancy that can go wrong, and if something like this ever happened to me, when I was all alone… Lily would be there. Of course, Lily would be there. And my dad, Geoff, who's always been my rock. Mom's been in Spain for years with her new husband, Miguel, but we talk on the phone. She's here for me when I need her. My family and my friends are all I'd need.

And surely, I would find the strength to try again if something happened like this. I always find the strength to try again, all by myself, because I am strong, and I am independent and I don't need a man.

Why am I still shaking?

I'm lying to myself, that's why.

CHAPTER FOURTEEN

THE SOFT JAZZ drifting from my speakers takes me back to a cramped New York apartment, and Mabinty's perfume lingering in the air with the incense sticks she used to burn to hide the smell of her burnt food. I was always the chef in that relationship. I shake off the memories and silence the music. My coffee has already gone cold in my hands. I pour it down the sink and check the time. I need to get to the asylum soon. I'm meeting everyone there. Rose, too.

I pick out a shirt and sweater, unravel the red scarf from the hanger on the back of the closet door and check my reflection just as my phone buzzes—a text from work about an upcoming fertility case. Work. That's what I should be focusing on, not Rose's questioning emerald eyes, or the way her smile makes my chest tighten every single time.

But as I reach for my jacket, guilt gnaws at me. I never told Rose about meeting Mabinty again. It was innocent enough—just retrieving the old record player—but why did I keep it from her? I outright lied to her, actually. Why?

"Because you're an idiot," I mutter, running a hand across my head. The truth is I don't want Rose to think there's anything left between Mabinty and me. But lying by omission? That's not me. Not usually.

I zip up my jacket hard and face the mirror again. "You're making a mess of this, Lucas."

Rose's face swims before me—hurt and confusion when I pulled away after that almost-kiss outside her place, weeks ago. I was trying to protect her, protect myself. But those walls I've built because of Mabinty, because of my dad? They're crumbling every time she looks at me lately.

I'm halfway to the train when my phone buzzes again. This time, it's Rose.

Hey, just wanted to confirm this place is absolutely perfect for a séance.

My fingers hover over the keys as I smile. Keep it professional, keep it cool, Bennett. But I can't help myself.

Oh, I bet. Did you bring the sage?

I hit Send before I can second-guess myself and hurry on toward the train. I'm a little late, she's already there, probably mingling with the others in the group. Her reply comes as I descend into the subway.

Tons of the stuff. :)

That simple smiley face shouldn't make my heart race, but here we are. I shove the phone into my pocket and board the train.

"You're in trouble, Bennett," I whisper to the empty carriage. "Big trouble."

I spot Rose across what used to be the Old Prairiewood Asylum parking lot, now overgrown with weeds and a few abandoned shopping carts. Her bright red, knee-length coat stands out like a beacon against the looming gray abandoned building. She's wearing it loose over dark jeans, her chestnut hair swept into a messy bun. My heart skips a beat as I approach them. I have unwittingly worn a scarf that matches her coat.

The urban explorers are already chatting with her, and I can't help but smile at how easily she fits in. As I approach, I overhear her discussing the structural integrity of old buildings with one of the group members. I didn't know she knew about things like this, but there's probably a lot I don't know about Rose, including what it's like to kiss her.

"Lucas!" Rose calls out when she sees me, her green eyes lighting up. "I was starting to think you'd chickened out."

I grin, closing the distance between us. "Never. I love a good ghost hunt."

She grimaces but her eyes are alight with the kind of spirit I haven't seen in a while.

The asylum looming behind us is a hulking mass of crumbling brick and shattered windows. The dreary sky casts an eerie pallor over everything, which seems to match the building's foreboding aura quite fittingly. I was only half joking about the ghosts.

Rose shivers slightly, glancing back at the structure. "This place looks a bit more intense than that theme park we explored last time."

I place a reassuring hand on her shoulder, ignoring the spark of electricity at the contact. "Don't worry. We've got some pretty experienced people here."

She nods. "Including you?"

"Including me," I confirm, but I can see the apprehension in her eyes. Before I can say more, one of the group leaders calls out.

"We've found a safe entrance around back. Let's move!"

As we round the corner, a light drizzle begins to fall

from the bleak-looking sky. The group crowds around a partially boarded-up window, discussing the best way in.

"Ladies first?" I offer, extending a hand to Rose.

She raises an eyebrow. "Such a gentleman," she teases, but takes my hand, anyway.

As I help her through the window, I'm acutely aware of her closeness, the warmth of her skin against mine. She stumbles slightly on the other side, and I instinctively reach out to steady her, my hands on her waist.

"Thanks," she breathes, her face inches from mine.

For a moment, we're frozen. My heart speeds like a train on a track as our eyes lock, and for a fleeting second it feels like everyone else disappears and we're back on her driveway.

But just as quickly as it appeared, the moment is broken as one of the other explorers calls out that they've found something interesting. We both step back quickly, our hands falling away from each other. The group gathers around an old medical table covered in rusted tools and empty vials. Rose looks a little green at the sight of it all as I position myself opposite her, but I can tell she's trying to hide it.

"Looks like this was some kind of doctor's office," one of the explorers, a tall guy with shaggy hair, comments.

Rose nods absentmindedly, her eyes scanning the room. "I wonder what kind of experiments they were doing here."

I shrug, still watching her closely. "Probably better off not knowing."

The asylum's interior is exactly what I pictured, a haunting tableau of decay with a musty smell, like various things have suffered and rotted here over time, birds and rats included. Peeling paint hangs from the walls like tattered skin, and rusted gurneys litter the corridors. Our footsteps echo ominously in the cavernous space as we step around them, poking our heads into rooms that are either eerily empty or packed with dilapidated furniture, old linen carts, metal bed frames with broken springs sticking out like weapons. One room is particularly odd. I follow Rose inside as the rest of the group wanders on past us, and she stands in front of a cobweb-covered dresser and closet, standing like hollowed-out skeletons.

"It's freezing in here," Rose whispers, rubbing her arms. Her coat is such a vivid red against the monochromatic room that I feel like we're in a movie as I walk up behind her and shine my flashlight into the drawers, pulling out pieces of old yellowed paper. Bills. "They say the cold spots are where the ghosts hang out."

She shoots me a skeptical look. "Really, Lucas? Ghosts?"

I grin. "I think this was the old reception room, or office," I say, handing her the bills. She studies them in intrigue while I tell her about the building's legends.

"There's the story of the Weeping Nurse, still searching for her lost patients. And the one about the Mad Doctor. His laughter supposedly echoes through the east wing on stormy nights."

As if on cue, thunder rumbles outside, and rain begins to pelt the broken windows. Rose turns on her heel and almost bumps into me as she leads the way back out of the room. I don't miss how she folds the old papers and puts them into her coat pocket. I'm so glad a part of her is enjoying this.

Room after room reveals remnants of a past best forgotten: grime-infested tiling in echoing bathrooms, threadbare mattresses with suspicious stains and down one particularly spooky corridor, iron bars. We peer into the end room, at the bottom of a long corridor, and I can almost see a shudder ripple down Rose's spine as she takes in the scene. I tell her about a haunted cell and she rolls her eyes. "Very atmospheric. Next, you'll tell me—"

A sudden crackling sound startles us both, causing me to bump into a rusty wheelchair in our path. A shower of pebbles crumbles from the cracked ceiling, echoing eerily in the silence. Rose grabs my arm, pointedly avoiding my gaze as she playfully admonishes me. "Watch where you're going, Lucas."

"It's probably a bird," I tell her as she releases me.

"Probably." When she looks back at me from the window, there's something about those green eyes sparkling under the dim light that makes me completely forget we are standing in an abandoned asylum filled with possibly deranged spirits.

I beckon her into another room attached to this one and we start inspecting a cluster of empty patient beds. Their sheets are all yellowed and stiff with age. A small pile of tattered books sits in a long-abandoned common area at the end. Rose picks up one of them, flipping through its brittle pages with fascination, before placing it gently back on the pile.

Then, another sudden creaking sound from the previous room makes her jump. I shoot her a reassuring smile, though I can feel the hairs on the back of my neck standing up as well. I'm not going to say it out loud, but it really feels like we're not alone, even though the group is still walking around upstairs.

"Let's get out of here," I tell her, and we're almost at the door when she lets out another shriek. This one is a cry of pain.

I'm at her side in an instant, doctor mode kicking in.

"It's just a scratch," she says, clasping her hand and pointing to a rusty spring sticking up from one of the beds.

I can see the blood welling up already. It's a bit more than just a scratch. I pull out a small first-aid kit from my pocket.

"Let me take a look."

I clean the cut, kneeling on the dirty floor.

"Always prepared, aren't you, Doctor?" Rose teases.

"Well, I know how trouble follows you, flower girl."

I dab at her wound with antiseptic and hand her a Band-Aid, and her laughter fades to a soft smile as her fingers brush mine. She knows how much I've come to care about her. Even when she does something as simple as graze her hand, everything stops until I've helped her. My heart is thumping wildly against my chest. The uncomplicated act of cleaning up her wound has somehow turned into an intimate exchange, and I am trying so hard to mask the electrifying tension coursing through me.

"I'm glad we're friends again, Lucas," she says.

The word *friends* hits me like a punch to the gut. "Are you sure that's all you want us to be?"

Rose's eyes widen. For a heart-stopping moment, I think I've made a terrible mistake, voicing that question out loud. She looks at me for a brief second more before dropping her gaze to my lips. The unspoken question hangs heavy in the eerie air between us. "You're killing me," I tell her, and she moans softly, closes her eyes, bows her head low.

I gently cup her face, my thumb grazing her soft skin as I tilt her chin up. Her breath catches in her throat, followed by another moan that's dripping with every ounce of the longing I feel, too. Then, I'm not sure who moves first, but I'm kissing her, or she's kissing me. We're kissing, passionately. Her lips are soft and urgent against mine, and I pull her closer, all the weeks of pent-up longing pouring out in this one incredible kiss.

Suddenly, the sound of footsteps echoes nearby. Too

close, considering we're alone. We spring apart, breathing heavily.

"Did you hear that?" Rose hisses.

I nod, scanning the empty hallway. "It must be the others," I say, but I'm not convinced.

Another peal of thunder, closer this time, and Rose grabs my hand. We dash through the corridors, half scared, half exhilarated, bursting out into the rain-soaked parking lot. As we stand there getting drenched, Rose starts to laugh. I've never heard her laugh like this. This is something pure, untamed. It's a kind of laughter that starts deep down in the belly and jumps up through the throat to paint the air all kinds of colors I can't even describe. It's contagious, infectious even. Just the sound of it fills my senses until I lose myself in its resonance and I can't help but join in.

"Some urban explorers we are," I tell her, taking off my scarf and wrapping it around her neck.

Rose grins up at me, raindrops clinging to her eyelashes. "We're the worst," she says, and this time, it's definitely she who kisses me first.

CHAPTER FIFTEEN

The aroma of sizzling peppers and cumin wafts through Lucas's apartment. It's so cozy in here, especially with the smell of his Tex-Mex menu mingling with the pitter-patter of rain against the giant windows. I've never really minded the rain in Chicago. After today's events, I love it.

I lean against the sleek kitchen island, watching him expertly flip tortillas on the griddle as part of the meal he casually hinted he'd prepare for me weeks ago. I'm kind of flattered he remembered and offered to cook it tonight, for everyone.

Some of the urban explorers are chatting animatedly in the living area, gathered around on the two couches facing each other. They were planning on going somewhere else for food, but Lucas offered a more homely shelter from the weather. I was planning on going home myself, but after that kiss, and the offer of Tex-Mex, I thought why not, and accepted the invite to his place.

His movements when he cooks are fluid, graceful, confident—just like when he's in the operating room. I can still feel his hot mouth on mine when I close my eyes. I shouldn't have…but I wanted to. It's been a long time since I've been kissed like that.

"Rose, can you grab the salsa from the fridge?" Lucas asks, flashing me a quick smile before grabbing up some avocados.

I nod, and my fingers brush against his as I hand him the cold jar. The simple touch sends a jolt through me, and I'm right back in the asylum, kissing him like a crazy person. I couldn't have stopped if I'd tried.

The apartment is a testament to Lucas's stylish, modern taste—all traditional furnishings, metallic touches, exposed brick walls. The floor-to-ceiling windows make a breathtaking showcase of Chicago's skyline and I love how the city's lights are twinkling at us through the rain-streaked glass. But what caught my eye on the way in was the grand piano in the corner. He's set it up to be the star of the whole apartment. I bet he's an incredible player to have done this. I love the way its ebony surface is gleaming under the soft lighting, almost begging someone to play it. The thought of him playing just for me sends an illicit thrill right through to my bones, but I push it aside. I'm here as a colleague, nothing more. That kiss was a mistake.

I think.

A very sexy, super-hot mistake that I want more than anything to happen again.

I join the urban explorers as they gather around the dining table, their excited chatter filling the room. It's an apartment for hosting, not like our house, which is filled head to toe with toys and old baby stuff, which Lily says she's keeping for me, of course.

"Did you hear those weird noises in the asylum?" Cheryl shudders. "It was like…whispers in the walls or something, so creepy. And footsteps."

Mark, another explorer, shakes his head. "Probably just birds nesting in the rafters. Old buildings are full of them. You hear what you want to hear in these places."

Someone points out that they didn't really want to hear ghosts, and if they did, they would've done the séance. The conversation turns to nothing but white noise when Lucas appears with a steaming platter of fajitas. Our eyes meet, and for another electrifying moment, I'm transported back to that dimly lit room, feeling his lips on mine, his hands…

"Earth to Rose," Sarah says, snapping me out of my reverie. "What do you think? Ghosts or birds?"

I clear my throat, willing my cheeks not to flush. "As a doctor, I'd say there's usually a logical explanation for these things. But who knows? Maybe some mysteries are meant to stay unsolved."

Lucas smiles thinly and slides into the seat next to mine. I'm acutely aware of his closeness as we dig into the food, and my eyes won't stop stealing glances at him, despite me willing them not to. The way his hands move as he gesticulates, the deep timbre of his laugh—it's all so distracting. I take a sip of my drink, trying to cool the heat rising within me.

After a moment, Sarah leans in, her voice dropping to a conspiratorial whisper. "Speaking of unsolved mysteries, I could've sworn I saw you two sneaking a kiss back at the asylum. What's the story, huh?"

My fork clatters against the plate. Heat rushes to my face, and just like that, I am struggling to maintain my composure.

"I…uh—" I stammer, searching for words. Mercifully, my phone buzzes in my jeans pocket. "Excuse me," I say, practically leaping from my chair. "I need to take this."

I hurry into the hallway, beyond grateful for the reprieve. It's Lily. I answer, trying to steady my breathing. "Hey, Lil."

"Rose! How'd it go at the Old Prairiewood Asylum? Did you summon the dead with your séance?" Lily's voice is bright, teasing.

I lean against the wall, closing my eyes. "No séance, but… I kissed Lucas."

There's a brief silence, then an excited squeal. "What? Oh, my God, Rose! Details, now!"

I can't help but smile at her enthusiasm. "It just happened. In the moment. It was…"

"Amazing? Just average? Not like you imagined? Come on, give me something!"

"It was…intense," I admit, my voice low. "But Lily, it can't happen again. We work together, it's—"

"Oh, stop it," Lily interrupts. "You deserve this, Rose. Don't I keep telling you that? Accept it. It's been ages since—" She pauses abruptly. "Oh, shoot, you're still with him now?"

She sounds worried and I straighten. "Yeah, why?" Then it dawns on me. "Oh, no, Lily, I totally blanked. I'm supposed to be watching the twins tonight. It's date night for you and Theo!"

She pulls a face. I know her so well that I can literally hear it. "That is why I was calling, yes."

Reality crashes back in and I groan, pressing my forehead against the cool wall. "I completely forgot. I'm so sorry, Lily. I'll head home right away."

"Don't you dare rush home," Lily insists. "You always make these sacrifices and you know I appreciate it, but it's not expected of you. I'll ask Mrs. Hernandez next door to put the twins to bed. She's always offering to help."

I hesitate, suddenly torn between responsibility and the unexpected freedom dangling before me like a gold-plated Lucas-scented carrot. "Are you sure? I don't want to upset them. They love my stories."

"Positive. They'll love her stories, too, I'm sure. Have

fun, sis. I want all the details later. He's so very sexy, imagine what those hands could…"

"I'll be back in the morning for the grocery shop," I say quickly, then I cut her off, sucking in a deep breath as guilt and excitement bubble in my chest. It's been so long since I've been in a man's apartment, I almost don't know what I'm supposed to do next, but when I walk back in, the coffee is being served and they're still swapping stories and theories about the asylum.

Lucas catches my eye, raising an eyebrow in silent question. I give him a small nod, feeling a flush creep up my neck, and it only gets hotter when he rests a hand on my knee under the table, like he's claiming me. I like it.

Hours pass in a blur of laughter and animated discussions. As the night wears on, the light fades, the rain continues to pound at the glass and I really feel like I've made new friends, despite having to dodge a few difficult questions from Sarah about the kiss she saw outside.

When the group begins to gather their things, I linger, pretending to be fascinated by the Chicago skyline, visible through Lucas's floor-to-ceiling windows, and his vintage record player. My heart races as I hear the last goodbyes at the door, followed by the soft click of it closing.

Lucas's footsteps approach, and I can feel the tension crackling between us instantly. Neither of us speaks for a moment. The silence hangs heavy as the raindrops patter with what feels like a million possibilities.

"So," he says finally, his voice low.

"So," I repeat.

He smiles. "I didn't expect you to stay."

I turn to face him, acutely aware of how close he's standing. "I didn't expect to, either."

His eyes search mine, and I feel the last shreds of my resolve wavering.

"Rose, about earlier—"

"We probably shouldn't talk about it," I interrupt.

Lucas takes a step closer, and I instinctively back up, feeling the cool glass of the window against my shoulders through my shirt. "Maybe we should," he murmurs.

The air between us feels electric now, fully charged with a new kind of energy. I know I should leave. I should tell him it's time to get the train, time to remember my professional boundaries and what happened last time I launched into something with a colleague, but I can't bring myself to move.

"Rose," he whispers, his voice barely audible. "I meant it when I said you are killing me."

He reaches out, his fingers ghosting along my jawline. As his lips meet mine, all thoughts of propriety and professionalism vanish. In this moment, I'm not Dr. Rose Carter, divorcée, dedicated endocrinologist, responsible aunt. I'm just Rose, a woman on fire, who is allowing herself to feel and to want for the first time in far too long. This time the kiss is three times more passionate than before and I melt into Lucas, my hands tangling in his shirt as I lose myself in the moment, the heat radiating off him only fueling my desire for him. Body to body, skin on skin.

In this moment, there are no thoughts of consequences or regrets. It's just me and Lucas, and I feel like I float through every touch and every kiss, relishing it so I can dredge it back up from my memories later. Somehow, after he presses me gently to the piano keys with a noisy clunk, we end up on the piano stool and he grins against my mouth.

"Are we going too fast? I'll get us a nightcap?" He half stands, still leaning over me, and kisses me again before groaning and tearing himself away. I catch my breath, my fingers brushing the polished surface of the piano for want of something else to do with my hands now that he's clattering around in the kitchen.

The keys are cool beneath my fingertips as I plunk out a simple melody, one I learned as a child. It's been years since I've played, but muscle memory takes over. It's far from being good. I hear Lucas's footsteps behind me, followed by the clink of glass against glass.

"Your drink, my lady," he says, his voice low and intimate in the now quiet apartment.

I nod, accepting the tumbler of amber liquid he hands over. It looks like it's going to burn, but so what. Tonight I'm feeling reckless. "Thanks."

Lucas slides onto the bench next to me, our thighs touching. The warmth of his body, just one limb of it against mine, is intoxicating. "I didn't know you played," he teases.

"Very funny," I reply. "Want to show me how it's really done?"

"If you insist."

I move aside, and after he sips his drink, his long, slender fingers replace mine on the keys. Suddenly, the room is filled with a hauntingly beautiful melody. I recognize it immediately—"Clair de Lune" by Debussy. The music swells and ebbs, Lucas's hands moving with graceful ease, like he's completely at one with the music. Hypnotic. Like his kisses. At one point, he even closes his eyes. I realize I'm watching him in awe and wonder.

"That's incredible," I breathe when the final notes fade away. "Where did you learn to play like that?"

Lucas's eyes meet mine. I spot a hint of vulnerability in their deep brown depths. "My mom insisted on lessons.

She said a true gentleman should be able to play at least one instrument. My father played, too. He was pretty good."

"So why did you need lessons? Why didn't your father teach you?"

Lucas shrugs. "He didn't have time. That man was always too busy for me, remember?"

I stare at him, surprised by the sudden bitterness in his tone. He studies the keys, too thoughtfully as he continues. "And the worst part? I've become just like him, haven't I? All work, no real life outside the hospital."

"What about breaking into abandoned buildings and playing piano?" I say. I want to add "what about me?" but I think it's too soon. "You seem to have a lot more going on than you give yourself credit for," I say instead.

"I guess I find room for the things I want," he replies.

I swallow hard. "And what do you want most?"

"I don't know. That's why I work so much. I never really considered anything else other than Mabinty, and the prospect of having her kids, and now I'm…not with Mabs, and I'm definitely not having kids so…"

"She was right," I murmur, suddenly aware of how close we are, and how deep this conversation is getting. I also don't want to hear how opposed to having a family he clearly is right now. "Your mother, I mean. You are a true gentleman."

His hand reaches up, tucking a strand of hair behind my ear. "Rose," he whispers, and then his lips are on mine again. The kiss is different from our earlier ones—slower, deeper, filled with an intensity that makes my head spin. This is too much.

"I should go," I say breathlessly, standing up quickly. The few sips of drink I just had are already going to my head.

I quickly grab my bag and head toward the door. But

before I can open it, Lucas's hand reaches out to stop me. He turns me around and kisses me again, softer this time but still full of longing.

"Good night," he whispers against my lips.

"Good night," I reply, but in seconds, his hands are roaming over my body again, igniting a burning inferno inside me that would take diving into the freezing cold river to extinguish. I press myself closer to him, desperate for more contact. Our bodies move in sync. It feels like we've been doing this dance for years, and his fingers intertwine with mine as we move away from the door and into his bedroom. Inside, his hands find my waist, pulling me close.

As we fall onto the bed, I can't help but think how different this feels from anything I've experienced before. Even with David, my ex-husband, it was never like this. Lucas touches me with a reverence that makes me feel wanted in a way I've never known.

"Is this okay?" he asks, his voice husky as he hovers above me. I'm tearing at his shirt now, desperate for more of him.

I nod, unable to find words, letting my fingers do the talking. "More than okay."

What follows is a passionate exploration of each other's bodies that blows my mind with its intensity. Lucas is attentive, responsive to every gasp and shiver. His knowledge of the female anatomy seems to translate into an intimate understanding of my body that literally leaves me breathless and gasping and clutching at the sheets like a wild woman. I'm so in awe of him, but somehow my body knows just how to respond, just how to pleasure him, too. By the time he slides on the condom I am too worked up to do anything but kiss him, and when we move together, it's pretty evident our connection goes way beyond the physical. It's as if Lucas sees me—truly sees me—in a way no one else has before. The intensity of it all is so overwhelming I find I'm blinking back tears—oh, my goodness! Embarrassed, I swipe them away and he asks me if I'm all right, if I want to stop, and I cup his face in my hands, smiling through my tears. "I'm perfect," I assure him. "Don't stop."

The night stretches on in a magical blur of passion and tenderness and whispered words and a million emotions I didn't think I was capable of processing. The way he looks at me and caresses me, it's like he truly appreciates everything about me, every curve, every line, every freckle, and I hope I prove how much I appreciate him, too. When we finally collapse, spent and more than satisfied, Lucas pulls me close, his arm draped protectively over my waist.

"Stay," he murmurs into my hair, already half-asleep. There was never any question that I wouldn't, once we got naked. Besides, the last train left hours ago.

I nestle closer, under his arm. I'll remember this forever, I think, as I allow myself to drift off in his embrace, and when I wake, I blink in shock at the sunlight streaming through the window, before remembering where I am and what just happened.

I take a moment to breathe, to watch this beautiful man beside me, still sleeping peacefully, his breathing deep and even. Carefully, I extricate myself from his hold, trying not to wake him. A clock on the wall shows it's late, gone 10:00 a.m., which isn't surprising, considering we spent most of the night awake, but it's Sunday and I need to get back home. I have chores to do, I promised Lily. I drop a kiss on his lips and tell him to stay where he is, and he mumbles something about making me coffee, then promptly falls back to sleep. I can only smile. He doesn't need caffeine and neither do I; we both need more sleep, but I can't ignore my responsibilities any longer.

As I gather my clothes, my gaze falls on a shelf in the corner. The gifted buckle from the Texan ranch is a humorous feature piece that makes me smile. Records are stacked neatly across several shelves, their spines showing multiple genres, mostly jazz. Something jigs in my mind. The vintage record player in the lounge.

Keeping my footsteps at bare minimum volume, I creep back into the lounge and pad over to it, rubbing my eyes. Sure enough, it's there; I wasn't imagining it. I saw it last night of course, but it barely registered. My mind was all caught up on Lucas.

I rub my arms, the questions and disappointment mounting as fast as the thrill of the evening fades and fizzles out. Isn't this what Mabinty was going to return to him? And didn't he specifically tell me he didn't meet up with her to retrieve it?

He lied.

CHAPTER SIXTEEN

I watch as Rose's fingers glide over the ultrasound wand, the cool gel catching the light as it spreads across Mrs. Chen's abdomen. Her green eyes never leave the screen as she studies the grainy black-and-white image flickering to life.

Mrs. Chen is lying tense on the exam table, gripping the edge of her gown with pale knuckles. Her eyes dart nervously between us, trying to read something—anything—from our expressions. Rose clears her throat softly, her voice laced with the kind of compassion she hasn't extended to me for a week now, not since she snuck out of my apartment that morning.

"Mrs. Chen, I'm seeing multiple small cysts on both of your ovaries. This pattern is consistent with a condition called polycystic ovary syndrome, or PCOS." She glances briefly at me before turning back to the screen, and Mrs. Chen's breath hitches.

"So that… Is that why I haven't been able to get pregnant?"

Her voice trembles with the strain of months—maybe years—of trying and hoping and sitting in rooms like this with strangers probing and prodding her. It's nothing we haven't been through before, but knowing what Rose is going through, or *was* going through with the trial and the sperm donor, makes it hit home harder for me now, too. Not that I know where Rose is at with it all lately, because she doesn't appear to be talking to me.

I step closer, choosing my words carefully. "PCOS can make it harder to conceive, yes, but it's not impossible. The cysts can affect regular ovulation, but there are treatments that can help."

Mrs. Chen presses a hand to her chest, visibly absorbing the information. "So…there's still hope?"

Rose softens, tells her there is definitely hope, which surprises me. Usually, she leaves that part up to me, while she takes on more of a practical approach. Is she phasing me out in any way possible now, because I'm a colleague and she's slept with me, and now she's terrified people will know and start talking, like they did about her and her ex?

As we discuss treatment options, I want to kick a foot through this invisible barrier that Rose has pushed up between us. The first few days admittedly I treated it like a game, something fun we were sharing, me the cat, her the mouse. Only, she hasn't let me catch her yet. Ever since that night, my mind keeps flashing back to the warmth of her soft skin, all her curves and lines, the way she let down her guard, just for a moment, just for me. And now she's acting like nothing happened.

I push the thought aside, forcing myself back into the present.

Mrs. Chen's voice interrupts my wandering thoughts. "What about IVF?"

I nod, folding my arms as I lean against the counter, choosing a reassuring tone to tell her we'll start with less invasive approaches, lifestyle changes and medication, and Rose wipes off the ultrasound wand as Mrs. Chen processes the information, her hands finally relaxing their grip on her gown.

We wrap up the appointment, scheduling Mrs. Chen's follow-up. As she walks out, her shoulders seem lighter, but Rose is more tense than ever. She keeps her eyes on the paperwork, her voice cool, efficient. Cold, even. "We should probably go over her file in more detail later. I'll send you the updated report."

The ache in my chest tightens. "Sure," I murmur, but she's already halfway out the door. I can't take it anymore. I catch her arm gently, my frustration finally boiling over.

"Rose. We need to talk. What's going on? Do you...do you really regret what happened between us so much that you're making out like it didn't happen? I feel like one of those ghosts in the asylum here!"

Her green eyes finally meet mine. I watch a storm of emotions swirling in their depths and for the briefest of moments I think she might open up, but then her walls slam right back into place.

"Doctor Bennett, this isn't the time or place for personal discussions," she says, her tone clipped. "We have patients waiting."

As she pulls away and strides down the hall, I feel like I've been punched in the gut. What the hell happened to the woman I made love to that night? Did I dream it? I thought we connected on a deeper level, deeper than I ever connected with Mabs, now that I think about it. I thought she felt the same, but now it feels like we're back to square one—or worse.

I run a hand across my chin. This is so frustrating. I want to be mad but I'm just...well, I'm pretty hurt, actually. I'm not sure where we stand at all now, or how to fix this. All I can do is wait, I guess.

I straighten my lab coat and head to my next appointment. The day stretches on, full of patients who need my focus and expertise. But even as I immerse myself in my work, it doesn't help like it usually does. I need to know what happened.

I catch her again in the parking lot, and she pulls her red coat tight around her when I call for her, ask her again if we can talk. I must be coming off as a crazy person, but this is what she's done to me. Rose just sighs. Her green eyes scan mine for a moment before she steels herself.

"Lucas, look, it was...lovely. But I don't do emotional connections, especially not with colleagues."

Her words sting, but I push past the hurt. "Rose, I'm not your ex. I'm not David," I tell her, stepping closer. "I know we work together, but I'm not going to hurt you or make things awkward. What happened? Don't you trust me?"

She shakes her head and almost laughs, which irks me more than I let on. "What's so funny?"

She shakes her head again, tightening her jaw, and buries her chin in the collar of her coat. "I don't want anything from you, Lucas. The trial has been successful. I thank you for setting that up for me. I'm doing very well on it, so they say. There's a high chance that a sperm donor insemination will take this time."

I look at her, stunned. "You had the procedure again?" For some reason, the thought of it makes me slightly nauseated.

"Yes, I did."

"Wow, that's...um..." I swallow the stab of disappointment as it hits me, watch the leaves swirling round us in a sudden breeze. "Why didn't you tell me?" I ask her. I can't hide the disillusion in my voice and I hate it.

She lowers her head. "I didn't think you'd want to know,"

she says, and I press my hands to my head, stepping back from her. "And I was right, judging by your reaction."

"I'm just surprised you did it, after we…"

"After we what, slept together?" She sounds incredulous now. "You don't want anything else from me, Lucas, that was one night of fun and you know it."

I stare at her, completely thrown. "Yes, it was one night of fun, but I was thinking it might turn into a few more nights of fun, and maybe something else," I admit.

Rose stares at me open-mouthed, and I turn and pace away. I can't look at her anymore, knowing what she's done. This situation is pressing all my buttons about kids and families. I don't know what I want but I know what I *don't* want. I don't want to keep living in a world where Rose is being so cold and distant with me. I want *her* in my life. I know that now. I want us to at least try to see if we can be something, and to see if we can navigate what we do and don't want together.

When I look at her again, she has her arms crossed, leaning against the wall. I swear she is blinking back tears. "But… Lucas, you lied to me. You met up with Mabinty when you said you didn't."

I stare at her now, racking my brain, and she rolls her eyes like I'm an idiot, pushes herself off the wall. "The record player? The records? I saw them in your apartment. I can't start anything with a liar, Lucas, especially not one I work with, and who doesn't even want kids."

I'm still staring. So *that's* what this is about? A record player?

"You want me, but you don't want a family. And you're also a liar."

"I'm not a liar, Rose. Why are you so intent on building this case against me?"

"Just forget about it," she clips, swiping at her eyes and straightening her back. "You don't have to explain yourself. You were together a long time."

"Yes, we were," I agree with her. "And no, I shouldn't have to explain myself! You should just trust me."

"I don't," she says, her voice wobbling now. "I don't trust you. I want to, but how can I?"

I don't know what to say to that. This is her issue to deal with, a result of that stupid man she married. What can I do?

Huffing a sigh, she turns around again and makes for her car. I almost follow her but I stop myself. How can I make her understand when she's already made up her mind about me, and us, and the fact that she's now probably expecting a baby ASAP with a random dude she's never met? Now I'm not hurt, I'm mad, actually. What is up with these changing emotions? What is this woman doing to me? When she pulls away from the suddenly too quiet parking lot, I can't help but feel like I've just lost something I never really had in the first place.

The days blur into another week, a monotonous cycle of patients and paperwork. Chicago seems bigger than it ever did, a giant, cold, vast city where Rose and I coexist but barely interact, much like Evergreen General. I catch glimpses of her in the hallways, her brown hair swaying as she rushes past, always with a purpose. In joint appointments, she's efficient and polite, but never personal. A workaholic, like she said she was.

In meetings, we maintain a facade of professionalism. "Doctor Carter, your thoughts on this case?"

"The patient's hormone levels suggest we should adjust the treatment plan." She talks to me, but her eyes never meet mine. I try to ignore the persistent memory of the feel of her skin against mine. The way our bodies spoke to each other, how we guided each other, how damn good it felt inside her, body and mind. Now there's only silence. And she might even be pregnant!

One evening, still trying to get her out of my stubborn brain, I stash the record player in the closet where it can't torture me. I shouldn't have lied about meeting Mabinty, I think, as I shove it behind the rail of coats and jackets. It was the smallest white lie to me, a nonissue, something I said for Rose's benefit…kind of… I've known Mabs practically my whole life. It's not as easy as you might think, cutting ties completely. Besides, I wanted my damn record player!

But understandably, it's huge to her. Rose has been broken and lied to, and kept in the dark, and she thought I was different. She'll probably never trust me again.

In the kitchen, my gaze falls on the wedding invitation stuck to my refrigerator. Lily and Theo's names are embossed in elegant script and I trace the edges of the card. Her sister's upcoming nuptials. The wedding is this weekend already; how time flies. Everyone from Evergreen will be there. I rip the card out from under its magnet and toss it into the trash. The thought of seeing Rose all radiant as I know she will be in her bridesmaid's dress, laughing with others while barely acknowledging me, is too much to bear. I'd crack, or say something, or both, and that wouldn't be fair to anyone.

I reach for my phone. I'm sorry, Rose, I type, but please tell Lily and Theo I won't be able to attend the wedding. I hit Send before I can change my mind.

CHAPTER SEVENTEEN

My phone buzzes over the soft rustle of tissue paper filling the living room as I carefully finish wrapping another faux flower stem. Lily's working alongside me, tucking each silk blossom into its designated glass bottle for the homemade table decorations, and she looks up when I put the device back on the floor a little too hard. My stomach just plummeted through the carpet.

"Lucas can't make it to the wedding," I announce.

Lily's hands pause midwrap. "Oh, Rose. That's a shame."

I force a shrug, trying to ignore the sharp pangs of disappointment tearing through me. I know we haven't exactly been seeing eye to eye but a part of me still expected him to be there on Saturday, with the team. I don't know why.

"It doesn't matter," I say, unconvincingly. "He lied to me about meeting Mabinty. I can't trust someone who does that. It's better off this way."

Lily eyes me sideways. She hands me another flower to wrap. "Not all men are like David," she says gently. "Did you ever think maybe Lucas only lied because he likes you and was afraid of scaring you off?"

I snort, focusing intently on the delicate petals between my fingers. "Right. Because deception is such a great foundation for a relationship."

"Oh, so you want a relationship with him, do you?" She

quirks an eyebrow and smirks, and I wave her off by flapping a flower in her face. "You're being too hard on him," she continues, instantly stirring up the whirlwind of conflicting emotions that's been dormant in my belly since she took my mind off him with this wedding stuff, for all of an hour, probably less.

Part of me wants to believe that Lucas lied because he didn't want to scare me off, but David's trail of lies that ultimately led to me discovering his betrayal left me so scarred, is it any surprise that Lucas's lie was a trigger? I have to trust when to remove myself from situations that are bad for me. I tell Lily so and she sighs. "I just want you to be happy."

I manage a small smile. "I know. And I am, in my own way. I have my work, I have you… That's enough, isn't it? And I have a good feeling this time. I'll get pregnant. It's going to take. I can feel it."

"That's wonderful," Lily says, but her brow furrows slightly. "But are you sure you're ready to close the door on other possibilities?"

I nod, forcing my mind back to the sterile room at the fertility clinic just the other day: the cold stirrups, the awful, unromantic clinical process, the total opposite to how I felt that night with Lucas in his bed, and in his arms. Maybe that's why, despite my best efforts, I couldn't stop thinking about Lucas the whole time the event was happening. His warm brown eyes, his gentle hands, the way he always seems to know exactly what to say to put patients at ease, the way he knew exactly what to say and do to *me* that night.

"I…" I start, then falter. I have to come clean with my twin at least. "The truth is, Lils—and I know this is terrible—I couldn't stop thinking about him. About Lucas.

Even as she was performing the procedure, part of me was wishing…well…"

Lily's eyes widen, then soften. "Oh, Rose."

"I know, I know," I say quickly. "It's ridiculous. Maybe you're right. I've been pushing him away because I'm scared of how much I like him. I am terrified of getting hurt again. Our futures don't align. He doesn't want children, and I… I'm choosing motherhood."

"Maybe you're not giving him enough credit," Lily suggests gently. "People can change their minds, especially when they meet the right person."

I shake my head firmly. I said pretty much this exact thing to him once, and he seemed to contemplate it, but he hasn't said anything to make me think he wants kids, since. "No. I can't build a life on maybes. I already made up my mind."

"I understand," Lily says, although I can tell she's not convinced at all. She knows me, and I can read her face. "But why don't you just ask him to the wedding yourself? Give him a chance to explain, at least."

"Absolutely not," I say, more sharply than I intend. "He's made his decision. He won't be at the wedding, and I'm not going to give him any other signals that I want him there. That's final."

Lily raises her hands in surrender. "Okay, fine, have it your way. I just hate to see you close yourself off like this. You don't have to always be so independent, you know."

"I appreciate your concern, Lil. I do. But this is what's best for me right now."

I grab for another flower and wrap it so tightly that it breaks. I let myself fall back on the carpet, blinking at the ceiling while she offers to pour me a glass of wine. I refuse, obviously. I could be pregnant already. But I can't help wondering if I'm truly convincing Lily I don't want Lucas around, or totally failing to convince myself.

The alarm blares through the clinic. My heart lurches. The emergency code rarely goes off in the fertility department, and my thoughts go to Emily Hanson. Please, not her. She's here now, with Lucas, I think? I move fast down the hall into Room 3B. It's not Emily I find.

Annika Ackerman is curled up on the bed, her face twisted in pain. She's thirty-four, three months pregnant via IVF, and alone. No partner today. No support. Her skin is ashen, and she's gripping her stomach with one hand, the other clawing at the sheets. Lucas is already with her.

"Tell me," I say, moving to his side.

"I—I can't breathe," Annika gasps, her words ragged. "My chest—something's wrong."

I glance at Lucas as he fiddles with an IV. This isn't right.

"She was short of breath and having hot flashes while waiting, but the chest pain hit as soon as she got up to follow me," Lucas says.

My stomach twists. "What's her status now?"

"Vitals are all over the place. Blood pressure's crashing, heart rate's spiking."

He radios down to ER. "We might need backup up here. Possible thromboembolism."

I check the IV, my own voice tightening. "Pulmonary embolism? A clot?"

"One of the risks post-stimulation, even though we hardly ever see it."

Lucas is listening to the radio. "They're sending people up now."

Annika's gaze locks on to mine, her eyes wide with

panic. "I—I can't—" She can hardly speak and her body is trembling. We need to stabilize her now, or this could get worse before anyone's even made it up the elevator. I think of Theo downstairs and pray he's on shift. My hands work before my mind catches up. If the clot moves and blocks anything vital she could go into cardiac arrest.

Annika lets out a low, pained groan. Her hand grips my wrist, cold, shaky. "Am I dying?" she whispers, and it makes my chest constrict.

"No," I say firmly, and Lucas echoes me, though a ripple of fear travels up my spine. "No, you're not dying. You're going to be fine."

The room feels smaller, the air heavier. I can hear Lucas barking orders, but it's all background noise now. We've barely spoken and now we're literally fighting for someone's life together. It puts everything into perspective, really, all the silly grudges we hold on to, all the things we leave unsaid.

It feels like a lifetime before Theo rushes in with the heparin and administers it swiftly. Annika's body responds with a series of jerks, and for a horrifying second I think we might be losing her. "Breathe in. Focus on me," I tell her.

She locks eyes with me, but there's a glassiness there. She's fighting it, but she's fading fast. I swallow. I can't do anything now; it's out of my remit. Theo barks more orders at the guys he came in with and Lucas puts a steady hand to my arm. I lean into him, needing his calmness. These situations rattle me more than they should, knowing I could be pregnant. I won't know for sure, not for a couple of weeks yet, but I might be.

They're pushing more oxygen now, trying to stabilize her as her body fights the clot. Annika's breathing is still ragged, but she's holding on. My voice cracks and I have to leave the room. Lucas follows me, and I turn into him. "We can't lose her, not like this," I tell him, and he puts his hands to my shoulders, steadying me.

"We won't." He knows this is a close one but I can see he's not going to give up, and neither should I. Back in the room the seconds morph into an eternity as the team works tirelessly to save her. The frantic pace of it all finally slows as Annika's vitals begin to stabilize. A little of the suffocating fear recedes from my bones and Theo nods at Lucas, recognition of a job well-done.

Theo presses a hand to my shoulder briefly as they wheel her out, down to the ICU where she'll receive round-the-clock care, and where I will be sure to check on her shortly. As the double doors swing shut behind them, it's just Lucas and me left standing in the emptied room. His gaze sweeps over my face before landing on my trembling hands, still clenched tightly around my lab coat.

"She's in the best hands," he tells me.

"I know." I let out a long sigh. "I thought she might be Emily."

He looks at me in surprise, gently tells me Emily's appointment is next, and I know he knows I'm applying worst-case scenarios to every single one of our pregnant patients. He knows me, and he knows why. I meet his eyes. I want to tell him I'm done with acting like I don't want him around, that Lily was right. I've been pushing him away because I like him so very much, more than I want to, but the words stick in my throat. What if I'm pregnant? He'll want nothing to do with me then, so why would I walk willingly into another disappointment?

I'm saved anyway by my phone, but it's a message from the pianist. My stomach drops as I read it, and I rest my head back against the wall with a sigh.

Now? Really?

"Damn," I mutter. "Of course this would happen now, when my nerves are already shot."

Lucas throws me a questioning look and I shake my head. "The piano player for the wedding. He broke his arm, falling off a ladder. The wedding's tomorrow. I need to make some calls."

I excuse myself, making my way to the cafeteria. I get a coffee, and fresh adrenaline takes over as my fingers fly over the phone screen, reaching out to every musician I know within a fifty-mile radius. No luck. Panic starts to set in. I thought I had everything under control, but I don't. I need to pull it together.

When I return to the exam room, Lucas is finishing up with Emily Hanson's latest exam. I tell her hi, and Lucas looks at me over his glasses. "Any luck?"

I shake my head, defeated. "Nothing. I'm out of options."

Emily looks between us, her hand on her belly. I explain what has happened. Over the recent weeks, Emily has come to know about Lily's wedding, and I've actually come to consider her as more of a friend. I'm excited to meet her and Nathaniel's baby soon.

There's a moment of silence as the three of us think. Then, hesitantly, Lucas speaks up. "I... I could do it. If you want."

I blink, surprised. "What? I thought you couldn't come. You RSVP'd no."

I realize Emily is still looking, but at this point, I don't even care. He told me flat out that he wasn't coming to the wedding, and I haven't questioned him on that decision since, despite wanting to. But now, not only is he changing his mind about attending, he also wants to replace the pianist. I look at him, considering it. Right now he's my only option.

"Are you sure?" I ask him.

"Absolutely," he says, his dark eyes meeting mine. "I um…maybe I was too quick with that RSVP, huh?" He looks at Emily, who suppresses a giggle, then back to me. "Anyway, look at what Theo—Doctor Montgomery—just did for me…for us," he says.

Us.

He said there could have been an us, and again I pushed him away. Too scared that he'd change his mind for one reason or another. But he's not David.

I take a deep breath. "Okay. Thank you, Doctor Bennett. Really."

As Emily leaves, wishing us both luck, Lucas lingers. "Rose, about Mabinty… I'm sorry. I should have been upfront with you. I promise, no more white lies."

My heart clenches. I want to tell him it's okay, that I forgive him because I kind of have a feeling I know why he did it, but that would open up a whole other can of worms. What if I'm pregnant already? I can't afford to let this friendship slip into anything other than purely platonic territory, not this time.

"Maybe I overreacted," I tell him instead. "I'll see you tomorrow. Thank you again."

Without another look at him, I leave the room, then the hospital. I guess the next time I see Lucas, it'll be at the wedding. I'll just have to be okay with it. But at some point on the drive home, it strikes me that when Emily looked like she knew something was going on with me and Lucas, I didn't even worry. I wasn't the least bit concerned what people would think. There are bigger issues in a hospital and Lucas *isn't* David. He's proven that already. And all of this is why it's going to be a thousand times harder letting him go.

CHAPTER EIGHTEEN

I CAN'T TAKE my eyes off her. The soft curves of her shoulders, the way her chestnut hair is cascading down her back—she's breathtaking in that dress. A magnificent honor. As if sensing my gaze, Rose turns and our eyes lock. The Botanic Garden takes on an ethereal quality as I step onto the cobblestone path and start toward her across the courtyard.

Fairy lights are twinkling in the trees over the throngs of people milling around the tall reception tables, all looking suave in suits and gowns, sipping from flutes of champagne. Her lavender dress catches the light in all the right places, highlighting her incredible figure as she chats with a man I assume is her father, Geoff. I've heard her mention him a few times. And her mother is here, too. She looks just like Lily and Rose, and she's here with a man. Her second husband, Miguel, I think. I've heard Rose mention her, too. A jolt of longing courses through me as she finally excuses herself and makes her way over, her heels clicking against the stone. I straighten my tie, suddenly aware of every move I make.

"Lucas." Her tone is warm but guarded, just as I expected. "Thanks for coming. And thank you again for agreeing to play piano for the ceremony."

"Of course," I reply as her green eyes dart around,

searching. Then I lower my voice. "Rose, please don't act like I'm a stranger."

"Did you come alone?" she asks, ignoring my plea but still failing to sound casual.

"Yes, just me, just like I said," I say, accepting a flute of fizzing liquid as the waiter passes us.

"Well, I'm glad you're here. Lily will be thrilled."

"How is she doing?" I ask in an effort to keep the conversation going. I wish I didn't still want her. She's already made it pretty clear that our one night together was as far as things will ever go, that her priority is motherhood, not a relationship. And I know I don't want any part of that. So why can't I get her out of my head?

"Nervous, excited. You know Lily," she replies, still looking around her. I frown. It's like she doesn't even want to be seen with me. "I should actually go check on her. But I'll see you up there?"

"Absolutely. I'll be at the altar."

She looks up sharply and I shrug. "At the piano?"

Rose's smile doesn't quite reach her eyes as she tells me she'll see me later. I watch her make her way back through the crowd, leaving her perfume lingering behind. This is every bit as awkward as I thought it would be. What am I even doing here? I feel like I owe it to Theo, though, and Lily, too. I've been practicing the songs nonstop in my apartment, over and over, losing myself in the music, thinking about Rose, of course.

When it's time for the ceremony, I settle onto the piano stool, my fingers poised over the keys. I let the lilting melody of Pachelbel's Canon fill the air as Lily appears at the end of the aisle. She's a vision in ivory lace, her dress hugging her curves, flaring out into a dramatic train on the red-carpeted aisle. I play on while all eyes stay glued to her, and damn if I can't stop seeing Rose in her place. The perfect bride. They're not identical, but they look pretty damn similar from here.

Cameras snap, and more fairy lights set a storybook scene around the ivy-clad pillars and white silk-draped chairs. Tears glisten in Lily's eyes as she takes her first steps toward Theo, waiting in his tailored gray suit at the altar. They really are the perfect couple, everyone agrees. But even as the twins appear in their little wheely cars, throwing petals out behind them, and my fingers keep on with the melody, my gaze keeps drifting to Rose, following her sister. Our eyes lock again and for a moment, it's like we're the only two people in the room. I fumble a chord, my fingers suddenly clumsy on the keys.

Rose's lips quirk into a small smile, and I feel a flush of heat rush to my face. I force myself to focus on the music, on Lily's evident, radiant happiness as she meets Theo at the altar and takes her stance opposite him. But my traitorous eyes keep finding Rose.

As the officiant begins to speak, my mind wanders over long conversations with Mabinty about our own wedding. The arguments about venues, guest lists, even the damn napkin colors. It all seems so trivial at this moment, but now I can see beyond those trivialities. I think we both secretly knew it would never happen. I think she knew it, too. We were both dancing around the inevitable for far too long.

"Do you, Theo Matthew Montgomery, take Lily Anna Carter to be your lawfully wedded wife?"

I wonder if Mabinty's found someone new. The thought doesn't sting like I expected it to. Instead, I feel…nothing. The realization is quite liberating. I hope she finds happiness.

"I do," Theo's voice replies, clear and confident.

I transition into a softer piece as Lily and Theo exchange rings, and the twins giggle, rallying around them. Rose catches my eye again and this time, I don't look away. There's a warmth in her gaze now that draws me in, a different look, almost…regretful.

"You may now kiss the bride."

I play the final chords as Lily and Theo share their first kiss as husband and wife. The applause drowns out the music, but I can't tear my eyes away from Rose. She's clapping, beaming at her sister, but again and again, her eyes keep drifting back to mine, especially when she catches the bouquet.

Of course, she would catch the bouquet, and of course I force my eyes away when she does, but the same thing continues between us all the way through dinner. The speeches make everyone cry, including Rose from her seat at the head table. The pull toward her is magnetic, almost visceral. It doesn't help that I'm seated between two colleagues and positioned directly in her line of sight. I try to focus on my meal, on the conversations around me and the three-piece band when they start to play, but my attention keeps drifting back to Rose. The way she laughs at something Lily says, the graceful movement of her hand as she reaches for her glass—it's all so captivating that I keep missing people's words, even when several attractive women talk to me and try to tell me how great my piano pieces were.

After the plates are cleared and the band encourages everyone onto the dance floor, I watch as Rose excuses herself from the head table. At first, I think she's going to the ladies' room, but she pauses and turns around, then starts walking straight toward me. My heart rate picks up as she approaches and stops before me, a new determination set on her face.

"Doctor Bennett," she says, "care to dance?"

I can't help smiling as I stand, smoothing my jacket. "I thought you'd never ask, Doctor Carter."

She bites back a smile of her own, but even as we step onto the dance floor, surrounded by people we know, the tension between us makes it feel like we're plugged into electrical sockets. Her perfume fills my senses as she steps closer to me. We move together as the music swells around us and our bodies find a natural, effortless rhythm like they did in my apartment that night, skin on skin. I need to move on from this. But she's stuck in my head like a record, even when she's not right in front of me.

"You look beautiful," I tell her into her ear. The words tumble out before I can stop them. "I haven't been able to take my eyes off you all night, you know that?"

A blush creeps up her neck, but her gaze remains steady. "Is that so?"

"You know it is," I hear myself growl. "Rose, I—"

She cuts me off, her fingers tightening on my shoulder. "Lucas, let's not complicate things. We work together. People here can see us. It's—"

"I'm not your ex," I remind her again. I want to do bad things to her in this dress, tell her all the things I've been keeping in, in the only way I know how. By using my hands, my fingers, my entire body. She sighs, long and hard.

"I know you're not my ex. I'm so sorry I compared you to him. You're the opposite of him. You're…"

"I'm what?"

I pull her slightly closer, emboldened by the music, the atmosphere, the way she just fits right against me. "I'm yours. I want you. And I think you feel the same. You wouldn't have asked me to dance if you didn't. You wouldn't have agreed to let me play. I feel you watching me, Rose."

Rose looks up at me. "And I feel *you*. All the time. Everywhere."

The torture is clear in her emerald eyes and for a moment, I think she's going to pull away. Instead, she leans in and moans softly, right before her hand sweeps up to the back of my neck. Her lips press to mine in a kiss I know she didn't plan on, any more than I did. It's soft, lingering, filled with the aching I've been feeling, too. My hand cups her face; the other finds her waist but just as quickly, she pulls back. The aching transfers to her voice when she whispers at me, directly into my ear.

"It's a three-minute walk to my hotel room. Do you want to get out of here?"

The sex is just as incredible, if not more incredible than before. We move together like our bodies already know each other inside out. But I tell myself not to read into it, to just enjoy Lucas Bennett as we fall backward onto the hotel bed. He strips off my clothes with a fervor that sends shock waves of lust right down my spine and through every single inch of me.

I've been feeling his eyes on me all day and it's been turning me on so much, I couldn't deny myself another taste of him, whatever the consequences might be. I am done pushing him away. If he's happy with a casual thing, until I become a mother and start my new life, the life I've always dreamed of, then I'll be just fine with that.

His hands are rough and determined as they throw my shoes to the floor with my dress, but gentle as they trace delicate lines across my body. I could burst into flames of desire under this man. I can feel myself getting lost in his touch, forgetting everything else except the pure lightning-bolt pleasure through my veins as we become entwined on the hotel bed. I hear myself let out a deep, throaty moan that echoes off the cobalt blue walls.

"Oh, God," I mutter. "This is insane, Lucas."

His fingers trace circles around my palm as he continues kissing my neck, sucking and licking, picking up where we left off all those weeks ago, only he's a beast unleashed right now, someone who's clearly decided he wants me and wants to show me exactly how much. I'd be pretty terrified of what this all means if I wasn't so completely enraptured. "This is what you do to me, Doctor Carter."

I can feel his erection pressing against my stomach now, and I can't help but grind against him in anticipation. Why have I been denying myself…this? He pulls away from my neck, sucking on my earlobe as he whispers, "Do you want this? Do you want more of me?"

His voice is rough with lust and I nod and reach for him in turn, unable to form any words as he starts trailing kisses down my chest and teasingly nipping at my nipples. It feels like I'm being branded by fire, but I want more. I've never let a man this close to me emotionally, as well as physically, and I arch into him as he lowers his head between my legs. He takes a deep breath through his nose, inhaling me deeply, letting his fingers tease at me.

"So beautiful, every part of you, Rose." His breath fans across my skin, sending chills down my back. "I could never get enough of you." His lips on me make my toes curl as he begins to lick and suckle, and I gasp and writhe underneath his swirling tongue. He is driving me wild, tracing figure eights, and I grasp for him, pulling him closer to me with my legs, rocking my hips against his mouth. The friction only heightens the sensation coursing through my body. All I can think is how much more of this incredible feeling it's possible for me to handle without exploding.

He must be thinking the same, because he groans and repositions against me and thrusts. I shudder at the feeling of being one again. I love how our tongues dance hungrily as we move in sync, finding that rhythm we always find together, faster this time, harder, more animalistic. Maybe it's the thrill of the hotel room, the noise of the wedding downstairs, knowing we've been dancing circles around each other all this time, but it's so raw and intimate, and when we finally slow, it's like our bodies might have known each other before, in a different life or a different time, maybe. I fall into the magic of it all, taking over, climbing on top of him before we both finish this too soon.

My nails dig into Lucas's shoulders, leaving small red marks as I urge him closer. Slapping skin, rustling bedsheets, steamed-up windows. It's the most erotic encounter of my life so far. We make love two, three, maybe four more times. I lose count. It all blurs into one breathless tangle and we can't get enough of each other, but eventually, we can't hide out for much longer. People must be looking for the maid of honor by now.

The taste of him lingers on my lips as we walk back to the wedding party. My heart is still a speeding train. I'm torn between the urge to reach for his hand and the need to maintain a respectable distance. I sneak a glance at him as he goes for a well-earned drink, admiring how his suit hugs his broad shoulders, and how he's covertly hidden the wrinkles in his shirt quite expertly under his jacket and tie. I hope my face isn't too flushed. My lipstick was so smudged I just had to do my whole makeup again.

He catches my eye and smiles, and I feel high from our dirty little secret. We avoid each other for the best part of an hour, before he corners me in a quiet hallway away from the crowds.

"I've missed you," he groans, urging me close, pressing his lips to mine.

"That was…" I start, unsure how to finish the sentence. I'm too busy kissing him, melting right back into him.

"Incredible," Lucas offers, his deep voice tinged with amusement.

"Amazing," I agree, grinning under his mouth.

"There you two are!" Lily's voice cuts through the moment. My sister appears in a whirl of white lace, her face flushed with happiness and champagne. "Where have you been hiding?"

I open my mouth, but no words come out. Lucas smoothly steps in. "Just catching up. It's been a while."

Lily's eyes dart between us, a knowing smile playing on her lips. "Well, don't let me interrupt you *catching up*, whatever that means, wink-wink. But save a dance for me, Rose. We need photos of the flower girls on the dance floor!"

As she swirls away, I let out a breath. Lucas chuckles.

"Shall we?" he asks, gesturing back toward the party.

Throughout the evening, we gravitate toward each other like magnets. A brush of hands as we reach for champagne. Stolen kisses in quiet corners that leave me breathless and wanting more. But despite my happiness, something keeps niggling at me. If I am pregnant, this will all end. I cannot have one good thing without losing the other. I tell myself over and over not to let it bother me. I know I've been trying to psyche myself up for success after so much disappointment, but still, the chances of it actually working are slim, right?

CHAPTER NINETEEN

Three weeks later

THE DOORBELL CHIMES and I pull open the door, instantly overcome with the strange anticipation that always hits me when I see Rose. She looks nervous, her hands wrapped around the strap of her purse. I guess it's been a while since we've seen each other, since she took some time off to look after the twins, and I went to Atlanta for a conference, and to see Mom.

"My flower girl," I say with a grin, stepping aside to let her in. She smiles a little wider, but there's something off in her expression. I can't quite place it. "Come on in," I add, shutting the door behind her. The smell of garlic and herbs fills the apartment and I tell her I'm making something simple, comforting. I hope she'll like it.

"It smells amazing," she says, and I lean in, dropping a kiss on her cheek as I take her coat. She looks at me, her expression unreadable, but she doesn't lean in to kiss me back. Okay. Noted.

We walk to the kitchen together, where I've got pots of sauce simmering on the stove. I feel strangely proud, though I wouldn't normally admit that. "I'm trying out a new recipe from my mom," I tell her, giving the sauce a stir. "How've you been?"

"Busy," she says, her voice a bit strained. She starts twisting a piece of her hair around her finger. "The twins are a handful, but Lily and Theo had an amazing time in Barbados."

I nod, tossing in a bit more seasoning, watching her out of the corner of my eye. She seems jittery. Something's definitely off. "And how are the newlyweds?" I ask.

She forces a smile. "Blissfully happy. They're moving in to the new house soon."

She shifts her weight, glancing around the kitchen like she's not sure what to do with herself. "How was your business trip?" she asks.

"Productive, but long," I say, glancing at her. "Met a few guys doing some amazing new research—could be a game changer..." I trail off when I see her expression. It's way too tense for such casual conversation.

I hand her a bowl of cherry tomatoes, figuring maybe the simple task will get her to relax. "You can halve these for the salad."

We work side by side in silence, though I can feel her anxiety radiating off her. Every so often, I brush her arm when I reach for something and I try to catch her eye, but she avoids my gaze. I can't take it anymore.

"So," I say after a moment, pausing with the spoon, "are you gonna tell me what's really on your mind?"

She sets down the knife and takes a deep breath. "Lucas, I..." Her voice falters, and I watch her struggle with whatever she's trying to say. Her fingers are trembling slightly. Then, all at once, she blurts it out. "I'm pregnant."

The words hit me like a punch. I freeze. The spoon slips from my hand and clatters onto the stove, splattering sauce everywhere. I don't care. I'm staring at her, my mind reeling, trying to process what she's just said.

"I did a home test first," she says quickly, her words spilling out in a rush. "Then I went to the fertility center for confirmation. It's positive."

I turn to the sink, gripping the edge, trying to steady myself. I take a deep breath, but it doesn't calm the tension coiling in my stomach. After a long pause, I manage to speak. "I should have expected this," I say. "The trial was a success, that's amazing." I shake my head. A mix of emotions that I can't even begin to sort out are roiling through me. "I'm happy for you, but…"

"What if it's yours?"

I whip around to face her as her question hits me like another punch. "Wait. You think it could be *mine*?"

She goes pale, like she's about to crumble right in front of me. "I'm not sure," she whispers, avoiding my gaze. "I'd just had the procedure before the wedding…and we were together, several times. I mean, it's possible, right?"

Possible. I search my memory, but it's all a blur—a series of red-hot moments where I lost myself and everything else faded away. Did we use protection every time? I can't even remember, and that realization makes me feel sick.

"Jesus, Rose…what the hell?"

"I'm sorry," she whispers, looking like she's about to cry. And maybe I should feel more sympathy but right now I'm furious at myself. I know we've both made mistakes here, but this…this changes everything.

"What will happen if it's yours?" she asks.

I can hear the panic in the undertone and I start pacing.

"Rose, I never intended to be a father," I say, trying to keep my voice calm, despite the fear that's rising up from my core the harder I try to push it down. "It's not what I wanted. It's not what I planned for. I told you I didn't want—"

"I know. I know, but you said you wanted *me*. Doesn't that mean anything?"

I let out a laugh. I can't help it, it's the shock. The absurdity of the whole thing, the irony. Her face falls, and I feel a pang of guilt, but I push it down and keep pacing. I'd be a terrible father; I'd regret it. I wouldn't ever be around, I'm too busy! She starts glancing toward the door.

"We'll have to do a test, together…you know that as well as I do. Oh, God, this is such a mess."

She grabs her purse, her movements jerky and tense. She's on the verge of breaking down, and I want to reach out, tell her it's going to be okay…but I don't even know if that's true. I drag a hand down my face, trying to sort through the utter turmoil taking over my chest. If it's mine, I can't… I mean, I can't be a father. I'd only mess it up, or regret it. I went over all this with Mabinty.

"I'm sorry," she whispers, her voice cracking. "I totally respect your decision to not want anything to do with me. I said I would do this alone and I will, whether it's yours or not."

"Rose, wait—" I start, but she's already halfway out the door.

"I'll let you know when the test is scheduled," she says over her shoulder. Her voice is flat and controlled, though I can see the tears in her eyes. And then she's gone, leaving me standing in the middle of my kitchen, the sauce still bubbling on the stove. I feel like the ground has just shifted under me, and I don't know how to get my footing back.

I slip through a gap in the chain-link fence, my boots crunching on broken glass and other bits of trash from years ago. The crumbling facade of the abandoned Chicago post office is a hulking relic of Art-Deco grandeur, now being left to decay. This is the first urban exploring adventure I've taken alone, without Lucas, but it doesn't intimidate me. I've got scarier things going on right now.

I think back to the test we took three days ago, to see if it was his. He didn't have to do much, just swab his cheek and hand it to me, but the whole exchange felt weird and dirty and he barely met my eyes as he handed the sample over. I felt as crushed as a dead beetle and I've been crushed ever since, having to work around him, feeling his eyes on me, the pitying looks. Like he wants to talk to me but knows there's nothing to say.

He did try to call me last night. He wanted to find out the results. I didn't have them then, so I sent him a message by way of answering his call.

No news yet.

I watched my phone all night for a message back, but it didn't come, and then the anger really sank in. At him, and myself, for getting into this stupid situation. For trusting him! He promised he wasn't like David and stupidly, I started to let my guard down. I even hoped for one tiny split second that maybe I wasn't pregnant, so I could be exactly what he wanted. As if that wouldn't have been doing myself the hugest, most unforgivable disservice! I promised never to bend for another man. Why should I?

Inside, I flick on my flashlight, illuminating a huge, cavernous sorting room and rows of very cool-looking rusted mail chutes. Dust motes swirl in the beam as I pick my way carefully across the plaster-strewn floor. What a mess. This place is only marginally messier than my life.

My mind drifts back to Lucas as I explore. The way he

looked, standing in that kitchen three days ago, his sauce dripping all over the place. He was so repulsed by the possibility this child could be his, and now… I don't know how to tell him.

My phone beeps. Lily.

Have you had the results yet?

She knew I was getting them today, but I escaped with the news and came out here. I can't escape forever, though. And I owe it to Lucas to tell him first.

My flashlight beam catches on an old sorting table. I lean against it, lost in my thoughts. The cold metal seeps through my jacket and I click a few photos on my phone, absent-mindedly, lingering on one of us at the wedding. We look good together, I think. But I'm not what he wants; he already made that very clear.

"He has every right to not want a family, just as I have every right to want one," I say aloud as if any ghosts or birds that might be lingering here might hear me and agree. "But I know he'd be good at it. He'd be a great dad. He's just convinced himself he wouldn't be, because of his own father."

I sigh to myself. I am going to suffer the same fate with Lucas Bennett as Mabinty did.

I push off from the table and continue my aimless wandering. My footsteps echo off the high ceilings as my brain churns through the situation and what to do; how it blew my mind, having to do that paternity test the other day, and seeing the results this morning, staring up at me in black-and-white.

I stumble over a fallen beam, catching myself against a

wall. The momentary shock clears my head, and Lucas's face is all I can see—his incredible smile, the light in his eyes when he talks about his work and his adventures, and his food. The way he looked up on stage that time, doing his thing alongside me. The way he looked at me when he told me I should just trust him.

"God, I've been an idiot," I groan, rubbing my face. "I never should have trusted him." The tears sting my eyes. "But I couldn't help it. I'm in love with him."

I sink to my knees on the filthy floor and sob, pouring out my distress into the silence. On reflection, abandoned buildings are great places to fall apart because no one can hear or see you, but I am pathetic, and I am pregnant and I have no idea how to tell him. "Ridiculous. My whole life is just ridiculous!"

After what feels like an eternity, I finally pull myself together. I just have to do it, I decide. I just have to tell him. Right now.

My heart shifts in place as he answers my call. I can literally feel it thudding erratically under my sweater. "Rose?"

"Lucas." I can tell he is nervous. "I have the results from our test."

"Don't tell me," he says quickly. "I don't want to hear it right now."

I suck in a breath as my heart breaks all over again. Then I sigh so loudly that a pigeon startles in a cracked window frame. "If that's how you really feel…"

"No, I mean I want to see you. I want to hear this from you in person," he says. "Where are you?"

"I'm…" I look around me at the mess. This is no place to meet Lucas. Besides, I don't want to ruin these adventures for myself in the future by connecting them with bad memories, and I am rather enjoying these urban explorations. I will enjoy them without him.

"Meet me back at the Botanic Garden," I tell him. I figure whatever happens, we will both need air.

CHAPTER TWENTY

THE SCENT OF jasmine hangs in the air, as heavy as my thoughts as I pace along the winding path to the spot where she said she would be. Lily's wedding in this very garden was so beautiful. It feels like forever ago already, and my mind keeps replaying those stolen moments with Rose. If I could go back in time, knowing what I know, would I still have done it? Would I still have made love to her?

My heart feels like it's about to burst out of my chest and I'm digging my nails so hard into my palms that it hurts. I know I've hurt her, but I've been doing some soul searching these past few days, and whatever the results are, I know it's Rose I want. I'm in love with her. I have to tell her that and let the cards fall where they may, I guess. It's just that every time I try to imagine myself as a dad, my own father's face swims into view. I hear him telling Mom I was too expensive. I see him closing that damn study door on me.

I shake my head to clear the image. "You're not him," I remind myself firmly, and not for the first time since she told me this child might be mine. "And you're not Rose's ex, either. You are better than that. You are better for her."

Suddenly, I see her, standing in big winter boots and her red coat. A vision. The sound of my footsteps makes her turn around.

"You got here fast."

I smirk. "I probably got a few speeding tickets." I reach out to sweep a stray lock of hair behind her ear and I take a deep breath, steeling myself. She takes my hands. Is it fear I see flicker across her face? My heart is thudding. How is it possible that I'm actually standing here hoping to God the child inside her isn't someone else's? Hoping it's mine.

She has to force herself to meet my eyes. "Lucas, the baby...by some miracle, it's yours. Not the donor's."

I stare at her, feeling my eyes widen in shock. My grip on her hands tightens, and I can feel a slight tremor in her fingers. She looks away, probably expecting me to lose my cool once and for all, worse than I did in my kitchen, for which I am not proud at all. But I find I am laughing, with relief more than anything. "So...so it's really mine?"

She frowns in surprise and nods, the words falling out of her quickly now. "I know this is a lot to take in. You're probably in shock. I want you to know that I don't expect anything from you. I can handle this on my own. You don't need to be involved if you don't want to be."

As the words leave her mouth, my heart constricts. Deep down, I know that's not what she truly wants. I can see it on her face. "Rose..." I swipe a hand behind her head, and she gasps softly, stepping closer as I urge her to me. "I know you like to think you're strong and independent and more than capable, but I am going to be by your side through this, okay?"

She blinks at me. "But you said..."

"I'm so sorry. I said a lot of stupid stuff in a moment of shock."

I guide her to a bench and sit beside her, my voice low. "I never thought I'd be here, telling you all this, with you, pregnant! But I was an idiot. I was so caught up in my head,

I shouldn't have reacted like I did, or left it this long without telling you I love you."

"Oh, Lucas." She presses a hand over her mouth at my words, and her eyes fill with tears as I take her other hand.

"Can you ever trust me again? I never wanted to hurt you, Rose. You're the best thing in Chicago besides the pizza. I was just unprepared!"

I pause, looking down. "I've got some hang-ups from my childhood, from my dad, as if you haven't realized that. I spent my whole life thinking I'd end up like him—working too hard, always too distracted. So, I've been convincing myself I shouldn't bring a kid into the world."

She reaches out to me. "I know, but Lucas, you're so much more than your job. And I've seen you with kids—the twins adore you. You're amazing with them."

"I want to believe that. I really do," I tell her. "And you should know it was never like this with Mabinty. We'd grown so far apart. But you…" I pause, my thumb caressing her cheek. "Meeting you has changed everything. You've shown me something else, flower girl. I knew you were different the second that smoothie came between us."

Rose sniffs and I press my lips to hers. She kisses me back, then cradles my face. "What are you saying here, Lucas?"

I kiss her again. "I'm saying I want to make this work. Us, the baby, all of it. I'll even find a new position at another hospital so we don't have to work together. I don't want to complicate things for you professionally."

She stares at me open-mouthed, like she's stunned by my offer. "No, Lucas. You don't need to do that. I'd be proud to work alongside you. I told you before you're nothing like David. Maybe I convinced myself you were a few times, to protect myself, or to stop myself falling for you, but it didn't work. I'm in love with you."

I lean in, resting my forehead against hers. "This is wild," I murmur. Then I feel my mouth stretching out into a grin. "When I set you up with that trial, I knew I was helping you, but this…"

"You took that helpfulness to a whole new level." She laughs now, which makes me laugh, and for the first time in a long time I have the feeling that everything really will be okay. I'm not going to be afraid of being a father. In fact, it's growing on me the more I think about it. I would do anything with and for this amazing woman.

She presses her mouth to mine, and I wrap my arms around her, savoring the feel of her, drawing her strength and courage around me and making it my own. The gentle breeze carries the scent of a thousand flowers, and I can't help picturing the new life growing inside her. Our life.

"I know we have a lot to figure out," she says, opening her eyes to meet my gaze.

"We'll do it together," I tell her. "I promise you, Rose, I'll be here. For you, for our child. Or children? It could be twins, right?"

"It could be," she replies, and for a second she looks quite bewildered. It makes me laugh. If it's twins, even better. Even more to love.

I lean in, closing the distance between us again, and we kiss like we never stopped, like our mouths know how to fuse together as well as our minds and bodies do. Is this what it feels like to have it all?

She cups my face in her hands again. "I love you, Lucas Bennett," she whispers, her voice thick with emotion.

Tears prick at my eyes and I'm so choked I can barely whisper back, "I love you, too, Rose Carter."

I pull her into me again, and in this moment, with the breeze tickling my skin and my arms around Rose, I feel a sense of peace I've never known before. Whatever the future holds, I know I've found the woman I will love for the rest of my life.

The air is crisp as we make our way through the quiet back streets of the empty neighborhood. The early-morning light casts an ethereal soft glow on the worn buildings around us as we trudge ahead with flasks of coffee. It's almost surreal to be out here, bundled up in jackets and scarves, with Lucas beside me and our baby girl, Eliza, nestled quietly in a sling against my chest. She's just a few months old, all soft cheeks and bright eyes that take in everything around her, and I'm not sure she knows yet how lucky she is to have her very first adventure with both her parents right here.

Lucas is grinning like a kid as he points out the route he mapped for us last night. We're exploring a half-abandoned gin distillery and Eliza's twin sister, Francesca, is gurgling away from her carrier on his back. Our fraternal twins are our world these days. Just adorable. Their smiles have everyone wrapped around their little fingers.

Lucas's excitement is infectious, and a flutter of a thrill grips my stomach as we approach the tall entrance, covered in graffiti. I can't believe he manages to find so many of these places, and they're always exciting. Or maybe I'm just excited to be seeing them with him... To think my life used to be all work, work, work and now it's so much more. We're always finding new ways to play and explore, even more so with Eliza and Francesca in the picture.

This particular place has been around since the Prohibition era, he tells me, but it's been years since anyone used it for anything but the occasional art installation.

"This way," he whispers, and we squeeze through a side gate. The rusty creak makes Eliza stir against me. She lets out a tiny contented sigh before settling straight back to sleep. I don't know how she does it. Lucas glances over. His eyes crinkle up in wonder and love before turning his head to blow a kiss at Francesca. Then he meets my gaze with a look that makes my own heart ache with absolute happiness. How did I get this lucky?

It's strange and wonderful at the same time to see this side of him—the once guarded man who didn't think he wanted children at all, who now practically melts at the sight of his own daughters! The girls can do no wrong in his eyes. He barely takes his eyes off them.

Inside the old building, the sunlight filters onto my back through the stained-glass windows as we walk. It's so cool in here, not eerie at all. Steel shafts and pipes glint in the beams of light, giving the place an even more mysterious, almost magical, feel. The air feels layered in here somehow, dense with the faintest traces of juniper and spice, as if the ghost of gin is still lingering in the rafters and clinging to the walls. I watch Lucas trail a hand along a line of old barrels stacked against one wall, breathing in the sour edge of long-evaporated alcohol. He was wary of me joining him on these outings while I was pregnant, and now, despite me promising to tread carefully, he is guarding my every move, stepping out in front of me and motioning me forward when the path is danger-free. I love this man!

Lucas pulls me gently toward a central chamber. "Check this out," he whispers, guiding us toward what must have once been the main brewing room. The space is huge, with towering copper vats and intricate pipes that wind along the ceiling like veins. Nature has reclaimed parts of it. Vines have crept through cracks in the walls, and a small tree is sprouting defiantly near the entrance.

"Imagine what it used to look like," I whisper.

"Oh, I am." Lucas's gaze shifts from the room to me, then down to Eliza, still sleeping peacefully. "This might be my favorite adventure yet," he says, and I melt.

His attention shifts to something across the room and he gestures for me to follow. We step carefully until we reach an arched window frame; the glass is long gone now. It opens out to a view of the city skyline, bathed in gorgeous golden morning light. "It's breathtaking," I say. "I can see why you wanted us to come here at such an ungodly hour."

Lucas smiles that half smile that always makes my heart skip, before gently taking Eliza from my arms, cradling her close. One girl on his back, one close to his chest.

"Rose," he says, his face turning serious. "I have something I need to ask you."

I frown. "What is it?"

He reaches out and tucks a strand of hair behind my ear, his thumb grazing my cheek. And then, in one graceful motion, he lowers himself to one knee, still holding Eliza in his arms.

I clasp a hand to my mouth, my heart racing as it all sinks in. Oh. *Oh*.

"My beautiful girlfriend," he begins, and my heart leaps up to my mouth. "You've changed everything for me. I thought I knew what I wanted, what I didn't want, and then you came along and… Well, I threw a drink on you, and you went on to prove to me that the best plans in life are the ones you don't even make yourself. I'm so lucky to have met you."

I laugh through my tears and he reaches over Eliza to squeeze my hand.

"You've given me more than I ever thought I deserved—a family, a home, and a love that feels like something out of a dream, truly. I can't imagine my life without you now, and I don't want to." He takes a deep breath, looking up at me. "Rose—will you marry me?"

I'm crying now, full-on sobbing as I nod. I can't even find the words. "Yes," I finally manage. "Yes, Lucas, yes."

He rises and passes Eliza back to me, and as the sunlight streams onto us all through the open window, he leans down to kiss me. I feel like my heart might explode out of my chest—I can't wait to tell Lily.

When he pulls back, he presses his forehead to mine, and suddenly, we're both laughing and crying like lovestruck idiots. He slides the most beautiful ring onto my finger and instantly it catches the light, almost blinding me. This is totally crazy. It's so like him to propose to me here. But with Lucas by my side and our girls the picture of happiness and contentment on their first ever urban exploration, I know this is only the beginning of our adventure.

* * * * *

*If you missed the previous story in the
Twin Baby Bumps duet,
then check out*
A Daddy for Her Babies

*And if you enjoyed this story,
check out these other great reads from
Becky Wicks*

Nurse's Keralan Temptation
Tempted by the Outback Vet
Daring to Fall for the Single Dad

All available now!

MILLS & BOON®

Coming next month

SECOND CHANCE IN SANTIAGO
Tina Beckett

Vivi tried on a fake smile.

'Hi! I didn't know you were at Valpo Memorial. At least not until I saw you in the operating room.'

That dark gaze stared her down for a minute or two. 'Didn't you?'

Cris's words took her aback and she frowned. 'I'm not sure what you mean by that.'

'Surely my name was on the list of hospital staff when you came here looking for a job.'

He made it sound like she'd been desperate or something.

'Actually, I didn't 'come here looking for a job.' I saw a posting at the hospital where I was *already working* as a scrub nurse and applied. I didn't scour the website looking for familiar names.' She threw in, 'Besides, I might not have even recognized your name if I'd seen it.'

That was a mistake, and he knew it because one side of his mouth curved. 'Oh really? I got a few letters that seemed to indicate otherwise.'

Yes, she had written several long pages of prose that reiterated what she'd said the last time she saw him…that she would love him forever. That she would never ever forget him.

Her face heated. 'I was a child back then.' And she didn't talk about the fact that he hadn't written her back because she didn't want him to know how soul-crushing it had been that he hadn't cared enough to respond.

The way she'd never responded to Estevan's texts? No. That was not the same. She was convinced that he'd never really loved her—or he wouldn't have been able to jump into another relationship so quickly. It seemed she was forever doomed to love men more than they loved her. But not anymore.

'It seems we both were.' His face turned serious. 'And now we're both adults, so I assume we can both work at the same hospital—the same *quirófano*—without it causing a problem, correct?'

Continue reading

SECOND CHANCE IN SANTIAGO
Tina Beckett

Available next month
millsandboon.co.uk

Copyright © 2025 Tina Beckett

COMING SOON!

We really hope you enjoyed reading this book. If you're looking for more romance be sure to head to the shops when new books are available on

Thursday 19th June

To see which titles are coming soon, please visit
millsandboon.co.uk/nextmonth

MILLS & BOON

afterglow BOOKS

Afterglow Books is a trend-led, trope-filled list of books with diverse, authentic and relatable characters, a wide array of voices and representations, plus real world trials and tribulations. Featuring all the tropes you could possibly want (think small-town settings, fake relationships, grumpy vs sunshine, enemies to lovers) and all with a generous dose of spice in every story.

♪ @millsandboonuk
◉ @millsandboonuk
afterglowbooks.co.uk
#AfterglowBooks

For all the latest book news, exclusive content and giveaways scan the QR code below to sign up to the Afterglow newsletter:

SCAN ME

afterglow BOOKS

KAREN BOOTH
He's on track to win her heart...
NOT SO FAST

Much Ado About Hating You
They're enemies at work...but can love write their happy ending?
Sarah Echavarre Smith

- Sports romance
- Enemies to lovers
- Spicy

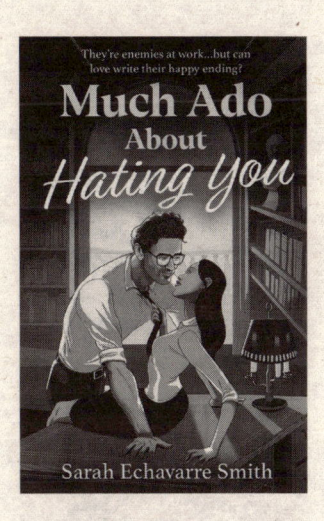

- Workplace romance
- Forbidden love
- Opposites attract

OUT NOW

Two stories published every month. Discover more at:
Afterglowbooks.co.uk

FOUR BRAND NEW BOOKS FROM
MILLS & BOON MODERN

The same great stories you love, a stylish new look!

Conveniently ARRANGED
LYNNE GRAHAM · LORRAINE HALL

WANTED: HIS HEIR
MAYA BLAKE · DANI COLLINS

DEFIANT Brides
Tara Pammi · Michelle Smart

THE BILLIONAIRE'S LEGACY
ABBY GREEN · NATALIE ANDERSON

OUT NOW

Eight Modern stories published every month, find them all at:

millsandboon.co.uk

LET'S TALK
Romance

For exclusive extracts, competitions and special offers, find us online:

- **f** MillsandBoon
- **X** @MillsandBoon
- **◉** @MillsandBoonUK
- **♪** @MillsandBoonUK

Get in touch on 01413 063 232

For all the latest titles coming soon, visit
millsandboon.co.uk/nextmonth

OUT NOW!

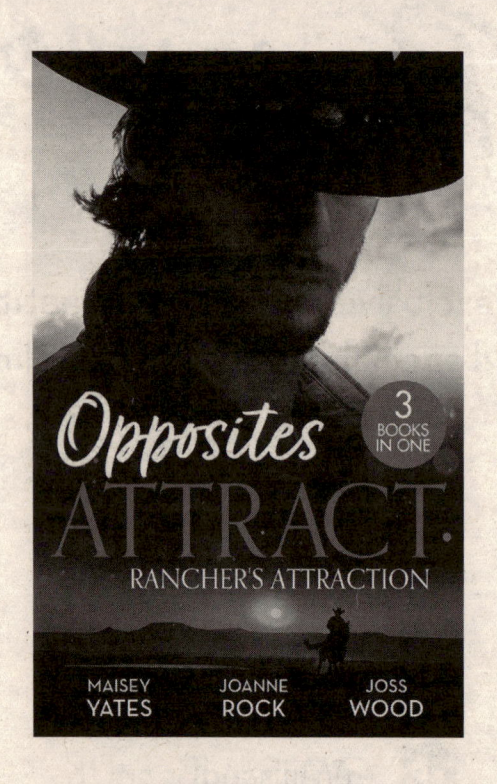

Opposites Attract: Rancher's Attraction

3 BOOKS IN ONE

MAISEY YATES · JOANNE ROCK · JOSS WOOD

Available at
millsandboon.co.uk

MILLS & BOON

OUT NOW!

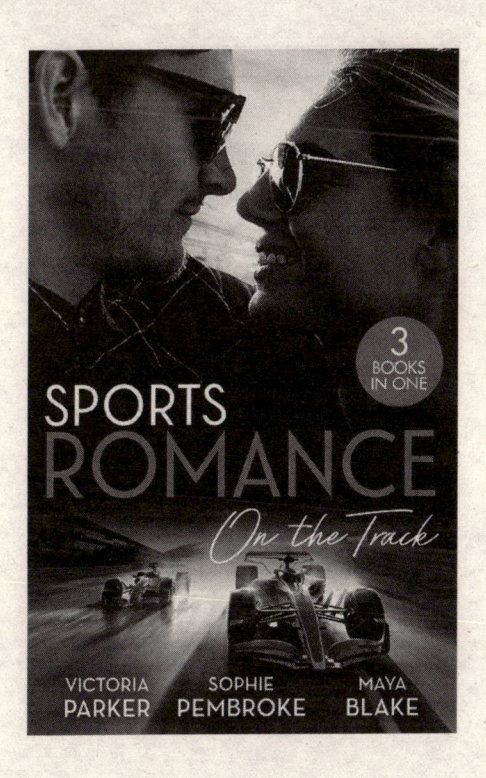

SPORTS ROMANCE
On the Track

3 BOOKS IN ONE

VICTORIA PARKER
SOPHIE PEMBROKE
MAYA BLAKE

Available at
millsandboon.co.uk

MILLS & BOON

OUT NOW!

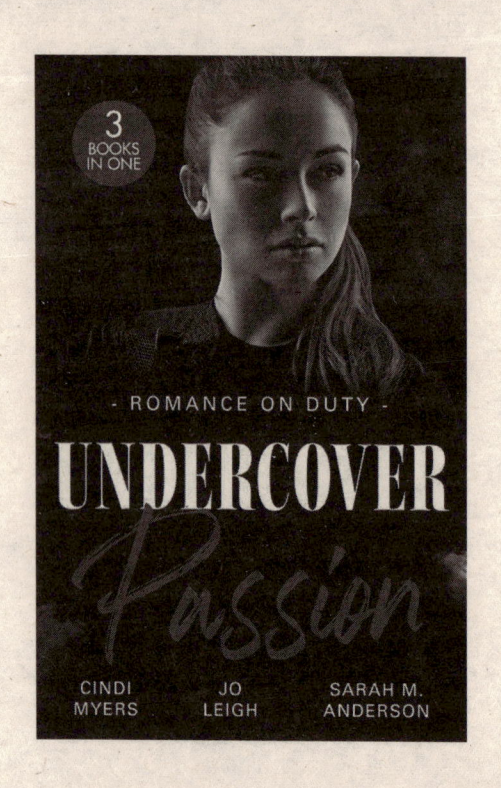

— ROMANCE ON DUTY —
UNDERCOVER
Passion

3 BOOKS IN ONE

CINDI MYERS   JO LEIGH   SARAH M. ANDERSON

Available at
millsandboon.co.uk

MILLS & BOON